THE UNWAN

CW00417783

A Jo Wheeler Mystery

GUY SHEPPARD

SOCCIONES

ISBN: 9798607212995

Cove design & typesetting by Socciones Editoria Digitale
www.socciones.co.uk

Other mystery novels set in Gloucestershire by Guy Sheppard

Countess Lucy And The Curse Of Coberley Hall
Sabrina & The Secret Of The Severn Sea
The Silent Forest

Author's note

When Sidney Arthur Thomas Sheppard died, he left behind hundreds of love letters written by his wife Marjorie. These letters, mostly sent him during the Second World War, have survived in little cardboard files dated 1939-1944. They offer a window into extraordinary times when people faced difficult, sometimes impossible choices. Above all, the often poignant missives show a neglected wife's growing frustration, to the point of rebellion, as she is forced to fight a world war and a war with herself.

This novel mixes crime fiction with biography, where all letters quoted are inspired by real correspondence. For historical photographs see blog at: www.guysheppard.wordpress.com.

WORLD WAR TWO TIME CHART

28 July 1939: Marjorie Wallis and Sidney Sheppard get married. Honeymoon on the French Riviera.

1 September 1939: World War II begins.

December 1939: Marjorie and Sidney are forced to abandon their Hanger Hill flat in London.

7 September 1940: Blitz on London begins.

Sidney goes to work for Messier (French aircraft undercarriage maker) in London, but is evacuated to Warrington because of the Blitz. Joins Morgan Crucible but is again evacuated from London to Wilnecote, near Tamworth.

January 1940: Marjorie joins the NAAFI (Navy, Army & Air Force Institutes) at Ruxley Towers, Claygate, Esher, Surrey.

Sidney joins Tungum Tube Co. in London but is once more evacuated to Cheltenham.

24 November 1940: First major raid on Bristol.

11 April 1941: Good Friday raid on Bristol.

21 May 1941: Last air raid of London Blitz.

Spring 1942: German bombers attack cathedral cities in "Baedeker" raids.

June 1943: Sidney enters a mental hospital in Oxford and then Ash Hall Nursing Home in Stoke-on Trent.

January 1944: Baby Blitz begins against London and other cities.

May 1944: Marjorie demands divorce.

13 June 1944: First V1 flying bomb is launched at England.

8 September 1944: First V2 rocket attacks begin.

7 May 1945: Unconditional German surrender.

8 May 1945: Victory in Europe Day.

ONE

I would apologise if I thought it would do any good. Instead I'm dogging your wife's footsteps when we're not even friends. You can be sure the dislike is mutual and I'm doing my best to dismiss her, except something wasn't right the moment we met in the cathedral porch a few minutes ago – her showing up like this has to be underhand, even pernicious. She means trouble or she wouldn't be here.

She looked so conceited as she spat in my face. 'Not *you*?'

'I could say the same.'

'Oh *please*.'

She always this polite? She always this charming? I really ought not to worry about her at all. It's not as though I don't have a baby to see to at home.

'You've missed the Sung Eucharist,' I declared bluntly and banged my stirrup pump and scoop at her feet on the floor of the nave. I'd just descended the 225 stone steps from the top of the minster's tower where I'd been scanning the wintry sky for German bombers high over Gloucester. As a result, I could barely feel my frozen fingers and toes. 'The service started forty-five minutes early, on account of it being All Saints' Day.'

'You think I can't see that for myself, *thanks*.'

'Just saying.'

She started scanning the congregation with an urgency she failed to explain. If she wasn't here for the service, she wasn't about to give thanks to the dead. Nothing else added up, either. Nothing else can? There was an

1

ugly defiance in her face when she muttered, 'Don't mind me, I'll stay where I am.'

Your no-good spouse certainly knows how to dress well for someone in her mid-thirties. I have to say I feel quite the tramp in my blue boiler suit, duffel coat and sloppy tin helmet. While I'm clomping about in my big boots, she sports shiny black, square-toed Oxfords. That little black pillbox hat, with its short gossamer veil which sits just below her eyes, looks rather pretty on her Kirby-gripped red curls. I'd kill for her Alligator bag because it boasts a special pocket large enough to hide these ugly gasmasks most of us refuse to carry any more. I'm surprised, though, that she doesn't fasten the buttons on her beige poplin trench coat or otherwise secure its broad belt, because there's absolutely no heating in the cathedral. As for that calf-length black woollen Utility Atrima dress, it cost at least eleven coupons. Tied at the waist, it really does hug her slim figure! It's certainly a lot more flattering than the regular box-cut patterned suits I own. When a woman is only allowed to buy one new outfit a year, thanks to all these government posters telling us to make-do and mend, it's hardly surprising if most of us are finding it a bit of a struggle to look our best. Is that proper red lipstick she's wearing? I think it might be.

'I'm Jo Wheeler, in case you've forgotten,' I growled, showing off my blue and white armband that says FIRE WATCHER. 'I'm the one who looks out for the enemy round here.'

She ignored the offer of my hand with feigned sorrow. It's such a little thing, joining palms instead of fists, but to her I'm still a leper? 'Last time we met I did something of which I'm not very proud.'

'I thought you'd broken my nose.'

Her sneering eyes settled briefly on the black and white bull terrier at my feet. 'Does your dog fire watch, too?'

'Bella goes where I go. Luckily these new buzz bombs that are wreaking so much havoc in the south-east haven't reached us yet. But then you'd know about them, wouldn't you?'

Your wily wife thought me a great nuisance for trying to block her way like that, but I'm a victim of my own stubborn nervousness because I'm also waiting for you, my love. She smiled along the edge of her spotted veil.

'Don't worry, Jo, I know for a fact this is where he meets you.' Know, as in betrayed. Something about her presence struck me as involuntary, but not forced. She flexed her fingers as if she found her new leather gloves too tight all of a sudden. Did *you* pay for them, my love? I rather think you did.

'Damn all this rationing. Will it never end?' I said and offered her a precious cigarette which, to my astonishment, she accepted almost graciously.

With her head bent over my Zippo lighter, her home-rinsed hair smelt of vinegar. 'Sooner I'm done here, the better.'

'Me, too.'

She hated having to talk to me like this yet didn't demand to be alone. It's easy to feel rather small and insignificant in this vast space where time has both stood still and suffered so many changes. Gone is the nave's flat, trabeated ceiling with its gilded timbers. Hidden, too, are most of the graves and crimson tiles where ugly stone slabs now cover the original floor. I turned to her in this weighty, plain and now colourless world and my eyes grew narrower. 'Why did you say you want to see him?'

'I didn't.'

'I'm sorry, I didn't think it was a secret.'

'What does it matter to you?'

'We're not much good to anyone if we can't be friends.'

'That's a fair point.'

'So why?'

'I'm not going to be Marjorie Sheppard for much longer.'

'You think I don't know?'

'*I* think you should stay out of my way until I've done what I need to do.'

'Which is?'

'I need Rufus's signature on something.'

'Doesn't mean I can't wait.'

'You might regret it.'

'Are you threatening me?'

At that moment the congregation rose to exit the cathedral.

'Thank God, he's coming at last,' cried Marjorie and gave you a wave.

Your face filled with a mixture of sorrow and alarm, my darling, which was why I took a step back into shadow. It was clearly an awful shock to see your treacherous wife scurrying towards you. You looked quite lost for a moment? I wanted to say how hideously alarmed I was on your behalf, but I didn't. I didn't want to seem that vulnerable, which is why I've decided to retreat behind a pillar before my presence embarrasses you any further.

So here I am, loitering alone like a spy in the south aisle. Should your unscrupulous spouse rush to kiss you, I will not make a fuss or reveal how concerned I am – I won't be that bumptious.

Don't worry, I won't suddenly pop up to say boo. It isn't that I'm proud of my good fortune, but I'm not about to step forward and proclaim my big moment to the world. I'll not leap in the air or twirl in your arms, but if you are the man I take you for I don't expect a joyous smile. In just a few seconds you mustn't embrace her. So what if your brow is all furrows and frown? So what if your bottom lip is trembling? Should I worry? My look may be one of sheer hate, but I have my fists firmly under control.

I'm sure I'll soon discover if I'm in any danger.

***

If only your eyes were not quite so sunken and tired, my darling, I might not worry about you so much. But I do. When I see you stride down the nave, it's a treat to observe someone quite so upright and imposing. I feel my heart leap in my throat. I absolutely love your thin black moustache. A prominent nose and gently receding chin give you an air of a proper gentleman. I know these Utility suits are absolutely awful – you can't even buy them with turn-ups due to the shortage of cloth – but inside yours you are thin, gaunt, almost skeletal. This is what this war is doing to you. To us both. You look more like forty-seven than thirty-seven. When you run your hand over your receding black hair you permit yourself a slight, sad smile. Those pearly white teeth look almost too perfect to be true.

My first reaction is to keep pace with your sneaky spouse by way of the next aisle. What's the point of snooping on her if I can't hear what she's

4

saying to you?

Marjorie purses her lips and blows smoke at the roof. That's real lipstick all right, not the dry, chalky stuff I use. Ever since my GI went to war I've had to make do with something akin to actors' greasepaint. It has a terribly bitter taste and woe betide I ever shut my mouth before it dries. Every morning I walk round the house gasping like a stranded fish. Luckily, she's not about to waste hers on a kiss. I could never be that dignified.

It's no use, I miss the first words she utters. I could point out that the acoustics in the cathedral are some of the best in the world, but clearly your wife will have to sing or shout before she overcomes the echoes.

I know this is a public place and it won't do to give way to emotion, but you can take it from me that I'm pretty nervous under all this control. It's the sort of person I try to be when I'm not drinking. My good friend John Curtis will vouch for that. I can say this because he's the one who helps me home when I pass out on the cobbled courtyard of the Fleece Inn – thank goodness they've stopped rationing Guinness! For a verger he can be annoyingly forgiving: '*We all have to make a fool of ourselves occasionally to remember who we are.*'

I bet he'd say the same about you and Marjorie, right now, if he had the chance: '*Here are two people who have known each other a very long time, but who are so bottled up and concerned not to make a fuss that they've forgotten why.*' I've been intending to introduce you to John for a while now, my love, but I fear you might consider him too opinionated. And you'd be right, he does tend to let fly without thinking, ever since he witnessed people die before his eyes in the London Blitz. He has a survivor's guilt like me, I suppose. He's a bit pedantic and bossy, though not in a bad sense, not in a way that makes you feel small. He has no time for pessimists and has only sympathy for those who find the current world too hard to bear. Most of all, he believes I'm not a lost cause, only an incurable romantic, which is lucky for me.

I'm thinking all this when I see your shifty wife turn and walk you along the nave. As you pass by I catch a snippet of her weasel words: 'I'm so sorry, Rufus, that I didn't acknowledge your letter before, but I have only just got back from a week's holiday in Ilfracombe with Peggy…'

It confirms what I already know about her. This is not the full-bloodied upper class accent of someone who attended finishing school, but more a London suburban drawl. Yes, it sounds to my ears rather ghastly and snobbish, but then it belongs to someone blatantly on the make. She has a very good opinion of herself, or would like to have.

You both come to a halt before the walls that support the cathedral's organ. Here you linger as if imagining the rich tabernacle work and statuary that once adorned the screen in pre-Reformation days. The two altars are gone, and with them all the colour and gold. To see any splendour now you will have to enter the choir, but you don't do that yet, you choose to loiter.

You strike me as wistful: 'It's no use you pleading with me, Marjorie, nor do I think it helpful for either of us to recriminate…'

Your wife goes to give you an uncalled-for touch on your arm. She doesn't look as if she's pleading, but it could be a trick: 'You seem to expect me to be brimming over with happiness, dear Rufus, but that's hardly possible when there are so many things to be settled.'

I was correct, she's here to make trouble. It sickens me to eavesdrop on you both like this so fragrantly.

Actually it doesn't.

It pleases me no end.

'Come Bella, we need to go nearer.'

Bella doesn't move. Nothing is wrong, as such. Nothing else is going on, although sometimes a dog sees more than its owner?

If only John would appear. He can eavesdrop, too. I'll plead, threaten, even promise to go to the flicks with him if he'll help me out here. All I need is to allay my fears because I'm afraid of what's about to happen. If I was more squeamish, you and Marjorie could roam where you like, my darling, I would let her alone.

You both have things to settle because of me.

From the north transept you mount the steps to the ambulatory. Here monks once followed the same route round the apse on their principal Sunday procession when they sprinkled holy water on every altar before the supreme Mass of the week. Yet you are too busy talking in whispers to watch where you're going. It's one more indication of something I refuse to admit – I'm not wanted in your world at this moment.

'You're not the person I remember,' floats in the air, or have I misheard? When you both walk past Gloucester's famous alabaster king lying on top of his tomb, neither of you turns, however briefly, to consider his exquisite death mask. From here anyone else would pause beneath the great east window that normally floods the choir with its silvery grey light inset with blue and red jewels and streaks of yellow. Except the glittering glass has been carefully dismantled for safe storage 'for the duration' in the crypt. This is the most splendid window I know, a hymn of praise after the benediction of the Blessed Virgin Mother which followed her legendary coronation. Will this war not end until we have destroyed everything we have ever valued? None of us should have to start from nothing. What do we think we're doing with our future?

I'm so busy inwardly raging I've lost sight of you, my darling. Panic strikes as if from nowhere. I can't believe I could be so stupid. It's like a kick in the groin. I start along the south ambulatory as far as the south transept to complete my circle of the presbytery and choir. I have to stop for a moment to remove my tin helmet because my head feels so hot. My legs are weak. I'm shaking.

The stairs! You and your sneaky spouse have ducked through the little stone doorway in the corner of the south transept that will take you high over my head? I don't know why I'm so convinced of this, but I am.

I'm puffing like mad on my cigarette but its smoke hardly calms me at all. Voices sound in my head. I feel myself burning, yet the cold stone floor chills me to the bone. This is like one of those panic attacks I have in the night. It's both past and prescient, like a dreadful warning.

I have to go after you.

I have to be certain…

It takes me a while to summon the courage to scale the narrow, winding steps hidden deep inside the walls – I'm groping my way up blindly in total darkness. I didn't bargain for any of this today. I don't want to act on impulse, only something is screaming at me not to delay another minute. 'Stop here, Bella. No, on second thought, come on.'

Bella sneezes and shakes her ears. The least a dog can do is to expect her owner to know her own mind?

Beyond the top of the stairs, a long passage follows a veil of decorative Perpendicular carvings that have been laid over the original, plain Norman building. Not everyone may know this, but at this end of Gloucester Cathedral one chapel is built directly on top of the other on three levels. The first is in the crypt, the second is on the floor of the minster itself and the third is at the level of something called the triforium high above the choir. I'm in its great stone walkway almost at roof level, from which spectators once watched lavish ceremonies unfold on the ground floor of the church below. The way is a terrible squeeze in places, though lit by glazed windows on one side and a row of unguarded apertures on the other. I can't say for sure why I'm doing this, but I'm running.

My head throbs. I can't breathe, because I can feel the weight of masonry shift at my shoulder. The great half-barrelled thrusts of the triforium, which act as flying buttresses *inside* the building, cry out at the great weight of choir walls and groined roof just above me – I fancy I can feel lead and stone bear down on my head until my brain wants to burst.

Originally this lofty gallery continued right round the east end of the Norman church, but later, when the choir was remodelled, the apse and corresponding part of the triforium were swept away to make room for the enormous east window. Of the original chapels only the small east one remains. In order to reach it, a narrow gallery crosses two 'bridges' outside the window. That's where I hear it, for the lowest sounds are instantly magnified from one end of the passageway to the other, due to its peculiar acoustics. It's your voice, my love:

'You said yourself, Marjorie, that it is rather pointless living our separate lives…'

That's where I go, from the south triforium to the north – I chase after your floating words like little birds. Except you and your wife haven't stopped to admire the pieces of an eighteenth century reredos and other relics that reside in one of the radiating chapels. Nor have you left the triforium to enter the north transept, since that is blocked by the apparatus of the 32ft organ stop…

I'm totally dismayed as I execute an abrupt about-turn. How can you elude me in my own cathedral? An icy shiver runs down my spine. No, I confused myself when I heard your whisper. You must have been behind me all along?

'Bella, come. We need to double back.'

Next minute I'm knocked sideways. It isn't you, my darling – not that I see their face in the dark corridor. The stiff collar of their raincoat shields their chin and their hat dips low over their eyes as they dash past me. The air smells momentarily of peppermint. Someone has been sucking sweets while keeping vigil…

A cry pierces the air. Mine, too. 'Hey! Watch where you're going, will you?'

How far they descend into darkness I don't know, since I'm too busy hurrying towards raised voices…

Because there continues above the cavernous Romanesque nave a second, smaller triforium running above its main arches. It can be reached by the same spiral stairs my assailant just took. I'm in a dizzyingly high gallery where each of its empty stone windows offers a vista to the vast drop before me.

'Marjorie? Where are you? What do you want with my fiancé?' I should never have waited to find the courage; I should have acted sooner… You may be 'Rufus' to her, but to me you'll always be Sidney. It's not as though I haven't tried to be fair. Charging at the nearest 'window' in the side of the triforium, I rock to stop my own fall. Is this what it takes to beat your wife at her own tawdry game? What sort of woman is she? She has behaved so cowardly the way she has led you on, except now it's clear what she always intended. I warned you there was no future for us until we were rid of her…

I told you what would happen if you made me wait too long.

A deadly vertigo grips me as I lean towards the distant flagstones.

I can hardly bring myself to peer fifty or so feet to the nave's hard, grey floor directly below.

'Sidney!'

I can't bear to imagine what lies there. I can't even watch where people are shouting and running…

TWO

'Two people fall off a balcony and you freak out, Inspector? That's not like you.'

DI Lockett shot pathologist Oliver Lacey half a smile. Gloucester's Bearland Police Station might resemble an elegant mansion situated on the corner of Castle Lane and Bearland, but on a day like this it could feel as much of a prison as the real one next door. Before him lay Sidney Sheppard's naked corpse complete with crooked limbs, facial bruising and bleeding from nose and ears. For a moment he gave his own hair a quick stroke. He was trying out a new, scented violet Brilliantine and wondered if his colleague would notice. If he was 'freaking out' it was only because the cause of death might be obvious when the motive was not.

'How can one of them fare so much better than the other?'

Oliver shrugged his lean, square shoulders at him. 'Sheer luck. A sharper object is more likely to penetrate the skull than a hard blunt surface. Maybe Sidney fell back and struck the edge of a projecting base at the bottom of a stone pillar while his wife landed beside him on flat ground? Or she crashed on top of him and he broke her fall? Either way, she gets away with broken limbs and a fractured skull.'

DI Lockett stared at the corpse grown strangely pale and doll-like. 'It all looks an awful mess to me.'

'To the more clinical eye we have here a depressed fracture which has caused the skull to indent into the brain cavity.'

'So?'

'Our victim has a basal fracture in the floor of the skull. Particular damage has occurred at the top of the neck near the spine. If you come my side of the slab for a moment, you'll see where the occipital bone has impacted the lambdodial suture at the back of the cranial b…'

'What happened to his eyes?'

'They popped out when he hit his head. For the same reason he bit his tongue in half. Do you want to see?'

'Not right now.' Oliver's all-embracing knowledge of bodily things never ceased to amaze him, but he disliked all this faffing about with cadavers. The dead were beyond his help – he was more the sort of inspector to chase after the living. In the last few years he had seen so many bombed out, looted houses, robbed corpses and dodgy black market goods sold for ridiculous prices that he had a very long list of suspects to reel in. Not a week ago he'd paid a spiv £2 for a pair of stockings for his sister's birthday, only to discover they had odd seams. It was enough to make you lose faith in human nature. 'Look me in the eye and tell me they didn't *choose* to jump. This isn't a crime, it's a confession.'

'I would go so far as to suggest our victim has recently received psychiatric help.'

'What's that got to do with anything?'

'It would explain the teeth.'

DI Lockett reached for his white enamelled cup. Its contents were no better than varnish, but after his transferral from Bristol to Gloucestershire Constabulary last year, he didn't like to make a fuss about anything, not even terrible tea. There had been a time when everything at a crime scene had been gathered up and taken back to the police mortuary to be examined by a forensic pathologist. But examiners like Oliver were a new breed. They insisted on visiting the crime scene in person. They wouldn't let anything be moved until every object had been recorded in relation to everything else. It relegated himself to second best at times.

'What about his teeth?'

Oliver stroked his oiled black hair. For a thin young man with very bad eczema on his forearms he could be remarkably good-tempered as well as good-looking. 'Upon impact on the cathedral floor all the male victim's new dentures shot out of his mouth in the direction of the choir.'

'So?'

'Doctors have been known to advise the total removal of a person's teeth in order to cure medical disorders associated with bad nerves.'

'Ouch. What else is there?'

'There's no sign of any weapon, unless the trauma to the head has destroyed the evidence. No torn clothing. As you say, it's as if they both decided to step over the edge together.'

'Don't forget, tonight is our darts match at the Black Dog. Eight o'clock sharp. Losing side buys the last round. Oh, and you're driving.'

'I don't remember saying anything about driving.'

'Too late. You just did.'

DI Lockett screwed the lid shut on his silver, disc-shaped baccyflap and slid it back inside his jacket pocket. Now that his pipe was well and truly alight in his mouth he had no excuse to delay. Oliver hadn't commented on his new hairstyle but, hey-ho, it was still early days. Tonight was the real test. His new cufflinks should have elicited more of a response, though. It's okay, he thought, it's a start.

He walked back to his office where he picked up a Criminal Record Form to survey its contents:

Name: Sidney Arthur Thomas Sheppard.

Address: "High Grove", Cheltenham.

Height: 6ft ½ inches.

Build: slim.

Complexion: sallow/pale.

Eyes: blue. No spectacles.

Hair: black, brushed back, oiled.

Nose: long, Roman.

Lips: thin.

Teeth: all dentures.

Chin: recedes.

Ears: large.

Hands: long fingers, well-kept.

Dress: pinstripe grey business suit. Polished black shoes. Grey hat.

It asked a lot of anyone to fathom what was going through a man's mind as he fell to his death, but he had to try. He had to establish some rapport with the deceased in order to care.

That was one way of putting it. He picked up the second victim's C.R.O. As with Sidney he began with the name and address taken from the National Registration Identity Card found in her pocket: Mrs Marjorie Sheppard, 12 Anchorage Gardens, Claygate, Surrey. Same surname, different address. Since when did husband and wife live in separate places? Still his heart missed a beat. Could he imagine himself ever making a suicide pact? No, he couldn't. God forbid it should ever come to that. God forbid anyone should discover…

He puffed rapidly on his pipe as he cast his eye down the list of Mrs Sheppard's physical description:

Height: 5ft 8 inches.

Build: slim, round-shouldered.

Complexion: florid, uses cosmetics.

Eyes: hazel. No spectacles.

Hair: red, wavy.

Nose: thin, pointed.

Lips: thick (crossed out), well-shaped.

Teeth: clean, some fillings.

Chin: pointed.

Ears: small.

Hands: short fingers, varnished (red) nails.

Dress: beige trench coat, black woollen dress and expensive stockings. Square-toed Oxfords.

At that moment the door flew open and DS Biggs leaned in. 'Our visitor is still kicking up one hell of a fuss, sir. I think you'd better come at once.'

'Yes, yes, sergeant. Tell her I'll be right there.'

'Very good, sir.'

'And knock next time you enter. How often do I have to tell you?'

'Yes, sir. Sorry, sir.'

DI Lockett propped his Bakelite pipe in his mouth, bundled his notes together and marched down the corridor. This wasn't going to end well, but he already knew that, as he entered the shabby interview room.

'Sorry to keep you waiting madam. Has anyone offered you a cup of tea yet?'

'I'm not here for tea.'

Opposite him stood a woman of about thirty. She wore a knee-length, dusky blue dress that buttoned up the front with brass buttons. A cinched waist and wide, ruffled shoulders completed the functional look that befitted current military fashion. Next moment she slipped her black and white rayon scarf from her head and began winding it in knots round her fist as she paced in circles. She had rolled her black hair with curling irons to leave one curl on top of her head in a victory roll.

He pointed to a chair. 'Please sit down and we'll get started. It's Mrs Jolantha Wheeler, is it not?'

'You can call me Jo. Mind if I smoke?'

'Be my guest.'

'You told the constable at the desk that you have something for my ears only?'

'That is correct.'

His agitated visitor began rummaging inside her leather shoulder bag to produce a packet of Woodbines. She didn't wear her wedding ring, he noticed. He scratched his eyebrow as he waited for her to fire up her stainless steel Zippo lighter and direct her cigarette to her lips with her blackberry-coloured fingernails. Her greasy red lipstick had dried out in the heat of the office and was beginning to crack. That wasn't the only thing he blinked at twice now that he had the chance to study her more closely. That had to be brown cream, not real stockings, smeared on her legs? One leather toe of her blue pumps was worn out, but was not all this to be expected in wartime? You had to be in the services to look really smart these days. Even then it was better to be in the Navy or the WAAF to get the best uniforms, while anyone in the Army or ATS came a very poor second. It was now the fifth year of conflict. There had been nine bombing raids over Gloucester alone with 150 casualties and 25 lives lost. Shortages of just about everything had grown worse – he was still looking everywhere in the empty shops for a new shaving brush.

'I have here the written statement of what you said you saw happen in Gloucester Cathedral on the 1st of November.'

'That's why I wanted to see you.'

'You have something to add?'

'Not exactly.'

'Then why are you here?'

'An innocent man may have died because of me.'

DI Lockett frowned. Jolantha Wheeler's voice came across more of a snarl than a grumble. She had all the bearing of a well-educated woman, who no doubt knew highfalutin words he didn't. These well-educated types soon got a bit above themselves, in his opinion. In fact, her accent might sound somewhat cut-glass but she seemed too worried to be pretentious this cold winter morning. He resolved to listen, then send her packing.

'What we have here, Mrs Wheeler...'

'Please call me Jo.'

'...looks like a double suicide.'

'All the evidence says it isn't.'

He took a quick puff on his pipe. 'You know this how?'

'The man who died is Sidney Sheppard. We first met in the Cadena Café in Cheltenham one Saturday afternoon when I went there for tea and cake. He was sitting all alone at a table next to mine. We got chatting. Don't get me wrong, he was always the perfect gentleman. When we visited a pub we never drank at the bar, only in the lounge. On the day he died I went to meet him at the end of All Saints' Day Service in the cathedral, except that red-haired bitch suddenly showed up to spoil it all. My Sidney didn't kill himself, Inspector, because he and I were about to get married.'

DI Lockett eased his pipe from his mouth and gazed into its bowl of red-hot Fine Shag. He looked at the coarse tobacco the same way a fortune teller might fathom tealeaves in the bottom of a cup.

'You know the deceased? You didn't say so in your statement.'

Jo looked flustered for a moment. 'Well, I'm saying it now, aren't I?'

'Was it your habit to rendezvous with men at the cathedral?'

'I'm a widow, if that's what's bothering you.'

'How long have you and he been acquainted?'

'He first told me he loved me seven weeks, six days and three hours ago. Sidney was such a clever man. You should have heard him talk about some of our idiotic politicians we have now – he couldn't abide any stupidity or corruption.'

'If I might stop you there for a moment…'

'I'm not finished. You have to realise, Inspector, that Sidney was the most generous of people. He was always buying me boxes of chocolates. He's a great fan of Noel Coward's plays, as am I.'

DI Lockett resumed puffing on his pipe. Said nothing.

'Listen to me, Inspector – Marjorie was definitely lying in wait for him. She had it all worked out. Ask the other witness. He'll bear me out.'

'You say in your statement that someone collided with you at the head of the stairs that lead to the top of the choir and nave. Can you describe him to me?'

'It all happened so quickly. He had his collar turned up and his hat pulled down.'

'We'll come back to him in a moment. How long did you and Marjorie exchange words in the cathedral?'

'Not long enough to finish my cigarette.'

'What did you talk about?'

'His frightful wife behaved like a nice person, but she wasn't. She was setting a trap. You'll agree once you start to investigate.'

'Let me rephrase that – did you and she already know each other?'

Jo curled her lip and twitched her nose, as if at a bad smell. 'Does it matter?'

DI Lockett felt obliged to rise to the bait. 'You really saying she lured her husband there?'

'She's a cunning minx.'

'You did just imply you didn't know her, right?'

'I tell you Marjorie is a born liar. She didn't even use his real name, she called him 'Rufus'. She did it to my face. Poor Sidney…'

'We found solicitors' papers in her pockets which required Mr Sheppard's signature. Do you know anything about those?'

'That explains it.'

'Explains what?'

'As soon as I followed them round the cathedral, I could see something wasn't right.'

'You followed them?'

'I knew I had to do something.'

'What did you do?'

'I waited to hear what that bitch was saying.'

He looked into the bowl of his Bakelite pipe again. He didn't much care for Fine Shag but he couldn't find any Three Nuns Tobacco anywhere, not for love or money. Or Jolantha Wheeler's words left a sour taste in his mouth.

'Don't look at me like that, Inspector. I wasn't planning to make trouble, I just needed to know what she wanted with my Sidney.'

'What did she want, in your opinion?'

'She apologised for ignoring his letter. Said she'd been holidaying in Ilfracombe with her sister. Funny time to go on holiday, if you ask me…'

'And?'

'He said *he didn't think it helpful for either of them to recriminate.* She said *there were so many things to be settled.*'

'You think she ambushed him in order to sign the divorce papers?'

'I see that now, of course I do, Inspector. Not that it changes anything.'

'It's a good enough reason to pick a fight.'

'Why else would they quarrel?'

'Not them. You.'

Jo picked ash off her lip. 'Since you put it like that.'

'You overheard enough to get very upset, did you not?'

'Listen here, Inspector, when you've seen your own family burn to death, it comes as a great relief to meet someone who is willing to sit down and take you seriously. Sidney understood my pain. He'd been ill himself, thanks to this horrid war – he'd suffered a crack-up like me.'

'What crack-up would that be?'

'Well,' said Jo, looking as if she might have said more than she intended. 'I was ill, yes, in 1942. I was in Coney Hill Mental Hospital. Why do you want to know that?'

'Who sectioned you?'

'My bloody mother. Who else? That stuck-up bitch has always considered me half crazy.'

There it was again, that word 'bitch'. That made three times already. Clearly Jolantha Wheeler was never slow to express her opinion of other women who double-crossed her. It was something he might have to bear in mind.

'Just to be clear, you've been married before, but lost your husband…'

'Are you deaf? I just told you – in the Bristol Blitz. Jack and I ran a confectionery shop in Castle Street. Bombs obliterated it and killed him and Emmy. I never even found their bodies in the debris…'

'Emmy? Who's that?'

'Our one-year-old daughter.'

'But you still have a daughter, don't you?'

'That's Jacqueline. After I recovered from my breakdown I met an American called Joshua Jackson and we had a fling. Jacky is his child. Since then he and I have lost touch. He either died in the D-Day landings or he's fighting somewhere in Europe as we speak.'

DI Lockett wasn't about to pronounce judgement on what he thought of GI brides, he wasn't going to condemn illegitimate pregnancies, either – not to her face, anyway. But from his time in the city he did know that some Bristolians had renamed a lane near St Philips and St Jacobs churchyard "Contraception Street" on account of all the condoms that could be found lying about – that's because American soldiers, black and white, were dropped off and collected there every night by army trucks so that they could go drinking and dancing. It was a somewhat secluded place where lovers liked to meet. Without doubt, this woman sitting before him had been unlucky in her choice of men.

'Let's get back to the cathedral. You decided to eavesdrop on what Marjorie and Sidney were saying. And after that?'

'The crafty thing realised I was following her because she deliberately gave me the slip at the Lady Chapel. That's when I guessed she'd climbed the steps to the triforium…'

'The what?'

'It comes from the Latin word "transforare", which literally means any passage within the thickness of a wall.'

'The real point is, it's high.'

'Very. You can see down into the choir from up there, where the passage follows the north and south ambulatories.'

'Ambulatories?'

'It's where the monks processed from one side of the presbytery and high altar to the other when the cathedral was still a monastery...'

'But in your statement you say Marjorie and her husband weren't to be found there...'

'No, they weren't. That's because a second triforium...'

DI Lockett rolled his eyes. That weird name again.

'...leads off the first. You'll see what I mean, Inspector, as soon as you reconstruct the scene of the crime.'

'So Marjorie and Sidney are standing in this second passage that overlooks the nave when you finally catch up with them again?'

'As I said, the man in the hat must have seen them better than I did.'

'Ah yes, *the man in the hat.* But you can't describe this mysterious person even though he ran right into you?'

Jo reddened. 'It was pitch-black on the stairs.'

'That gets us nowhere.'

'Such a valuable witness can soon be found, I'm sure, Inspector.'

DI Lockett frowned. 'You think he saw Marjorie attack Sidney?'

'*Attack* is exactly right.'

'I'm not sure it is.'

'You and I both know there's no going back on this, Inspector.'

'But it's a total mystery.'

'The thing is this. Sidney would have told me if he'd known Marjorie was going to be at the cathedral, he would never have put me through such... such a HUMILIATION.' Jo flicked dark hair from her face. 'He wasn't the sort to reject someone for looking a bit of a fright, he wasn't like most men. He saw past the surface... to the person within. Nor was he the sort to love someone and leave them.'

DI Lockett winced. He had grown accustomed to seeing one-armed and one-legged men on crutches limp along the streets, he'd met blind men in pubs and seen pilots who had lost half their faces, but to see an otherwise handsome woman so badly injured still came as a shock. He was looking at her burnt head where her ear should have been. He could see how a former beauty might resent her unblemished rival, how she might harbour some residual hatred for most men, too, for their crude indifference. It accounted for her slight deafness. He tried to hide his unfair, unjustifiable reaction as best he could.

'Well, thank you for your time, Mrs Wheeler,' he said, glancing at his stainless steel watch with its centre-seconds. 'We'll be in touch if we need to talk to you again.'

'Of course we'll talk again. You need me to prove that devious bitch guilty.'

'But you didn't see it happen, did you?'

'I heard Sidney cry out as he fell.'

'So there may not be a crime to solve?'

'Then I want to know why not!'

'Don't worry,' said DI Lockett soothingly. He had to get rid of Jolantha Wheeler this minute. 'We won't leave any stone unturned. Just one question. Is there any way Marjorie could have known about you and Sidney? You do realise that it was she who filed for divorce, don't you? She set the whole thing in motion on the 17th of September, only a few weeks ago.'

Jo screwed her cigarette into the ashtray and stood up quickly. She snatched her bag off the table.

'How the hell should I know? That's your job. I should never have let her wander off with him in the cathedral. It's all my fault. If only I hadn't been so cowardly, if I hadn't given her free rein... That way, she would never have got away with it. Even if she didn't push him, she is somehow responsible, I can feel it in my bones. But you're right, I'm being a bit daft. You can't try a dead body in court, can you? She's gone and that's an end to it. Good riddance, I say.'

'You know she isn't.'

'What do you mean?'

'Marjorie isn't dead, she's in a coma. Doctors put her chances of waking up again at no more than 50.50.'

Jo looked aghast. Her eyes nearly popped out of her head. 'What! Which hospital is she in? Is it local? Can I see her?'

'I'm not at liberty to say.'

'Why the devil not?'

'Her family have requested privacy.'

'I only want to take her some flowers.'

'Why would you do that?'

'You don't believe me, do you?'

'I could telephone ahead, I suppose. Marjorie's mum and dad could meet you at a pre-arranged time outside the ward – they could go in with you while you sit with her.'

'And ruin the surprise?'

***

'Lt-Col. James Huntley, 6th Baron Sherborne,' said DS Biggs, typing up notes on Jolantha Wheeler, born Dutton. His boss had the door open to his office and he could see him at his desk filing his nails. 'How's that for a dad?'

'Uh-huh.'

DI Lockett was pre-occupied. While it was true that blackout had recently been reduced to 'dim-out' and the threat of further mass air raids on the city seemed unlikely, there was little room to relax. Virtually every day V1 Flying Bombs were hitting London. He'd encountered one such terrifying FLY whilst staying with his aunt Beryl in Lavender Hill on Sunday 18th of June. It crashed in a yard alongside the railway line and damaged a bridge over Battersea High Street shortly before six o'clock in the morning. He could see the crater and fires raging from the shattered window of his bedroom.

Now there was this other new-fangled rocket that was proving truly unnerving because you couldn't hear it coming. The trouble was, no one in government had admitted what was going on, they'd tried to pass off the first detonation as an exploding gas main when everyone else knew better. That's why his aunt wasn't the only Londoner to nickname the new rocket a 'flying gas pipe'. A day or so ago Winston Churchill had finally been forced to come clean and inform Parliament that Britain was under siege. Was it any wonder if they all expected to be blown up in their beds at any moment? If the weapons could reach London, Ipswich and Norwich, how soon before they hit Gloucester?

He really wanted another excuse to visit Oliver. It was the pathologist's birthday and it was time to pluck up the courage and give him his present – a green and gold tiepin – in the mortuary. Only the dead could be guaranteed not to look and listen.

'God knows what we should make of her, sergeant. Our Jolantha's got a bee in her bonnet about something.'

'Wasn't she the one who found that local bigwig dead in the Forest of Dean last year?'

'Please, no more. I had hoped never to clap eyes on her ever again.'

'The local press called her a hero. She certainly made you look small.'

'That's only because she fancies herself as some kind of private detective.'

'What do you suppose she really wanted? She marched in here as if she owned the place. Wouldn't be quiet until I assured her that she could speak to you in person.'

'She's a ruddy nuisance, that's what she is.'

DS Biggs reached for a fruit gum. It secretly amused him to see his boss get the fidgets. 'Perhaps we should try taking her seriously, sir?'

'You heard what she said: she lost her family in 1940. Since then she has sought solace in men, of whom Sidney Sheppard is but the latest?'

'That doesn't make her a goodtime girl.'

DI Lockett sighed. Jolantha was the sort of person to take big risks. She took on the bigots, which made his fellow ex-Bristolian difficult to dismiss. She had dated a black GI and given birth to his child when American troops were strictly segregated at home and abroad. In Bristol he'd seen soldiers go to different pubs and clubs to avoid their black comrades, but this wasn't because of the attitude of British men and women so much as fellow Americans – they hated to see white girls kissing black GIs. It made her a bit of a rebel. He sympathised – he'd like to be that brave, too. When the Colston Arms refused to accept that black and white soldiers should not be served together, he made a point of drinking there every night. A pub like that was a beacon of liberality. He only wished it could do the same for him and Oliver.

He cleared his throat noisily. 'Mark my words, sergeant. Everything suggests our Jolantha is a real wrong'un, but you're right. We can't let her make total fools of us, can we? Go to Sherborne. Find out everything you can about her. Ask her family.'

'You mean drop everything and just go, sir?'

'Did she not just admit she was in an asylum?'

'Just to be clear, sir, doctors don't use the term 'asylum' any longer. They're all mental hospitals now.'

'Asylum. Hospital. Loony bin. What do I care? Damn it, Jolantha Wheeler walks in here as bold as brass and says two people didn't plunge to the ground by accident or suicide. She *says* she bumped into some man in a hat on the cathedral stairs, but admits she was first at the scene. She didn't see Marjorie push her husband over the edge but still *says* she's to blame. Why would she do that? Why question the facts as we know them? It's almost as if she's trying to throw us off the scent by throwing it in our faces.'

DS Biggs shuffled papers next to his ink blotter on his desk. It worried him because his boss sounded as though he had a score to settle. 'Very compelling, I'm sure, sir.'

'Isn't it just!'

'But not conclusive.'

'A born liar will tell anybody anything.'

'With respect, sir, no one could have predicted that two people would fall from the top of Gloucester Cathedral on All Saints' Day. Not even Jo Wheeler.'

DI Lockett shut his office door so hard he shook every sash window in the building.

'She could if she pushed them,' he boomed through the glass.

THREE

I'm walking Bella in the monks' former graveyard while thinking of you, dear Sidney. I'm retracing medieval paths around the cathedral which are so much more secluded after Gloucester's busy streets – it does no good to frighten people by talking aloud to the dead.

I'm trying to look my best for you in my grey single-breasted trench coat with pointy collars, brown leather gloves and black Oxford heels. My damson velvet hat with a yellow feather is American, but I hope you won't mind if I follow fashion for once. As I turn right from the minster's south porch, I do my best to avoid Dean Drew in what was once the Abbot's house – he hasn't yet forgiven Bella for digging up old bones.

Jacqueline blinks at me from her pram. It wouldn't surprise me if she doubts whether I'm her real mother because she spends so long with Mrs O'Brien, but what are good neighbours for? I wonder if she'll grow up to ask me who her father is? I'm sure you would make a good parent if you were here right now, my darling, I'm sure you'd know what to say to this chubby brown face that looks at me so sternly as we pass from sun to shade beyond the end of the south transept. We're going as far as the remains of the old infirmary and back.

I think about you all the time. I can't believe you've gone, it's so incomprehensible, so unexpected, so unjust. Your 'departure' is a test of faith itself. You'll have me protest something from the depths of my heart?

I'm not so good at showing my love, am I? Instead of floods of tears I'm furious. People will confuse my hostility for madness, but really I'm frightened. I don't want you gone, dear Sidney. I wish you'd told me what was wrong in time for me to help you. Did we not vow to tell each other everything?

It turns out I'm not the only walker keen to take advantage of the wintry sunshine. This other visitor wears a red Rayon gabardine raincoat with large pockets and a detachable hood. Her dark brown hair is tightly rolled back from her brow. She's very pretty with a strong chin and a rather broad nose which is a bit like a boxer's, but she has big black bags under her eyes which suggest a certain sadness, somehow. She can't be much older than me.

My fellow mother suddenly steers at me with her pushchair. She looks startled. 'Sorry. I was miles away.'

'My fault. It's these Utility prams. They don't go round corners.'

'No, they don't. I still have one just like it at home. Thank goodness Janet is nearly three now and I don't have to use it. My name's Dora, by the way.'

'Mine's Jo. Visiting the cathedral, are you?'

'I'm about to go back to London.'

'Aren't these new travel restrictions a nuisance?'

'Tell me about it. We're living with my sister Flora in Twickenham after our house was hit by a doodlebug at the end of June. Fortunately, my husband George arrived home on leave from the RAF a few minutes after it happened and we managed to salvage most of our furniture.'

'Gosh. Sounds as if you were lucky to come out alive.' I point to my scabby looking miniature bull terrier. 'We both know how that feels, don't we Bella?'

'She looks as if she's been through the wars, all right.'

'I rescued her from blazing ruins in Bristol.'

'I'm afraid I've had my dog gassed. Many Londoners have. Broke my heart, it did. But pets aren't allowed down air raid shelters and I couldn't bear to leave him to the mercy of all the bombs.'

'I'd rather die than abandon Bella…'

'What a lovely baby. What's her name?'

I should keep moving. A child like mine doesn't go down too well with some people, but Dora doesn't blink an eye.

'Her name is Jacqueline, but everyone calls her Jacky.'

'How wonderful! I wanted to name mine Jacky, only George wouldn't let me. I had to settle for Janet.'

Those sad furrows on her brow deepen – she's being oddly thoughtful again.

'Well, Dora, I'm fire watcher here, although I'm hardly needed now because no rocket has hit us so far, *touch wood*. Allow me to show you around the cathedral, if you have time.'

'I'd like that. So how old is Jacqueline?'

As I say, I'm not one for idle chatter about babies, except I play along. They are rather fascinating but apt to monopolise you. 'She's six months.'

'Is she teething yet? I remember Janet sitting on my knee at five months or so, trying to eat her way through a large apple, which was pretty hard going since she had no teeth.'

Now I know Mrs O'Brien has told me that Jacqueline's little troubles are associated with teething, but I can't say for sure.

'We've had a few crying sessions lately.'

'I remember when Janet became the proud owner of one tooth. It looked so peculiar, stuck in the front all by itself – I remember hoping it would have a companion in time for Christmas. It did its work quite well, though. I was soon covered with little bite marks where she kept trying it out on me.'

We venture through the south porch and the cavernous stone walls, pillars and floor of the nave automatically mute our voices. If its beauty inspires dread in me, then it's because this is where you died.

'I'm still waiting for Jacqueline to say her first word.'

Dora smiles. 'When Janet discovered her voice at twelve weeks she began cooing. The trouble is, she preferred to do it late at night and I would never allow myself to sleep until I heard it.'

'I don't sleep much, either.'

'Don't worry, they soon grow. Janet is not in the least bit shy and talks extremely well for her age.'

I want to complain that Jacqueline won't play by herself, but Dora isn't listening. Instead she's staring up at the stone apertures that line the triforium high above the nave. She's looking at it as if she'd have me explain: 'I expect you know this place used to be the monastic church of St Peter? It was built by the Normans in the twelfth century, but when

Henry VIII dissolved the abbeys…'

'Is that where he fell?'

I freeze. There is an odd pounding in my chest, my head throbs; my knees feel too weak to support me. I look in alarm at my companion and wonder whether I just heard her correctly.

'Oh, you mean our famous 14th century Prentice's Bracket in the south transept? The carving showing the apprentice stone maker plunging to his doom is…'

'I mean Micky Sheppard.'

On the outside I don't move a muscle but my brain is on fire. I'm seeing melting stone and falling floors. You never told me you knew anyone called Dora, my love. For a moment she might as well be speaking in tongues.

'*Micky* Sheppard? Are you sure?'

She is almost too busy examining the paving stones at our feet to reply. She's looking for traces of your blood, for certain, where Bella is sniffing and whining.

'I first met him in 1931 when I was nineteen and he was twenty-four. We'd both just joined Jantzen Ltd. after it opened its first factory in England to manufacture women's swimsuits. I worked as a secretary in the mill while he was soon put in charge of sales and advertising. When a mutual friend told me what happened, I had to come and see for myself.'

I still can't believe what I'm hearing. 'No one by that name died here on November 1st. His name was Sidney.'

'We all had nicknames for each other before the war…'

'Really?' I'm not about to let on I know you so well, my love. Your workmate has come to see where you hit the floor. It's too crazy for words. 'He and his unlucky wife didn't fall this side of the nave, they fell over there.'

'Over where?'

'You'll have to see it to believe it.'

'But how does anyone fall *inside* a cathedral?'

'A very high passage cuts through the walls. Another such gallery continues round the ambulatory above the choir. No one really knows why they were built or even if they were ever much used. The dean has been exploring them, looking for hooks – he's convinced that tapestries were hung from the apertures to celebrate festivals, hundreds of years ago.'

I'm rabbiting on because I don't like this any more than she does. There's still a stain on the stone where you bled to death, dear Sidney.

Dora squints and blinks at the rounded, unglazed windows high above us and a tear rolls out one eye. If she wasn't leaning heavily on her pushchair, I think she might topple over. 'How on earth do you climb all the way up there?'

'Spiral staircases lead off north and south transepts.'

'He and his wife were fighting, were they?'

'It seems that way.'

'Were you there when it happened?'

'Nearby.'

Instantly I regret being so rash. Now she will assume I have all the answers – I'll never get rid of her.

'What do you think caused them to fall? Was it an accident?'

'Why don't we go and sit in the choir for a moment, Dora?' I'm worried someone will hear us talking too loudly.

I'm busily directing us both towards some of the sixty elaborately carved and canopied stalls of dark oak which provide seats this side of the screen, where Bella lies down and keeps guard.

Dora is suitably impressed. 'This is such a beautiful place. Perhaps it goes some way to explain why Micky came here on the fatal day.'

'Why should you believe that?'

She looks startled. It's my tone of my voice – I've forgotten to pretend to be disinterested.

'Perhaps Micky and Marjorie went up to the triforium to get a better view of the nave? Maybe one leaned too far from a window and the other reached out to save them?'

Tight-lipped, I select a pair of dragons locked cheek to cheek on the nearest wooden misericord for your friend to rest upon, dear Sidney – they're a writhing mass of ribbed wings, slanted eyes, nostrils and claws. I'm sitting us both down where monks once eased their aching legs as they recited or sang the divine offices of Matins, Lauds, Prime, Terce, Sext,

Nones, Vespers and Compline.

Dora puts a hand in her pocket to retrieve a pretty, black satin purse embroidered with chrysanthemums and cranes. Inside is a glass into which she peers hastily at her red lipstick.

'I had to come today. I had to see where he died because I'm not sure I'll be able to make it to his funeral.'

'You knew him that well, then?'

'It was love at first sight.'

'Love? Really?' This has to be some kind of trick? That can't be why she's here. I can't believe I'm talking to someone who has the audacity to call herself your paramour, my darling. She should go back to where she belongs.

'Whenever Micky was away from the office I missed him so much. I tried to lose myself in work, except there was no antidote. We talked about Edward VIII and Wallis Simpson, but even they weren't as much in love as we were.'

Huh!

The king and his divorced lover?

I hardly think so.

'Sounds romantic,' I say through clenched teeth.

'If Micky and I were to get wed, I would have to go through all the scandal of being a divorcee like her... It's worse for a woman, as you know. Wallis Simpson has been made persona non grata.'

'All this was some time ago, right?'

'If it hadn't been for the baby, I might have left my husband by now. I always felt Micky and I were two exclusive people. No love was as great and sure as ours. I kept telling him I didn't know what I'd done to deserve it but we would cherish it until death do us part. We had such great plans for the future.'

I grit my teeth. 'That must have been tricky.'

'Before the war we all holidayed together in France which was idyllic. There was me, my husband George, Micky and his future wife Marjorie and her friends Bernard Sharp and Kath, as well as other pals from Ealing. We drove all the way to the French Riviera and once went skiing in

Austria…'

She's alluding to that whole other, pre-war life of which you spoke so fondly, my dearest. She's before my time. Or is she?

'You telling me that you all knew each other and yet you and Sidney managed to keep your affair a secret?'

Dora blushes. She's aware her daughter is asleep in her pushchair but somehow fears she might be listening? Which is ridiculous for a child so young.

'The Ogre got a little suspicious at times…'

'The Ogre being?'

'My husband. Before George joined the RAF I never had much private life. Whenever I could escape his attentions for a few minutes I'd write to Micky or we'd get a moment alone somewhere when I could tell him how I felt. I didn't want George to be hurt, but I wasn't sorry when he was called up. Lack of sleep during the London Blitz made him very touchy.'

'Don't tell me he hit you?'

'I once spent three weeks in hospital on his account.'

'How come?'

'We all liked to go horseracing before the war. Micky, George and I bet on "Ready Cash", but it fell at the 2nd fence in the 1937 Grand National. It was supposed to be a red-hot tip. Micky lost the most as usual – £1 – because he was always staking far too much to get us some money to secretly kick-start our new beginning. But George vented his wrath on me…'

Now I understand, the furious beating of my heart abates somewhat. I knew there had to be an explanation. How noble of you, my darling! I knew you wouldn't simply be in love with this dog killer. You wanted to save her from her brutal spouse – anything less would have been beneath you.

If she and I sit here and chat any longer, we might fight.

How will that end?

Bad for me. Worse for her.

Okay, I'll tell you what she and I will do, we'll discuss you in detail, dear Sidney – we'll get it over with and then we'll be done.

FOUR

CONEY HILL MENTAL HOSPITAL

Dear Violet, don't you feel that what you did was absolutely despicable and the way in which you did it even more so? You have destroyed half my life because life is made up of shared experiences, memories and friends and when you departed all of those were lost. Five years or more have passed since we first met, but they have not brought me understanding of events so hurtful, still less the uncivilised way in which they happened. Must I do the regretting for both of us? I have not the slightest wish to be vindictive, I just cannot face that what we have is wrong.

You do not seem to realise that you have never been honest with yourself and therefore cannot possibly be honest with others.

If you really want to blame me for the breakup of our relationship, there is nothing I can do about it. The simple fact is that, but for Sidney, we would have been married by now. You have been mixing with someone who was unscrupulously using the circumstances of the war to exercise his own petty indulgencies.

You may think a butterfly life in a butterfly world is more satisfying, but I am not sure you would think that if you allowed us to live together.

When I listen to a haunting song or read some beautiful poetry, I feel our parting, and particularly the manner of it, like a tragedy.

Sidney never gave me the impression of being the right style for you and frankly I don't know how you found it possible to do what you've done.

Rest assured, I do still believe that you, like me, think it is worthwhile to live a noble life. For that reason alone, you must agree that you're much better off without him. Love H.

FIVE

The choir's great clerestory windows bathe Dora and me in an almost unbroken sheet of light. If light signifies truth, dear Sidney, I like to think we can be truthful here. Which is why I have to know more! It goes against my every instinct, but it's either that or tear my hair out. You may be gone, but what you and I had was real. It was amazing. I'm right about this, I know I am. All I wanted was for our love to be like this place. And it was – it was beautiful.

It's not as if we're talking about conspiracy, blackmail or extortion, we're simply two grieving women – we're grieving for you, my love. No matter what this cuckoo in the nest may say, she has to be the imposter round here.

'So Dora, when did you last see Sidney – I mean Micky?'

'Several months ago. He'd been very ill.'

'How did he sound?'

'He'd lost hope, somehow.'

'I can't imagine him ever doing that.'

Your sweetheart looks askance at me. 'You knew Micky, too, Jo?'

I've let slip my mask again. She mustn't suspect what I'm thinking, she mustn't suppose me her bitterest rival.

'Like I said, I was in the cathedral when it happened. The police want to call it suicide.'

'That's what worries me.'

'*Really?* Is that what you think?'

'Micky's biggest fault was that he was always overworking. I used to get quite worried about him when he went on holiday without his friends and told him he was at the seaside to rest his mind as well as his body. I said if he came back to me with the faintest lines on his brow I would send him straight back. I had a lovely, safe feeling, knowing that I was still everything to him, but he knew how George sticks. I blame myself for what happened – I should have jumped straight out of my marriage the first time my husband raised his hand to me…'

'You said he was a bad loser.'

'That's when I said I couldn't be Mrs Simms for the rest of my life. The Ogre sent stupid letters to the hospital which I tore into a thousand pieces. George took it for granted that gifts of flowers etc. and promises of good behaviour could wipe out the previous six years.'

I'm trying to stay calm and not scream. 'So you saw Sidney – Micky – most days at work, did you?'

'I always felt very Mondayish and a bit off colour if he wasn't in the office. Even now I have this picture of him peeping over the heads of the swimsuit buyers and flashing a little smile at me whenever he could. At times it felt as if I would never get five minutes alone with him. Sometimes it was possible for him to see me briefly in the evening at 6.30. George knew nothing of this, of course.'

I'm trying not to go all holier-than-thou on her. 'Still you stayed married?'

'Oh how I wish I'd had more strength for the fight with the Ogre. I could see he was trying to make up for the past, but somehow I found his attention quite repulsive.'

Perhaps now is not a good time, yet I feel some stirrings of sympathy for your sweetheart, dear Sidney. On the other hand, she has let you down by her own admission. I can't exactly see myself ever taking her side.

'Are you saying that you and Sidney were lovers before *and* after he married Marjorie?'

'Not lovers. We were in love. There's a difference. I was never sexually unfaithful to my husband.'

'But you and Sidney never gave up hope of eloping?'

'Things grew complicated when I became pregnant. Also George was a different man after he joined the RAF. I used to joke about the leopard really can change its spots. He loves his daughter. But Micky and I remained devoted…'

'Until his death a few days ago?'

'I often thought it was time we came down to earth and realised that life for us would never be any different. At the same time, I did think we should make the best of it under rather trying circumstances. I supposed nothing really mattered as long as we knew that each loved the other.'

Quite frankly, the discovery appals me. She adored you *until a few days ago.* 'It must have been quite a strain.'

'Micky could get very insecure. I had to tell him "Of course I still love you, darling," or "Of course I didn't think you were a nuisance." Why I couldn't convince him that my feelings hadn't changed, I don't know. I remember writing to him after he married Marjorie, "I miss you very much and, as things are now, I regret not having taken the plunge with you." There is so much unhappiness in the world that I didn't want to add to it. On the other hand, I still supposed everything would come out right one day, although I feared even then that we'd waited too long. I was twenty-eight and feared I had nothing to show for it.'

'It does no good to blame yourself.' I'm feeling that cynical again.

'We were all having such a bad time that I was blind to the obvious. Bombs were falling everywhere and we were lucky to escape for so long. The noise was unbearable. At the same time, I did seem to sleep through the air raids. I told Micky that if "we were together I'd make you sleep, too." A mutual friend told me he had heard from him and he didn't seem very cheerful, so I wrote at once and asked him, "What's the matter, darling? You're not keeping anything from me, are you?"'

'But someone found out about you?' I say hopefully.

'Micky's letter was once handed to me while I was talking to our mutual friend Kath and she immediately suspected something. It turned out she had a boyfriend and suggested I rope Micky in for myself. I didn't know how to take that remark, only hoped she wasn't being spiteful.'

Did you really care about this airhead, dear Sidney? I honestly have no idea how you could. There's not much I can do about that right now, only try to dig for more truth.

'Sorry to keep asking, why *didn't* you simply run off with him?'

'I ask myself that question every day. I could have saved him I know I could. With George away in the RAF I'd have my bedtime coffee by the fire before going to my empty bed. It was all wrong that Micky wasn't with me. But I must confess I missed my husband and one can't break the habit of years in a few days.'

I simply can't accept that Dora loved you so recently, dear Sidney. It makes our own great passion seem so brief and fragile. You and I also had something that could have been saved, if only you'd given it a chance. Didn't you want it? With me, alone?

'I should mind my own business?'

'No, really, don't go. It's good to talk. You've no idea how hard it is not being able to tell anyone your greatest secret. I remember when Micky and I saw "Snow White and the Seven Dwarfs" together – I love those Disney films and I can never get George to take me to anything.'

I don't know where I'm going with this, I only know I have to question your friend some more. I want to hear her damn herself with her own words, I want to confirm she is somehow unworthy. 'By the sound of it, Sidney came straight back from his honeymoon to pursue his affair with you.'

'Put like that, it sounds awful, doesn't it? As if he didn't *want* his wife, or something. But his new job saw him travel all over the country. I joked, "What a restless soul you are." I think he was terribly lonely.'

'Or he considered his love for you to be deeper than his love for his bride?'

'It's true he kept sending me presents and money. Sidney was the most generous man I know. The one time I refused one of his cheques he became very miserable – I didn't know whether to be hurt, annoyed or sorry for him. I didn't mean to be distant. I told him my feelings for him hadn't changed, but with the Ogre at RAF Langley I wanted to enjoy my newfound freedom – I wanted to see what it was like to live as most people do when they're between leaving school and getting married. It was my way of saying I got wed too soon, I suppose. In actual fact, I was already a little old for that and I more or less went on in my own humdrum way.'

My lip curls. She makes my blood boil. 'But Sidney – Micky – chose to believe you belonged to him?'

'I warned him not to become too dependent.'

'How did he react to that?'

'As I say, my getting pregnant three years ago put a different perspective on things. I was terribly happy about it and realised at once that it was what had been missing from my life. George had one foot in heaven and it gave him the anchorage he needed. Of course I had to tell Micky. It's why I feel so guilty. My great happiness was tinged with sorrow when I realised how much I must have hurt him – I could only hope he too would find something in his marriage to make life worthwhile, after all. I didn't know if I'd ever see him again. I left that up to him but begged him not to hurt me.'

I am puzzled, I confess. I don't feel I know you suddenly, dear Sidney. Not like this. Not as the admirer Dora says you were, *of her*.

'Tell me what happened next?'

'After four months' silence and with Janet due to be born in one week, Micky got back in touch.'

'He took the risk!'

'We had to be careful. I wasn't staying at home to have the baby, so I had to tell him not to answer my letter until he had some news. I didn't want his note to fall into the wrong hands.'

'So you dared to resume your liaison?'

'Another two months went by, then in May 1942, he wrote to me again. Janet was very tiny but made up for that in health and strength. I was living with my parents at 14 Shirley Road and wasn't too good – I ended up having internal stitches. George managed to get home on leave regularly to see I was doing the right thing by our infant.'

Again I feel sick to my stomach. 'You and Sidney started meeting secretly, did you?'

'I told him that if he was ever in London he would always find me at home after 5.30 and on the Green near Turnham Green Station during the afternoons. There could be no morning visits before 12 p.m., as there was always so much to be done for baby and she would *not* wait for anything.'

'Did he come?'

'No, but I told him I'd like to have him drop in for coffee as he always did in the old days. It was so like him to remember my birthday in October when I even forgot it myself. He sent me a cheque which was useful. I kept saying it was so hard to write as one would talk, but I would like to see him soon.'

I'm puffing frantically on my Woodbine. Bella lifts her head from her paws, lowers one ear and registers my annoyance. 'So you wrote regularly rather than visit?'

'I liked to tell him how Janet was progressing. It was silly things. I said "You'd love her now" or "She's no longer on a baby diet", or "She runs about and chatters a lot". I often wished he and I could share her. All the time he was falling dreadfully ill and I had no idea.'

'Ill?' I say innocently.

'I did tell him "You're being very foolish to try to work yourself better". How I wished for the old days, I might have talked some sense into him. Instead I kept telling him about Janet's cold or slight attack of croup, or I moaned that she had her father's temperament and we both knew what that meant. Last Christmas I was shocked to learn that Micky had been in a mental hospital for months already and was due to stay a lot longer. I couldn't even help him financially. I certainly hadn't realised he was in such a bad way. I could only sympathise and felt helpless which was all very wrong. I did offer to go and see his sick mother because her hospital was so close to where I was living. Sometimes I talked to Janet about him and told her he was dreadfully ill. She said "Poor little soul".'

I'm doing my best to take this all in my stride when really I want to declare my interest – you didn't worship this smug, hypocritical mother-wife, did you, dear Sidney? You worshipped only me.

'Anything else?'

'I was awfully sorry to hear of his own domestic trouble, that he and his wife weren't getting on. It's enough to make anyone feel suicidal. In May this year, two days after Micky came out of the nursing home, Marjorie told him she wanted a divorce. It didn't help his recovery, did it? Of course I promised to keep the news very, very much to myself… But I've said far too much already.'

Dora has talked herself to a standstill, I realise. Should I feel indebted to her? I call Bella who is up to no good at the tomb of King Edward. I've heard all I want to hear because you're mine, not hers. It's all right. There is no you and her. There never was, even if the gullible fool is fearful you killed yourself because of her inaction.

'Didn't you say you had a train to catch, Dora? I know a quick walk to the station from here. Let me point you in the right direction.'

'You're right, I can't stay a moment longer. Goodbye. It's so nice to have met you.'

A heavy shadow divides us. The weighty secret she has unwittingly unloaded on me makes me her confessor, not friend, my love. Your ghostly presence treads between us, I'm sure.

Your dead step is an extra echo on the hollow floor.

***

I'm at the entrance to the south alley by way of the north transept when John Curtis emerges from the cloister garth. In his hand is a garden rake. He's the last person I wish to see right now because I owe him 10/-. His fingers are filthy but he looks resplendent in his verger's purple cassock. He doesn't explain why he's wearing his finery in the garden today, only dusts soil off his gown that covers his cassock while I push the pram along.

'Who was that woman, Jo?'

I quickly draw him away from the stone carrels where monks and novices once did their reading and writing. His portly figure, as always, belies both the ceremonial importance of his job and its menial, daily responsibilities – he looks half chalice-bearer and half gravedigger. He bends over the pram, pulls a face or possibly a smile, to say hi to Jacqueline.

'She says she's an old friend of Sidney's. She *says* her name is Dora.'

'Excuse me?'

'I don't like it, either.'

John wrinkles his black moustache and blinks at me through his spectacles. 'I hope you were discreet.'

'Please believe it!'

'So why was she here?'

'She just wanted to see where he fell, but can we trust a word she says?'

John looks down at his feet. Utility suits come with no turn-ups these days but he has bought his trousers too long and sewn his own. Unfortunately, his needlework is no good and one trouser bottom in coming undone on his muddy boot. He wrinkles his red nose. 'If Dean Drew sees us...'

'I only have 'gaspers', I'm afraid.'

'They're too harsh for me.'

'Yes or no?'

'My last lot of Player's Medium Navy Cut No 9 were rubbish. I'll swear they're putting sawdust in fags these days.'

'Aren't they just? I miss my Black Cats. All the best brands have been withdrawn 'for the duration'.'

'Will we see hide or hair of Dora, again? How serious is it?'

'Apparently she and Sidney were in love but not lovers, if that makes any sense.'

'Like me and you, then?'

I don't answer that, only shift my feet on the stone pavement as I light up. Except no amount of frantic puffing can disguise my frustration. 'We can't have every Tom Dick and Harry nosing about, it's too... *unnerving*.'

John amuses Jacqueline with his bunch of wrought iron keys to the cathedral doors. Each one is bigger than her whole hand, but she likes the way they clink and rattle. 'Dora wasn't there when it happened, so she can't know a thing.'

'That's easy for you to say. You weren't there, either.'

'Sidney's gone, Jo. No one can pin anything on anyone...'

'You think?'

'I realise you were infatuated with him, but I never thought it would come to this.'

'You have no idea...'

'And you should stick to your story...'

I whistle Bella who's seen a pigeon fly through the presbytery. 'Don't you see? The truth is bound to come out when Marjorie wakes up.'

'But, Jo, there's no sign she will ever wake up.'

'That doesn't mean I shouldn't do something.'

'You should let the facts, or rather the lack of them, speak for themselves.'

'Don't forget I was seen by someone on the stairs. It's only a matter of time before they're found, or they come forward voluntarily.'

'It may mean nothing.'

'If the police don't buy my story...'

'What story? What have you told them, Jo?'

'I told them his pernicious wife pushed him. What else?'

John spits his cigarette at me. 'You told them *that*?'

'Marjorie was there as much as me. It's her word against mine. Surely it's reasonable to argue that I'm not the only guilty one here?'

But it's not just John who wails, it's Jacqueline: she's crying because she needs burping or changing, or something. 'No person should mean more to you after they're dead than when they were alive, Jo. It isn't healthy.'

'Then answer me this. Do you suddenly expect me to believe that everything Sidney and I had together was one big lie?'

'You really think it might be?'

'Clearly, he and Dora were in touch right up to the end.'

'Yes, okay Jo, but is this a line you want to cross? More to the bloody point, I told you to let Detective Inspector Lockett stew in his own juice. Do you even remember what you said to him? You should never have gone back to Bearland Police Station! What if your show of innocence failed to impress him?'

'And take the blame for something that he thinks only he can explain? Why should I be so stupid?'

SIX

It's midnight and I'm lying in bed listening to Bella hunt mice as usual in my little, rented home at 18A Edwy Parade in Gloucester. The sudden squeals don't wake Jacqueline who continues to sleep in her cot-cum-drawer on the floor beside me. This war expects everyone to cope, remain calm and not break down. I'm not one of those scaredy-cat mothers who gives birth to babies in order to dodge conscription, I do my bit at the Gloucester Shirt Factory in Magdala Road sewing army uniforms three days a week. Trouble is, all that tough serge makes my fingers red raw and soaking them in bowls of alum has done little good so far.

The blacked out house reeks of damp clothes that I've put through the wringer as well as smoke from the chimney that I've tried to sweep myself. I've laid out my comb, face cream and powder on my dressing table and I've put my Kirby grips neatly in a dish as usual. I'm in most need of a new toothbrush right now.

There are more serious worries. Feeding Jacqueline has never been easy. What with my failure to sleep, the threat of air raids and the endless queues for the simplest thing, is it any wonder I've hardly produced enough milk for her these past few months?

But that's not all. To close my eyes is to relive a whole other existence. I never spoke to you enough about my previous life, did I, dear Sidney? Honestly, I can think of nothing else some nights – I wake screaming and can hardly breathe. No one knows what it means to lose everything, to the point of insanity, until they've done it themselves. Nobody but you knew how someone like me can sink so low. When I think of Sunday, 24th November 1940, the scenes are so vivid I can smell my baby burning in

41

her father's arms…

Now you're gone I have no one left to hold me. I'm back in the dark – I'm walking beside Bristol's badly damaged St Nicholas's Church at the end of Baldwin Street. Walking helps. If you were here I wouldn't dream so much. You'd keep me close and there'd be fewer failures when I lapse and let in the sadness…

The images that flood my head tonight are stark and savage. Over there is the city's Floating Harbour busy with boats. Bristol Bridge sees a pony and cart, several cars and a great many pedestrians follow its rusty tramlines to go across the water. A smartly dressed woman pauses to post a letter in the bright red pillar box that stands on the corner of Baldwin Street and High Street. Like her, I'm trying to behave normally – that's the point of this madness: to act as if nothing has happened is the new challenge.

When I cross the road I'm in a place that has been turned inside out and upside down in heaps of hot bricks in what used to be Bridge Street. I'm holding a handkerchief to my face in clouds of smoke that issue from stumps of walls, I'm picking my way along a road that has been reduced to a footpath by great screes of rubble from buildings that have literally been shaken to pieces. I can see the outline of floors and attics of shops whose identical frontages have been reduced to ground level. Basements are awash with debris. The only places that stand with sufficient walls to deserve a number are Nos. 20 and 21. Everything else is fit for demolition. I'm stumbling about in silence and stillness as long shadows penetrate the jagged masonry.

I'm not entirely alone in an otherwise total absence of pedestrians and shoppers. Helmeted rescuers struggle to stretcher an injured man from a hole in the ground, while a dead woman lies buried up to her chest in a mountain of rubble. Her face is set in a frozen gasp like a fallen statue. Firemen's hoses snake at my feet as survivors wander about, as do I, to see what bombs have done to their businesses. Yet I don't talk to any of them, except in a blur, I only continue along my own peculiar path through hell.

I planned to bring you here one day, dear Sidney, to explain how, when the Luftwaffe tore the heart from this great city they took mine with it.

It feels good to be here because I'm doing something rather than nothing.

I'm retracing old steps because my guilt is as big as my sorrow.

I suppose what I'm saying is that I still want to show you how things were before you and I met, I'd like you to know that I'm not really this mad, sad widow who spends her time in mental hospitals. I'm really the happy mother who took tea on this exact spot, in Lyons & Co. at No. 4A in Castle Street, where I was waited on by smart young girls dressed in white caps and pinafores before everything was consumed by falling incendiaries.

I don't know if the dead can ever return but if you can hear me now, my darling, this is why I deliberately got close to you. If love means anything to you, then here lies the physical evidence of my loss – it's written in the smashed bricks and broken timbers of my flattened sweetshop. I never thought I'd have to resurrect such scenes to show you, but I'm glad to. You're still my best chance. To walk down the aisle with you would have seen me strong enough to put all this carnage behind me – start over – but you mustn't think I'm irredeemably given to grief. With you at my side I'm sure I can rise from the ashes again like a phoenix, even if you can only live on in my heart.

I know you didn't *choose* to leave me behind.

If that sounds emotional and sentimental, then I'm sorry. I'm sure even ghosts get bored easily when it comes to sorrow. Fact is, I'm stuck in a place I can't escape. I feel I'm descending into an in-between state every night where life and death get reversed. Each time I enter these ruins I'm convinced I'll never, ever find my way out again. Then suddenly you are back beside me in bed.

SEVEN

It's a cold, gloomy day, as nearly as grey and sombre as this Cotswold stone villa. I hope you'll forgive me for treading in your footsteps like this, dear Sidney, but whenever we drank beer in The Monks' Retreat Bar this is the place you mostly referred to as home. You only mentioned it a few times, but I took care to hang on to your every word. Before, snippets of information like this were interesting, not vital. Now they are.

An iron gate reads "High Grove" in Greenway Lane, Cheltenham. All the adjoining railings that once made up the rest of the fence have been melted down for the war effort, so I can step through the gate or straight off the pavement into the front garden. Bella chooses the latter, whereas I opt for decorum.

Today I've made a big effort. I'm wearing my rabbit fur coat (dyed to look like sable), gloves and cork-soled shoes, while I've also donned my bullet brassiere and my best scarlet and white spot-printed Utility shirt dress with white buttons that cost me seven coupons. Of course nylons have proved a sticking point, but I've used tea and gravy to brown my legs and have drawn the seams up the back of my calves with a crayon.

I just need to give my cheeks a last dab of powder from my tortoiseshell compact. I'm in such a tizz that half the powder flies up my nose – I can't help but give a sneeze just as someone answers my bang on the door. 'Be good, Bella. Absolutely no whining or growling.'

With suitable solemnity Bella flattens her ears. Anyone can accuse her of being unapproachable, unpredictable and sometimes downright snappish, but they can't ever accuse her of not being bold.

I toss the metal compact back into my bag and smile my best smile.

This will have to be good.

'Yes? What do you want?' An irritable, middle-aged woman peers at me over the rim of her glasses. Her green herringbone Tweed suit is very good quality but has seen better days. There are lots of bobbles and marks on one of the jacket's large pockets from which protrude the handles of some red secateurs. Her brown eyes flash, her broad shoulders stiffen proudly, her long, aquiline nose wrinkles its nostrils at me and her face hardens. Clearly, I'm interrupting her rose pruning.

'Are you Mrs Tuffley?'

'And who, young lady, are you may I ask?'

'I'm Mrs Jo Wheeler. I believe Sidney Sheppard lived here.'

'So what? He's dead now.'

Her forthrightness takes me by surprise, so much so that I'm forced to blink back a tear.

'It's all been a terrible shock. I was there when he fell. He was such a nice person. I can't believe he's gone.'

I can feel Mrs Tuffley mentally scoring points against me as she studies my dress, demeanour and pet dog from under her shaggy eyebrows. But my show of contrition has worked, she has taken the bait and is, without doubt, ready to let me in. We can all do a lot with a tear.

'Jo Wheeler, you say? Doesn't ring a bell. And I usually have a very good memory for names.'

Of course you had no reason to discuss me with your landlady, dear Sidney, yet I feel certain my name must literally have been on your lips every minute of every hour? I'm also very excited. Some of the things you said to me begin to take on flesh and blood, so to speak. Mrs T. is definitely a bit of a dragon! You were right, too, when you said the house stinks of horse leather and polish. I wonder, for a moment, if that hat and coat hanging up in the spacious hallway are actually yours? It's all very silly of me, I know, but I'm half imagining that you're still here. If only I had Bella's finely attuned nose I might be able to smell you, too.

We stand about in the rather spartan parlour. Paintings of horses, mostly hunting scenes, adorn the walls while two very large armchairs fill the space by the window otherwise blocked by a golf bag. Mrs T. focuses hard on the white band on my finger where my wedding ring used to be, which only seems to add to her partial but as yet ill-informed belief that there is something odd about my visit this morning.

I have to say I don't much care for her beady eyes.

I'm here to interrogate, not be cross-examined.

'So tell me, my dear, what do you want with Sidney that's so urgent?'

'It's like this: I 'fire watch' at Gloucester Cathedral. I was waiting to see him there after All Saints' Day service, when his dreadful wife turned up. I feel convinced it is because of her that he died.'

'How so? She's as good as dead herself.'

'I'm here as a friend to investigate, that's all.'

Mrs Tuffley tut-tuts. 'What kind of world have we created for ourselves in the last five years, that two people can hurl themselves to their deaths in such a place? It's positively sacrilegious. I intend to write to the local newspaper about it.'

'Precisely. I'd call it an outrage.'

'All the same, it's such a shame.'

'Or one pushed the other?'

'Pushed? As in *murdered*?'

'Well, what else would you call it?'

'I'd call it a tragedy, Mrs Wheeler. A husband and wife have died in most mysterious circumstances, but I don't see how you can leap to such controversial conclusions.'

'Someone has to uncover what we're dealing with here, Mrs Tuffley, I think you'll agree.'

Her smile strikes me as cynical and not a little insolent. Her whole attitude I can class only as unpleasantly disagreeable. She doesn't even offer me a cup of tea.

'Why me?'

'I'd like to see Sidney's room, if I may. You haven't re-let it yet, I hope?' Oh God, I haven't thought about that. What if all your things have already been removed from your lodgings? *All the evidence.* Panic grips me. There is a weird cramp in all my joints; my brain aches; my lungs can't suck sufficient air. I wonder if I'm about to feel faint, when I remember to breathe.

Mrs Tuffley doesn't say anything about Bella, so I assume she can come, too. Our host smells of lavender-water as she leads us upstairs. The house is a veritable maze of passages and Bella is all sharp intuition. Corridors head for what I assume is some sort of attic at the back of the building. To sniff you out, my love, she has to sniff for clues. *Sleuthing*. In a word, that's the only way to describe her right now. And the switch happens in the bat of an eyelid.

'As you will have gathered, Mrs Tuffley, I'm particularly interested in your opinion of Sidney's questionable wife. How well did they get along?'

'What do I know? She's never lived here.'

'Excuse me?'

'Marjorie would arrive late on Saturday and leave early on Sunday. Nine weeks would go by before I saw her again. She and her sister Peggy rent a flat in Claygate in Surrey.'

Of course you did once admit to me that you and your inferior spouse had been forced to separate because of the war, my love, but I didn't expect anything quite so final. It confirms my greatest suspicions. And I thought this might be a wasted visit!

'How did they seem? Did they ever kiss?'

'Briefly, yes.'

'How about passionately?'

'Not that I saw. It was more a peck on the cheek.'

'But they did share a bed?'

'Oh yes.'

'Was Sidney pleased to see her when she visited? Was he sad to let her go?'

'You do ask some strange questions, Mrs Wheeler. Lucky for you, I take a healthy interest in all my tenants, but I'm not a nosy parky.'

'Did they ever quarrel?'

'Things were a bit tense, to say the least.'

'Did she make threats of any kind?'

'More barbed remarks.'

'But it's safe to say they irritated each other?'

'She's a deep one, if you ask me. I could never quite make her out. She didn't like me much, for sure.'

'Think about it.'

'A weekend together was enough.'

'But that's not to mean Sidney chose to live apart?'

'Good gracious no. He only came to Cheltenham in December 1940, to start a new job at a local tube-bending firm called Tungum Tube Co., because he had to. He'd studied metallurgy at night classes at London University and had a good brain for that sort of thing. That's why he was soon made Works Manager producing fuel pipes for Spitfires and Hurricanes...'

'That much I know.'

'Then you'll also know he was obliged to drive to places in Scotland or in the Midlands during the worst of the bombing. He saw Coventry Cathedral go up in flames. That didn't leave him much time to visit his wife in Surrey, but he did his best. And to think at the time they'd only been married eighteen months.'

You once told me that you sat in your car on the hills overlooking Leeds, I think it was, dear Sidney and watched it being bombed. It was very bad weather and with no heating you nearly froze to death. When you arrived back in Cheltenham you staggered into a pub and downed two straight whiskies one after the other. You made it sound like a great adventure. I never realised how abandoned you must have felt. All thanks to your errant wife!

Already this hints at how little she cared about your safety?

It suggests a serious lack of empathy which fits a murderous mind.

Mrs Tuffley huffs and puffs up our last set of stairs. She's really very unsteady on her feet! She could trip at any moment. *One little push and she'd be gone*... I doubt it's arthritis, it's more likely that she's done it falling off her horse while hunting foxes.

'So what did Sidney and Marjorie do together when she deigned to visit him in Cheltenham?'

'Occasionally they went to a dance or attended the theatre.'

I can't imagine you ever wholeheartedly enjoying your wife's company, my love, not when I know for a fact you've been so reliant on me these past few months. You said we were soulmates when we last kissed. I'll always treasure those words. I can't believe anyone could say such a thing unless it came from the heart.

It's all right. Nothing will change how much you wanted me.

Of course, there is one question I need to ask: 'What kept Marjorie in Surrey all this time, in your opinion? What's the great attraction?'

Mrs T. turns the brass doorknob and opens a door to a room high up in the eaves.

'She works for the NAAFI.'

***

For the first time I can see where you sat, slept and dreamt of me, dear Sidney. I can feel myself sweating. It is a rather non-descript room with a low, sloping ceiling on one side and one small dormer window, but to me it feels like home. This is where you wrote me such sweet letters. I was afraid that coming here would turn out to be a terrible mistake, but it isn't, I'm feeling vindicated already. It's as though you're still living and breathing. I expect you to return at any moment.

Mrs T. stands over me like a grim headmistress. She doesn't trust me one inch. 'I was going to give his suits to my neighbour, but Sidney was so unusually tall and thin. There wasn't an ounce of spare flesh on him.'

'May I?' I ask and start going through pockets one by one.

'There's no money, if that's what you're hoping for, Mrs Wheeler. I took it to pay the rent.'

It's a disappointment, of course, given that I've rushed here so promptly. You were always so generous to me that I'm sure you won't mind if I pawn a few of your things? It's not as if you need them now, my darling, and I do want to buy something nice to remember you by. Your funeral will be any day now and I simply must look my best. One pinstripe suit yields a few pennies in one of the pockets and a rather nice gold fountain pen.

Next minute I give a heavy sigh at the sight of your faux leather toiletry case on a table. It's ridiculous, I know, but something so intimate and close to you, rips my heart apart. I want to wail when I pull the zip, open the bag and screw the lid off one of two Bakelite canisters with chromium plated metal coverings. In my grasp is your wooden handled shaving brush. How many times have you held what I hold now, I wonder, as I run its amazingly soft badger hair over my chin? A Gillette Safety razor with a chrome-plated top lies in an open cardboard box while an unused 'Blue Gillette Blade' rests in its paper wrapper. That blade, like me, waits for you. Just to touch your nail file, scissors and comb recalls the feel of your long, slim fingers. You were always so neat and tidy, which is why I first noticed you. Few men bother to groom themselves so well these days.

'There's a camera in the drawer in the cupboard,' says Mrs Tuffley, growing tetchy. 'You'll find a lot of letters, too, in the drawer below. Take what you like. They're no use to me.'

'Really?' This PRONTOR II camera has to be worth a bob or two. I also stuff my bag with your handkerchiefs and shirts, since every type of material has a value in this time of shortages. Besides, I can wear them to work. 'What letters might they be?'

'How do I know? I haven't read them.'

That's a lie, for sure. I wrote letters to you, dear Sidney, except when I open the drawer I see several grey files, not envelopes. Each one contains a year's worth of correspondence from 1939 to 1944. That handwriting isn't mine.

I stuff everything into my bag anyway. Anyone can write a letter and stick a blue King George VI stamp on it – it's not the same as being with you face to face, as I was with you. There are several books, too. One is called "Disraeli". You were always so passionate about politics, dear Sidney. If it was one thing you raged against, it was the privileges of the rich and upper classes. Disraeli was a passionate man and so were you. You really did think you had the answer to every injustice.

'You should probably leave now,' said Mrs Tuffley.

'Oh? So soon?'

I'm not wrong when I say Mrs T. is as blind as DI Lockett. She's afraid I'm about to go off with the sheets and pillowcases when I'm only imagining myself lying next to you, my darling – I'm running my hand over the exact spot where you last laid your head. Can no one but me see that you didn't deserve to die the way you did? Is it really up to me, and me alone, to do something about it?

Bella and I make our way back downstairs. Blast it! I've probably appeared too anxious, too fraught, too *loving*. Before I go, I must do my best to behave sincerely and sanely.

'Did Sidney ever tell you he was in trouble at all, Mrs Tuffley?'

'That's none of your business, surely?'

'Did he have any other women in his life that you know about? Have you ever heard of someone called Dora?'

'Didn't he tell you? I gave him notice to quit a few days ago.'

'Really? Why's that?'

'Goodbye Mrs Wheeler.'

I'm being herded along the hall before I can ask anything else useful. 'Perhaps you and I could take tea together in the Cadena Café, Mrs Tuffley? Would next week suit you? Here's my card.'

As I step out the door she kicks it shut in my face.

'I take it that's a no.'

That really wasn't very nice of her.

By the sound of it she did the same to you, dear Sidney? Bad manners can get a person into serious trouble.

She'll come to regret it.

Bella thinks so, too.

***

But that old bat isn't the only reason I'm here, I'm just getting started.

"Home Farm" is not a very large concern, just a house, a few barns and some stables to the rear of "High Grove". I'm braving mud in my shoes as I do my best to skip the puddles in the yard without splashing my coat. Someone is tacking up a horse as I approach with a smile. An amiable looking man in his early forties, with a receding forehead and short, dark brown hair parted down the middle peers at me over the saddle he slides along his mount's back. He tightens the girth up a few holes, then waits for

51

the horse to breathe out before tightening it again. For a jockey he's quite tall.

'Mr Gerry Wilson?'

'Yes.'

'My name is Mrs Jo Wheeler. I knew your fellow lodger Sidney Sheppard.'

'Did you? He never spoke your name.'

This is a setback, to be sure, but I persevere. 'You heard what happened to him and his wife in Gloucester Cathedral?'

'It's a great shame.'

I'm very excited to be in the presence of one of the most famous men in England, not least because I do like a flutter on the gee-gees, as well you know, dear Sidney. Mr Wilson is my hero, too. Not many riders can say they've won the Champion National Hunt Jockey seven times.

'Sidney promised to take me to see the Gold Cup when this war ends.'

'God knows when that will be. Troops have been living and training on Cheltenham racecourse for over a year now. They've churned the going all to pieces with their caterpillar tracks and wheels.'

'It's so frustrating. How's a girl to make any money?'

'At least Newmarket and Ripon have seen some action.'

'I've heard Aintree is going to be a P.O.W. camp for all these soldiers we've been capturing in Italy.'

'Can you believe it?'

'Sidney considered you his one true confidant. It's thanks to you that he and I got some winning tips, Mr Wilson.'

'Please call me Gerry.'

'He was particularly impressed when you rode out with him on a carthorse called Glen. He said it really flew over the jumps with you, but wouldn't do a thing for him, or anyone else.'

'That'll be the big Welsh cob the farmer hires out by the hour. Sidney rode him once or twice, but mostly he sat on one of my brood mares which he preferred.'

'When did you last chat to him? Can you remember?'

'It must have been a couple of weeks ago. We didn't talk long because I'm busy training horses now, not racing them. This will be my first season on my own.'

'How did he seem to you?'

Gerry leads his horse to a mounting block before replying. 'I expect he told you he's been very ill.'

I'm doing my best to stay out of the way of the stallion, because now it knows it's about to go for a gallop it's getting very excited. Big feet are stamping the ground all round. 'Yes, he did tell me. Why do you suppose that was?'

'Whatever it was it made him physically sick. You'd think someone was poisoning him, or something! Doctors told him it was simply overwork, but that's not the whole story, I'm sure.'

'Did you ever meet his wife Marjorie?'

'A snappy dresser. Daughter of an engineer, I believe.'

'She ride out with you, too?'

'Never.'

'Was there anything obviously wrong between her and Sidney, do you think, from years ago? Mrs Tuffley spoke of a tension between them. Or would you say Marjorie's desire for a divorce came out of the blue?'

'It can't have been easy with one of them living here and the other in London.'

I have one hand on the horse's bridle – I'm convinced Gerry knows more than he realises.

'Tell me what you and Sidney talked about. Did he confide in you about Marjorie, at all? Did he suggest she had it in for him in any way?'

Gerry shoots me a look. For all his positive and genial demeanour, he can be a hard man in the saddle. 'We only ever talked about racing. For instance, I told him tales about Miss Dorothy Paget.'

I laugh. It's the first time I've done so since you died and for a moment you might be back at my side. 'Sidney loved it when you shared your stories with him. Who else but Miss Paget would sleep all day and spend all night betting £4 million at a time on a horse?'

'He told you what happened when her Rolls-Royce broke down on a trip to the races…?'

'She bought a passing butcher's van to go the rest of the way.'

'To this day she travels everywhere with two cars in case she ever finds herself stranded again. You see two Rolls-Royces arrive at a racecourse together and you know it's Miss Paget. She says men make her vomit and she refers to her servants by the colour of their shirts, not their name. I always get on well with her, though.'

'Sidney said she must be terribly unhappy?'

'It's only thanks to Miss Paget that I got to ride one of the greatest racehorses in history.'

'You mean Golden Miller. Sidney loved that horse. Me, too. It's a legend.'

'The point about Sidney and me is this, Mrs Wheeler: neither of us had a particularly good start in life. We've both had to survive on talent alone. That can be hard work because we've nothing much to fall back on. Sidney was a generous man, but if he had a fault I'd say that he was almost too anxious for doors to open for him. The well-to-do can be like that, can't they, they can be indifferent. They don't see some casual rejection or jibe as harmful. I speak as someone who has spent years riding horses for an owner who is often appallingly rude, unapproachable and very domineering. For all Sidney despised the rich he wanted to be accepted by them. But he relaxed with me – he could be himself and stop acting.'

'Are you saying Sidney had too thin a skin for what he aimed to do?'

'Marjorie had great ambitions for him, certainly.'

It's just as I thought, your suspect wife sucked the soul out of you, dear Sidney. It wasn't enough to abandon you, she had to imply you were a failure, too?

'Except Sidney could be so witty and funny. At times he didn't have a care in the world. He could be the life and soul of the party. No one made me laugh like him.'

'A good ride out on Cleeve Hill breathed new life into him, Mrs Wheeler. But something was constantly gnawing at him inside, I suppose, not of his own making.'

'Suspicion….?'

'No.'

'…. that his own dodgy wife was no longer on his side?'

'Suspicion hardly covers it.'

'If it wasn't suspicion, what was it? What was eating into him?'

Gerry jerks his horse's head from my fingers and turns to leave the yard. He looks sideways at me with his usual cheerful smile that hides his core of inner steel.

'I think it was fear.'

***

Bella jumps into the sidecar as I kick-start my Brough Superior Combination back into action. I really ought to telephone Bearland Police Station, I ought to report what progress I've made to indict your killer, dear Sidney, but I know this is unreasonable. DI Lockett has to be given a chance to make a fool of himself and it won't do to feed his suspicions too soon.

That doesn't mean nobody has to pay for my disappointment.

Dead men can't speak, but I can.

EIGHT

DS Biggs was feeling literally on top of the world. The roar of the supercharged 1,125cc four-cylinder engine was music to his ears, as he bowled along the A40 at a toe-tingling forty-five m.p.h. towards Sherborne in his Austin 10. It wasn't every day he got to drive the shiny, black police car all by himself, this high on the Cotswolds.

Arriving at a set of large iron gates topped with faded armorial panels, he entered rolling parkland. He could have been back in the eighteenth century, except a large part of the surrounding farmland had been given over to RAF Windrush for the training of pilots on its grassy fields. So much so that, in 1942, two steel net runways had been laid to ensure all-weather availability and the impressive complex of Blister hangars, Nissen huts, pillboxes and Watch Tower had seen a lot of action. Despite less need for new bomber crews just lately, the airfield was fully operational as a Relief Landing Ground. He knew this with confidence because his brother Ben worked here as a mechanic servicing North American Harvard and Airspeed Oxford training aircraft.

Three times enemy planes had tried to bomb the heart out of this place, mistaking its lights for nearby RAF Rissington.

But none of that was the slightest help to him now as he stood outside the biggest house he'd ever visited.

Should he wear his hat on his head or carry it respectfully in his hand, he wondered, as he stepped up to the imposing front entrance in the mansion's north side? On his head might convey more authority.

He'd thought about it on his journey here.

He'd thought about it quite a lot.

An unsmiling maid dressed in a Peter Pan collar and French mop cap trimmed with fancy hem stitching opened the door to him. 'Tradesman's entrance is round the back.'

'Good morning, miss. My name is Detective Sergeant Biggs from the Gloucestershire Police. I'd like to speak to Lady Dutton, if I may.'

'I'm afraid her ladyship isn't well.'

'It concerns her daughter Jolantha.'

'Who? In that case, detective, you'd better follow me. Please wipe your feet.'

How anyone could feel at home in such a cavernous building, he didn't know. Perhaps the larger your house the greater your imagination became, as if you learnt to grow into your surroundings? It made his own little terraced property look like a rabbit hutch. He trod pine board floors in the hall and entered some sort of reception room where the bewildered maid left him to twiddle his thumbs.

He had no wish to be uncharitable, but it did seem to him that the woodwork could do with a good wash. The rug underfoot was also curling at the corners, he noted. His mother had been in service with a wealthy family and he knew some of the tricks – always apply a hot iron to the reverse side of carpets to kill moths. Looking about him, he observed with a knowing smile how faded red curtains had been turned upside down and reversed at the last spring cleaning.

The maid eventually returned pushing a pale-faced woman in her fifties in a wheelchair. Her blue eyes were burning, her cheeks were pinched, her lips were shrunken and her greying hair looked dishevelled as if from some drenching sweat in the night. She fiddled with one of the silver buttons on her long-sleeved jacket and plucked compulsively at its light blue chiffon lining.

'You wished to speak to me, detective? What's this all about?'

DS Biggs bent his head briefly, then regretted it. Should the law bow to its betters? Probably not.

'The thing is, your ladyship, there's been a fatal incident in Gloucester Cathedral. On November 1st Sidney and Marjorie Sheppard fell from…'

'Not too close, detective…' Lady Dutton gave a sudden, violent cough into her handkerchief, then banged her fist on her chest as if to suppress the pain.

'Perhaps I should speak to your husband, instead?'

'He's not here. He's busy arranging to give up Sherborne House, all thanks to this war. Have you seen what the RAF has done to half the estate? We live with the constant racket of aircraft coming and going.'

'I don't wish to inconvenience you…'

'Get on with it, man. The whole county must know about Sidney Sheppard and his wife by now.'

'It appears your daughter was present when the tragedy took place.'

'Did Jolantha tell you that?'

'She heard the victims' cries as they fell.'

'That's what I thought.'

'She was very convincing.'

'Oh *really.*'

'Did I say something wrong?'

'Jolantha will tell anyone anything to get attention, detective. She's not to be trusted.'

DS Biggs reached for his notebook and pencil. 'You mean she's a fantasist?'

'She didn't have a spell in a mental hospital for nothing.'

'Are you suggesting she's unstable?'

'I should know.'

He took a deep breath. 'By 'unstable' do you also mean violent?'

'What kind of daughter points a shotgun at her own mother?'

'She really did that to you?'

Lady Dutton used a skeletal arm to shift position in her chair. Her predicament had seen her lose so much weight that the smallest effort quickly fatigued her. 'You'd better believe it.'

DS Biggs struggled to articulate the exact purpose of his visit.

'Did your daughter tell you that she and Sidney Sheppard were courting? Did she ever bring him here?'

'No, but Jolantha has always been a headstrong, difficult girl, detective. Not like her brother Hugo. She has never been able to accept her proper station in life and behave like a lady. And to think I called her after Iolanthe. In Greek her name means pretty blue flower. In reality, she's been nothing but trouble.'

'I'm simply trying to establish the exact nature of the relationship between your daughter and the deceased.'

Lady Dutton pulled her grey woollen blanket up her knees as far as her gown's belt and buckle.

'I'm sorry, how does that help me?'

'…?'

'I've been very ill, detective. I could have died. Why isn't my only daughter at my side? She only comes here to scrounge free petrol from one of the estate's farms to use in her brother's motorcycle, since farmers can still get fuel. She should be arrested. Instead she's gallivanting about, doing what she likes with whomever she likes. Sidney wasn't the first – she's already had a child by an American GI. Jolantha is no better than a Yankee bag.'

He was familiar with the term, but shocked to hear it nevertheless. Any woman who spent too much time with American soldiers was likely to be called a 'Yankee bag' these days, but he wasn't here about that. 'So you can't tell me if she had reason to quarrel with Sidney for any particular reason?'

'She falls out with all her men eventually.'

'Does she harbour grudges?'

'Don't we all?'

'You say Jolantha has been ill in the past. Is she fully recovered and coping okay now, in your opinion?'

'I wouldn't say that.'

'What would you say?'

Lady Dutton wiped her hand across her brow and suddenly looked feverish again. 'Jolantha craves unconditional love and heaven help those who don't give it to her, detective. Dreams shatter when they fall to earth. She can be positively vengeful. Ask her psychiatrist in Coney Hill Mental Hospital. Now I really must lie down. Please see yourself out, won't you.'

A spluttering plane was circling perilously low over Sherborne House and adjoining church when DS Biggs walked back to his Austin 10. He could see why the Dutton family might wish to move on. At least one Wellington bomber had crashed in flames on the nearby runway when its engine failed; it was a miracle that nothing had ever struck the home itself.

He was all set to climb behind the steering wheel when, growing curious, he turned about and embarked on a quick tour of the gardens. He inspected the stable block and meat house and stopped to admire the remains of an impressive Pleasure Ground that ran south, uphill and away from the mansion with its terraces, brick walls and clipped yews. But he saw nothing untoward as he entered the orangery to smoke a much-needed Player's Navy Cut No. 9 in the warmth of its paraffin stoves.

'Can I help you, detective?'

He was wrong to think he could snoop about without being noticed. 'Excuse me, sir, I'm DS Biggs. I hope you don't think I'm taking liberties?'

A man in his thirties turned his head his way and he was immediately aware of the horrible disparity between the grin on the veteran's lips and the terrifying holes in his head. Blank eyes focused on him, but saw nothing.

'The maid has told me why you're here, detective. But you shouldn't believe anything my mother says about my sister, she's a vindictive old witch. She should be in a sanatorium even as we speak. Instead she's doing her best to give us all TB. It's one reason I stay out here. I'm Hugo, by the way.'

'Her ladyship does seem to have it in for her daughter, I must admit.'

'That's why she lied to you.'

'Lied? Surely not? Does she often do that?'

'My sister isn't as vengeful as my mother wishes you to believe, Detective. Jolantha is just trying to make sense of her life, like us all.'

He very much wanted to reach for his notebook, but feared that Hugo would hear him scratching tell-tale words on paper with his pencil. How he had known it was him in the orangery, he didn't know, he could only think it must have been the sound of his police boots on the stone floor.

'Did your sister talk to you about a Sidney Sheppard, by any chance? I have reason to believe they were very close.'

'Sidney? Oh yes. Jo had set her heart on him and I was so happy for her. She even threatened to run away with him. I was about to give her the money to buy a wedding dress for the big occasion. Of course Sidney had to hurry up and secure his divorce first...'

'That's not going to happen now.'

Hugo banged about with his white stick as he shuffled closer to a table and carafe. 'Can I interest you in a sherry, detective?'

'That's very kind of you, sir, but I'm on duty.'

'I presume Mother told you we're vacating Sherborne?'

'She did.'

'I know every inch of this place. It's going to be a challenge finding my feet somewhere new.'

'Forgive me, but how did you...?'

'Lose my eyes? I was sitting in the top of a tank when a German grenade hit the turret. On the bright side I lived to tell the tale. Plenty haven't. Mother can't forgive this war for what it has done to her only son and heir. She's half out of her mind with outrage and horror and feels a need to vent her disappointment on somebody else – that somebody happens to be her own daughter.'

'Did Jolantha mention Sidney's wife Marjorie, by any chance?'

'I know they clashed at his brother's wedding last May.'

'Last May? Are you sure?'

'I hope you're not shocked, detective, by our little family ways.'

'The thing is, when we interviewed your sister at the police station she gave us the distinct impression that she didn't know Marjorie at all well. I'd go so far as to say she let us believe they were perfect strangers.'

'That's Jolantha for you. She gets muddled. Ever since she was dragged unconscious from a blazing building during the Bristol Blitz, she's had trouble remembering basic things. Sometimes she can't be sure what she has and hasn't seen. She's a casualty of this conflict, too, detective. There was a time recently when she nearly lost faith in everything. She went to the brink with drink. Discovered bliss in Guinness! That's why this wedding to Sidney was so important to her. I sometimes think I'll come out of this war better than she will, but she's strong. I believe in her. You should, too.'

'Hmm. I see. Well, thank you for your time, sir.'

'That's quite all right, detective. I felt I owed you an explanation. My sister's really a very sweet soul.'

DS Biggs marched back to his car. He'd come here secretly hoping to rule Jolantha out of his inquiries. Instead he reached for a hasty cigarette to replace the one he had so foolishly squandered among the oranges and lemons. So she had lied – she did know Marjorie after all. It sounded trivial but the more he thought about it, the more concerned he became. Did that mean Marjorie had chosen to know Jolantha, too?

On balance, he felt bound to side with Lady Dutton rather than Hugo, for now. Jolantha might get muddled, but that only proved she was not to be trusted?

NINE

Jacqueline and I may be stuck in our shabby little parlour in Gloucester, but I'm tuning into music from foreign stations on the wireless. In my head it's 'Wings for Victory Week' all over again. The jazz music makes a welcome change from the BBC and its hours of boring organ concertos. With you gone, dear Sidney, there's no stopping that time before you and I existed – I'm reliving jitterbugging on the dance hall floor to raise funds to build more Spitfires last year in Bristol.

As I swing to the music, it feels as if everyone in the whole world is with me tonight. Factory girls and those in ATS uniforms do the quickstep with merchant convoy sailors. Smart airmen clap hands with WAAF women. Meanwhile an army boy squeezes his knees together in a straight, narrow line pressing down on the balls of his feet as he does the Shorty George…

I cup my hands behind my head and swing my hips as fast as I can while the piano blasts in my ears. This place is so packed I was afraid I wouldn't get in at 10 p.m. My GI dance partner takes me in his arms – I'm pecking his forehead frantically with mine. We both shake our kneecaps. I kick my feet one by one, when suddenly he bends down and I swing a leg high over his head to flash my thighs. Next minute I'm head first over his shoulder from floor to air.

In all the excitement and noise I can hardly make myself heard: 'What's your name, soldier?'

'Joshua Jackson. What's yours?'

'You can call me Jo.'

Everyone watching us is applauding and shouting, 'Take that thing!'

I can't stop staring at my handsome swinger. He looks so smart in his olive drab uniform with its khaki mohair tie and gabardine shirt. I hold on hard to his hands as I skate him in circles in his leather-soled shoes round the shiny floor. Once he shouts 'Cut a rug, baby!' Otherwise we don't talk too much. He's hungry for me and I'm hungry for him – it's gone beyond talk, it's on a whole different level. We're back at the beginning as if we've only just met – it's the ball of the foot then the heel, in two slow 'dig' steps, followed by one foot back and one in place but very quick. We each take a step to the side, then execute two 'shuffles' – it's side step, almost-close-other-foot, then side step in 4/4 time with syncopated rhythm.

I'm as drawn to his dark eyes as I am to his drawl. He's from America's Deep South and can't believe his luck that he's got to jive with someone like me. But I'm the lucky one who's grateful. No one I know can swing hips like him!

I'm over his back in a backward flip that sees me land on my feet, only to have him slide down my leg like an eel.

He's strong but respectful. On the dance floor every person is equal. We're wagging our heads at each other and pointing furiously before doing spins – we're jumping and clapping as I take the lead, then he leads me on. It's swing those hips again. It's shake those knees. It's wiggle that arse. Most of all, it's jump for joy...

We crook our elbows and strut chicken-style. We jump and kick our heels and walk with purpose before we wave goodbye.

Another night a gang of white GIs will catch us canoodling in a doorway and start a fight. The American Military Police in jeeps will arrive dressed in their pretty white caps, white gaiters atop their olive drab uniforms and MP armbands, looking as if they couldn't hurt a fly. These 'snowdrops' will beat Joshua black and blue and threaten to have him hanged by the neck until dead in Shepton Mallet jail not twenty miles from here, because their word is law, even in Britain.

But that's not this night. Right now I'm seeing only smiles, while I walk Bristol's blacked out streets in my memory. Joshua and I are in each other's arms at the side of the brewery, near the churchyard, as he struggles to fit a condom which gets all tangled up in his fingers until I can't wait any longer... We're kissing and giggling as he has his hand up my skirt while I pop the three large pearl buttons that undo my raspberry pink camiknickers from below…

My head's still spinning with laughter and dance tunes until all I can think of is I'm alive.

I never told you about my brief time with Joshua, dear Sidney, I never got the chance. I guess you might not have been too pleased, but then again it was my choice, my fling, my cri de coeur – this was me grabbing life by the horns again, if only for a short while and with no hope of marriage.

Then you came along and made me your marvellous promise. Which is why I can't let this business of your death go unchallenged. Don't tell me I have nothing to lose.

TEN

John Curtis and I are partway up the narrow, spiral stairs by which we left the south transept – we're carrying our stirrup pumps and buckets of sand and water up to the top of the great tower. These low, ancient doorways were not built for someone his size, but as cathedral verger he alone holds the keys to all the locks. He's only five years older than me, yet he's huffing and puffing and banging his elbows on the curving stone walls which doesn't improve his temper. Beads of sweat bubble on his brow like drops of rain.

'Bloody steps. They get steeper every time.'

'I thought you'd resolved to do more exercise?'

'I've cut out eggless pancakes for breakfast.'

'Didn't I say you should run round the cloisters with me and Bella every morning?'

'And you should stick to "The Women's League of Health and Beauty".'

Bella mounts the steps in leaps and bounds and wonders what all the fuss is about. We're squeezing ourselves past the massive bell of Great Peter of Gloucester as well as the glass house enclosing the clock. Still ascending, we come to the peal of ten bells and machinery by which the chimes are set in motion at one, five and eight o'clock.

Once we're on the tower's roof we have a fine view of the dimmed-out city below.

The massed formations of German bombers may have stopped coming but on the morning of August 31, twenty flying bombs were launched at Gloucester between 04.30 and 05.00 hours from the North Sea. Luckily only eight made landfall and they came down in Suffolk and Essex, but there might yet be rockets. That's the trouble with fire watch duties, you never know when to expect the Luftwaffe's next big surprise.

John blows on his cold fingers as he takes up position next to one of the tower's spiky stone pinnacles. 'No wind tonight. That's good. Perhaps we won't freeze to death for a change.'

I'm already scanning the moon-lit sky though my binoculars as he breaks out carrot sandwiches all round. 'Want one, Jo?'

'You know what I think about your carrot sandwiches.'

'I've gone easy this time on the mustard sauce.'

'I think I'll stick to my fish paste and parsley.'

'Have you seen sense yet? Have you stopped fretting about Sidney's unfortunate "accident"?'

'Nobody, it seems, doubts a thing so far.'

'Listen to yourself. This isn't your life's mission but your life you're talking about. You're not doing anyone any favours by stirring up trouble.'

'Has it not occurred to you, John, that I might have been set up? Someone could yet try to make me take the rap for his fall.'

'Just let me ask you one thing. You can answer it or not, it's up to you.'

'Now what?'

'What are you afraid of?'

'Justice.'

'I keep telling you, there's no way you need blame yourself for any of it.'

'This isn't about lives lost but the life we had coming. Sidney was about to be my future and I his.'

John nods but I'm not sure he fully understands. 'Or you wanted someone to replace Jack and Joshua and be a father to Jacqueline?'

I refuse to listen. It might appear that I'm looking at a peaceful sky, but really I'm seeing searchlights, tracers and the bright white glow of exploding bombs. I'm back in Bristol in 1940 and '41, mentally wandering a place suddenly turned upside down…

My road is blocked by fallen walls that have flooded each thoroughfare with rivers of debris. Curiously, most individual bricks look largely undamaged – it's as though whole buildings have simply become unstuck, loosened and prised apart into their constituent pieces. I have the crude notion that if I could wave a magic wand, everything would simply rise up and, like Humpty Dumpty, cement itself back together again. You helped bury what happened to me, dear Sidney, but now you're gone old memories resurface…

As if the solution to everything lies in the past as much as the future?

When I shut my eyes I'm straight back to the place where I once went to have my hair done. I'm picking my way over a sign that says "guaranteed permanent waving" which has plunged from the hairdressing salon on the burnt-out first floor of WILLSONS at Nos. 72 & 73 Castle Street. I'm standing beside fallen sans serif neon letters that advertised its café on the ground floor where I took tea most Wednesday afternoons.

I live with these dead ruins every minute of every day, my love. I'm neither here nor there, only in limbo. On my left, Cock and Bottle Lane is pretty much impassable, thanks to mountains of smoking timber, although I can see as far as the Bristol Co-op whose stylish, curved frontage now resembles the smoky bridge of a shipwrecked liner. Everything is black, burnt, gone.

Back in Castle Street, the stench is odd. As I've told you before, I don't often smell anything in my dreams. This one is different. As I negotiate more screes of rubble the heady taint of burnt beer barrels wafts my way from the cellar of the wrecked pub "Standard of England".

I'm looking for "Jack and Jo's Sweet Store" in a street growing increasingly anonymous. Whole sets of premises have simply vanished from the face of the earth. When I do find my shop it is almost indistinguishable wreckage.

Into my dream steps a fellow observer to gaze at the embers. He carries in his hand a brown paper bag of sweets, but when he looks my way his damaged face scarcely has lips to suck or chew…

'Should I know you?' I cry, only he's gone already in a gust of smoke.

It's only one of my customers following old routines now lost forever…

I'll not be handing him any more humbugs or peppermints any time soon…

I know you witnessed complete devastation in the Midlands, dear Sidney, I know you saw the Blitz in London, too, but what I'm treading now is the almost complete destruction of what used to be me before I knew you… I bought furniture here at No. 27 from a house furnishers called Cunnons. My brother had repairs done to his Brough Superior Combination at nearby Castle Wall Garage while Jack drank with friends in "The Warriors Arms". I had two pictures for our marital home framed by J.H. Welsh at Nos. 23-25. It was there, too, that Jack and I had our wedding cake decorated…

But the right-hand side of Lower Castle Street has suffered almost total erasure. "The Onion Oyster Bar" at No. 8 is gone. So, too, are the Bristol Loan Office, billiard room, pub, dining rooms, the lamp and store factors and printers.

This part of the street has always been terribly narrow – it backs on to the old castle wall and juts out beyond its neighbours. Here the roadway pinches to a place where two tramlines merge in an awkward bottleneck controlled by a one-eyed points boy who has to stop and start the cars. I once gave him a stick of liquorice to keep him warm as he kept watch with his pole in the pouring rain. I'm standing before an open trapdoor in the pavement out of which the congregation crawled unscathed from the cellars, after bombs blitzed The Welsh Congregational Church on the 24th of November…

You must be wondering why I feel the need to tell you all this in such excruciating detail, dear Sidney, but even ghosts deserve some connection to places they once loved. People suffered in these streets. Do you see their spectral shapes where I don't? Perhaps you should be the one to take me on a guided tour of my former haunts, not me, in this new netherworld? What could you show me? What did you?

Yet it's not all ruins. While the much loved 17th century Old Dutch House stands gutted on the corner of Wine Street awaiting demolition by the military authorities and my own street has been unofficially dubbed "Blitz Street", nearby Castle Mill Street and Castle Green have fared a bit better. I'm walking past the occasional intact shop and even in Bridge Street some places look reasonably okay. I could say I'm like one of these lucky survivors, that I've come through the blitz when those close to me haven't. Only I don't feel lucky.

You'll be glad to know I'm about to return to the point where I started, I'm on Bristol Bridge where my dreams invariably end at their beginning. Tomorrow night I'll make the same pilgrimage to call for my husband and daughter as I do most nights. I'll sift hot timbers with my bare hands, because in my nocturnal existence between life and death I don't experience any physical pain, only heartfelt emptiness and longing among the burnt-out churches, shops and houses and their abject silence.

'Jo? Are you all right?'

It's John, pressing a hot cup of tea into my hand. I struggle to catch my breath but I'm grateful – he's reminding me that I'm supposed to be keeping watch, hundreds of feet up on top of a tower.

'Sorry, I was miles away...'

'Did you really plan to marry Sidney?'

'We had something. Why wouldn't we get wed?'

John frowns and tweaks his moustache at me. 'You know you can never make things right, don't you?'

'Yes.'

'But you can make things worse.'

'That's a risk I'll have to take. This ignorant world of ours – this dark world at war – needs to know he alone was the light of my life. As it is, I feel totally unforgiving.'

ELEVEN

'Not too far now, sir,' cried DS Biggs into the teeth of the wind. They could already look back and see the tiny shapes of military vehicles parked on Cheltenham Race Course in the valley below. From this height they looked like children's toys. 'Take my hand. This last bit might prove tricky.'

DI Lockett shivered inside his trench coat as he was forced to negotiate an unexpectedly steep twist at the top of the tortuous path. 'If I'd known we were going mountain climbing I would have worn my boots.'

'We've come this high, sir.'

'But we'll catch our deaths up here.'

'If the cold doesn't kill you, I will.'

'What's that, sergeant?'

'You're absolutely right, sir, it's freezing. All the more reason to press on.' DS Biggs struck out along the edge of the limestone escarpment through patches of snow. At just over one thousand feet, Cleeve Hill was technically a mountain and the icy wind lashed his face while his hands froze. They were on their way to the death scene at the edge of the common.

He'd been told that on a clear day you could see the Black Mountains over seventy miles away, or look into the Evesham Valley, but today the horizon was shrouded in cloud.

They were at the highest point in Gloucestershire and one of the oldest. Was it any wonder that the Iron Age earthworks before them sometimes went by their other name of 'Cleeve Cloud Fort'. It was also a golf course.

The spot they had to aim for lay beyond the hill's ancient banks, cross ditch and its mysterious ring that may or may not have been built to pen animals. They were crossing a place that had been farmed 6000 years ago, but it was the cutting of stone on an industrial scale that had created such vertiginous cliffs.

'This has to be where she went over, sir.'

DI Lockett approached the edge with caution. The quarrymen had blasted their way into the north-western part of the common where their drills had dug straight into the scarp face of the hill. One careless act and a gust of wind could sweep him into the void. He was looking at a sheer drop of hundreds of feet to hard rocks below.

'What was she doing up here, anyway?'

'Mrs Tuffley was a keen golfer, sir. She made a point of playing in all weathers. Those are her clubs you can see scattered all over the cliff face.'

'And this happened when, you say?'

'A farmer looking for a stray sheep found her body at eleven o'clock this morning. For a while the weather had taken a sudden turn for the worse when a hill fog came down…'

'So she could have wandered off the edge in the mist?'

'Everyone I've spoken to says she knew these rocks like the back of her hand.'

Certainly the artificially created cliff had no ledges, bushes or trees to break a person's fall. One nudge and you were gone. He screwed up his eyes and watched police officers guard the scene far below.

'No signs of foul play on the body, sergeant?'

'No, sir.'

'Suicide?'

'Apparently she was reckoned to be a bit of a battleaxe – a very tough lady. Not exactly the suicidal type. But there is one thing I've discovered which might be of interest.'

'What's that?'

'The ex-National Hunt jockey Gerry Wilson lodges at Mrs Tuffley's "High Grove" not too far from here. He confirms that's where Sidney Sheppard stayed as per the address on his ID Card. More to the point, Jolantha Wheeler stopped by a few days ago. It explains the presence of her visiting card in the deceased's pocket.'

'Jolantha Wheeler? How odd.'

'She was asking all sorts of questions about Sidney, apparently.'

DI Lockett looked again into the abyss. The landlady's broken and bloodied body might have been loaded into an ambulance hours ago and the whole area cordoned off, but the scene still sent a chill down his spine. Death had been mercifully quick – her skull had smashed like an egg on a crag.

'How well did Mrs Tuffley and Sidney Sheppard get on, I wonder?'

'He always paid his rent on time and she cooked regular meals for him. She even drove him to a mental hospital in Stoke-on-Trent when he fell ill. Why do you ask?'

'So definitely no bad blood between them?'

'Only this. A week ago she suddenly gave him notice to quit his digs. I don't know why.'

'Or she didn't fancy a 'madman' living under her roof?'

'To be fair, sir, Sidney Sheppard had been certified sane by his doctor.'

'Try telling that to her neighbours.'

DI Lockett turned abruptly from the cliff's edge and started back along the brow of the hill at some speed. If he'd heard anything to arouse his suspicions, he didn't say so, he only dwelt on a world full of petty unkindnesses. Such slights delivered daily could wear a person down to the point where they did something very stupid? He thought he knew how that might feel. When he stood in a pub drinking beer with Oliver he had to be on his guard not to make the wrong gesture or smile the wrong smile in case he got noticed by a hostile crowd. When the world refused to countenance your feelings, or deliberately set out to destroy them, it could soon result in burning resentment.

Mrs Tuffley may have been too hard on Sidney at just the wrong time.

It could be difficult to forgive.

For some.

DS Biggs did his best to catch up. 'Did you know they used to race horses up here, sir, before they built the new racecourse down in the valley?'

'No, I didn't.'

'Crowds of up to 50,000 attended an annual two-day July meeting. It must have been quite a sight. A by-law still prohibits "gambling, betting or playing with cards or dice at any time on the Common".'

'I bet it doesn't mention murder?'

TWELVE

I'm standing outside "Thanet Court" on the Hanger Hill Garden Estate in Ealing, dear Sidney. Your former block of flats is black and white and half-timbered, until I feel I'm in some fantastical 'Tudorbethan' England.

I must have passed eighteen similar fake mansions with their tall Tudoresque chimneys on my way here.

Bella jumps out of the motorcycle sidecar to wee on the nearest privet hedge, in what amounts to an enormous grassy courtyard. You spoke of us possibly moving in here for a while when the war ends, my love. How long did you and Marjorie live under this roof in your future marital home that never was? We're talking about a few months? Less? Either way, I'm here to banish the spectre of your hateful bride.

Now she's gone, it can be mine.

I long to feel your presence as I approach 'ye olde worlde' oak front door whose low, sweeping roof is more suited to a lychgate in a churchyard than someone's Home Sweet Home. The main thing is that Bella and I are following the evidence. Consider this physical proof of what we were going to have, my love. I fully expect to see somebody stand beneath the tiled porch through which you once walked to our love's abode – I'm waiting for a spectral 'you' to greet me at any moment.

'Good morning. Are you Mrs Wheeler?' The gravelly voice of a middle-aged man in a neat, grey suit puts an end to my wishful thinking. There's a thin black moustache over his top lip and his hair is slicked flat with Brylcreem; his fingers are dyed yellow with nicotine. Most people have given up wearing vests with their suits since they regard them as a waste of cloth in this period of shortages, along with raglan sleeves, turn-ups and half belts. But not him. A loop of silver watch chain dangles from his waistcoat pocket.

'Yes, I'm Mrs Wheeler.' I hold out my gloved hand as he looks aghast at my oilskin leathers and helmet.

'How-do-you-do. My name is Mr Dew. I represent the Hanger Hill Garden Estate and I manage the letting for the Cooper family who owns everything you see around you.'

Is this the same person who welcomed you, years ago, my love? I should think so, since the Estate prefers to conduct all letting of flats itself, not via other agents. To take this man's hand is to connect with you, dear Sidney – I regard it as a brief grip across time.

'We spoke on the phone about flat No.18.'

'We have a second, larger property that you can view, too.'

'Sorry. Only No.18 will do.'

'Hanger Hill Estate is an excellent choice, madam. It is only ten years old and one of the finest in London. One especially good feature is its relative privacy – there are only three ways in by road. You will probably have noticed the very scenic 'duck pond' at the junction of Monks Drive and Links Road?'

'Well, I can't say…'

'You simply must let me show you the rose garden at the north end of Princes Garden.'

'If we could just go inside?'

But there's no stopping his spiel. 'What you have here is a little bit of the countryside in the big city. Consider it the ideal, romantic expression of rural Metroland. Nearby is the Hanger Hill Club where you can drink and play tennis.'

Just to hear *that* club's name sees my blood run cold, my love. I recall how much it rankled when you told me how Marjorie arranged to meet you there, along with her brother Norman and his wife Nessie, for a reunion of pre-war friends in June 1943? The last '65' bus went about 8.30, but she could go up to town and catch the 10 o'clock down from Waterloo. You never made it because that was the day you collapsed shaking in front of a factory in Leeds – you had a total mental and physical breakdown.

Your shameless spouse went to the club without you. To miss your chance to catch up with the likes of old pals Bernard and Kath must have been a terrible blow as your former social life continued on a parallel track without you…

'Are you okay, madam?'

It's Mr Dew, attracting my attention again.

'Do I look as if I'm not okay?'

'Well, ahem, as I was saying, you are choosing to live in an exceptionally quiet and attractive location. All you'll hear in the evening is the sound of birdsong. I love it.'

'I'm sure you do.'

'You like birds?'

'Not so much.'

Mr Dew neglects to mention that elsewhere on the Estate I counted five fire-scorched houses in complete ruins. Many other buildings have lost tiles off their roofs or have wooden boards for windows. It is a sobering thought that, had you gone on living here, my love, you might have been killed by a bomb or rocket as you strolled along.

'Would you care to see inside now, madam?'

'I thought you'd never ask.'

Next minute Mr Dew leads the way upstairs to flat No.18. I'm rather apprehensive, even though I'm here to pick up where you left off.

'A few windows were smashed by a bomb which fell in the field near the cricket pavilion, but otherwise this place has escaped the war thus far. Please note, Madam, that the delightful lounge comes fully furnished. Mrs Sheppard personally bought the linen chair-back covers for 1/11d each in Bentalls to protect the furniture.'

I feel my toes curl. 'Oh, she did, did she?'

'They still look quite nice and they've certainly protected the material quite a lot.'

My eye settles on a carpet sweeper and then a coffee table which requires some polishing. Did your woeful wife buy those, too, dear Sidney? I don't like this any more than you do. I suddenly feel like a revenant myself. All I hear is silence. All I sense is stillness. All I feel is absence. I don't want this to be a place for ghosts only. The sight of the chair-back covers comes as a nasty shock, I must admit.

Nevertheless, it's a relief to find anything tangible of yours, because I know for a fact that Marjorie and her younger sister Babs cleared most of your newly acquired wedding gifts out of here ready for the subletting. You told me how she did it without you because you were already far way in Warrington – ten hours by train from London – in your new job. I can just imagine them trying to stow all your belongings inside suitcases and carriers ready to take them to Auntie Allie's – I wish I'd been here to see them trying to get a dinner, breakfast and tea service along with an hors d'oeuvre set and cocktail shaker on to a No.112 bus! I can just imagine them leaving a trail of pastry forks, grapefruit spoons and fish knives half way across Ealing. In the event, the two cases were too heavy to carry far and they had to call a taxi. It cost them 3/-, worse luck, if I remember you correctly. Unfortunately, there was such a lot left, they had to dump a good many items at her parents' place in Creighton Road. At least her mum and dad hadn't yet moved to Esher.

I should have realised the plan was to preserve your flat for your future return.

I didn't know Marjorie tried to play the fussy housewife.

Too bad it's my job to keep house now and not her.

'Before we go any further, Mrs Wheeler, I must tell you some more about the flat – it really has had two sets of model tenants since the Sheppards left so abruptly at the end of 1939.'

'Just to be clear, when did they first take out the lease?'

'It was during that summer, five years ago. But as you can see, the only things that show slight wear and tear are the walls and ceiling and they are not your concern.'

It's true, the only damage I can see is a slight cigarette burn on the dining room table.

'The carpets, madam, are almost unworn and the lounge suite looks very clean, I think you'll agree. The last tenants here, the Linds, were very particular. For instance, they broke the Morphy Richards iron and immediately took a lot of trouble to get it repaired. Likewise, the towel rail in the bathroom. The only reason they are leaving is because Mr Lind's wife is going to have a baby in April and they are going to live with her parents at Leigh-on-Sea. He has a job at Park Royal and is going to travel all that distance every day, poor man...'

You might not think I want to hear all this, dear Sidney, but actually I do. I want to discover who lived here in your stead, who used your things, who trod your carpets and slept in your bed. I want to feel close to the life you created but never had, before your atrocious wife spoilt it all.

'The Linds, you say?'

'Mrs Lind is a Norwegian and her husband is Swedish. They both escaped the Nazis in Norway in 1943. They arrived here without any china, linen or plate, but other people on the estate rallied round to get them started. That's the kind of friendly place you'll be moving into.'

'Is that so?'

Mr Dew's rat-like face contains very beady eyes. I can't say I altogether trust him.

'Of course there are one or two minor points still to be settled, Mrs Wheeler. The black-out curtains belong to the Linds, not the Sheppards. That goes for some of the china and that wireless you can see over there on the sideboard. Naturally I'll draw up a new inventory, once you confirm the day you want to move in.'

'Uh-huh.'

Bella is sniffing an Indian rug in what I take to be the spare room.

I leave her to it.

Sometimes a dog knows best.

Your kitchen is absolutely charming, my love, though I doubt Marjorie appreciated it as much as I do. Best of all is the vista. It's quite spacious and has superb views across what should be sports fields, except they've been dug up for allotments to aid the war effort. It gives the flat a very airy feel. Because there are no houses facing it, this window opens straight into the London sky. I'm looking at a lung that can let the city breathe freely. I can see why you chose this property above all the others. You have a very good eye.

'As you can observe, Mrs Wheeler, the gas cooker is spotlessly clean and still looks new.'

'Thanks, but I'd rather make up my own mind.'

'Ahem. Quite. Perhaps we should proceed to the master bedroom next?'

'Lead on, Mr Dew.'

'The linen clothes basket, electric clock, bathroom cabinet and brass vase all come with the flat.'

'I see.'

Mr Dew holds open the door to your bedroom and I can hear my heart beating as I enter.

I open a walnut veneered wardrobe and coat hangers hang inside, though I doubt they're yours, dear Sidney.

Mr Dew is being very pushy. 'There is one thing to be settled. The leaseholders' representative proposes to sell the oak bed, mattress and bedding. I suggest a price of £10 complete. He also wants you to purchase the cream-tiled kerb from the fireplace in the lounge.'

'When were you told that?'

'Mr Wallis rang yesterday. He's the father of Mrs Marjorie Sheppard…'

'You don't say?'

Suddenly I'm furious again. How dare your father-in-law decide the fate of your belongings. I have a good mind to take the flat here and now and claim my rightful inheritance.

But I say nothing.

It's not so easy treading in the ashes of a broken dream when you and I could have done so much better – I would have made you a lot happier than Marjorie ever did, my darling. This is where you and I were going to sleep, make love and conceive our children. I wouldn't have been your frigid spouse but your passionate consort.

Truth is, this place was nothing except a burden to you. It must have been a constant reminder of what you should have been doing instead of being forced to live away from your inconsiderate bride.

'I have one question. Should I ever have to sublet in the same way the Sheppards have done, how would I be paid? How have you been paying them?'

'We send the rent to Mrs Sheppard, as per instruction.'

'Not to her husband?'

'The Hanger Hill Estate office does not pay money straight into bank accounts, but sends regular postal orders for £2-10-10. These being crossed, Mrs Sheppard has been obliged to pay them into her account *in person*, since Mr Sheppard has not been living in London.'

I could have expected no less. Your money grubbing wife managed to talk you into getting her hands on all the income from the flat, did she not, my love? It's another black mark against her in my book. Not that I don't sympathise a bit. I've had a quick look at the figures: there's always something to be deducted from the rent, such as 18/6 per month for rates and in January they will be taking 30/- for cleaning the hall etc. You weren't getting much of a bargain, were you, darling?

'Excuse me, madam. Did you hear a word I said?'

'What? Sorry.' Mr Dew is anxious to get back down to business. 'Please do carry on.'

'A flat of this type is £15 a month. You can pay the rent at the Estate office which you'll find at 2-4 Queen's Drive. If you'd like to take out a three-year lease, then the Estate will redecorate everything for you.'

I'm sorely tempted. I can't lose by it since I can, it turns out, always sublet it for a profit the same way you did, dear Sidney? There's maybe a catch in it, of course. 'I'll think about it and let you know very soon, Mr Dew.'

'May I remind you, Mrs Wheeler, that demand for these properties is high.'

I know what the Estate wants, it wants to get a couple of hundred tenants or so to sign long leases and then sit back and relax. For a shifty, nasty-eyed man, Mr Dew has more or less given the game away. I don't envy you dealing with him one bit, dear Sidney.

'Bella, come.'

'Please allow me to walk you to the office, madam. It's not very far…'

'Sorry, but I have to be somewhere.'

I'm back at your stalled beginning, my love. All your hopes for future bliss were invested in this flat only for complete strangers to reap all the benefits. Except, those other people have been happy here. I'm almost glad. If you and Marjorie couldn't live here as man and wife, it is wonderful to think that you provided such a pleasant home for two people running for their lives from the forces of evil. It is somehow typical that, in the face of your own misfortune that you should be able to help someone else. This place doesn't feel half as cursed as I'd feared, just soulless without you to give it meaning.

Back on my Brough Superior, I pull on my gauntlets, helmet and goggles as Bella jumps into the sidecar. I'll not be returning. It's too late for that now. I can't live here without you, after all – I can't live in rooms that feel so full of *her*, not you. The unwanted do not always stay unwanted in our own minds.

On the other hand, I'd be a fool to come all this way and not do something about it – it'll be a shame to waste a very real opportunity.

I need to see with my own eyes where your negligent wife ran off to live without you, my love, five years ago. If I am finally to be rid of her I have to smoke out that den of iniquity she called her real home, at least. Never let it be said I didn't come prepared.

That's why I've packed a five-gallon jerrycan of petrol in the sidecar.

THIRTEEN

CONEY HILL MENTAL HOSPITAL

Dear Violet, I hope all is well with you and life continues on its serene course of afternoon siestas on the settee with chocolates, followed by a little bridge, perhaps. It is not easy to write to you because you seem to have an inconsistent view of what is true and fair.

In the period between going to bed and falling asleep, I must have lain awake and thought hundreds of times, in fact thousands of times, about the great love between us. You obviously got many things wrong when you spoke so kindly to me in Bristol, years ago – you greatly compounded my difficulties by saying the exact opposite of what you thought or felt.

I fear you have never been able to face the enormity of what you did to me at the beginning, still less the enormity of the way in which you did it. You have made no attempt to be honest with me and I doubt whether you have been with others. I must admit that I view your silence with mixed feelings. Once again there is the apparent desire to insult or wound me, if not directly, then by inference, which I feel arises from your own intense feelings of guilt.

There has not been much I could do to fulfil our love when so often lately you have been completely hostile – I had to conclude from your outburst about not wishing to be the mother of my children that your love and loyalty lay elsewhere. Yet so many times in the distant past you greeted me happily with free peppermints and sherbets in your sweetshop. You were nice to me when nobody else was. It's so unfair. Life without you makes no sense to me, but only seems unbelievably squalid... Love, H.

FOURTEEN

So it turns out your wife's Claygate flat isn't a patch on the one you and she rented in Hanger Hill, dear Sidney! But I can see, even in the dark, that it is compact and easy to manage – Marjorie did very well for herself while she left you to suffer, my dear. Albany Crescent runs from the shops in Station Parade round to Foley Road. No.12 looks modern and self-contained and is built on a site which used to be known as "The Anchorage".

I'm here because I have to be able to explain why she did what she did to you in the cathedral.

There can be no room for ambiguity.

I have to be able to point the finger.

Call it character assassination.

Or getting to know your enemy.

I have to do it since she's failed to die.

Her priority is a home close to work at Ruxley Towers where the NAAFI is based. The rents may be steep in Claygate, but as to the cost of food I'm assured that office staff can enjoy a really sensible lunch at the NAAFI restaurant with fresh vegetables every day. In fact, there is a very large choice of food – soup, two fish, roast, several hot sweets and three cold. You, on the contrary, my love, had no such subsidised food to buy in Cheltenham. Is it any wonder you looked so thin when I first met you? I say this courtesy of the absurdly lewd publican in "The Foley Arms", where I'm staying for one night.

I got better sense out of the barmaid. 'Suffered much enemy action in Surrey, have you?'

The horse-faced girl with a nasty rash on her neck served me my pint of stout and took my enquiry in the spirit it was intended. That is, I was convincing in my concern.

'During the London Blitz incendiaries hit a few homes – three in Orchard Way, including Mr Hawthorn's from Evens & Co and one in Hare Lane. At one time "Milbourne House" had twenty in the grounds and Arbrook Common was littered with them. We felt horribly exposed in the glare as the Jerries hovered overhead while the firemen were trying to put out the fires. Now it's these damned rockets we have to dodge...'

It is amazing how accustomed you become to chatting about death and destruction after a while. That attack by a V2 on Woolworths a few weeks ago in New Cross, southeast London, killed 168 alone. Nearby Esher was hit in August and so was Cheam. Even as I look up, a faraway rocket zooms like a comet through the sky. I'm risking my life in "Doodlebug Alley" tonight for you, dear Sidney.

That's not good news.

Well, it is for me.

One more 'blast' won't raise any eyebrows.

I have with me those little grey files I rescued from Mrs Tuffley's clutches. Here is everything your hussy of a wife has been sending you for the last few years and more, by way of correspondence! As I say, always get to know thine enemy. I would never have presumed to pen such pitiful words on the 29th of September, 1941, for example, I would never have written such a begging letter. It only goes to show how far she was prepared to live beyond her means. At the very least Marjorie kept getting her sums wrong: 'My darling Rufus, could you possibly let me have £2 towards the rent? I've hardly spent a penny on myself this month (besides the usual everyday expenditure), but still have been unable to save the whole amount. Unfortunately, I had to give Peggy the Hanger Hill flat money as I borrowed from her on my return from Cheltenham. Sorry to be such a nuisance. All my love, Marjorie.'

I lean on my motorcycle as Bella keeps guard in the sidecar. It's a cold night but she's curled up on her blanket beside the petrol bomb.

If I haven't gone inside yet it's only because I want to be sure I'm not wrong about anything. But I needn't worry. Marjorie's letter dated the 12th of May 1942 says a lot. When you suggested that your unreliable wife apply for a job at the NAAFI, dear Sidney, I guess you were trying to save the financial situation the only way you knew how, but who could have foreseen that she would create a whole new existence for herself virtually overnight, which you'd help pay for:

'My darling Rufus, I have been going to buy some woollen dress material since January, but as you know, my money just fritters away and I don't seem to have anything to show for it. I've still got my clothing card almost intact and Peggy has offered to lend me a £ or two to enable me to get one or two things *before* the people rush to the shops with their new coupons... Therefore, darling, if you can possibly spare me a £1 or £2 before the new coupons are out I might get a better choice. I'm considering buying only an elastic belt (they are getting terribly scarce), some stockings and perhaps a length of material. Later on I would like another suit, but I don't expect that for quite a time.'

Now I would have thought you could easily have got £5.5.0 a week for the Hanger Hill flat, as there is a long waiting list at the Estate office. I think you were giving it away, my love, particularly with furniture at such prohibitive prices. I think your tenants should have paid for the cleaning of the staircase and the extra rates? Your trouble is, you're too generous. And reckless? Even your spendthrift wife says here, somewhat ruefully: 'I've duly read the newspaper cutting about post war gambling and I agree it is a risk worth taking to get some money. Well, have some fun working out our system.' So you thought you could bet your way out of trouble by backing horses, did you? I'm not blaming you, dear Sidney, I only sense your desperation.

Which brings me back to your duplicitous spouse. If she really did get herself a whole new life straight after she married you, why does she pen you the following on the 20th of May 1942: 'My Darling Rufus, I have at last written a congratulatory letter to Pam Mackeroy and have told her we hope to see her, the baby and as many of the old crowd as possible next month. I understand from Nessie that Kathleen is not working yet, and is to be seen coffeeing with our Vera every morning in Ealing Broadway. If it hadn't been for this wretched war, I should have been one of the select band of young matrons dallying in Broadway each morning, too. *This time of the year always makes me long to be back at our own flat in Hanger Hill with you...'*

I'm here to exorcise all the falsehood and calumnies – I can't trust the police to do it for me any time soon. I won't wait for another rocket to pass by, I'll go and finish it right now. I have enough petrol to do a good job.

I'm doing it for the best of reasons. You are rooting for me, I know you are, dear Sidney. It's only right and proper that this bordello should be wiped off the face of the earth. That is your command – I hear you – like an urgent whisper in my head...

FIFTEEN

'Now is not a good time detective.' The resident medical superintendent of Coney Hill Mental Hospital scratched his uncombed hair. 'I can spare you five minutes, that's all.'

DS Biggs's heart sank. Whoever had built this three-storey, red-brick administration block with its tall clock tower had done their best to relieve any institutional bleakness with some fancy blue brick diapering under the eaves, but it was equally well suited to a workhouse, factory or even a gasworks. The grumpy superintendent's words called to mind the embossed stone tablet that he'd passed on his way in – he found himself reciting its words under his breath right now "Bear ye one another's burdens".

'I'll try not to be any longer than necessary, sir.'

'You don't understand, detective. They've shut Bristol's new mental hospital at Barrow Gurney and evacuated some of the patients here. Except we're full already. How I'm expected to cope I don't know, when twenty of my male attendants have enlisted in the army. I simply don't have sufficient staff to man the wards any more. I'm having to run here, there and everywhere. Is it any wonder one of my patients has absconded?'

'Absconded?'

'Don't worry. Captain Hector Knevitt is one of our voluntary admissions.'

'Lose a lot of patients, do you?'

'Listen here, detective, these are exceptional times. The Captain is simply exploiting all the upheaval to take off on his motorcycle combination, as usual. He's pining for his imaginary sweetheart again. All he ever does is write endless love letters to someone called Violet – he does it on official Coney Hill Mental Hospital notepaper that he steals from my drawer. I've been known to take pity on him and give him a few sheets just to keep him happy. He won't use anything else because he thinks he works here. He believes he's her doctor. As I say, he'll be back the minute he runs out of stationery.'

DS Biggs put pencil to pad and made a note of the name. 'Is he not a risk to the public, then?'

'Not at all. Hector is a kindly soul.'

'How long has he been gone?'

'I really can't say.'

'Let me guess. One week? A few hours?'

'Staff found his bed empty on All Saints' Day.'

'November 1st?'

'That's all I have right now.'

'You don't report such 'absences' to the police, then?'

Superintendent Beal suddenly busied himself with his papers. 'Hector is a forty-nine-year-old ex-Royal Fusilier (City of London Regiment) who was gassed in The Great War. It still gives him delusions and nightmares and he can't live for long on his own before we have to re-admit him. Writing letters calms him down. Our country is full of such forgotten, troubled men, detective, but he will never harm anyone, if that's what you're worried about. He's not that sort. He's like a child. Wouldn't hurt a fly. He'll be back soon, or one of our nurses will find him. Last month he turned up in a sweetshop in Westgate Street.'

'Good to know. I'm here to eliminate someone from our enquiries, that's all.'

'Still doesn't make it convenient.'

'We can't do it without your help, sir.'

Superintendent Beal narrowed his eyes. Once a person's sanity became the subject of the law, the distinction between validation and incrimination could be a fine one. He fetched a set of files, the top one of which read "Alphabetical Register of Patients."

'Name?'

'Jolantha Wheeler, born Dutton.'

Superintendent Beal gave a start. There was a slight flush in his cheeks; his eyes flickered wildly from side to side; his voice choked; his hands seemed at a loss what to do on the desk. Then, licking his crooked teeth, he took a deep breath and opened the register before him. 'Are you quite certain that's who you want, detective?'

'Is there a problem?'

'Perhaps we should defer your enquiry until after I've telephoned her family?'

'That's not a reason.'

'To me it is. This could cost me my job.'

'I'll be the judge of that.'

'For heaven's sake, detective, the Duttons of Sherborne are some of the most important people in the county.'

'I promise you I'll be the soul of discretion.'

'You'd better be. Let's see now. Here we are. Admission date June 8, 1942. Discharge date September 20, 1942. Previous places of abode, a confectionary shop in Castle Street, Bristol. She was one of our very few patients to bring her own toothbrush.'

'And you tell me this, because?'

'What I mean to say is that Jolantha had all her own teeth. Plenty in here do not.'

DS Biggs reached for his notebook and pencil again. 'Just to be clear, superintendent. Did Jolantha go mad, in your opinion?'

'We don't use that word any more. We aim to help sick people, not simply lock them up like lunatics.'

He scribbled 'mad?' on his pad. While Superintendent Beal's discretion was admirable, they both knew what he said wasn't strictly true. When his 90-year-old grandmother lost her marbles she had to be locked away on the top floor of a remote mental hospital in Yorkshire for ten years, along with other violent inmates who were no longer to be trusted with kitchen knives.

'So what name would you give to her state of mind, superintendent, back then? If she wasn't mad, what was she?'

'Her form of nervous disorder was what we term nowadays as 'mental stress'. In layman's language you might call it shock, strain or worry. It builds over time, due to a variety of causes, until something triggers a crisis.'

'What crisis?'

'In Jolantha's case she tried to shoot her mother Primrose with a shotgun.'

'What was the fight about? Do you even know?'

'Primrose didn't want any daughter of hers consorting with American soldiers.'

'Is that why her mother had her committed?'

'No, she admitted herself.'

DS Biggs raised his eyebrows. 'Like Hector Knevitt?'

Superintendent Beal stroked his square chin. 'It's only been possible since the Act of 1930. Jolantha joined our unit for voluntary patients without any requirement for certification.'

DS Biggs had to admit he was somewhat out of his depths here. He still had in his head the image of a straightjacketed woman being dragged screaming into a padded cell. 'Is that what you mean when you say she wasn't mad? Or is 'mad' simply not the *technical* term in your books?'

'Jolantha knew she was mentally ill, detective.'

'I consider it rather percipient of her.'

'She didn't want to be that person any more.'

'I'll have to think about that.'

'Put yourself in her shoes. When I met her she was a wounded, grief-stricken widow. She had seen her husband Jack and her baby daughter Emmy burn to death in the Bristol Blitz in 1940. The shop where they'd all lived collapsed on her when she tried to go to their rescue. That's how she lost one ear.'

'Such a thing would derange most people, I admit.'

Superintendent Beal reached for a cigarette. 'For the same reason we continue to treat shocked soldiers from the 1914-18 war, Jolantha blamed herself for surviving. She thought she should have been able to brave the flames long enough to rescue her family – she thought she should, at least, have died in the attempt. The fact that her brother Hugo had been blinded by a German grenade only made her even wilder.'

'Yet brother and sister seem close.' He wanted to add 'close enough to cover for her' but he didn't. That was the puzzling thing about Jo, so far she hadn't asked anyone to provide her with an alibi.

'Nothing could offset the real conflicts that stemmed from her family.'

DS Biggs crossed out the '?' after the word 'mad' in his notebook. 'We're back to the shotgun again?'

'You have to remember Primrose was under great strain, too, detective. Whole ways of life are changing as we speak. With so many sons killed or mutilated in the last war as well as this one, big country estates like hers are changing hands because there is no suitable male heir to inherit them. Primrose must have felt her world slipping away. She did her best to pass her frustration and disappointment on to her daughter, as though she could somehow reverse the decline. Jolantha was always expected to marry well and behave like a lady, but she was more interested in dogs and motorcycles and didn't feel the need to maintain her position in polite Cotswold society. Cracks in Jolantha's life first appeared when her mother disapproved of her marriage to Jack Wheeler because, being an orphan, he had no family of his own, no 'lineage'. He was only a small-time businessman and no Dutton daughter was meant to end up working behind a shop counter in Bristol. After all, it's trade.'

'But Jolantha defied her, anyway?'

'When the war hit Bristol and Jolantha lost everything she realised that she had no one to turn to. Her father was kind but remote, like so many fathers of his class. She didn't feel able to burden her brother because he had enough troubles of his own. She broke down, detective, and tried to blow her mother's head off with a gun, but the cracks in her life already existed. All it required was one final thing to shatter her to pieces, like a vase. That something was guilt.'

DS Biggs shifted awkwardly in his chair. From now on, he thought gloomily, he was not going to be able to question a suspect again without wondering what 'cracks' they were hiding. 'How did she react to being in hospital?'

'Jolantha worked in the sewing room with our seamstresses, folding garments and sorting clothes. She even did a little sewing under supervision. Later she spent time in the laundry alongside our laundry workers.'

'A spoilt, rich girl like that? Didn't all the clothes get mixed up?'

'Things like cardigans and knickers are communal items, detective. The main problem was finding garments to fit someone so thin.'

'But surely her family could supply whatever she wanted?'

'Jolantha wouldn't be treated differently from the others. Except for that toothbrush I mentioned. She wouldn't share that with anyone – she'd tear their eyes out if they went near it. You can get TB from someone's else's mouth.'

'She wasn't too proud to scrub and clean, then?'

'Not at all. She adapted better than most.'

'Can you be more specific?'

'She volunteered to help take the nightwear off the beds in the mornings. She took her new life here very seriously and didn't want to be a burden on anyone.'

Of course, Superintendent Beal was never going to show him Jolantha's case book, he was never going to reveal details about his patient and her condition day by day in her medical diary. But something else was wrong. Something had happened that might yet prove crucial. Call it a gut feeling.

'You aim to 'cure' most of your patients, do you, sir?'

Superintendent Beal frowned. The detective's grating voice bordered on cynicism. 'I can tell you quite truthfully that Jolantha responded very well to ECT.'

'I'm not even going to guess what that is.'

'ECT involves Ediswan Electric Convulsion Apparatus. The treatment uses electricity to induce a seizure in the brain.'

'Isn't that a bit drastic?'

'Jolantha was fully conscious the whole time. She was in absolutely no danger, detective, I can assure you.'

DS Biggs fanned himself vigorously with his notebook. His heart raced; he was feeling very flushed. His eyes blurred, his hands trembled. 'I don't know where you get that idea.'

An expression of professional pride lit the superintendent's eyes. 'Believe me, we took every precaution. Our nurses held her down by the ankles, hips and shoulders while a charge nurse supported her chin to ensure she didn't swallow her tongue and to prevent her jaw from dislocating. She also wore a gumshield. The head electrodes were dipped in saline solution and applied to her temples at each side of her head. These were removed as soon as the procedure concluded. Afterwards we placed her in the recovery position as usual, but she wanted to get off the bed and straightaway asked for a cup of tea.'

'Who paid for the treatment?'

'Her father.'

'And Jolantha agreed?'

'She realised that she had reached rock bottom.'

'Or her father paid you a sum you couldn't refuse?'

Superintendent Beal looked horrified. 'You seem to think we abused Jolantha in some way for the money, but nothing could be further from the truth.'

'I'll believe you.'

'We're running out of time here. Will that be all?'

'Oh God, yes.' Which was when he asked his most important question of all. 'So what state of mind would you say Jolantha was in when she *left* your hospital two years ago, superintendent? Would you say she was as right as rain?'

'Physically she was much better. She had put on weight and was smiling again. Of course…'

'Yes?'

Superintendent Beal's face acquired a more enigmatic and painful expression. The look was hard to read. The kindest word for it was 'thoughtful'. Other people might have called it 'realistic'. 'We aim to fix about eighty per cent of a person's mental health problems within these walls, detective. The rest they have to do themselves, back in society.'

'You say Jolantha was fine physically, but how do you know? How do you even see inside someone's head, anyway?'

'Trust me, her brain is likely to be fine, unless…'

DS Biggs stood up to leave. 'Unless what?'

'Unless she is still experiencing some minor problems with reality.'

'Which means?'

'Sometimes she may find it hard to 'place' events in the right order or recall exactly what happened. It did confuse and distress her before she left us, I must confess. At times she became quite violent, but it was never likely to be a great problem, in our estimation.'

'In your estimation? How so? What did you do to her just before she left Coney Hill?'

'We twice had to inject her with insulin shock treatment to tranquilize her, that's all.'

'But you thought it safe to release her back to her family?'

'Oh no, detective, we didn't 'release' her, as you put it. Remember she was a voluntary patient.'

'So what happened? Did you give her more ECT?'

'It was too late for that.'

'Why?'

Superintendent Beal closed the thick leather cover of the admissions' register with a loud bang. A look of pain passed across his eyes. He could have been thinking about Captain Hector Knevitt again.

'Nurses found Jolantha's bed empty on the morning she was booked in for more treatment…'

'You mean to tell me she did a runner!'

SIXTEEN

'You lost, or something? Can I help you?'

I stop dead in "Anchorage Gardens", then turn to face whichever busybody has just followed me up the block's concrete stairs. Bella barks. My pursuer has gingery hair and prominent cheekbones. The mouth is rather mean but it is the hooded eyes I note most – she dares to stare right through me. Clearly she has been to a dance or something, because she is wearing a very smart fur coat and a red beret. That coat has to be American Opossum – you don't acquire a garment like that for less than twenty-two guineas.

I tighten my grip on my can of petrol. 'I'm looking for Flat 12?'

'I live with my sister Marjorie in Flat 12. I'm Peggy.'

Of course! This is the person whose first words were, "Goody, now we can go to the flicks" when you sent your deplorable wife a 10/- note, dear Sidney, even though you were struggling to pay £7.7.0 to bailiffs at the time to cover the expense of drinks at your wedding. In one of her letters to you even Marjorie calls her a 'little devil' and 'mean as ever'.

I consider one sister to be as bad as the other.

'Get inside.'

'What? Where?'

'Your flat. Of course.'

'But I don't know you.'

'Oh, but I know you.'

Your sister-in-law is as tall as I am and is not inclined to give way, but I play my trump card – I signal Bella to bite her heel.

Peggy's confused, but she doesn't think to scream for help. Which is just

96

as well. As it is, she soon unlocks the door and lets me in.

I don't wipe my feet on purpose.

'Who are you? What do you want? Have we ever met before?'

'Sit down and shut up.'

'Is this something to do with Marjorie's fall?'

'Let's not get ahead of ourselves.'

The flat is not quite the extravagant whorehouse I expected. Dress patterns and pieces of neatly cut fabric litter the living room where your wife last altered one of your old suits for herself or stitched herself a new outfit from pieces of cloth bought with government coupons. A library book lies open on the arm of a chair where someone has half-knitted a green jumper from recycled wool. I cast a quick look into the spare room where you very occasionally stayed, my love. It's empty.

When I return to the lounge, Peggy has the audacity to abandon her chair and point at the door. 'If you don't leave at once I'll go downstairs and ring the police from the phone in the hall.'

'No, you won't.'

'Are you here to hurt me?'

'What do you think?'

'I've never done anything to you. I don't even know you.'

'I'm here to do right by Sidney Sheppard. He and I were planning to start a whole new life together when your sister killed him.'

Peggy's jaw drops. Okay, so now *I'm* getting ahead of myself, but it's worth it to see the look on her face. It's an expression of absolute terror.

'My sister didn't kill anyone…'

'But will anyone believe it?'

'…because *he* was so cruel to *her.*'

'Don't take me for a fool. Don't tell that to the police.'

'So you are here to make trouble?'

'That depends on you.'

Your sister-in-law sinks on to the hideous brown sofa and huddles in a huff inside her fur coat. 'My sister went through hell with that man. He talked the talk but never delivered. You have no idea what a sham their marriage was.'

This is old news but confirms we had something that you and Marjorie didn't, my love. I pull up a chair back to front and sit astride its seat. It's time to get down to business. I'm being highly unladylike by spreading my legs in such a fashion, but I have one eye on the five-gallon jerrycan at my feet – I have to be able to reach it in a hurry. It's precious stuff and cost me a small fortune in coupons. Meanwhile Bella chooses to chew a self-fabric belt and buckle on one of the dresses your deceitful wife has spent so long carefully mending, my love.

Peggy is all fluster and bluster, for all the good it will do her. 'I'm not to blame for anything that went on between Marjorie and Sidney. I have my own worries. My husband David is a P.O.W. in a rat-infested camp in Poland… I haven't seen him for years.'

'You don't get it, do you?'

'What do you mean?'

'I'm here to see the place that you and Marjorie had Sidney subsidise – is this not where the two of you colluded and went behind his back? This is her little love nest, isn't it? Here, she could fuck God-knows-whom.'

'Whatever it is you're after, it has nothing to do with me or Marjorie. Sidney is the villain here…'

'Stop saying that.'

'Listen, my sister and I took this flat on November 1st 1940. It only came about quite suddenly – we didn't plan any of it. Marjorie and I had the most awful row with Mother and Daddy one Wednesday evening…'

'What you mean is that you both had husbands who were 'off the scene'. You couldn't go gallivanting while you both lived at home, so you hatched a plan to give yourselves more freedom to go to the flicks and dances. You're as much to blame as Marjorie for how things turned out…'

'You're wrong. It wasn't like that. A family row had been brewing for months. It started with something trivial, but before it was over so many things were said on either side that it was utterly impossible to go on living together. Marjorie and I dashed upstairs and started packing our things. We would have liked to have left on the spot, but it was eleven o'clock at night and an air raid was in full swing which made it rather too difficult. Anyway, Marjorie and I decided we would try and get a furnished flat with a spare room for David or Sidney to stay over…'

'You expect me to believe you did it on the spur of the moment?'

'It will take me hours to tell you all the things that were said, but Sidney's few shillings' worth of laundry was one of their grievances. Daddy was making Mother out to be an absolute martyr and slave and she always echoes everything he says. Marjorie completely lost her temper and told them how petty and uncharitable they were. Daddy asked me how she dared say such a thing after all he had done for her and Sidney. I ask you! Marjorie told him he'd hardly done a thing for them and said they were unnatural parents in that they did far less for their children than most people…'

'Oh, *please.*'

'They seemed to healthily resent the fact that she and Sidney, although newly married, had not the usual expenses of running a home. They forgot the fact that one of the reasons *they* wanted *her* to go to Esher with them was to avoid having some Canadian pilot, or whoever, billeted on them. I think if they got two guineas a week out of Sidney they might have been a little friendlier, but the steady persecution she had to put up with in the last six months or so made it impossible for her to live in such an atmosphere…'

'So?'

'She could never relax in that place and she certainly didn't see why at 30 she should have to put up with living with her parents. I felt exactly the same. Do you know, they even begrudged us having a bath, in spite of the fact that mother wastes money left, right and centre betting on the dogs. That's when we said we were coming here.'

I have to hear this to believe it. I've never witnessed such a performance. 'These pyjamas are absolutely lovely, aren't they? Pure silk articles are so scarce nowadays and fetch such high prices.'

Peggy eyes Bella's bared teeth anxiously. 'They belong to Marjorie. Sidney posted them to her at the beginning of last year.'

'No doubt he sent her these rather fine camiknickers, as well? Definitely pre-war quality.'

'Sidney's landlady at "High Grove" in Cheltenham acquired them from someone she knows down in Devon…'

'You won't be seeing her again.'

So saying I toss the knickers to Bella to chew.

Peggy rushes to save the precious garment but thinks better of it. 'Damn you, you'll ruin everything! Why are you doing this?'

I stop to light a slow cigarette. I even wave one at Peggy, but she shudders and declines my offer because that's the sort of person she is – she has no manners.

'I'm doing it because Sidney tells me to.'

'How can that be? He's dead.'

'If he was dead he wouldn't be in my head.'

'Are you crazy?'

'Not crazy, just unforgiving.'

'What is there to forgive? Marjorie and I are simply two lonely wives who want a bit of fun. There may be a war being waged, but life has to go on. Where's the harm in that?'

'Thanks to Marjorie, Sidney suffered a complete nervous and physical breakdown. He broke himself financially trying to pay for his own place as well as this one and you both repaid him with betrayal.'

'Have you any idea how difficult it is to find a place to live anywhere in Claygate? Everyone wants to be able to walk or cycle to the NAAFI.'

'Your sister is a gadabout. She should have been a better wife, but I'm afraid she's not one of the finer women of this world.'

'Marjorie may seem a rather frivolous person to you, but underneath I can assure you she is quite sound. She doesn't deserve to be lying in a coma in hospital right now because of *that man*.'

'Oh, no?'

'She certainly didn't set out to do anything to jeopardise her future with him. All she wanted was to settle down and do all the things they'd planned in their flat in Hanger Hill when they got married. He's the one who blew it all. So please don't concern yourself with our few harmless parties.'

'Huh!'

'Our NAAFI nights are extremely prim and proper, and there's absolutely no petting.'

'Right!'

'There is none of the "Aldermaston" atmosphere about them, and all we do is have a few dances and then tromp into another room for a drink or two. The housekeeper makes tea for everybody about 12.30. You must agree it's all very respectable…'

I whistle Bella and we play a game of rag doll. No dog likes to let go of its latest 'kill' once it has gripped it firmly between its teeth with much happy grumbling and growling.

'So how is it that Sidney told me that Marjorie danced half the night away with another man on her wedding anniversary?'

'What of it? Sidney visited here in July 1941, but my sister had already been invited to a NAAFI celebration and he agreed she could go without him.'

'But she stayed out to the small hours!'

'She wasn't being heartless and unsentimental – she thought a lot about him and had us all drinking toasts to him for hours. We went to "The Mitre" at Hampton Court for dinner – it was roast duck and champagne – it was a real treat. Marjorie didn't even get tight you'll be pleased to hear.'

'But she could have joined Sidney in Cheltenham at any time these last three or four years? What wife doesn't want to be with her husband?'

'On the other hand, she's very happy in her present job in which she is exempt from munitions or the services. She hates the idea of having to work in a factory – it's so noisy and dirty. Yes, Sidney did keep asking her why she found life so interesting here, but she considers she has one of the most rewarding jobs in the Corporation. She loves her work and says the "days go on wings". She's never felt so fulfilled.'

'Or he was right to smell a rat?'

'No, he was jealous of his career wife.'

'I'll ask you again. Please don't lie to me this time. Did you, or did you not, dissuade your sister from going to live with Sidney in Cheltenham, just so you both could have a jolly good time here, at No.12 "Anchorage Gardens"? Think carefully before you answer.'

'I…'

'It's a straightforward question.'

SEVENTEEN

Coney Hill Mental Hospital

Dear Violet, I have resisted the temptation to fret and fume despite ample provocation in your silence. Your attitude is not big on fairness, but that is not unusual if you'll forgive my saying so, and is in stark contrast with what you have said in the past. You quite definitely said every day in the shop in Bristol 'It's so lovely to see you' and 'You must sit by me in church on Sunday'. It was so kind of you to remember my birthday – you always signed it with an X.

But I will not quote any more from those distant days. As I have said before, there is an old saying, 'Only the truth hurts'.

The things you hoped for with Sidney, even if garnished with lashings of luxurious living would not, in my view, have equalled an intimate, loving relationship full of mutual desire and constantly striven for by both parties. We, on the other hand, were together far too long for my love for you ever to die.

As we are still both living, despite the bombs, we might yet enjoy forty or fifty years of married life together and for my part I can assure you that our future will prove a very loving relationship. If, as seems obvious, you thought to keep yourself from me for Sidney, you will surely jump at the chance to come to me now that he is out of the way? But is that to be?

I deeply regret anything I have done which has caused you pain, but your past behaviour had me believe that all was well between us. I didn't think you would say, 'Consider me your dearest friend' and 'Let me help you any way I can,' if you didn't mean and feel it. I'm not a violent person. I only ever killed two men, to my knowledge, in the whole of The Great War. If my past letters have grated with you, I'm sorry. Rest assured, I'm only doing what I am because I cannot believe that what you thought you had with Sidney ever represented your true self. Love H.

EIGHTEEN

Peggy would dearly like to light a fire in the flat's little fireplace but her eye keeps returning to my petrol can. As a result, 12 "Anchorage Gardens" feels cold and cramped. She refuses to accept that I'm not here for myself, I'm here for you, dear Sidney. To all intents and purposes I am you. Dead or alive, you have returned.

'Why is your dog destroying Marjorie's clothes? What's wrong with you?'

Bella looks up mournfully with a mouthful of camiknickers in her teeth. She flicks one ear forward then back, as if to say, 'Who, me?'

'The thing is, Peggy, I needed to see this place for myself. I'm glad I have. It'll help make sense of the rest.'

'The rest?'

'The whole business of the fall in Gloucester Cathedral.'

'How can you say that?'

'Let's admit it. There's everything to suggest your sister killed Sidney because he wouldn't go along with her obscene behaviour any longer…'

Peggy's blue eyes widen. 'What obscene behaviour?'

'Marjorie is a real flirt who can't be trusted?'

'Please come away from the wireless. We've only just had it mended.'

'Your sister went behind Sidney's back and brought him low, quite shamelessly.'

'That's tommyrot. Of course some of the men at the NAAFI fancy her – they say she's the nicest girl they know, but it's always good to be popular, isn't it?'

'Try telling that to the police.'

'Anyway, she and I chaperone each other. Yes, we go to a dance at the

Hanger Hill Club when we're in Ealing on a Friday night, or on Saturday we go to Surbiton to see "I Married A Witch" or something similar, but then we have to rush back for fire guard. That's the thing about war, no one has much time for themselves, do they? You have to snatch moments of happiness when you can.'

I'm admiring the shiny wooden wireless more closely. It does, I admit, look expensive. 'Spare me the sob story, please.'

'If Sidney hadn't been so jealous, he might have been kinder to her.'

'No, I think we can say he hit on something…'

'He didn't want her, but he didn't want anyone else to have her, either.'

'…something he didn't see coming.'

'My sister is a good person.'

'You reckon?'

'She takes her wartime responsibilities very seriously.'

Naturally, I expect Peggy to lie for Marjorie, my love, but she can't pull the wool over my eyes. But for her, none of this need have happened. 'Or she was always working overtime and doing fire guard duty even at Christmas, to give herself excuses to stay in Claygate where she had her lover. Anything but join Sidney at "High Grove" in Cheltenham, if you ask me!'

'I find your accusations almost too childish for comment. However, as Marjorie is not here to defend herself, I will comment. You don't seem to have the slightest idea what conscription for fire guard duties entails. In the first place it has nothing to do with the NAAFI.'

'Oh no?'

'It is a National Defence Regulation and the NAAFI just does as it is told and provides 35 people a night, which is the number laid down for a building of its size… The only official grounds for exemption are illness, annual leave and husband home on 7 days leave. Anything less than that doesn't count. What shocked Marjorie was Sidney's nasty remark about it…'

Bella has grown tired of chewing knickers and lies down on the carpet. She utters a growl whenever Peggy strays too far. As do I.

'Let's face it. Your sister is a lazy snob.'

'What makes you say that?'

'I know for a fact she despised her own husband because he wasn't in the Services.'

Peggy lights herself a shaky cigarette from her packet of Park Drives. She breaks the first matchstick against the box and reaches for another. It's one up to me. I've hit a raw nerve, evidently. 'But don't you think that seems to be the general attitude of Service people towards civilians? Take Bernard Sharp, for instance, Sidney's best friend from his Ealing days. He has been quite scathing about people who are not in the Services, excepting Sidney – for whom he has the greatest respect.'

'My point exactly.'

'Also the wives of men in the forces are inclined to look down their noses at women with civilian husbands. All the half-a-dozen or so girls with whom Marjorie and I have lunch at the NAAFI or with whom she does fire watch, have husbands in the Forces and they have been rather patronising towards her. The one or two with husbands abroad are also rather bitter, but I suppose one must make allowances for those… To pile on the injustice, Wing Commander Bryant holds the opinion that Service men and women will have the first choice of the decent jobs after the war.'

I roll my eyes. 'You do know Sidney tried to join the RAF in April 1939, don't you? That's three or four months before he got married.'

'Should I even care?'

'I've listened to you. Now you listen to me.'

'If you insist.'

'I do. If anybody's the responsible one here, it's Sidney, not your bloody sister. In the month up to the war he applied to five territorial recruiting centres at Hammersmith, Mattock Lane, Hom Lane, The Ryde and one other. The trouble was they all took the attitude that the war would be over very quickly and anyway they had no equipment. He was told to come back in six months' time.'

'No one doubts his commitment to the war effort.'

I know I've all but lost her already, dear Sidney, but I will argue your case. You didn't tell me all this for no reason. Your defence is her damnation. 'My point is, Peggy, when he was called up to have a medical in Tamworth, it was discovered that his previous employers had stamped his insurance card "Reserved Occupation. Not to be enlisted without authority of the Ministry of Labour", or words to that effect.'

'As I say, no one's calling him a coward…'

'Will you *listen* for a moment? I'd like that. He then switched jobs to work for Tungum Tube Co. – then based in London – to get back to his wife again, only to be evacuated once more to escape the Blitz, this time to Cheltenham. There he began making vital fuel lines for fighter planes…'

'For pity's sake, are you mad? What are you trying to prove here?'

'Don't interrupt. Two years ago the German Messerschmitt plane could gain an extra altitude of 5000ft over the Spitfire, which gave the enemy fighter a big advantage. Spitfires couldn't climb that high because when they did so the petrol cocks leaked due to the erratic behaviour of the co-efficient of expansion of their stainless steel plugs in the brass and Duralumin bodies of the petrol cocks…'

'*What?*'

'Shut up. Sidney happened to call at Vickers Weybridge when this problem was being discussed. He knew that the co-efficient expansion of Tungum alloy tubing was very close to some stainless steel and might be more stable. And so it turned out. You could say Sidney helped save the day in the Battle of Britain. Whether he would have been better manning some ack-ack gun in London is debateable.'

'Okay, so my sister worried far too much about looking nice and making friends, only that's not a crime. What was really criminal was her husband's erratic behaviour, for which I do, in part, blame myself unfortunately…'

'I beg your pardon?'

'I'd rather not talk about it.'

'Sorry, you have no choice.'

'Look here, whoever you are, do you have any children?'

'I have a daughter called Jacqueline.'

'Then you'll agree that motherhood is important.'

'Think what you like.'

'Marjorie was twenty-nine when she got married. She's now thirty-four. That's a vital period in any woman's life…'

'What of it?'

'If I can just explain for a moment? When our mutual friend Pam Mackeroy had a baby in 1942, Marjorie became very worried. She said to me that she supposed she had another year or two to decide whether to follow suit, but Sidney said things were difficult enough these days without deliberately adding to their responsibilities. On the other hand, she thought people should, war or no war, seize the future. It's all right for me, because I'm younger. If David comes back alive we still have time to start a family.'

'Really? Marjorie is the maternal type? I don't think so.'

Peggy bridled and bit her lip. 'She told Sidney that she was working so hard that she would have to have a baby soon to have a 'rest'. She was being flippant, but with everyone else having children she felt she was going to be left out in the cold. The one topic was going to be what the children said and did, and it's possible she would be rather envious in her middle age. You're right, it was a change of front on her part, but they say most women feel that way after they have been married a few years. The trouble was she didn't think Sidney was very keen on having children, although he liked them and knew how to treat them and get the best out of them. We agreed that Malcolm, our brother Norman's son, took more notice of Sidney than he ever did of him or his wife, Nessie. We even told him he would make an ideal father. At the christening, Nessie said to my sister, "Marjorie, you must have one – they grow on you and are well worth all the horrid business of having them". Sidney wasn't even at the christening.'

'Marjorie was a frigid bitch and you know it.'

Peggy pouts and appears quite speechless for a moment. 'Of course I bitterly regret it now, naturally I do. I was so silly, but I thought I was being helpful at the time…'

'What on earth are you talking about?'

'If really you must know, my sister has always suffered very bad periods. At the end of each month she is rotten for a while but nothing happens. For instance, at Christmas 1942/3 she spent a couple of happy days with Sidney but rather spoilt it by passing out on the last day. When she got the curse one Friday at the NAAFI office and fainted the A.C. recommended she take "Adexelin" vitamin capsules, as they'd done his wife some good. When she married Sidney it was at the very end of July and she was due to suffer as usual while staying on the French Riviera. That's when I gave her something to stave off the bleeding…'

'You *gave* her something?'

'All I can say is it had a lot of apple cider vinegar in it.'

'You got this how?'

'From the friend of a friend whose granny used to swear by it. You take it at night whenever you need to stop anything happening.'

I raise my eyebrows. Peggy flinches. I guess she knows what I think. 'Is that what did happen?'

'Marjorie drank too much vinegar or it somehow fermented in the French heat. I don't know, but she was violently ill for days with diarrhoea.'

'Sidney never told me that.'

'Why would he? Don't you see? It meant he and Marjorie never consummated their marriage while on honeymoon.'

'It's unfortunate, I agree, but hardly the end of the world.'

'That's not what I'm saying.'

'What are you saying?'

'Sidney never went near her physically again. My sister 'lost' her husband, her dream of marriage and her future in the space of a few days in August 1939.'

'And you think you're to blame, not her?'

'What else could it be?'

This throws me, I must admit. I came here to condemn, not redeem. I order Bella to stop chewing things for a while. 'Are you saying that Sidney never made love to his wife in the following five years?'

'Believe me, Marjorie is still a virgin at thirty-four.'

'Or she held out because she didn't want *his* children?'

'That might have been true after she met Frank a year or so later, but it certainly wasn't true in 1939 and 1940. My sister was very keen to be married to Sidney but she found him preoccupied and distant. She rather blamed herself. I even saw her sign one of her letters 'your loving but rather thoughtless wife'. She said she was sorry she made him so miserable. It was bad enough living with such uncertainties – no home, no job, no husband, because he'd been evacuated elsewhere to work – but she couldn't be sure of his affection, either. Months could go by without them even seeing each other. Every now and then he'd say she was still important to him, but they weren't lovers. Were you his lover? Did he ever fuck you?'

Now I can't put my hand on my heart and say you and I ever...

'That's not what I want to discuss right now.'

'You're right, Marjorie couldn't stand his rejection any longer, but she didn't kill him.'

I pick up my can of petrol and think where to start burning this place to kingdom come, only she hasn't yet told me why you would be so squeamish, my love.

That's not to say I credit one word of it.

I cannot believe you spurned your wife simply because she had her period on your honeymoon.

No man would be that stupid.

Peggy is spinning me lies and I won't tolerate it any longer. I don't trust her. She is a vindictive person like your wife. She is saying these odd things about you to poison me against you.

'Bella, come! We're out of here.'

But Peggy isn't about to let me go so easily. Damn it. 'I don't know what you really hoped to gain by coming here today, but it's not true that my sister considered Sidney to be her meal ticket for life.'

'Too late, this place is burning.'

'She may have settled at first for a boring typing job at her father's engineering firm when they were all still living in Ealing, but the war changed all that. It changed *her*. She had a stroke of luck – she was made secretary to Group-Captain Prall, the RAF Member of the Board of Management at the NAAFI. The work was very secret. She came home on the first day saying she would have to stay off the drink from now on, because we all knew what it did to her tongue...'

'You'll burn, too, if you don't shut up.'

'I'm telling you this because I don't want you to think my sister was a parasite. She worked very, very hard and was soon earning 77/6d per week…'

I walk out the door even as your sister-in-law spouts more nonsense. I have Bella at my side and my can of petrol is still, inexplicably, in my hand when Peggy shouts after me: 'You have to trust me on this. Whatever finished Sidney and Marjorie dates back to the very start of their marriage.'

'Sorry, but I don't believe a stomach ache could do such a thing.'

'You still won't listen?'

'Why should I?'

'Because Marjorie told me something terrible soon after she returned home from honeymoon.'

'Save it.'

But your sister-in-law has run after me as far as my motorcycle. She sees me load the jerrycan back into the sidecar, except that's not the focus of her attention any more – I am. Peggy attempts to take me by the arm as I swing a leg over my machine and Bella jumps aboard alongside me.

She'll have me stop just long enough for her to have the final word in my ear. 'When Marjorie recalled – and she never forgot it – how Sidney loathed her while on honeymoon, she went hot with shame. Shall I tell you what else she said?'

'What?'

'She said, "I bet there was never such an unwanted bride".'

I twist the throttle and prepare to ride home to Gloucester. As I turn the Brough Combination in a tight semi-circle in the road, Peggy screams after me from the pavement.

'Wait. You never said who you are?'

'Me? I'm the one he should have made happy ever after.'

NINETEEN

Coney Hill Mental Hospital

Dear Violet, you seem to find some satisfaction in regarding me as weak, but these things are of course a matter of opinion and perspective. I have always had an instructive urge to do what to me seems the right thing from the point of view of morality and justice.

I am just as vulnerable as anyone else – maybe more so as I have no means of knowing – and make no special claim to moral rectitude or righteousness. But I have fought off sexual temptation because I always felt – and experience has generally proved – that doing the right thing gives the best chance of happiness and perhaps success, but certainly happiness.

If you regard me as being weak, am I to understand that, conversely, what you have tried to do shows strength of character? Without putting too fine a point on it or in any way wishing to be offensive, what you did was to deceive, to lie, to cheat – and finally make a decision which you know in your heart was wrong. You would have ended up married to a man you would quickly have realised you could not love and who, sadly, for whatever reason, could not express his love for you in the magical way intended by nature.

As far as I am concerned it will be heavenly to make love to you and I will revel in doing so – but unfortunately you treat me with contempt and physical rejection and there is no greater destroyer of love and romance.

But I will persevere and if you had not been so headstrong I might have won you over by now. Love, H.

TWENTY

I'm all dressed up in my mourning-clothes ready for your big day, dear Sidney. Bella has stayed home with baby Jacqueline, which is why I'm feeling a bit guilty, although I'm sure Mrs O'Brien will cope all right as usual.

Now I'm in the neighbourhood with time to kill, so to speak, it strikes me as unfair not to take your abysmal wife some flowers, my love. I might as well pay my respects, since she should be as dead as you.

I bet she didn't bring you anything when you were in hospital, I bet she was never this thoughtful and decent?

Right now I'm marching along Du Cane Road in London with a bunch of horribly expensive red roses. I've gone to no end of trouble to get them. I think you'll agree it proves I'm a finer person than she is, which is why you loved me so much better than her. The more I think about it, though, the more I wonder if I'm doing myself any favours – that air raid siren sounds a bit too close for comfort.

But I don't see any enemy planes in the sky and no ack-ack guns are firing, so it must be a false alarm. Can anyone vouch for that? There are no answers, only choices.

Either I go on or I go back.

So far it has been most confusing. Because your wife is in 'Hammersmith Hospital' I naturally concluded that Hammersmith was where I should go. That's why I took the Metropolitan Line. Now I've had to backtrack and take the District as far as East Acton Tube station, since it turns out the hospital really lies here, opposite Wormwood Scrubs Prison. Anyone would think she's trying to hide from me.

I'm worried my roses will wilt from lack of water.

Okay, so I didn't *buy* them exactly – I wouldn't waste my money – I picked them in the Dean of Gloucester's private garden early this morning before he had breakfast.

I feel tired and dirty. My train here was so crowded I was forced to stand all the way and the sight of so much bomb damage from the carriage window was rather alarming, to say the least. For example, there's a very large hole in the roof above platforms 6 and 7 in Paddington Station – I'm beginning to think Gloucestershire has escaped rather lightly lately, whereas the capital continues to take a real pasting.

A man keeps pace with me on the opposite, bomb-cracked pavement.

He's sucking sweets from a brown paper bag.

I do, for a moment, think he's familiar, except I can't see his face all wrapped up in his hat and scarf.

Do you think I'm dreaming you?

I'm in a wasteland where everyone is muddling along. I skirt a new water main that has been laid *on* rather than *under* the road, to make any future repairs easier to mend. As usual I could do with some ciggies. I stop before a big wooden board that covers a newsagent's shattered window, except when I peer through the greaseproof paper that 'glazes' the small hole cut in its centre, all I see is empty boxes and pictures of what the shop may or may not still sell. A sign outside reads 'Business as usual'. I try inside. No luck today. Try again tomorrow.

So here I am at last outside the hospital with its fancy green clock tower and weather vane. A spiv loiters at the door, hoping to accost nurses when they change shifts. His battered leather suitcase yields a packet of cigarettes and two pairs of stockings. It's worth coming, after all!

It's not yet visiting time so I won't have to compete for your wife's attention with her obnoxious lover or relatives. For a red-brick, former workhouse, Hammersmith Hospital isn't too grim and forbidding. I'm treading a vestibule paved with mosaics, while on the walls is a dado of most exotic-looking encaustic tiles. No wonder they once called it 'Palace on the Scrubs' and 'Paupers' Paradise'.

That doesn't mean, of course, that I'm entitled to be here as I sidle up to a trolley piled high with dirty linen and help myself to a white coat. I remove my black pillbox hat and veil to look more 'medical'.

I don't advise anyone to stand in my way.

So, Marjorie, my dear, where are you? Which floor? Which ward? I'm here to confirm how you're getting on.

TWENTY-ONE

'Didn't I say she's loopy?' DI Lockett slid open the lid on his baccyflap and took out a pinch of tobacco. The door to his office stood ajar and he could eyeball his sergeant in the adjoining room. 'We have here someone who didn't finish her treatment.'

DS Biggs had just written up his visit to Coney Hill Mental Hospital. It didn't look good, there was no doubt about it.

'To be fair, sir, Jolantha Wheeler *volunteered* for psychiatric treatment after she tried to gun down her mother…'

'Not before she told us it was Primrose who got her sectioned.'

'She may not have meant to lie to us, sir, she might not remember. I say we give her the benefit of the doubt. After all, she was able to recognise that she was under terrible strain and a danger to others.'

'Huh! Strain? Is that what you call it? We have a violent lunatic and possible killer on the loose who discharges herself from hospital and you want to talk about 'strain'.'

'That was two years ago.'

'Hmm.'

DS Biggs reached for his lukewarm cup of tea. It was no use trying to reason with his boss at a time like this. DI Lockett was in a very strange, almost 'loopy' mood himself. He'd seen it happen before, usually when he returned from the morgue where he liked to spend not inconsiderable time consulting with pathologist Oliver Lacey. More often than not, he could barely get a civil word out of him as if he had something to hide. Today was one of those days when the worry etched in his boss's face verged on pain akin to denial.

'Superintendent Beal did not appear to consider Jolantha a great risk to herself or the public, sir, after treatment.'

'No relapses?'

'I have no idea.'

'No visions? No voices?'

'Your guess is as good as mine.'

'No hallucinations?'

With each 'no' DI Lockett stabbed the air with the stem of his pipe to ram home his accusation.

'It appears that her mental collapse in 1942 would never have happened, sir, had it not been for the loss of her family in horrific circumstances. We can hardly blame her for getting ill, since illness is not a crime.'

'Don't get clever with me, sergeant. You know perfectly well what I'm driving at.'

'What's that, sir?'

'Jolantha was subjected to extensive electric shock treatment during her stay in hospital. For all we know it changed her brain. ECT is still in its infancy. She may not be the person she thinks she is.'

'How so, sir?'

'Strange impulses may enter her head.'

'There's always that chance, I suppose.'

DI Lockett's look hardened for a moment. 'Suppose I'm right? Jolantha has told us what she thinks occurred in the cathedral on All Saints' Day, but has she? What if she can't recall *step by step* what really happened?'

DS Biggs considered the pens and pencils spread neatly on his desk. One pencil struck him as out of line with the others by half an inch. 'You can't seriously think she's invented the whole thing to get our attention?'

'A man has died and a woman lies in a coma, that's all we can say for sure. The rest she has rearranged in her head to suit herself.'

'So what do we do now, sir?'

'I want you to go immediately to Esher. Talk to Marjorie's family. Find out if they have reason to believe that their daughter was being stalked or threatened by anyone.'

'Petrol's tight, sir. It's not as if we're not subject to rationing like everyone else.'

'Damn it, man, take the train. Take the coach. What do I care? It'll be well worth it to make sense of this mess. From divorce documents found on Marjorie's person we know she went to the cathedral to confront Sidney. Jolantha was waiting and watching. Why? She said she knew Sidney would attend matins, but not Marjorie. I don't believe a word of her muddled, self-regarding testimony, I think she was there to see him sign. She wanted him to know that he couldn't delay any longer because they had to get married in a hurry. It wouldn't surprise me if she doesn't turn out to be pregnant with his child.'

DS Biggs exchanged a blue pencil for a red one. 'Sidney wouldn't be the first man to keep his mistress dangling. It's easy to make all sorts of rash promises, but harder to break with your wife of some years' standing. I bet he told Jolantha they'd run away together. War is the perfect excuse for all sorts of cowardly procrastination nowadays.'

DI Lockett looked all hot and bothered. He pulled at his tie and consulted the great heap of files that lay before him. 'A great many people will live to regret the way they have behaved these last few years. A desperate Jolantha will turn out to be one of them, you mark my words. She's no better than a floozy.'

'With respect, sir, we don't know that.'

'I can feel it, sergeant, in my bones. Sometimes it falls within the remit of men like us to make a stand. We have to uphold a sense of decency.'

DS Biggs straightened another pencil on his desk. 'You honestly think she planned something sinister?'

'Sidney Sheppard wasn't meant to die that day – of that you can be sure. Someone's plans went horribly wrong.'

'Or both women are in on it.'

TWENTY-TWO

Your wife looks so dead, dear Sidney, so why isn't she?

Perhaps she's dead on the outside but alive inside? I really was convinced that the nurses would have shaved all that lovely red hair from her head, only they haven't. I know I would have. When I roll a curl or two round the tip of my cold finger it feels lanky and needs washing. There's surprisingly little bandage across her brow and down one ear. All that plaster on her legs and arms is quite comical, though – she looks like an Egyptian mummy.

Now I'm sitting on her bed I can squeeze her limp hand quite comfortably. I think I'm suited to play the part of doctor rather well.

Can she hear me? I promise I'll try to be polite from here on and not call her 'bitch' any more. I hate that word and anyway it's not very ladylike.

I must say, I'm very impressed with Hammersmith Hospital. Everything is on a war footing. The top floor of the building is closed to reduce the risk from rocket attacks and all the main operating theatres have been shut down and improvised ones established in the basement.

You can be confident Marjorie is receiving the best care, even if I do think other people should take priority. She's in here with the very latest wounded. I had to wander various wards before I found her, I had to pass beds full of air raid victims recently pulled from the rubble. Men, women and children have been crushed to the point where their bladders and kidneys can't function. They're crying in agony, poor things while your wife sleeps like a child.

Perhaps because of the confusion, no one has questioned my presence. I have in my hand a rather nice card, as promised. I made it myself. I know

Marjorie can't see it, so I'll describe it. My offering is tied with a beautiful blue moire silk ribbon and is a page within a page like a very thin book. On the outside there is a picture of four revellers holding up glasses in a pub – one man's jacket is coloured blue and white like an old-fashioned naval jacket – while set in the card's wide cream border are the words 'Happy Memories'. The whole thing is not more than five inches by four and will sit quite nicely beside the water jug and roses on her bedside table. Inside is even better. It reads '*May Christmas bring you all Joy and Happiness and the Coming Year hold for you Good Luck and Good Health*, Is the sincere wish of Jolantha Wheeler.'

So I lied about making it myself – I bought it on the spur of the moment from W. H. Smiths in the foyer of Paddington train station, but Christmas is still six weeks away and I can't be sure to return in time to wish her the compliments of the season.

I'm here to confirm your untrustworthy wife's complicity in your demise, my love.

This is her chance to own up to her share of the guilt.

But since she can't talk, how can she admit what she's done to you?

Is she even human any more?

Look at her.

She lies like a statue.

Can she even remember you, or is her brain turned to mush? I can't be sure any more.

All I see is you, dear Sidney, lying crushed on the cathedral floor. It falls to me to remind the world that ours will always be the deeper devotion, despite your diabolical wife's inexplicable, continued presence in this world…

Have the police even been here to grill her yet? I'd like to know how she intends to explain herself, since you could say the three of us are in this together.

I just want to confirm that she won't recover.

Don't worry, I'm not going to poke her eyes out, though I could – I can do what I like to her.

I hope she doesn't mind me popping in like this. I had an awful time on the train, but I've said that already?

I've come to tell her that your funeral will take place in South Ealing Cemetery. So you see, I'm here as much for you as her, my love.

If this were a fairy tale she'd be a princess and I'd be her Prince Charming. That's not to say I don't have in my bag more usefully incriminating letters. I haven't looked at every single one of them yet by a long chalk, but I will – I'm here to damn her with her own testimony, ever since you two started courting. I'd like to return every day and read them all back to her because I hate to think she'll go to her grave without you on her conscience.

(That's to say, I need to be sure we don't get our stories in a twist, should the police try to blame me instead of her.)

I have to give you credit, dear Sidney, you realised the value of keeping the evidence. DI Lockett will surely buy what I have to show him now. If I can demonstrate how much Marjorie quarrelled with you, years ago, I can reveal how she nurtured hatred for you in her soul. Whatever Peggy says, I know I'm right about this. I can prove to the world your wife is unworthy – I can show motive. You only have to look at her today to see how her love was less than mine. It's all written down in these pages, because secretly she intended to beguile, then harm you.

The police will inevitably come round to my way of thinking: she always had it in her to do what she did to you in the cathedral.

'Should you suddenly begin to hear me, Marjorie, twitch your nose or bat an eyelid or something, because this is what you penned to Sidney on November 11, 1932, almost seven years before you two got married. You were twenty-two and already causing him unbearable heartache: "My darling Rufus…" (Why the ridiculous nickname, I'll never know), "I want you to try really hard and forgive me for my past indiscretions. I am going to do my utmost to atone and if you will only give me time, I think I shall be able to prove it to you. Of course I want you, darling. You must realise that, and I want to be happy with you to the end of our lives. Please believe me, angel, and try to forgive me. Tons of love, Marjorie."

'I'm sure I wasn't so flighty at your age. You strike me as very silly and flirtatious. Instead of letting Sidney go after some falling out or other, you came crawling back because I don't suppose anyone else would have you.

121

I reckon you were *always* wrong for him, because I have in front of me something else you wrote *only four months after your honeymoon.*

'It's as good as a confession, in my opinion, on the 19th of November 1939: "My darling Rufus, I realise what a fool I was to hold you to marriage. But, dearest, although it's awfully hard for you to believe it, I really do love you a tremendous lot. I, selfish as usual, thought I could make you happy enough when we settled down in our own flat in Hanger Hill. Please, don't think I'm trying to start an argument. Far from it, darling, I'm just trying to tell you how sorry I am because I've treated you so badly, and I'm simply longing for the time when I can do something towards making you happy, comfortable and contented. Please don't look on me as a burden, darling, but as someone who loves you very much."

'You have the cheek to go on: "I hope you enjoyed your trip to the Midlands, also Ambrose's Band. Rimmie, in reckless mood last Sunday, took my sister Babs and me for a good run in the car. He tried to cheer me up, but all I could think of was you. I hated losing you so soon. For your information, darling, the curse arrived on time. Take great care of yourself, dearest one, All my love, Marjorie."

'Don't worry, I'll leave out the tedious bit about you renovating your mother's fur coat 'for a consideration' – apparently the shops wanted five pounds for doing it.

'Don't forget Marjorie, waggle a toe if you can hear me. There's a similar, cunning mixture of passionate endearments and casual indifference that you sent *my* Sidney in this next missive, from your parents' house in Esher on January 23, 1940: "Darling Rufus, thank you for your letter and the money. Both were very welcome. You didn't say when you were coming, but I expect it'll be Friday night, but do please let me know. I suppose you will be going to your mother at Waverley Avenue to collect your evening clothes or perhaps you are not going to bother to change. Dress is optional, by the way. I expect, however, you would rather change and I would much rather you did, if it's not too much trouble for you.

"I'm longing to see you again and to hear all about how you got the new job. The salary is not too bad, but of course you are worth double that amount.

"I agree with you, darling, we shall have to live very quietly and cheaply for a while. I don't think, however, you would be happy living here. I expect my people would get on your nerves and consequently you would get fed up with me. I think perhaps it would be better if you stay with your mother in Twickenham until we are able to take back the Hanger Hill flat. However, we can discuss all that when we meet at the weekend.

"I'm afraid I shan't have time to go to the doctor this week about my monthly pains as Daddy has got me some work to do. I expect I shall be busy typing most of the week, but the money will be very useful. I'm telling you this in case you want to do some shopping. I expect you'll damn and blast me again, but I didn't think for one moment you would be coming down this weekend.

"Darling, you didn't mention how you are in your letter. Have you recovered completely from the 'flu'?

"Rimmie phoned me on Sunday evening and asked if he could take me out Monday evening. He arrived at teatime. We went to the cinema at 6 o'clock, after which we propped up the bar in "The Bear" until 10 o'clock. In spite of the fact that he had to be up at 4.30 this morning, he insisted on going for a drive. We parked on Oxsholt Common where I had to listen to him telling me how wonderful I am etc., etc. I'd received your letter just before he arrived and I'm afraid I was thinking of your marvellous news all the time he was rambling on.

"I hope you can read this ghastly writing. We have run out of ink, and on top of that I'm writing this over the fire as the weather is so cold. I do hope you'll forgive this slapdash effort in pencil. All my love, Marjorie."

'Here's your new husband, with a new job in London (briefly), yet you don't want to live with him except in the Hanger Hill flat which you've already sublet! You're not exactly rushing into his arms, are you? I can just imagine you taking off your scarf and shaking out your great mane of flaming red hair, I can see how you might have toyed with my Sidney's affections from the very beginning to the end.

'It's all very expedient, you being so dumb. I rather resent you lying here so still and doll-like – it means you can't deny a thing I say. If I didn't know the facts, I'd suggest you're feigning. Anyone else should, by right, take this

123

pillow and place it over your smug little face… but that would only put you out of your misery too soon. The police must be informed how you played loose and fast with Sidney's affections, *and that you could never be trusted*.

'But I don't wish to be ungrateful. That crack on the head has almost certainly done for you. I wonder, vaguely, if I can push my finger right into your skull? Have you lost very much brain in your fall from grace?

'I didn't come here to be morbid, Marjorie, I came to say hi. I should perhaps move the flowers a bit closer, except they're so darned big. Can you even smell anything, anyway? It doesn't look like it. Can you smell me? How about I put my nose to yours. Can you smell me now, because I can smell you, you're all blood, sweat and antiseptic? I want you to know that I'm thinking of you every moment of every day. I'm praying for your slow recovery – I'm sure it will take years.

'Rest assured I won't let you alone.

'Perhaps you'll simply waste away to nothing, now that you're quite thin already. Then it will no longer be your word against mine.

'I need to think of myself now.

'Well, toodle-pip, sweetie-pie, until next time.'

***

I'm reserving a special place in my heart for your two-faced spouse, dear Sidney, for when I lay you to rest in the ground. She's the one I should be burying this afternoon, not you.

TWENTY-THREE

CONEY HILL MENTAL HOSPITAL

Dear Violet, of course you are fully entitled to think and believe what you like, but your hurtful silence makes it pretty clear that you have no need of old memories. You do not wish to recognise that they play any part in your life and even more obviously, you do not need letters from me reminding you of things past, since that is all that remains in common between us? I shall write no more. Love, H.

TWENTY-FOUR

I'm hugging my little black book whose cover says IN MEMORIAM in bold, gold letters; its 'order for the burial of the dead' still sounds in my head after the church service. I'll treasure it forever because it has your name Sidney Arthur Thomas Sheppard written inside it in lovely Gothic writing; I'm clutching definitive proof that the impossible has happened: you died 1st November 1944, aged 36. In reality you're now thirty-seven, because yesterday was your birthday.

I'm almost too warm in my black gloves, hat and veil and feel obliged to unbutton the storm flap on my gabardine coat in this sunny South Ealing Cemetery.

You'll be glad to know that there are at least sixty of us who progress slowly behind your coffin, my love. I'm here to make sure everyone does you credit. You never told me you had so many friends. Of course it's a great shame your meaningless wife can't attend.

No actually, it isn't.

She's not wanted.

The priest and clerks go before us and sing from Job: "I know that my Redeemer liveth and that He shall stand at the latter day upon the earth..."

You get the idea.

It's all very stately and dignified. I think you'd approve. Each step doesn't get any easier for me, though. I'm on my last walk with you at my side. I can't help thinking of what the sombre red text of my little black book says on its title page, I can't help but be a little frightened for you, dear Sidney. Am I consigning you to hell? *"Here is to be noted, that the Office ensuing is not to be used for any that die unbaptised, or excommunicate, or have laid violent hands upon themselves."*

Of course what's done is done, but suddenly I feel I have nowhere to send you except this frozen hole in the ground.

Other people look at me somewhat warily. It hits a raw nerve, I must confess – I'm the stranger at the feast, it seems. They're all wondering who I am and what I'm doing here as if I, and I alone, can excuse the appalling mishap of your death.

You know that I shan't do any such thing.

Not if I can help it.

They haven't a clue, have they?

I can't as yet identify anyone from your wife's side among family and friends. Clearly nobody from the Wallis family has had the nerve to show up on behalf of your bedridden wife? If that's the case, I consider it very bad form. Not that it matters. There can only be one widow here today and that's myself.

Your sister Dorothy is smartly dressed in a nice, if rather unfashionable black coat, hat and gloves. You'd be proud of her. You never told me a lot about her, except that she trained as an optician but now works in Sanders, the leading London goldsmiths. They specialise in clock and watch repairs, buy diamonds for cash and sell superb handbags. I must go there some time.

She's accompanied by her fiancé Jimmy Dewell. He works as a shop assistant in Sanders, too. You're right, he is a widower and far too old for her, but she has her arm hooked on his most affectionately. I've just heard someone whisper he's in the Salvation Army.

You may think it odd talking to you like this in my head as everyone else chokes back their emotions, but today is the last day you'll spend in my world, my darling. It's devastating. Soon you'll be beyond my reach forever and there's so much I still want to tell you.

But it's all right, nobody here can accuse me of anything. On the contrary they look suitably struck by my show of desolation.

I make a jolly good widow because I've done it before.

Your brother Frederick doesn't have your sense of 'presence', I must say. For a start he doesn't sport your lovely, curly black hair. He's come to see you off in his long leather motorcycle coat and helmet which I hardly consider appropriate. His mouth hangs perpetually open, which makes him appear rather dull and slow. No one can say he bothers to keep up appearances. As it happens, he passes me by without a second glance.

I'm sorry to see your mother is so much frailer than I expected. She must have been a great worry to you recently, what with the injury to her foot etc. How old is she now? Sixty-nine? She's not at all like that younger, more flattering photograph you once showed me of her in her prime. At the same time her neat white hair lends her great dignity. Black suits her. Being a former court dressmaker, she definitely knows how to parade.

This is the moment the minister asks God to keep you in his care: '...*earth to earth, ashes to ashes, dust to dust; in sure and certain hope of the resurrection to eternal life through our Lord Jesus Christ.*' That's my cue to elbow people out of my way and scatter a fistful of soil on the lid of your coffin as it sinks into the ground – because I know this is truly the end. I want to shout your name from the rooftops. We're burying my future with your past.

I feel utterly lost as the mourners disperse. Suddenly I want to vomit and the enormity of my loneliness hits me. There's no fixing this?

But I won't let it show.

Too late, I just did… I'm scurrying along the path like a frightened rabbit past acres and acres of gravestones when I see your mother, dear Sidney, standing with head slightly bowed before a high, white concrete cross. Her gaze fixes on its central word RESURGAM. Her voice is hoarse and broken-hearted – she is visibly shaking.

'Excuse me, Mrs Sheppard? Are you feeling quite well?'

'Never mind me, dear, I just came to remember my other son, far away.'

'The name at the base of the cross reads Anthony Philip Winsley, not Sheppard,' I venture to say as delicately as I can. 'What's that all about?'

'Philip was my firstborn, dear, at six o'clock in the morning at Kings Worthy in Winchester on the 7th of August 1893. He became Private No. 82651 in the London Regiment (Royal Fusiliers), but was killed in action on Wednesday, 24th of April, 1918, in France. Winsley is my maiden name. I gave it to 'im because his father would 'ave nothing to do with either of us. As a consequence, I was told to move on from the big house where I was employed as a lady's dressmaker at the time.'

'That's powerful men for you. They abuse us and leave us.'

'Only because they can.'

So that's why you didn't mention your half-brother to me, dear Sidney? Mabel isn't about to name names, but it's obvious she was seduced and betrayed by the head of the household when she was still in her teens?

'I'm so sorry to see him lie here.'

'It's not you who should be sorry, dear.' Mabel loses some of her strength suddenly but none of her anger as she leans on my arm. 'I've been assured that 'is name is inscribed, along with others from 'is regiment, on a panel set into the wall that surrounds the military graveyard at the village of Pozieres. 'is name is one of 15,000 who 'ave no coffins. Even half those who do 'ave graves can't be identified. He must 'ave been blown to pieces by one of the bombardments.'

'Excuse me?'

'If I 'adn't put up this cross, I'd 'ave nowhere to come.'

Then it dawns on me: no bones lie in this hollow ground. So you had a hero for a brother, dear Sidney, which makes me feel proud, too. To feel any less is to stop getting to know you. If I stop getting to know you, I might begin to forget. If I forget I might as well be dead myself.

'I've never been to France, although I do hope to go one day.'

'Neither have I, dear, but I've been told Pozieres guards a vital ridge of high ground between Albert and Bapaume... Philip was so unlucky. By the end of the year the war was all over. All 'e had to do was survive a few more months and he could 'ave come home safely.'

You must have been utterly confused and shocked, dear Sidney, when your older brother disappeared from your life. You can't have been much more than ten years old when he fell in battle.

'I've suffered losses, too, in this war.'

'A mother never forgets 'er firstborn, dear. Never.'

'Just saying.'

Okay, I lied about Philip, I'm not that interested in your long lost brother, I only want to talk about you.

'Are you coming to the wake, dear?'

I raise my head and find Mabel looking straight at me. She has your amazing blue eyes. 'That's very kind of you but I'm not kin, I'm his...'

'We're all kin today, dear.'

Her careworn, pale face is full of questions. I'm quite sure she's wondering if there's something I want to confess to her.

If only!

'I came by the No.17 bus, except I'm not sure where the wake is, or how to get there.'

'Don't fuss, dear, we 'ave room in the limousine. Come back with us to Twickenham. It's just a few miles.'

'I suppose you buried Sidney here to be close to his brother?'

'Ealing is where he grew up, dear. All my family are buried 'ere. That includes my parents, George and Jane Winsley...'

I'm sorry if I'm being obtuse, my love, of course you are going to be buried where your loved ones lie. Only I can't help feeling how nice it would be to have you all to myself in our own little plot somewhere, where I know for certain I will join you when the time comes.

My friend John Curtis says I have an extreme and irrational aversion to dead bodies and he's not far wrong. Except I can't expect a cathedral verger who digs burial holes to understand why I'm equally repulsed and fascinated by your death, dear Sidney. It's what binds us now.

Love shouldn't end at the graveside.

Your mother may adore her sons like no other, but I'm your lover. She hasn't felt my lips or seen the hungry stare in my eyes. She hasn't heard my hot whisper in your ear. Mabel's grief is but a shadow of mine.

Of course I should accompany her to your wake. It's time somebody learnt the truth about you and me.

TWENTY-FIVE

'What do you mean you can't find her?'

Ever since the inspector had arrived early at Bearland Police Station this morning, he'd banged about like a bear himself. DS Biggs stood before his boss's desk and did his best to look very small. It would do no good to offer him a fruit gum.

'Jolantha Wheeler has vanished, sir. I visited the shirt factory where she does regular afternoon shifts, but she didn't show up yesterday. She didn't fire watch at the cathedral, either. Nor is she at home, obviously.'

DI Lockett reached for a jar and began unscrewing its lid. 'Remind me. Where is that exactly?'

'18A Edwy Parade, sir. Here's the thing, though. She has left her six-month-old daughter Jacqueline and her dog with her neighbour, Mrs O'Brien.'

'So she'll be back soon?'

'For the baby, presumably.'

'I hope you're right. What else do we know?'

'Wherever she is, sir, she hasn't taken her motorcycle. It's parked on the road outside her house.'

'You mean to say she didn't even tell Mrs O'Brien where she was going?'

'No, sir, she didn't.'

DI Lockett gave a humph. It was true that many mothers desperately needed to work, except most nurseries had been closed down in case a bomb fell on them. Only recently had the government opened new ones in any number but these could be expensive. Husbands were away fighting and grandparents often moved to safer places. It was left to mums to keep

131

an eye out for other mums' children. That's not to say he wasn't consumed by dissatisfaction and doubt.

'There's something not right about our Mrs Wheeler.'

'You think?'

'Look me in the eye, sergeant, and tell me you don't think she's a bad parent.'

DS Biggs wriggled his toes inside his boots as he stood to attention. That strange, new cleansing lotion that his boss was busily rubbing into his hands said Glycerine and Cucumber on the jar. 'Mrs O'Brien says she is devoted to the child, sir.'

DI Lockett reached for his pipe. He rather subscribed to the current view that pregnancy was 'the prevailing disease' of the war. He started humming the song:

'Oh give me something to remember you by

When you are far away from me,

Some little something LITTLE something

When you are far across the sea.'

The way things were at the moment, all a girl had to do was to have a desire to please. Even a completely plain or downright ugly girl stood a chance with a soldier. That had to go for someone with one ear, too? Jolantha was, in his opinion, just another one making whoopee 'for the duration'.

He was really in a foul mood because Oliver had not let him hold his hand on the way home from 'The Black Dog' last night. Since 'dim-out' had replaced 'blackout', it was easier to get yourself noticed. Only the parks were dark enough to kiss someone safely.

'Everyone has something to hide, sergeant. We know Jolantha once threatened her own mother with a shotgun…'

DS Biggs badly needed a cigarette but chewed the end of his pencil, instead. 'If I were Jolantha, I'd threaten her ladyship, too.'

'So we're dealing with someone who has a propensity for violence.'

'We only have Lady Dutton's word for what happened.'

'But she called her daughter 'unstable'?'

'Her ladyship can be capricious, sir. Jolantha's brother Hugo said as much. I wouldn't trust anyone in that family.'

'She can't deny she was treated in a lunatic asylum two years ago.'

He bit his pencil harder. 'It's not a lunatic asylum, sir, it's a mental hos….'

'Mark my words, sergeant, we have a motive here: insane, jealous, vindictive. We need to look again at her medical history.'

'War affects people in different ways. I wouldn't hold it against her.'

'First Jolantha informs us she's known Sidney only a few weeks. Since then we've learnt they were seen together at his brother's wedding as long ago as last May. She also as good as denied recognising Marjorie when they met in the cathedral, even though they clashed at the reception. What else will she lie about, I wonder?'

'Both women may have met before, sir. That doesn't mean they *know* each other.'

DI Lockett jabbed the air with his pipe. 'You still not willing to trust me on this, sergeant?'

DS Biggs looked surprised. He was contemplating his broken pencil somewhat darkly. 'Why wouldn't I?'

'We could be dealing with a jealous rivalry. One woman may have provoked the other?'

'According to Jolantha, the man who ran into her in the cathedral triforium must have seen or heard something.'

'Anyone else see this so-called witness? Has anybody even answered our appeal to come forward with information?'

'Not yet, sir.'

'There you have it. He's another one of her inventions.'

'I'll keep asking.'

'You'll see, sergeant, I'll prove to you that our Jolantha is a hopeless romantic and fantasizer.' His eyes shone with the full force of an inner conviction. It was the same dangerous true-to-life gamble he took with Oliver. He could feel his heart pounding at the risk. 'Has not her own brother confirmed that she set her sights on marrying Sidney Sheppard? They were as good as engaged. Damn it, she was prepared to buy a wedding dress, ready to make him a bigamist.'

'I don't doubt it.'

'She's our number one suspect. She had most reason to see Marjorie dead on All Saints' Day… She flew into a rage when Sidney got into a fight with his wife about the divorce papers? She wants her rival out of her life once and for all, only the wrong person fell to their death. Now she harbours a grudge against the world.'

'But can we say for sure it was murder, not an accident, sir?'

'Marjorie was the one who was meant to fall and you know it.'

'All the same, Jolantha admitted her own presence quite willingly.'

'Did you not hear what I just said? She thinks she can outfox us.'

'Are you saying she arranged the meeting in the cathedral between Sidney and Marjorie just so she could make it look like…'

'Yes, that's exactly what I'm saying. That's why we have to keep tabs on her every movement.'

'I think I know where she might be, sir.'

'Where?'

'Just suppose she's gone to London – for Sidney's funeral?'

'Good God! Isn't that where Marjorie is? She's lying in a coma in Hammersmith Hospital. They moved her there to be nearer her family. Ring the matron at once and tell her that under no circumstances must she admit anyone to the ward during visiting hours. Then you'd better alert her parents!'

'You can't possibly think she might harm Marjorie now, can you, sir?'

'Why not? She tried once already.'

TWENTY-SIX

149 Waverley Avenue is a semi-detached, 'Tudorbethan' house in Twickenham with a half-timbered gable and fancy red and green flowers framed in its leaded glass windows. It's not very suitable for such a sizeable wake. That's not to say I'm not elated to be here. No matter how alien this vast London suburb may feel to me, I won't deny myself the smallest detail of your former existence, dear Sidney.

I desire to live and breathe the same air you did.

'Allow me,' says Mabel and directs me through your front door.

I follow slavishly. I can't resist. I'm secretly trembling like some shy girl who is visiting her sweetheart's home for the very first time. The walls wobble and I'm walking on air.

All those pompous mourners that assembled at your graveside now gather in the front lounge, where a lucky few rest their elbows and heads on the spotlessly white, crocheted antimacassars of a square-armed sofa and chairs. That's your brother Frederick and sister Dorothy over there by the bay window. I, too, tread the 'Seamless Axminster' carpet, but avoid eye contact with those whose names I know only from your wife's disgraceful letters: Kath, Bernard, Vera, Rimmie…

I'm all set to confess to your mother how much I adored you, my love, yet I feel at the mercy of so many conflicting emotions. Consider me your representative on earth – from now on you live through me alone.

I scowl, convinced no one will notice.

Suddenly somebody whisks Mabel away and I'm left drifting. The room is too hot and conversations get louder. I'm feeling a bit dizzy. It all hits me at once.

I'm expecting to hear only good things about you. Sure enough, it's not long before your name gets mentioned:

'Well, we'll certainly miss him. Shep always brought a certain buzz to a situation.'

'Bit of a maverick, if you ask me.'

'I hear that his Uncle Will once rented a cottage for the whole family in Ealing. Is it true his grandfather kept a pig at the end of the garden?'

'That illness of his has been a bit of a queer do…'

'Sheppard certainly had the gift of the gab. I could quite see him in parliament, couldn't you?'

'Oh God, yes. He always had an opinion on something or other.'

'He got obsessed. A diatribe is not the same as a debate.'

'You heard about his domestic troubles?'

'How is Marjorie?'

'From what I can gather they never lived together as husband and wife for longer than a couple of months.'

'What did happen on their honeymoon in '39?'

'One rumour has it he's impotent.'

'Or he's basically a very shy person in such intimate matters.'

'Do you remember how he made a big impression at Ealing amateur dramatics…?'

'Not to mention the local church. What is it he always said?'

'Faith makes the man.'

'He was a damned good football player in his day, don't you know.'

'Is it true he had a new sweetheart?'

'He can't have been serious about her or he would have told Bernard.'

'Just some bit on the side, was she?'

'Poor Marjorie. It's such a shame…'

'Do you really suppose what happened in the cathedral was an accident?'

'I hear the police may be having second thoughts.'

'Is it true there's a witness?'

'Marjorie will tell all when she comes round…'

I want to join in, if only to agree about your shyness, dear Sidney, except I can't – I hover but don't engage. It saddens me that people feel able to chat so freely about you in your absence. Nor, for the life of me, can I think why they're worrying about your slut of a wife – she can't feel a thing right now. It's me they should be consoling, not her. But don't worry, my darling, I'll think only worthy thoughts of you from now on. I'll try to be your guardian angel.

I'm breathless as I head outside in search of some much needed fresh air. Did you love this garden? You were never really one for the big outdoors, were you? I remember you saying that the best thing about London was that you could ignore the seasons. It made me laugh at the time. My secret plan was to introduce you to the delights of hiking, whereas John Curtis said I would never do anything with you because you sounded like such a dyed in the wool city person. I can't say for sure, only I can't accept anyone can be totally blind to the world's natural beauty.

Dorothy is busy feeding a pigeon under a gnarled apple tree, nearby. I know about this pigeon, but forget its name. Your sister pauses to push her perfectly circular and tinted glasses higher up her nose. With her hair cut in a bob she reminds me of a 1930s' flapper. At the same time, that ridiculously old-fashioned corset she's wearing pinches her waist and stiffens her back terribly. The result is a certain artificial confidence and poise, even elegance. I seem to recall that you told me she is unshakeably religious. I can see it might be true, without in any way being overwhelming.

I ought to confess our love to her, only I'm at a loss. How can I explain 'us' to someone like her? In my own mind I'm still your passionate mistress, my darling. Dorothy won't like me for pursuing a married man – in her eyes I'm the devil incarnate? But I'm not so sure. She seems a gullible soul.

To my great alarm, the pigeon runs straight for me.

'Sorry, I just stepped outside for a smoke.'

Dorothy is all smiles. 'Micky won't go anywhere because he can't fly. He's looking for Bubbles to play with.'

'Bubbles?'

'Our cat.'

'What's wrong with him?'

'He broke a wing in the Blitz.'

I have to give your sister credit; she has your compassion. Micky runs round her feet like a little dog. It's so funny a wounded bird should have your nickname?

Actually I'm not a big fan of birds. 'I was Sidney's best friend. You could say I knew him better than most.'

'Excuse me, have we met before?'

'I helped nurse him in Cheltenham.'

'That's good to know. Half Sidney's friends gave up on him when he got sick. Are you Patricia, by any chance?'

'Who's Patricia?'

'Sidney spoke a lot about someone called Patricia Francis. He was very fond of her. She's a chorus girl. He planned to take me to see her perform in "Night Time in Piccadilly", only I fell ill with flu and couldn't go.'

A chill runs down my spine. This is news to me but I soldier on. 'No, I'm not Patricia.'

'Then you must be Doreen or Dora?'

'Actually my name is Mrs Wheeler.'

'Sidney never mentioned you.'

'How about Jo or Jolantha?'

'There was a Gladys and a Joan, but no Jo.'

I don't wish to appear all prim and proper, dear Sidney, so I don't comment. You might have had a whole string of girlfriends for all I know, I might have been just one of many. You wouldn't be the first to take advantage of a lonely woman bereaved by the war. The possibility is a shock, though not a disaster. Why would you tell your sister your biggest secret? Besides, I know I meant the world to you. I believed you when you looked me in the eye and said, 'What I long for most is for this war to end and for us to have a settled life together.'

'So Sidney didn't confide in you about me *not even once*?' I say tentatively. Dorothy can see I'm disappointed.

'My brother lived a life far removed from mine, Mrs Wheeler, he was the star of the family. Whether it was swimsuits or steel he was a very successful salesman, like our uncle Will. It took this war to break him.'

'Or his pitiful wife,' I add quietly.

Dorothy bends down and lets Micky hop on her hand. 'The thing is, Mrs

Wheeler...'

'Please call me Jo.'

'The truth is – Jo – that before Sidney grew up to be such a success, we struggled to put food on the table. There were seven of us living under one roof at "The Cottage" in Ealing.'

'Really? That's news to me.' I note how she hesitates to talk or can't quite see where to begin. You were the same, my love. You never told me your whole story, you always fobbed me off with some sad smile.

'At first there was no running water and later a single, cold tap in the scullery. We had to pump everything from a well. In the bedrooms the only light was a candle and the whole place was extremely cold. Our father David was a confectioner for a while and then a restaurant car attendant. By 1911 he was unemployed. That's one reason why, in November 1912, he made us emigrate to New Zealand – all except Philip, that is, because he had a job as a wireman's mate on the District Railway. Sidney was terrified by the ship's steep gangway at Tilbury. He was not yet five and dreaded heights ever afterwards...'

'You left England? How extraordinary!'

'Anyway, we spent six weeks on the S.S. Ionic before we reached Hobart, where Sidney fell ill with measles and we had to go into quarantine for three weeks. From Wellington it was a nineteen-hour train journey to Auckland and Avondale, where our father's uncle lived.'

'So why aren't you still there? What made you change your minds?'

'His uncle was a pillar of the local church and couldn't abide Daddy's constant drinking. You can imagine what that meant. One day, Daddy attacked our mother in an intoxicated rage. Sidney rushed between them and tried to stab him in the leg with a blunt fruit knife. Daddy just laughed. After that we all had to leave in a hurry. Mother chose to return to England with us while our father sailed on alone to Canada. Some time after we reached home he sent us a postcard from Montreal. I still have it. It's a pretty, hand-coloured print showing the market and Church Bonsecours.'

'What does it say?'

'The card is addressed to his favourite Freddie. He says he hopes he will get on well at school and be able to read letters of his own very soon. He tells him to look after me and be a good boy. He doesn't mention Sidney. He ends by saying goodbye, with fondest kisses and a row of Xs. There's no address and we never heard from him again. Rumour has it he was killed while working as a lumberjack some time during The Great War.'

'You say you still have the card?'

'It's with some of Sidney's things that got left behind after he and Marjorie quit their flat in Hanger Hill. Would you like to see it?'

'May I?'

We go inside and up the stairs when I stop to stare at something framed on the wall. I'm drawn like a magnet to the expression of mournful dignity, solemn testimony and defiant celebration recorded on a scroll. As if to add weight to the starkest of statements, its script is penned in impressive Gothic lettering.

Dorothy pauses, too. 'Ah, yes, poor Philip. Mother never will get over it.'

This piece of framed paper marks your half-brother's death in 1918, dear Sidney. Hence the final line: "Let those who come after see to it that his name be not forgotten." I feel the same about you, my darling. Except you know that already. You may not be one of those men whose death hangs on a wall, but I will see to it that your passing does not go unnoticed.

Dorothy leads on. 'Ever since we lost Philip, Mother has been sure she will lose someone else. It's driven her half mad with bad nerves. During the London Blitz, she particularly fretted about Fred's two children, Pat and Phil. She couldn't sleep at night knowing they had to travel so far into town to go to school where a bomb might fall on them at any moment. That's why she persuaded Sidney to pay for them to attend the much closer Bishop Perrin Primary School on Hospital Bridge Road, just a short walk from here.'

'Couldn't Frederick do that?'

'Fred never bothered to get qualifications at school and has struggled to get a decent job ever since. His wife Grace had just divorced him, so Sidney had to finance everything himself. He even bought Phil a complete new cricket outfit for which he got no thanks at all.'

'But surely Grace should have helped?'

'She was last heard of in the East End.'

This is hardly music to my ears, although it vindicates why I've always had faith in you, my love. You took it upon yourself to be the head of the family even though you were the youngest. 'What will happen to Pat and Phil now Sidney's gone?'

'They've already left London to live at Thorney Weir near Iver, in the back of beyond. I worry about it constantly. Everywhere is rivers and lakes. What if the children fall in? Who will rescue them because Fred can't swim.'

'Fred can't swim? Really? That's a pity. You never know when you might need something like that? You can never be too careful, can you, near deep water?'

Your short-sighted sister is a kindly soul. Your dependent, overbearing mother, too, has been through the mill. But nothing excuses Frederick. Brother should support brother, in my opinion. You deserved better from him, my love. Instead he left you to shoulder his family's tribulations all by yourself. That's unforgiveable in my book.

He's another one who failed to stand by you in your time of greatest need.

He sounds almost as bad as Marjorie.

His name just moved up my list.

I feel an urge to rush downstairs and seek him out right now, I have to make him say what, if anything, he ever did for you in return. But that day is not today, it requires careful planning.

Revenge is a dish best served cold.

I think I've demonstrated that already.

Of course you could say this is all part of some sinister plan to salvage as much as I can of your life before it falls into the wrong hands, dear Sidney, but that's simply not true. The task remains to gather vital clues to bolster my case: *your wife has to be made to appear guilty in the eyes of the law.* I'm prepared to be defence and prosecution all rolled into one, to ensure she never returns to this world.

It may be highly irregular but the police have only themselves to blame – I can't help it if they're too slow to act, I must salve the hurt in my heart.

As it is, the thrill of anticipation is like a shock to the brain. I'm in your old bedroom where Dorothy points the way to some drawers in a cupboard. I'm a detective on your trail. Where does it end? You tell me.

Understanding is what I need right now. We're in this together, like it or not. If only you knew how sorry I am.

I can already see Dorothy taking out postcards, photographs and letters from when you were young – she's keen to reminisce about what was her childhood, too. Pity she doesn't appreciate what I'm really doing here.

What happens next stays between me and you.

TWENTY-SEVEN

Just my luck, thought DS Biggs, as his train ran late out of London. That V2 rocket that had struck a river pier close by Waterloo Station the previous night had blown off part of the station roof and damaged a signal box. But at least the air now smelt fresher after all those city fires as he disembarked at Esher station. Broken walls of gutted houses gave way to the beauty of the Surrey countryside. Suddenly he could be forgiven for thinking that the war had ended, so tranquil did it feel at the edge of the Great London Built-up Area.

He hadn't wanted to come but he had his orders.

A railway porter pushed a sack truck piled high with parcels along the platform towards him.

'Excuse me. I need to locate 33 Milbourne Lane.'

The porter grinned at him. Her eyes brightened. Delight and fascination filled her face; amusement was no less obvious. In fact, she struggled not to split her sides with laughter, he noticed, at the very sound of him.

'Strike a light, mate. What neck of the woods do you come from, then? That's a real country accent you have there, innit?'

DS Biggs frowned. He hadn't realised he even had an accent, not particularly. 'I'm from Gloucester, if you must know.'

'Never 'eard of it.'

'Can you help me, or not?'

The porter scratched her head under her ill-fitting cap. Her wartime jacket and trousers were not quite the right size, either, but she still managed to convey an air of authority by wearing a very smart tie. 'Okay, keep your 'air on. Milbourne Lane, you say? Let's see now. Go out the

143

station and turn right on to Portsmouth Road. Walk past Sandown Race Course into High Street. Turn left into Claremont Lane – you should go and see the grand Palladian mansion, lovely it is, Clive of India built it in 1768 – then turn left again into Milbourne Lane. You can't miss it.'

He could not decide what he resented most, being greeted as a country yokel or dismissed as a tourist.

'Past the racecourse, you say? I wouldn't mind a quick flutter on the horses.'

'Fat chance, mate. The whole place is full of crazy young men learning to drive armoured trucks. A doodlebug blew a load of them up in August. Shockin' sight it was. Men and women cut to pieces... The cousin of a friend of mine lost an arm.'

'Get a lot of flying bombs and rockets here, do you?'

'We don't call it "Doodlebug Alley" for nothin'.'

The cheery porter was correct: after marching along for ten minutes, he did indeed find himself in Milbourne Lane. This was the land of flower shows and games of whist, where a sign pointed to Esher Lawn Tennis Club and a shop window advertised a local golf course. He was soon standing before a white, semi-detached house that was bordered by thick hedges all round. Nor was it the largest dwelling in the road by any means, since most were detached mansions with mellow red bricks and long sweeping, brown tiled roofs all built in the 1920s or '30s. All the same, he reckoned you could fit three of his house into this pile.

That was fine with him.

Each to his own.

Yes, but he did worry. All those hard-working soldiers who were fighting abroad would want a share in prosperity such as this when they finally returned home after the war ended; they wouldn't easily go back to their factories without being given a bigger slice of the cake, having laid their lives on the line for King and Country? At the very least they'd want a bigger say in their own futures which meant a voice in parliament. He thought he might vote Labour himself if he got the chance? It made him wonder if Sidney Sheppard hadn't felt the same way.

He unlatched the garden gate and advanced up its stone path to knock loudly on the front door. He'd come a long way and wouldn't get home before tomorrow. His sore feet were troubling him. As a result, he was keen to avoid spending a bad night in a cheap hotel that was bound to have dirty sheets and bed bugs in a chilly room that would play havoc with his bunions. It was no use even thinking about staying in Esher – its "Bear Hotel" was totally out of his league.

Suddenly the door flew open and a voice growled in his face, 'Yes?'

'Are you Mr Wallis?'

'Read the sign, damn you. It says No Salesmen.'

'Sorry to bother you, sir. I'm Detective Sergeant Biggs. I'd like to ask you a few questions about your daughter Marjorie, if I may.'

'My daughter is very ill in hospital. There's nothing more to be said on the matter.'

'She may be in danger and I need your help.'

'How do you mean, *in danger*? She's in danger of dying already. What could possibly be worse than that?'

'If I could just step inside, sir? You wouldn't want the neighbours to…'

The thin little man before him had a bald head, a long face and a narrow, pointed chin. A pair of round, silver spectacles gave him a donnish appearance as he peered down his nose at him. 'My wife won't be happy if you tread dirt everywhere in those clodhoppers you're wearing. These are new carpets.'

'Sorry, sir. Police regulation boots.'

Mr Wallis led the way into a lounge where he steered him towards the flowery 'country cottage' style upholstery of a comfortable sofa. A large cocktail cabinet in a walnut veneer stood next to an Art Deco oak sideboard on which rested a dozen family portraits. There was no sign of any cheap Utility furniture that he had in his own home. He couldn't say that he liked it very much but the old-world charm of 'Jacobean' oak suited the semi's 'Tudorbethan' theme very well. By way of sharp contrast, a gaudy green and orange rug with modern geometric motifs lay at his feet on otherwise bare floorboards that had been planed and stained with shiny varnish.

'Would you like me to fetch my wife, detective?'

'Please do.'

'Ever since this debacle began Mrs Wallis has been visiting our daughter in Hammersmith Hospital while I go to work. The constant bus rides to and fro are exhausting her. She'll be having a little lie down, I expect, on the bed.'

Left alone for a moment, DS Biggs noticed a black and white photograph on the nearby sideboard. Sidney and Marjorie Sheppard stood arm in arm outside a church, surrounded by five bridesmaids all dressed in white and each holding a bouquet of flowers. Bride and bridegroom were smiling as if it were the happiest day of their lives. On the back of the frame someone had written London, July 28th 1939.

'You may smile, detective, but that wedding cost us a fortune.'

A small, rather stocky woman entered the room clad in a dress of purple silk velvet with padded shoulders and long sleeves. A large butterfly brooch with eye-catching red, black and green wings glinted at the neckline. Black calf court shoes gave her the look of a well-to-do headmistress or matron with their rounded toes and very solid heels.

'Sorry, madam. Please don't think I was prying.'

To his surprise she joined him at the sideboard and began to point out other photographs one by one. She smelt of lemon cream face massage. 'Doesn't Marjorie look wonderful? See how her dress widens into a long train that just seems to glide along on ripples of white net frills. It's such a shame she set fire to it.'

'Your daughter has burnt her wedding dress?'

'She shouldn't have. She'll regret it. I still have mine. You should have felt the material, detective, it was simply divine. It was covered with flossed-silk braid in a wonderful pattern of swirls and curves. Aren't the squared shoulders pretty? I think the neckline was just right, too, don't you? It should be, because we agonised over it for ages in The New Parade Outfitters on South Ealing Road. Nowadays some brides are forced to make do with dresses sewn out of parachute silk, poor dears.'

'Tell me, Mrs Wallis, did Marjorie have many other – ahem – gentlemen friends before Sidney, or was it love at first sight?'

'Marjorie was always greatly in demand, I can assure you, detective.'

'How old were they when she and Sidney got married?' He already had this written down somewhere, but couldn't be sure without looking in his notebook – he didn't wish to appear too formal before he put her at her ease.

'Marjorie was just twenty-nine and Sidney was nearly thirty-two.'

He didn't remark on that. It was not unusual for 'respectable' men and women to get hitched at such an age, given that it always fell to the man to find a job that would pay for a place they could afford to call home. Everyone knew that when two people got wed the wife was likely to fall pregnant soon afterwards. Of course it didn't always work out that way. He and Muriel had married when they were twenty and their only child had died at six months of diphtheria. They'd been trying for another baby ever since. It was ironical really. Thanks to this war, so many women were giving birth out of wedlock that all former constraints had flown right out of the window. What on earth had Sidney and Marjorie been waiting for?

'I must say you look very dapper on the big day, Mrs Wallis, in your fox-fur stole with flowers attached.'

'That picture was taken at the reception, detective. My beige dress suits me, don't you think, with gloves to match?'

'Charming, I'm sure.'

Mr Wallis re-entered the room, walked over to the drinks cabinet and poured himself and his wife a glass of gin. 'We should throw those awful photographs away. I don't know why we haven't done so already, since they only represent the past now. What do you think, detective? Are you a sentimental man?'

DS Biggs kept his nerve. 'It doesn't matter what I think, Mr Wallis, I only hope to put your minds at ease…'

'Well, we know that's not true. You said just now that you think Marjorie's life might be in danger.'

Mrs Wallis let out a small scream and slumped back on the sofa. 'Danger? Whatever do you mean, detective?'

'Have either of you heard the name Jolantha Wheeler? She usually calls herself simply Jo. We have reason to believe she might have attended Sidney Sheppard's funeral yesterday, in Ealing. Were you at the service by any chance? Did a woman approach you in a hostile fashion?'

Mr Wallis stiffened. 'What makes you think we would go to that man's funeral?'

'He was your son-in-law, was he not?'

'He and his whole impoverished clan can go hang for all I care, detective.'

'If you could just answer the question, sir.'

'We're not aware of anyone of that name, are we, dear? Who is she?'

'She was present in Gloucester Cathedral when your daughter fell.'

'You're not saying that this Wheeler person has anything to do with what happened to our daughter, are you, detective? You're not here to say it wasn't an accident, I hope, because I simply couldn't bear it?'

DS Biggs chewed the end of his pencil and considered how to respond. 'I want to know how well Marjorie knew Jolantha. Did she mention her to you, at all?'

Mr Wallis rose abruptly from his seat and his face was a mask of red indignation. 'I regret ever having set eyes on Sidney Sheppard. His marriage to my daughter was a disaster from day one. I always said it would be. I should never have given my consent. If anyone did want to kill her – God forbid – it would be that man. He was highly unstable. What do you expect from a Liberal?'

DS Biggs fixed him with a stare. 'So you know nothing about her, sir?'

'About Jolantha?'

'If you don't mind.'

Mr Wallis composed himself but didn't sit back down again, much to his wife's alarm. 'Marjorie never spoke that name, although…'

'Although what, sir?'

'I wasn't going to mention this, detective, except now I think I should.'

'Please do.'

'Isn't it obvious? Sidney didn't care about my daughter because he had this other woman in tow.'

'Jolantha was close to him, by all accounts, but it's her interest in your family I'm trying to establish right now. Are you quite certain your paths haven't crossed in the last year or so?'

'I swore to have no more to do with Sidney. Now, from the grave, he sends us this woman. Is that what you're saying, detective? You think she means to harm our daughter, or us? Damn the man. He resented everything his own shortcomings denied him. A rabble-rouser, that's what he was. He once walked into the headquarters of the South Ealing Conservative Club and shouted us all down, right in the middle of a meeting. No sense of decency, at all. Talk about self-loathing. He was a ruddy fool. Didn't I just tell you he was a Liberal!'

'That's quite enough, dear,' said Mrs Wallis, slapping her knee. 'Go into the garden at once and cool off. I won't have raised voices in my own house. It's too upsetting.'

'My wife's right, detective. We didn't ask for this. I'm too embarrassed and ashamed by the whole business. That man deceived us all.'

DS Biggs sat very still in the ensuing silence. He couldn't think anything for a moment. Here he was, trying to advise two very shocked and frightened people. They couldn't believe the miserable hand that fate had dealt them.

'What was that all about, Mrs Wallis? What does your husband mean by "deceived"?'

'What possible interest is that to you, detective?'

'If I don't ask I won't know.'

Mrs Wallis went to pour a gin and tonic for them both from the fancy cocktail cabinet. 'My husband and I haven't always lived here, detective, we used to live at 28 Creighton Road in Ealing W.5, not far from the cemetery. Sidney met Marjorie when she was just fifteen. She was very impressed by him. We all were. He spoke well and had passed Matriculation in English, Elementary Mathematics, Geography, French, Electricity and Magnetism at Ealing County School for boys. None of the Wallis children managed to do the same, to my shame. Marjorie thought him exceptionally clever. We soon discovered that he lived a few streets away in a rundown bungalow called "The Cottage" with his brother Frederick and sister Dorothy. We think a retired colonel from the colonies built it, or it might once have been a gardener's cottage with quite a large plot of land. Either way, it was completely out of keeping with everything else in our part of town. While this did bother us slightly, Sidney seemed such an ambitious, accomplished sort of chap who would soon rise above it. Marjorie had great hopes of him.'

'And Sidney was smitten by her, presumably?'

'Oh yes. They were both keen amateur actors with the Ealing St Mary's Dramatic Society of which he was the chairman. We once went to see him act in a comedy called "Aren't We All?" by Frederick Lonsdale in which Sidney played the Honourable William Tatham. Marjorie was convinced he might one day be a big name on the stage, though I must confess I found his performance rather wooden. I realise now that acting was his great strength, though, because he certainly fooled us. He was not what he seemed.'

'Are you literally accusing him of fraud in some way?'

'He'd say or do anything not to appear wanting.'

'Is that a yes or a no?'

'There was something 'off' about him, detective. Marjorie thought him the nicest man she knew, but he could be quite... I don't know what to call it. My husband says he was callous. Even that doesn't explain him. The only word for it is 'distant'. Sidney and Marjorie were forever quarrelling.'

'We found legal papers on your daughter's body which show she was actively trying to divorce her husband.'

'Wouldn't you, detective, if you had a marriage in name only? In 1939 Marjorie and Sidney took out a lease on a flat on the Hanger Hill Garden Estate in Ealing, except his new job with a Parisian clock company fell through the minute war broke out just after they got married. They were stuck with the lease but had no income. That meant they had no choice but to sublet the flat immediately. Worse still, Sidney could only get a new job up north in Warrington and wives weren't allowed in the accommodation provided. In January 1940 he found himself a better job back in London, except all staff were quickly evacuated to the Midlands because of the Blitz. Mr Wallis and I had bought this house in Esher by then, so Marjorie came to live with us while she and Sidney tried to sort out their futures. In reality they never lived together after that. He either stayed in digs or with his mother Mabel.'

'Sorry to bother you, but do you have her address?'

'It's 149 Waverley Avenue, Twickenham. His sister Dorothy still lives there, too.'

'How did Sidney and Marjorie correspond while apart?'

'By letter and by telephone.'

'What about visits?'

'They could be sporadic, owing to the demands of work and the difficulties of travel. For instance, it was a whole day by train to Warrington. He might as well have been on another planet.'

'Good point. How did Marjorie cope?'

'She joined the NAAFI in January 1940. Their headquarters are located near here at Ruxley Towers in Claygate. She works as a secretary to an Air Commodore. Sidney did manage to change jobs for a third time and went to work for a tube-manufacturing company called Tungum Tube Co., but it also quickly relocated out of London to Cheltenham on account of the bombing.'

'Cheltenham is closer to London. Did Marjorie not go to live with him there?'

'I want to be honest with you, detective. She and her younger sister Peggy soon found a flat of their own at No.12 "Anchorage Gardens", up the road from here in Claygate. The NAAFI is her whole life now. There was nothing for her to do in Cheltenham. She was needed here. She still is.'

'Doesn't mean he didn't want her.'

'You think? Then let me show you something, detective, and perhaps you'll see what we mean when we say there was something not right about our Sidney. Wait here while I fetch it. Help yourself to another drink, if you wish. Don't let my husband stop you.'

No sooner had Mrs Wallis left the room than Mr Wallis strode in from the garden and caught him with a glass in his hand. 'You should leave immediately, detective,'

'But your family could be in danger, sir.'

'I think I'd know.'

'Are you sure you haven't received any threatening letters? Has anyone been seen watching the house lately? I came here today to tell you that we believe Jolantha Wheeler may have embarked upon some sort of vendetta.'

'Vendetta? What sort of vendetta? Why?'

'I'm not in a position to say yet.'

'This is all mere speculation, detective.'

'Doesn't mean I'm not right.'

'You've disrupted our day quite enough already. My poor wife can't take any more. Neither can I. Don't forget your hat on your way out.'

'At least telephone me if you get any trouble, sir. Here's my card.'

'Good day to you, detective.'

'I hope you don't regret this.'

'You shouldn't have come. It was a very bad idea.'

'I'm only thinking of you and Marjorie.'

'I'm sorry, but that's how it is. Now go.'

A simple please would suffice, thought DS Biggs, as the front door slammed in his face. He was just settling his hat on his head when a steel window opened in a bedroom directly above him. To his astonishment, Mrs Wallis leaned out from its sill to gain his attention.

'Take this, detective. It's all I have from Sidney. It might go some way to explain the sort of person he really was. You might as well have it before my husband destroys it.'

No one hated surprises more than he did. He'd come here all fired up to warn a distraught mother and father about Jolantha, only to be told that Sidney was the one he should be blaming. He knew little about the letter he caught in his hand, except it would give him something to read on his way back to Gloucester.

A red sun was setting low in the sky as he boarded a railway carriage full of noisy soldiers going home on leave. Silvery barrage balloons turned pink in the sky as his train puffed out of Paddington. Air raid sirens fell silent and a temporary hush settled over the capital. Shame, no Spitfires, he'd really hoped there'd be Spitfires.

TWENTY-EIGHT

Whoever follows me also watches my house.

He turns up the collar on his khaki trench coat and shields his face under his hat and scarf – he's stamping his cold feet on the pavement right opposite 18A Edwy Parade. It's a bleak November evening, yet my keen observer is disturbingly persistent. I can't say for sure if it's the police or not.

Every so often he sucks a sweet from a brown paper bag in his pocket.

Anyone else might think he's my guilty conscience.

If you were here I'm quite certain you would go straight outside and confront him, dear Sidney. You wouldn't stand for this uncertainty and fear I'm feeling right now. What does he want? Why won't he say? It's definitely me he's tracking, but he walks off whenever I try to go near him.

Bella whines and goes to sit by the front door. It falls to any dog to read their owner's mood and respond accordingly. She guards the entrance with devotion, or she might have a yawn. Next minute she sticks her nose high in the air and sniffs repeatedly – that could be another mouse gnawing holes in the wall.

Jacqueline has finally fallen asleep on my arm and I put her to bed in her cot on the floor beside me. You'll be interested to know that she is still teething, after all, poor thing. I'm a bit all over the place at the moment. That's because I can't buy rubber knickers for her any more – one minute they're stocked in the shops and next minute they're gone. The same goes for rubber teats. We're even being told that rubber is uncomfortable and that our babies don't need nearly as many clothes as we think. But if we don't have proper nappies we have to cut up perfectly good clothes to make do.

I'm not about to question our love's worth, my darling, I won't let doubt worm its way into my soul. Housework at midnight helps. All this washing and cooking goes a long way to calming me when my mind is on fire. It's doing something physical, I suppose.

I've finished banging homemade, boiled nappies on the wooden washboard in the scullery, I've just rolled each one through the mangle to press out the water. I'm leaving them to dry next to my bras, girdles and slips on the wooden clothes horse near the gas-heated copper.

I'm running low on coal for the fire and it promises to be freezing. If you were here with me right now, I know you'd keep me warm. I did everything I could to save you, my love. It's NOT my fault you're gone.

Well, not exactly.

Truth is, there's a strange ache in my head and my chilblains hurt horribly. The district nurse did visit me once after I gave birth in hospital but since then, nothing! At least I'm in the Milk Scheme now for free milk, ever since I applied to the Gloucestershire Food Controller's Office. The Vitamin Welfare Scheme is also a godsend, because it means I can have access to free orange juice or vitamin A and D tablets to keep me healthy. It's all very well encouraging women to have children for the war effort, except we get worn out, too. I've declined all offers of cod liver oil, though. That stuff is hell. I should be grating onions ready to make some curried corned beef balls. I get most of my meat in corned beef now, ever since the meat ration became so stingy. I can't remember when I last managed to buy a 1/4lb of stewing steak, for instance.

Instead, I'm removing the lid from the shoebox in front of me on the kitchen table. It's very decent of your sister Dorothy to part with this collection of your personal possessions, dear Sidney.

This would be junk to anyone else, but to me it's a joy.

I'm shaking like a leaf, since the first thing I pick from the box is a newspaper cutting which features you. It turns out I have in my hand a photograph of Old Ealonians on stage in a production of something called "Autumn Crocus". You're wearing an open-necked shirt, a V-necked cricket jumper and a jacket with a handkerchief in your top pocket. I'm sorry, Sidney, but I have to smile – you had so much more hair ten years ago.

You do look a bit green, I must say. The same goes for a review of this other play presented by the Ealing St Mary's Dramatic Society at the Good Shepherd Hall in April 1932. This time you are the "Snapper" with a camera, 'snapped' as an irate husband enters the door. You have your eyes half closed as the lady caught on your knee clings to your neck in shocked horror. It's not just your skinny, clean-shaven good looks (no wartime moustache) that impresses me, it is the fact you appear so in control. How old were you then, 24 or 25? Your innocence is quite endearing…

Good-for-nothing Marjorie is on stage with you, looking demure, but she's not the one who gets the praise. What a write up "The Middlesex County Times" reporter gives you: 'Plenty of Sparkle in "The Unfair Sex". PROFESSIONAL POLISH AT SOUTH EALING. The casting was excellent and the tempo never flagged … You can decide for yourself which is the unfair sex… Sidney Sheppard gave a well observed rendering of the ultra-modern young writer of fiction… not a gesture was wanting to complete the performance.'

Bella gives up guarding the hall and lies down beside me on the floor in my heap of trophies. She must think I'm crazy sorting a dead man's debris, only given half a chance she'd dig up old bones, too.

I don't know if the dead can recall what letters they wrote or what was written to them, but this is someone called Rosa's to you. Do you remember 'Rosa', dear Sidney? I don't think she was your lover, far from it. It's dated January 22, 1928 when you were only twenty: 'Dear Sheppard, if I judge you rightly, you are, in my opinion, a person of character and the fortunate possessor of personality. Therefore, I entreat you to assert those gifts on Wednesday evenings from 7.30 p.m. to 10 p.m. at the Dramatic Society. Because really it jars me to see you wasting your time being flippant. What a great thing it would be to know that you have helped just one person to realise that there is no time to be wasted in educating oneself. You will, of course take this in the nature it is intended. Yours sincerely, Rosa Wolfinden.'

Now I did detect in you a certain hurtful casualness towards myself on occasion, dear Sidney. It seems Rosa saw it, too, at rehearsals. She detected a lack of solid commitment.

Yet she does, like me, consider you to be otherwise very serious and a fount of wisdom. Why else would she write to you from Kingston-on-Thames on October 22nd, 1928: 'Dear Sheppard, could you tell me what one must do to have faith? For years I have not been able to think of a personal God, an impersonal God, or a God of any kind. But then, this perhaps falls in with my philosophy of life. To live from day to day expecting nothing… Consciously, I have just realised that religion is rather important. But about the Virgin Birth, scientifically, it is impossible for such a thing to have happened… As you said, "Faith makes the man". Also, if one believes in one miracle in the Bible, one must necessarily believe in the lot. Don't you think it more possible that Christ was a Superman, ordinary in the sense of being a human, but extraordinary in his manner of living… Please write to me of your religion… Don't, on any account, say Dear Mrs Wolfinden again. Yours sincerely, Rosa.'

I cling to the letter feeling a little shocked, dear Sidney. Did you not twice deny to my face that you believed in anything spiritual, whereas now it seems there was a time, not so long ago, when you were firmly rooted in religion?

Hence this letter from Frank E. Harris from Brentford, who writes to you on the 17th of January, 1930: 'Dear Sheppard, will you please read the lesson for us at the Y.P.S. on Sunday night (19th)? We are expecting the Bishop to choose a passage of scripture – so if you can be at the church by 3 p.m. I can let you know the details. The lesson is to follow Family Prayers. Do please wait until people have 'settled' in their seats before beginning to read.'

Here you are, a dynamic young man at the heart of Ealing's church, school and clubs. I can see that even at 22 you wished to be the star of the show and not second rate? How laudable your ambitions were, but you don't take rejection well, do you, my love? You think it unfair.

You lose your temper.

As do we all.

Do you recall this note written to you on the 30th of September 1929, from the Old Ealonians Football Club: 'Dear Shep, I received your letter with mixed feelings. Having played with you last season myself, I was very sorry we couldn't find a place for you in the 2nd xi. I was, however, surprised and annoyed to find that you took exception to it. Gratitude for past service cannot be allowed to influence a selection committee... Two years ago Kit Williainson lost his place in the 1st xi after occupying it for 3 years. He promptly left us and was accompanied by howls of derision and vituperation. Tommy nearly made the same exhibition of himself last week, but his native good feeling saved him. May I hope that you will do the same? Yours sincerely, A. C. More. PS. Please treat personalities as confidential.'

But mere bric-a-brac is not what I'm after. I have in my hand something penned by your expendable wife long before you two got hitched. I can easily make this out to be evidence of her deadly culpability that will establish what a bad egg she really was. I will right your wrongs, dear Sidney, I really will, because the police have to be alerted to her self-willed and unpredictable temperament. I'll paint a damning picture of her, so help me God. For instance, how weak she was when she scribbled this to you on September 15th 1929. I could have done so much better at her age: 'My darling Sidney, I am awfully sorry but Daddy won't let me go tomorrow night. He said it is a nasty, morbid play with men and women saying outspoken things which I would never hear at home or in decent company. Also that it would be like a dose of poison to me and that he couldn't see why we couldn't go to a bright, merry show with plenty of good laughs... If you want to go, you could go with your boyfriends. I don't mind really. We could go to our usual haunt on Saturday.

'I love you with all my heart, my darling, and I will always be good for your sake as long as I love you. You are such a wonderful boy and I adore the ground you walk on. Oh to be safely married to you forever. Heaps and heaps of love, Marjorie.'

These weasel words are almost too much to bear. I hadn't realised just how cleverly the cunning minx set out to trap you. Three years earlier, on the 3rd of March 1926, she was prepared to snare you when she was not yet sixteen: 'My Dear, Silly, Sweet, Funny Sidney, thanks awfully for the last letter you gave me. It was the best of all you have written. I sincerely believe in you now with all my heart. I don't know how I possibly couldn't after that letter last night. You are quite right, Sidney, I do care for you. I have loved you for exactly a year since we went to Collins' party and I've only had my reward a little while. I think I have been exceedingly patient, don't you? Whoever said you were lukewarm and cold-hearted wants a thorough kicking. You're just a nice old dear. I must stop now, so goodbye for the present, with love (crossed out), Your Marjorie.'

She plays the same trick as a twenty-year-old in this, equally maddening screed dashed off at 'The office' on the 19th of April, 1931: 'Dear Rufus, herewith your sweater and the typing I did for you. I hope you are getting along all right without my guiding light. I must be pining – I can't eat, but that state won't last long although I hope to lose weight if nothing else out of this. Don't be cowardly and stay away from the tennis club as I have no intention of cutting you. I have told Greta we have packed it up so as not to be bothered with invitations for two in that direction. I have offered my services as a fourth at bridge at any time etc.

'It's a great pity I'm such a rotter and didn't know how to treat you while I had the chance. I realise it was all my fault now. This parting is much, much harder than I ever imagined it would be, still we learn by experience and I have come to the conclusion that the only way to be happy (when you're made like me) is not to think too much. Cheerio and good hunting. Yours, Marjorie.'

You and I never fought once, did we darling, whereas you and Marjorie were at each other's throats right from her teenage years. She made you want her by playing so hard to get – she hooked you like a wriggling fish ready to reel you in. I'm scrabbling about on the floor for more damning facts. It's not as if you didn't try to fight her off, because I have here the draught of a letter you scribbled in 1932: 'My dear Marjorie, my heart is heavy and my brain heavier. But it seems that you will never make any attempt to understand my difficult nature and consequently my mind is unlikely ever to be at rest. I have written to your people and the book is closed. Go to it and find yourself. Yrs. Sidney.'

So why on earth get wed in 1939? Can't you see it was never meant to be? I'm the one for you, not that hussy. The early evidence is all here in this little box. Yet I do envy all the time you two had together. You truly were childhood sweethearts. How I wish I had known you in your formative years, I would have been more loyal than her.

But for Marjorie you'd be at my side right now. She has ruined my life and must pay the price. I know it won't bring you back, but there's such a thing as poetic justice.

***

If I know what's best for me I'll go to bed right now, except I'm afraid to dream ever since you plunged to your death right in front of me, dear Sidney – I keep asking myself what I could have done differently. What was I thinking? Now I feel as if I'm lost in the dark. Why did you ask to meet me in the cathedral if you knew your irrelevant wife would suddenly appear? It doesn't add up.

I'm looking for absolution, I suppose.

No chance, not yet.

Not until I can show who's guilty.

Not until they get what they deserve.

I'm ready to do the right thing by you because I know you'd want me to, except you seem to be slipping further and further away from me…

I go to the window again and my ever present shadow guards my door in the dimmed street. I like to think that's you come back from the dead to watch over me as I go about my valuable work for posterity. I'll be your archivist beyond the grave, my love. Instead I can't get it out of my head that he's the one who barged past me at the top of the stairs on the day you fell to your death in the cathedral. He's the one who might have witnessed what I did in the triforium?

Whatever he wants can't be good. For all I know, my spy could be about to blab the truth at any moment.

It makes me think I'll have to be more careful from now on, because he and I clearly have unfinished business.

I should be scared half out of my mind.

Except I don't give a fig for him. Nothing will change what I have to do next. Bella gives a sharp bark. It isn't the bark she uses to get attention, it's the one she gives to express excitement. Other dogs might have real jobs to do – they hunt, save, sledge, fetch and guard, but she gets to ride in a motorcycle sidecar tomorrow with the wind in her ears.

TWENTY-NINE

For the first time he could remember DI Lockett had not shaved this morning – he'd been too busy mulling over something he should never have whispered in Oliver's ear late last night. It was too dangerous. Too 'deviant'. His thoughts were still in turmoil when DS Biggs kicked open his office door and coughed loudly. It was his subordinate's usual, irritating way of attracting his attention.

'What is it with you, sergeant? Why can't you ever knock?'

'Sorry, sir, but there's been a nasty incident in a sweetshop in Eastgate Street.'

'Really? You want me to make gobstoppers my priority right now?'

'A man threw the shop's owner to the floor and broke her leg in two places. She was trying to stop him filling his pockets with Black Jacks and Sherbet Fountains …'

'It'll be some spiv dealing on the black market.'

'I have a description…'

'More to the point, what did you find out about Jolantha in London?'

'Mr Wallis considered my visit to be in very poor taste.'

'Diplomacy isn't always your strongest point.'

'Everyone in Surrey seems to think I'm some sort of yokel.'

'They're not wrong, are they?'

'Mr and Mrs Wallis are adamant they haven't seen or heard from her. I think we're chasing ghosts, sir.'

'Can't believe you just said that.'

'Just one thing, sir.'

'Is it important?'

'No idea. But Mrs Wallis insisted on giving me a letter as I was leaving.'

'This concerns us, how?'

'Both she and Mr Wallis believe that the fall in the cathedral has everything to do with Sidney, on account of what they call his unstable character. They're pretty much prepared to say he might have gone so far as to harm their daughter in the heat of the moment.'

'But we all know who our chief suspect really is, don't we?'

'All the same…'

'A letter, you say?'

'Sidney Sheppard wrote it to Marjorie when they were courting.'

'Very well, let's hear it.'

DS Biggs had perused the neatly penned missive in his hand so many times that he virtually knew it by heart. He began by announcing the address and date written in the top right hand corner of the page: '"The Cottage", The Park, Ealing W.5. September 28th 1932.'"

'Which is significant, how, sergeant?'

'"The Cottage" was the Sheppard family home before the war, sir.'

'I really don't see why some old letter from years ago can help us solve deaths now, but carry on. What does Sidney write?'

'"Dear Mr and Mrs Wallis, I expect that what I have to say to you will be rather a joke to you, especially to Mr Wallis, but I shall be brief and to the point. Whenever I have the pleasure of a lady's company, I naturally feel some responsibility for her safe keeping, and I want you to know, therefore, that from today onwards Marjorie will not be in my company as, so far as I am concerned, any particular friendship which existed between us is ended. Marjorie was not with me last Saturday.

"Please don't think that the reason for this is that I want to monopolise your daughter, I do not. It is revealed, however, whenever such questions come up, that there is a difference in mental make-up between Marjorie and myself. She never wishes to give an expressed opinion or attitude, but asks that it be taken for granted that everything always turns out most advantageously, whereas I always express the attitude that seems to me to be the right one, knowing…"'

'Quite so. But then I'm a policeman. Go on, sergeant. What have you stopped for?'

DS Biggs rolled his eyes and resumed reading: "'... *knowing* that nothing can be done unless it is willed from the brain. Hence that thing I hold most clearly, mental understanding, seems impossible of attainment between us, and as this militates, at any rate so far as I am concerned, against progress, the matter is at an end. You, I should imagine, can now rejoice that both Norman and Marjorie are free of the paupers who encumbered them. With many thanks for the hospitality I have received at your hands. Yours sincerely, Sidney.'"

'Remind me, sergeant. Who's Norman?'

'He's Marjorie's only brother, sir. She also has three sisters called Peggy, Barbara (Babs) and Shirley. Sidney and Norman were very good friends, apparently.'

DI Lockett sucked his pipe. 'Sidney's writing style is suitably formal, is it not? He could be penning a business letter rather than describing his own love life. What age did you say he was when he wrote it?'

'Almost twenty-five. Marjorie was twenty-two.'

'And they'd known each other *how long*?'

'At this point, I'd say seven years, sir.'

'He certainly gets on his high horse, doesn't he? A 'joke', indeed!'

'He practically calls Marjorie stupid.'

'Whereas he's a thinker?'

'Bit of a firebrand, I'd say, sir.'

'Or a paper tiger?'

'A Liberal, sir. He once tried to shout down the chairman of the Ealing branch of the Tory Party.'

'We won't hold that against him.'

'It reminds me of myself and my sister when we were growing up. We always fought like cat and dog. Still do. The thing is, did Sidney always secretly despise and hate Marjorie enough to hurt her?'

DI Lockett filled his lungs with smoke and exhaled rather sharply. 'There's real bitterness in that use of the word 'encumbered', I must admit. That reference to 'pauper' says something, too. He's dismissing himself and his own family as a burden. How rich is the Wallis family anyway?'

'Mr Wallis is some sort of engineer. He's well paid, I imagine, but not exceptionally so. That said, they now have a very nice house in Esher. I think we have to see them as slightly snobby social climbers.'

'Now might be their chance to blacken his name once and for all?'

'Nevertheless, he went to great efforts to join their ranks, sir. He played cricket and tennis with their family and even joined the local Dramatic Society.'

'How do you even do that, sergeant? How do you fit in and get yourself accepted when you know you're so different?'

DS Biggs frowned. His boss really was in a strange mood today, both over excited and strangely terrified. 'He didn't have a father, or even his older brother Philip to show him what to do. All his decisions had to be his own?'

'Everything still points to him being a victim not a suspect. Suppose we go back to the beginning for a moment: Sidney marries a girl who comes from a relatively well-to-do family. They're not so posh as to reject him but they want him to conform to their views. There's a great deal of unspoken pressure. They expect him to provide a house for his wife and earn enough money to maintain a comfortable standard of living in London. They don't like his politics and he, by implication, doesn't care for theirs. To them he's riff-raff who doesn't suit their snobbish hopes for their favourite daughter. He makes things worse for himself by deliberately rubbing them up the wrong way with his political views – that letter he wrote them also borders on the downright rude. Clearly he has a lot of anger towards the world, for which I can only sympathise.'

'So how did someone like that get away with it, sir? How did he ever pass muster?'

DI Lockett averted his gaze and seemed suddenly to get something in his eye – it could have been the pungent smoke from his pipe or something else. He reddened and rubbed it. Last night he'd finally told Oliver he loved him. 'It all comes back to those amateur dramatics you just mentioned, sergeant. We're all actors, are we not? Sidney adopts the trappings of his more affluent neighbours, apes their behaviour and learns to pronounce his 'h's just to seem normal. That's not the whole story, of course.'

164

'What is, sir?'

'With his flashing blue eyes and tall stature, Sidney has genuine charisma, sergeant. He brings a sense of 'presence' to a room, like all good actors. But how far will it get him without the one thing he needs most – a sense of security? That's the constant worry. That's his one big weakness. The consistent theme of this letter is not hatred, it's panic dressed up as pride – its air of self-righteousness is him pretending to be above the Wallis's petty protests at where their daughter was on a Saturday night. He'd rather damn himself than take unfair blame. It's almost evangelical. None of it makes him a murderer, though, not by a million miles.'

'What makes you so sure, sir?'

'Sidney simply sought to obscure the truth about who he really was by acting someone better. It's how you get on in life…'

'He lived a lie, you mean.'

'The trouble is, sergeant, the most successful actor can strut his stuff on stage, only to find everyone suddenly boos him. Then where does he go? What then? He's caught like a rabbit in the lights.'

'You saying Sidney suffered from some sort of stage fright? In real life?'

'You tell me.'

'I have no idea.'

He could see that his sergeant thought this was a lot to read into one letter, but he felt convinced that he knew what he was about. 'It was something lacking in himself which made him vulnerable to other, more manipulative people.'

'So where does that get us, sir?'

'We have an address in Twickenham, do we not? You need to ask Sidney's sister Dorothy the same questions you asked Mr and Mrs Wallis. His brother Frederick, too, should be quizzed about Jolantha's recent behaviour.'

'As I said, sir, I think we're chasing ghosts?'

'It doesn't matter what you say, sergeant. From his letter I take Sidney to be a hopeless innocent. He was capable of falling in love but not loving. The thing is, did he ever pour out his heart to anyone else, only to break theirs? Did he change his mind and try to reject them before both parties felt 'encumbered'? Did he ever go so far as to write them a letter saying that 'mental understanding' was impossible of attainment between them, as he did to Marjorie all those years ago? Did he lose his temper and *provoke* them, too?'

'Who are we talking about?'

'Who do you think? For a man with things to hide, Jolantha Wheeler has to be his greatest strength and greatest weakness. What if they quarrelled? Someone like her doesn't forgive easily. Do we even know what she's getting up to right now? Have we found her yet?'

'Still working on that.'

THIRTY

CONEY HILL MENTAL HOSPITAL

Dear Violet, I know I said I wouldn't write again but the sands of time are running out ever faster and memories and questions from years past are always flooding in. There are some thoughts I would like to share with you. In doing so I have not the slightest wish to upset you, still less hurt you. I have never in my whole life wanted to harm you and when I have done so, it has been due to human frailty and immaturity.

If words mean anything at all, you were happy when you told me, 'You're the kindest man I know.'

You have never explained why you decided you were free to indulge in a man-hunt and were proud of doing so. Perhaps you wanted to live dangerously and seek adventure in tune with the prevailing lax wartime morality. Joshua had to go off to fight, but Sidney must have delighted you so much mentally, spiritually and physically that you immediately transferred your love and loyalty and tried to make a one-sided annulment of our love.

Ordinary decency and respect for your reputation might have demanded that you return home sober and at a reasonable hour, but you had not enough principle between you to moderate your pleasure even in these turbulent times. It makes me wonder what kind of person you really are. I thought better of you than that, (much, much better) yet you have offered me no explanation or discussion. I wonder if you ever stop to recall how many occasions, as the love of my life, you have kissed other men, quite apart from having a love child by one of them?

This war curtails entertainment and I don't know if Sidney had a place of his own, but you had the blackout to swallow you up, clasped in each other's arms, kissing and cuddling and all the other rituals of love's idyll. Yet every birthday and Christmas you visited me in hospital, or wrote to me to tell me all was well and send me all your love. And as the meetings went on week after week, month after month, and the familiarity no doubt grew and grew, and our love became more and more betrayed and debased, so did your own self-esteem and integrity – you kept on saying to me there was no one else.

Did you think it might be a temporary affair? But how much of our love and future together would have been left if I had not rescued you in time? Could you ever have come back to me, and would I have wanted you, after your latest fancy man even touched you? Now that man is gone, will you still deny you're mine? Love, H.

THIRTY-ONE

'You're quite sure it was Jolantha Wheeler who robbed you?' DS Biggs leaned forward on the sofa in the front room of 149 Waverley Avenue and frowned. That's what came of giving someone the benefit of the doubt. There was a strange chill in his spine; his hands shook; his heart raced. He wondered how their paths could have failed to cross and whether he should feel more alarmed.

Dorothy Sheppard appeared nervous in her owl-like spectacles. 'Well, detective, I didn't actually see her take it...'

'See, be damned,' corrected Mabel, patting her tightly curled white hair. She spoke with a slight lisp due to her lack of front teeth. 'Mrs Wheeler suddenly appeared at poor Sidney's funeral. None of us 'ad any idea who she was, she just said she was a friend of my son's. Dorothy thought she was being kind.'

DS Biggs took out his notebook and pencil. Waverley Avenue wasn't a patch on that big house he had visited in Esher, but it felt quite homely. You could live very comfortably in these London suburbs. 'The thing is, madam, I hadn't got Jolantha down as a petty thief.'

'She took a shoebox of precious photographs and postcards,' said Dorothy, very definitively.

'These were not items of any monetary value, then?'

'Well, how would you put it, detective?'

'She didn't make off with cash or silver, is what I mean?'

'No, she didn't.'

Mabel slurped tea from her cup. 'Didn't we just say? Jolantha Wheeler took advantage of our hospitality to rob us blind. She planned it all in advance. Her intention is clear to me now. There was a very odd look in her eyes, detective. Her pupils hardly moved, only stared straight out at you as if focusing on something inside her head and not in the room. Like a mad person.'

'Really mother, that's most unfair,' said Dorothy, shooing away Micky the pigeon before he pecked their visitor's ankle. 'She was, to my mind, rather calm and calculated.'

DS Biggs reached for his Player's Navy Cut No 9. It wasn't his favourite brand of cigarettes by any means – too mellow – but with all the shortages in the shops, he had to smoke whatever was to hand. 'Did she threaten anyone?'

'No, detective, she did not.'

'So it's possible she came to Sidney's wake simply to mourn his passing, saw some of his things and couldn't resist the urge to take them – as trophies?'

'It doesn't matter now, they're gone.'

DS Biggs scribbled *kleptomaniac?* in his notebook. 'I want to help you if I can.'

Dorothy pulled at her long flowery dress and spread it flat over her knees. 'Who do you think she is, detective? What does she want with Sidney's possessions? What's the connection?'

'I rather think she'd set her heart on eloping with him.'

'No! Honestly?' cried Mabel, spitting more tea. 'Sidney would do no such thing. He's a married man.'

'I don't think that mattered to Jolantha.'

Dorothy chimed in. 'You really think my brother planned to go on the run with this other woman, even before his divorce was finalised? Why didn't he tell us?'

'Unless he changed his mind. Unless he got cold feet at the last minute.'

Mabel was quick to break the sepulchral silence. 'Exactly so, detective! My son was extremely upset at the notion of losing Marjorie. After she refused to listen to him he was all fired up to fight the divorce in the courts. I can't imagine he'd ever promise to walk down the aisle with some other… 'bride'… bigamously.'

'It may not have been his idea.'

'You literally baffle me.'

'That's all I can say right now.'

Mabel rose, fiddled for a moment with her amber necklace, then stalked out of the room where her long black dress hissed and swished on the carpet. The excuse was to shoo Micky back to the garden, but really she was too upset to continue chatting.

'Please forgive Mother,' said Dorothy, constantly adjusting her spectacles on her the bridge of her nose. 'The funeral is still too fresh in our minds.'

'I suggest you think back. Jolantha tricked her way into your house and crept upstairs to look around, even as your fellow mourners were eating and drinking elsewhere in the house?'

'That's not how it was.'

'You're not making any sense.'

'It was my idea to look in the box, detective. At no time did *she* suggest we go anywhere, at no time was she that cynical.'

'We can argue about that some other time.'

'Whoever Jolantha is, she knows very little about us for someone who is supposed to be Sidney's sweetheart. I see that now. Is that even her real name? She might be a complete imposter?'

It was his turn to wriggle. 'Can you be more specific?'

'She was very surprised to know that Sidney had a half-brother called Philip who was killed in The Great War and about our failed attempt to emigrate to New Zealand in 1912. She was equally interested in our Uncle Will…'

'And Uncle Will is?'

'Mother's brother. He made a small fortune selling dried fruit. Had he not rented a bungalow for us in Ealing in those early days, we would have had no roof over our heads when we returned destitute to England. I was even meant to inherit sufficient money from him to start my own opticians, except in the end he chose to leave everything to the local church. Still, I mustn't complain. It was he who went on to buy this house for Mabel, to give her somewhere of her own to grow old.'

DS Biggs made frantic notes. 'Are you absolutely sure Jolantha didn't coerce you in any way?'

Dorothy blushed and the enamel brooch on her dress suddenly required her close attention. 'I didn't know what to say or how to help her. Jolantha Wheeler is not a lunatic, detective, she's lost in pain.'

'Did she tell you how she came to know Sidney so well?'

'No, she didn't. She was remarkably vague. What I will say is that she appeared very cut up about him, although I never saw her shed a single tear.'

'Yet you had no reason to disbelieve her?'

'We were all mourning my brother, detective – I was in a bit of a daze myself.'

'Tell me more about these mementoes.'

'I left her with a box of postcards, letters and photographs all relating to Sidney while I went to the lavatory. When I returned she and the box had vanished.'

'Was there definitely nothing of worth in there? No heirlooms?'

'As I said, it was purely sentimental value. For instance, there was a bronze medal commemorating Philip's death in 1918. I feel very disappointed in her. We took her into our confidence. Instead of which she robbed us of our memories.'

'I assume your brother Frederick was at yesterday's funeral?'

'Yes he was.'

'Did you see Jolantha approach him, too?'

'I didn't think to ask. Fred was too busy getting tipsy on glasses of sherry and gave me a wide berth. He knows I don't approve of his drinking. Then he left early. Come to think of it, though, she did ask me where he lived.'

'And you told her?'

'I rather think I did, I'm not sure. I had no reason not to. It's no secret. He lives with his new wife Wynne and her father Arthur Jones at Thorney Weir, near Iver. Fred's two children from his previous marriage live with him, ever since his wife Grace left him for another man.'

'Where will I find him, exactly?'

'Ask for "Orchard Cottage" by the river.'

DS Biggs took one last look round the room but saw nothing to help his

172

investigations. 'Thank you, Dorothy. You've been most helpful.'

On his way out he noted the scroll at the foot of the stairs that honoured the family's dead war hero. If Jolantha had meant to descend on them and strip them bare in some bizarre act of revenge, she would have helped herself to Philip's plaque, too, from the wall? No, taking the bronze medal had probably been a mistake, he concluded – she couldn't have known what was at the bottom of the box of bric-a-brac. She was in a state of shock at the death of her bogus fiancé, but if that was the end of the story she wouldn't still be so driven by it.

If he'd learnt one thing today, it was that she was prepared to go to extreme lengths to get noticed.

But would she kill for it?

He honestly had no idea.

All he knew was that he had to get to Thorney Weir as quickly as possible. Someone had to warn Frederick.

THIRTY-TWO

John, all muffled up in his big tweed coat, is only too happy to stretch his legs after riding ninety-five miles through the Midlands in my Brough Superior's sidecar.

But he's not happy with me.

'Coming here has to be the craziest thing ever, Jo.'

I toss him my goggles, leather cap and gauntlets. 'Wish me luck.'

'For Christ's sake, what darned good will it do to turn this into a whodunit? What is there left to prove? You were there when Sidney died – as matters stand, it's an open and shut case.'

I'm not angry with him – he's simply worried I'm crazy enough to incriminate myself. 'You really going to ask me that now?'

Ash Hall Nursing Home in Stoke-on-Trent certainly lives up to its name, dear Sidney – its castellated stone walls are the colour of grey ash. You must have thought it a very odd place when Mrs Tuffley drove you here late last year, to be incarcerated for the next six months. You must have supposed its Gothic turrets hideous and haunted? Did you feel like some latter day Count of Monte Cristo? Did you wonder if you'd ever escape from one of its dungeons?

'What's this notebook, Jo?'

'Give that to me.'

'It appears to be a list of names and addresses…'

'I said give it here.'

'Mrs Tuffley, Dora, Marjorie, Mabel, Dorothy, Frederick…'

I shouldn't have left my list of suspects tucked into the seat of the sidecar. It's so silly. I'm not thinking straight. But everyone makes mistakes, even when they have this much conviction inside them. At the same time, I'm haunted by the notion that I'm somehow wrong about everything, including myself. Poor John will never understand, he's only secretly jealous of you, dear Sidney. He's a good person really, though not a patch on you. He's my rock, my anchor. You'll have to forgive him, because you heard what he just said: he only wants to save me from myself.

'It's a list of people who might know important things I don't about Sidney.'

'What things, Jo?'

'I can't have Marjorie waking up and blackening a dead man's name when she alone has to be the guilty party! I can't have her proving things I can't, which requires drastic action.'

'….?'

'It's something Gerry Wilson said.'

'The famous jockey?'

'He said he thought Sidney suffered from a secret fear. He implied it made him very vulnerable. But I can think of only one reason why that might be true, or rather one *person*. I say this because Sidney was no shrinking violet. Not in most respects – he could be fearless. I'm desperate to discover what his nerve specialist thinks, because I refuse to accept he would ever have abandoned me if he'd still been in his right mind.'

'It's a long way to come to prove a madman sane.'

I ignore the sarcasm. I don't see my passionate interest in you as a mistake, dear Sidney, I see it as justice. Only your doctor will be able to tell me what happened *in your head* to make you so susceptible to your pointless wife's dreadful scheming? What hold did she have over you, that she could wheedle her way into your very soul to make you lose all reason? I must know, because there's no way that minx can evade what's coming to her now. *I'm here to find out what she did to you for years and years, I'm here to rule out any last minute eventualities.*

John orders Bella to stay put. He does it with a commanding voice yet sounds very calm. He's not being confrontational, only firm. Bella stops whining and wags her black, wiry tail. It's amazing. She'll not do a thing I tell her, lately.

175

'Don't you think, Jo, that your crazy desire to apportion blame borders on the vindictive? Whatever grief-driven guilt is tormenting you, don't let it turn you into a ghoul.'

'You saying this so I'll stop?'

'It's not too late to see reason and go home.'

'You don't think I don't want to? I detest mental hospitals.'

'This obsession with the dead is a mistake.'

'We're here now.'

John is still twitching. 'You can't change anything this side of the grave, Jo. You can't unpick a single moment of the past.'

But I'm through the Tudor-arch with its double doors and march straight up to a desk in reception. Round me is a large foyer, off which leads a broad staircase. I don't have to wait long – your doctor comes straight out of her office. I'm surprised to see that she is not what I expected. I don't know why this should affect me, since I'm here on purely medical grounds. All the same I can't help but feel a little envious. Nor is it much consolation that she is small, thin, short-haired and somewhat mannish. It's the thought of you pouring your heart out to another woman that I find so alarming.

'Mrs Wheeler? I'm delighted to meet you. I'm Dr Andratschke. I hope your journey wasn't too unpleasant. The trains these days are diabolical…'

'I have my own transport.'

Your doctor's sea-blue eyes have a delightful twinkle, I must say. 'I can spare you half an hour. Shall we go out on to the terrace? I was so sad to hear your bad news. Sidney was one of my more memorable patients.'

'I hope you won't consider my visit too unethical, Dr Andratschke…'

'Please call me Berta.'

'I'm here because the coroner returned an open verdict.'

'As I said on the phone, I can't let you see his files.'

'Just to confirm, I'm not here to make trouble. Poor Sidney is dead and nothing can change that, only he and I were very, very close.'

'It's funny he never mentioned you.'

'I'm just trying to grasp why things happened the way they did.'

Berta may not believe a word I say, but she can't think why else I might be here other than to mourn your untimely demise. She doesn't realise that her name is provisionally on my list, too, she doesn't know I'm here to discover as much about her as you, my love. I want to establish if she failed you along with everyone else, should she need to suffer the consequences.

We emerge on to a very broad terrace overlooking green slopes.

'Beautiful, isn't it,' says Berta. (Did you call her Berta, dear Sidney, or was it always 'Doctor'). 'You can see all the way to Bucknall and Hanley. When I stood here four years ago and watched the bombs falling on the city I thought it was going to be Prague all over again, I thought I'd exchanged one unsafe home for another.'

'It's a very pretty setting.'

'Coal is king here. You see it in the names of the fields before you, names like Coal Pit Field and Slack Pit Field. As a doctor I have to do the same, I have to dig deep beneath the surface. I have to know how to mine the rich resources in my patients' brains.'

'Please, Berta, can you tell me what was wrong with my Sidney? Is there anything I or anyone else could have done to fix it?'

'A mental illness is not like a broken leg. In my article entitled 'Mild Depressive Psychosis' that was published in The British Medical Journal on June 26, 1943, I point out that "there can be no hard-and-fast criteria in psychiatry, no infallible signs to guide one to the proper diagnosis."'

To say I'm disappointed is an understatement. I'm here for a definitive decision on what went wrong, my love. How else can I reduce its toxic power over me to something less scary? 'If diagnosis upon admission to Ash Hall is so difficult, how can you possibly hope to help anyone at all?'

'I was able to study Sidney for a considerable period in detail. I had him under observation for 24 hours of the day and I received daily reports on him from trained nurses. Any doubt over a diagnosis was resolved by the combined opinion of at least three psychiatrists, not simply me. Have no doubt, Sidney was safe in our hands.'

Berta may not appreciate it, but she's your voice now, my love. Whatever you said to her is in her notes and in her head. I have to tease it out of her because I can't talk to you any more in person.

'How bad was he, in your opinion?'

'When Sidney came here in the autumn of 1943 he was shaking from head to toe and could barely stand. He told me that his condition had first manifested itself when he arrived at some factory gates in Leeds, only to find he couldn't bring himself to go in – instead he panicked and collapsed.'

Something about your doctor's voice hits a raw nerve. It's almost too knowledgeable and professional. At the same time, I bet she 'fancied' you on the quiet? I can detect a real empathy for you in her voice which goes beyond regret. I get it. You never talked so much about yourself to anyone else. Of course, I don't suggest for one moment anything inappropriate ever happened, only no one can know you so well without falling a little in love with you, can they, dear Sidney? Or you with them? I have to accept that you opened up to her more than me? I try to steady my hand as I puff heavily on my cigarette. I should be more careful. I mustn't let the wrong emotions show, I mustn't be that petty and careless.

'The thing is this, Doctor: Sidney was clearly very stressed when he met his wife Marjorie for the last time in Gloucester Cathedral. I know, because I was there. Could her presence have sparked some fatal, mental reaction? Is there anything you can tell me that would stand up in a court of law? There is, isn't there.'

'Let's be clear. Sidney was jumpy, but he would never have *jumped* of his own free will, not in my opinion.'

'What if someone else was only trying to save him from himself?'

'He might fight back in his state of panic.'

'Is that really very likely?'

'No one could get through to him when he lost his mind. That's not to say a violent 'attack' was anything but temporary. In fact, I said to him "You're the sanest person in here". He helped organise games and generally helped run the place. All the other patients liked him.'

'Yet he obviously wasn't well or he wouldn't have stayed six months.'

'No one can work as hard as he did and not expect to suffer. If the body becomes totally worn out, so does the brain. All it requires is something to trigger a total meltdown of body and soul. Think of it as chinks in your armour.'

'His lack of home life with a proper wife wouldn't have helped, would it?'

'No, it wouldn't.'

'He was far too alone?'

'Yes, he was.'

'It's as I thought. Marjorie's unexpected arrival in the cathedral that day was clearly intended to catch him off guard. It upset his balance of mind. She, more than anyone, had seen how ill he'd been. Whatever she said or did, he was primed to 'fall' at any moment? It's something she would have known – in her heart of hearts?'

'Quite possibly.'

Berta is far too curious about me again. She studies the way I hunch my shoulders, fold my arms and dig my toe in the terrace. I'm thinking of the injustice you've suffered at somebody else's hands, my love. As a result, I'm all goose pimples inside my sealskins.

'Sidney was such a good, nice person. Why should he have to die at the hands of his own wife?'

'I can't say definitively what happened that day, but to understand somebody you have to go back to the beginning. That's what we do at Ash Hall. We use behavioural rather than medicinal techniques of group and individual psychotherapy. That's why the "Cassel Hospital for Functional Nervous Disorders" was established in 1919. Its original purpose was to treat 'shell shock' victims from The Great War.'

'I'd rather you tell me things Sidney said about Marjorie.'

'I'll come back to her in a moment.'

'Who else is there?' She can see my impatience. I'm here to convict, not condone, I'm here to build my case against the only real suspect there is. And then crush her.

But Berta is adamant. The word 'beginning' signals a whole different narrative for her. Whose side is she on?

Well, I don't know what to say, so I let her continue.

'The first thing I did when I became Sidney's doctor was to consider his childhood. He told me he was born in Ealing in West London in 1907, by which time its retired Indian civil servants who'd served the British Empire were nearly all gone. The "Queen of the Suburbs" was now the home of the lower middle class and the working classes. The District Line recently connected it to central London, as did trams along Uxbridge Road. It meant men could suddenly travel further to work...'

'*Really?* Your point is, Doctor?'

'Sidney was born in 1907, at a time when the capital was expanding rapidly. Victorian and Edwardian 'refinement' was swept away. South Ealing especially might not be so countrified and posh any more but it let in the poor. The Sheppards were one such family. Sidney's grandfather was a retired coachman, his father was a waiter, his half-brother Philip was a wireman's mate with the District Railway, while his mother Mabel is a skilled court dressmaker who has stitched parachutes for De Havilland. She also sold sweets in a sweet shop that she and her husband ran for a short time...'

'So did I until the German bombers decided to pay me a call.'

Berta smiles at my outburst. It's the smile of an indulgent mother, friend and inquisitor. She sees right through me.

'Despite such rapid growth and change Ealing was deeply conservative, a significant element to our story, I think.'

'Not sure I believe that.'

'You should. Sidney was raised in a very small bungalow next to a secondary school for girls in The Park. Nearby was Ealing parish church of St Mary's, the beating heart of the community. The incumbent of the living was Rev Charles James Sharp who arrived in 1916, when Sidney was nine years old. Rev Sharp was a man of very progressive ideas. His daughter Evelyn went to Somerville College, Oxford in 1922 where she graduated in Modern History. In 1926 she joined the Civil Service and is currently seconded to HM Treasury for the duration of the war. More significantly Sidney attended Ealing County School with her brother Bernard...'

'*This* is your story?'

'We're talking about an important family, Mrs Wheeler. Evelyn's uncles include an Archdeacon, a Judge of the Supreme Court in New South Wales and the chief cashier of the Bank of England. These are thinking people who help run society. It's my firm belief that this family inspired Sidney to want to do great things and become someone important like them... You could say he set himself challenging goals.'

This throws me until I'm not quite sure how to reply. For all her blather, I'm still your long lost friend and not your fiancé to Berta, dear Sidney – I don't think she realises what's at stake, for me. 'When he and I first met he seemed shattered. He didn't appear to have an ambition left in his head. He was running on empty.'

You doctor leans closer as a gleam of sunshine lights the valley before us rather beautifully. 'What do you think most stuck in Sidney's mind whenever he visited the vicarage next door?'

'How would I know?'

'It wasn't the size of the house or the extensive grounds, it was all the books in the library. They prompted him to re-invent himself in a few short years. Most of all he dropped his Cockney twang and learned to speak with a posh accent like BBC newsreaders on the radio. He also learnt to dress smartly and carry himself well. In a nutshell Sidney convinced himself that he could be whoever he liked, if only he could find a job that paid well enough to support his change of class. He would no longer be looked down upon by his new friends who were all materially so much better off than he was. If he couldn't match them with money, he could do so with the power of his mind.'

'Not to disappoint you, Doctor, but he succeeded. There was no stopping my Sidney. It was only when that... *that* woman set her eyes on him that his world fell apart.'

I stop myself just in time and relight my cigarette with my Zippo lighter. The look in Berta's face fixes mine. Latches on. 'Yes, he succeeded in joining a smart, suburban set, but at what price, Mrs Wheeler? For all the while he was trying to get away from his family, he felt doubly responsible for ensuring their welfare, especially his mother's, as she began to grow older. In short, he became obsessed by the notion that his new friends didn't have to shoulder the burdens he did – his biggest gripe was that they all seemed so carefree and happy because they had capital behind them to fall back on if they ever hit hard times.'

I'm less than happy at her summary of your early life, dear Sidney, I find it too clinical and one-sided. Of course you had a poor start in life and that may have left you worried and vulnerable, but that doesn't mean all those who are otherwise to blame can get off scot-free. You can be certain I'll make sure of that.

There's so much more your shrink doesn't know or hasn't told me. I'm secretly furious. Berta began by saying that she's bound by patient confidentiality, except she mustn't be allowed to hide behind her fine spiel, my love, because I didn't come here to be made a fool of.

Why listen to your undesirable spouse's false words in the cathedral, my darling? What part of your brain fell under her spell, that you could want her over me?

Because, despite everything, you were out of hospital and certified sane at the time.

Does Marjorie not realise she can hang for what she's done?

She's the unwanted bride, not me.

She knew just how to mess with your vulnerable mind.

I want her gone.

To think you were the most articulate person I ever met, my love. You could argue black was white. I never met anyone who had such a way with words.

If I'd given you half a chance, would you have gone down on one knee and begged me to save you?

'So, Doctor, tell me more about his no-good wife.'

THIRTY-THREE

'What if I'm too late?' thought DS Biggs grimly and clung harder to his steering-wheel. 'What if she's struck already?'

He'd just spent the night in a hotel in Iver where someone's idea of breakfast was a piece of burnt toast, a teaspoon of jam and no butter. Now he was obliged to navigate his way past a canal, a reservoir and a boatyard – he was in the borderlands where West London became wild country. Worse still, the Austin 10's headlights were next to useless in the ground fog as he bumped along a narrow dyke. If he tipped the police car into the reeds he could kiss goodbye to any promotion.

Dorothy Sheppard never warned him there would be so many unmapped lakes.

He didn't even know where to look next.

Did she think to tell him?

Did he think to ask?

Suddenly a lone figure loomed next to the water. The foggy apparition, formless and featureless, yet somehow suggestive of some predatory phantom, turned out to be a harmless angler.

He wound down his window and the cold winter air wet his face. 'Excuse me sir, is this the way to Thorney Weir? I'm looking for "Orchard Cottage".'

The hunched figure, dressed in a trench coat and cloth cap, clung to his rod and line. 'Not so loud, damn you! The bream has just begun to bite.'

'I appreciate that, sir, only I fear I'm lost.'

'Sounds about right.'

'Can you help me or not?'

The angler half-turned his head and wiped snot off his nose. 'You'll have to walk the rest of the way on account of the fact that there's no road over the River Colne.'

'You come here a lot, do you?'

'Ever since I got discharged from the army with a bullet in my back.'

'So you might have seen someone unfamiliar around here in the last day or so?'

'Like who?'

'Like a dark-haired woman, for instance. Thirty years old. Riding a motorcycle and sidecar. Answers to the name of Jo Wheeler. Probably had a black and white bull terrier with her.'

'No one like that ever comes this way.'

'Don't be so sure.'

The thing that most struck him as he trudged along was the mixture of stillness and silence. Only the roar of a nearby weir soon reached his ears. It was idyllic in many ways, except all he could think about was how this was the perfect time and place to murder someone – he expected Jolantha to lunge at him from out of the brume at any second.

Moments later he saw a rickety wooden bridge span the river.

'Can't see DI Lockett doing this,' he muttered, as he set foot on cracked planks above raging rapids.

The mist parted to reveal a solitary, two-story house at the edge of the riverbank. To call it a cottage was a slight misnomer, to say the least.

'Stick to the plan,' he thought and lifted his hand to a green door's heavy, cast iron knocker when it suddenly flew open.

'Not so fast! Can't you see it says *No Cold Callers*.'

Whoever had just spied him cross the bridge barred his way. The owner had very white hair and long, equally white sideburns that met beneath his chin. A raised white collar and fancy bowtie suggested that he was dressed in his Sunday best, even if his trousers had frayed turn-ups and needed a good ironing. He looked positively Edwardian, but no amount of eccentricity explained the double-barrelled shotgun in his face.

He waved his warrant card at him. 'My name is Detective Sergeant Biggs. May I come in, please?'

'Last time I had uninvited visitors they were two army deserters who stole all my chickens.'

'Know what I think? I think you need to put that gun away.'

'You think?'

'Better for me. Better for you.'

'Huh.'

'An Englishman's home is his castle, is that it?'

'This house used to be a pub, detective, on account of all the labourers who worked in the brickworks and gravel pits nearby.'

'That explains its size and remoteness.'

'It pulled its last pint in the 1930s when the final quarry closed down. Ever since then I've lived here with my wife, until she died last year.'

'That's bad luck.'

'Isn't it always?'

'Will you be Wynne Sheppard's father, by any chance?'

'I'm Arthur Jones, yes.'

'Forgive the intrusion, sir, but I have concerns for the safety of you and your family.'

'Why do you think I have this?'

DS Biggs pushed aside the shotgun and made his way into the parlour. The whole building smelt horribly damp as if the swollen river had plans to reclaim it.

'I need to speak to Frederick Sheppard, if I may? Consider it urgent.'

'My son-in-law goes sailing on Sundays to avoid going to church.'

'When will he be back?'

'I guess that's up to him. He likes to fish on the lake. What's the panic?'

'Why don't you put the kettle on, Mr Jones and then you and I can have a little chat while we wait.'

A Bakelite wireless cabinet rested on a table. He picked up a wax-paper coupling capacitor and cast his eye over resistors and vacuum tubes. A box full of tools lay nearby. Whoever dabbled in such things shared his growing interest in two-way radios. Bristol police cars already had them. Alas, the Gloucestershire force was not yet fully equipped and he still had to stop his Austin 10 at the side of the road and make calls from a special police box. That's what was bothering him right now. If anything happened, he was out of contact because Mr Jones clearly had no telephone.

His reluctant host returned with two cups of very strong tea. 'Forgive the mess, detective. Fred loves to fiddle with radios of all descriptions. You could say it goes with his job.'

'His job?'

'That's right. He tests radio equipment in dive-bombers and fighters built by Fairey Aviation at Hayes. It takes a brave man to do that, believe me. He was flying in planes from Great West Aerodrome until the whole site was recently requisitioned by the Air Ministry to build an airport for all London. Rumour says it will be called Heathrow. What a daft name! It'll never catch on! As it is, test flights have been moved to Heston Aerodrome.'

'Your son-in-law sounds a practical sort of fellow.'

'What's all this about, detective? Hasn't Fred suffered enough? His brother has only just been committed to the earth. Doesn't make any sense, if you ask me?'

'That's partly why I'm here. To make better sense of something. How well did Frederick get on with his brother Sidney, do you think? Did one help the other, or did they go their separate ways? We all know what brothers can be like, don't we?'

Mr Jones rolled his eyes as he passed him an ashtray. 'Chalk and cheese, detective. That's Frederick and Sidney. Whereas Sidney carried all the weight of the world on his shoulders, Fred doesn't give a damn about anything except new inventions. He could do so much better if only he would knuckle down and pass a few written exams, except he won't bother. No wonder his boss tells him, "Why can't you be like your brother?"'

'Fred resented being in Sidney's shadow, did he?'

'That's the honest truth. I would, on balance, have preferred Sidney as a son-in-law. For a start, he saved Fred's bacon during the Blitz by paying for his two children from his previous marriage to have private education. Sidney was the one who dressed so smartly and was so full of get-up-and-go, whereas Fred can be decidedly lazy. Why else do you think he and Wynne have ended up living here? Now my daughter is expected to raise another woman's offspring. That's where she is now – she has taken Pat and Phil to feed the ducks on the river. Marry a Sheppard and you marry trouble, if you ask me.'

DS Biggs glanced at his watch. 'Did the brothers ever quarrel about anything? How about *someone*?'

'As I say, chalk and cheese. Let me tell you something, detective, then you decide.'

'Meaning what, exactly?'

'There have been a few flashpoints. Their mother Mabel is seriously ill and could die at any time, ever since she dropped an iron on her foot last year and contracted cancer. My daughter has been very worried that Fred will lose out, come the sale of the family house at 149 Waverley Avenue in Twickenham. She was convinced that Sidney would go off with her husband's share of the inheritance, since he has always been the apple of Mabel's eye and she might leave him absolutely everything.'

'Mabel would do that?'

'To solve Sidney's financial problems, on account of his compulsive betting on the horses.'

'How serious are these debts?'

Mr Jones gave a wry smile. 'It was not Sidney's debts that caused a falling out between him and Fred, it was his imminent divorce.'

'Go on.'

'Sidney was obsessed with his wife's unfaithfulness. I mean, furiously so.'

'And?'

'He raged at Fred about letters Marjorie wrote him. Sidney said he was going to use the correspondence to establish – in a court of law, if necessary – that she had no *legal* grounds to divorce him. Fred desperately tried to talk him out of it. They quarrelled bitterly over it. After the failure of his own marriage, he didn't think fighting Marjorie was a good idea at all, especially as Sidney couldn't afford it.'

DS Biggs penned frantic notes. 'Did Fred tell you what was in the letters?'

'I know Sidney got very worked up about them. He kept harking on about how Marjorie had written, "I keep telling you, my darling, there is nothing to worry about. There is nobody else, although I admit I do like my present life." Another letter went something like this, "I certainly had no wish to convey a 'take it or leave it' attitude regarding our future and have always wholeheartedly agreed with all your plans." He told Fred he'd kept everything Marjorie had ever written to him year by year in cardboard files, ever since they'd met years ago.'

'Sounds like a precaution.'

'Precaution?'

'To hold her responsible for whatever went wrong.'

'Or justify whatever *he* did, detective. You'd hardly call it the behaviour of a rational man.'

DS Biggs fingered his watch again. If Frederick didn't come home soon he wouldn't be able to warn him face to face…

'So Frederick thought Sidney had brought it all upon himself? Why's that? Did he think he'd been unfaithful to Marjorie and didn't deserve his help? Is that it?'

'Well, Sidney certainly once had a very glamorous job working for Jantzen Knitting Mills Ltd., selling women's swimwear. He knew all the models and travelled a lot. He was the star of the Sheppard family, detective. He earned big money and looked like a film star in his smart pinstripe suits. Women were besotted with him. But was he ever sexually unfaithful to his wife? No, I very much doubt it. Unlike Fred, Sidney was never very practical – he lived in his head. He used to say he valued his brain over his heart…'

'Until his heart broke him?'

'As you say, this war hasn't helped, has it.'

DS Biggs scribbled a note on his pad: *A philanderer. Yes, or no?* 'So Sidney went out of his way to support his brother and his children financially, but when the boot was on the other foot and Sidney was ill, broke and jobless, Fred did nothing except criticise? He didn't stand loyally by him in his time of trouble?'

'You could say that. It wasn't just the lack of loyalty. Fred was, how shall I say, *largely indifferent* to his brother's predicament.'

'Did Sidney ever confide in him about someone called Jolantha Wheeler?'

'No, he didn't, but I think I know who you mean.'

DS Biggs suddenly forgot to write any more. His eyes grew wider; his tongue became tied; his breathing turned to a short, sharp whistle. He wondered what interested Mr Jones so and whether it was good or bad. It was the other reason he was here. 'Would that be last May at your daughter's wedding?'

'How can I ever forget?'

'Just to be clear, the woman I'm talking about has a burnt ear.'

'I don't remember seeing her at Ealing Register office where Fred and Wynne tied the knot, but she was definitely present at the reception afterwards. We all went to "The Swan" in Iver. It's a lovely old black and white coaching inn. You should try it while you're here. That's when I first noticed her, standing at the bar next to Sidney. No one could tell me who she was at first, or who'd invited her.'

'You mean she appeared out of nowhere?'

'I'm sorry to say my daughter invited so many friends from her place of work that I didn't recognise half of them.'

'Tell me what you do know about her.'

'It was all a bit troubling. Sidney had only just left mental hospital after recovering from his nervous breakdown. You could see he was like someone walking on eggshells. He was back at work but had only just begun driving to factories all over the country again to visit customers. On the positive side, he'd been fitted with new teeth…'

'Excuse me?'

'Doctors thought they could cure his stomach cramps by removing all his teeth in one go. The wedding was his first real chance to socialise again, except he still looked very weak and ill. Marjorie came with him to the reception, only she wasn't exactly much help.'

He scratched his head. 'Your point is?'

'My point is, detective, that Jolantha, not Marjorie, was the first to spring to Sidney's aid when he suddenly felt faint at the bar.'

'*Faint*, you say?'

'Jolantha helped him outside to get some fresh air.'

'Did they talk, at all? How did she sound?'

'When Jolantha came back into the pub half an hour later, Marjorie picked a fight with her. She hit her with a right hook to the nose.'

'Where had she been?'

'Sitting in the car with Sidney.'

'Did she fight back?'

'Not really. She collected her coat and left shortly afterwards, despite her bloody face.'

'Did she go off with Sidney?'

'I believe so.'

'Did you see it happen?'

'One minute she was here and then she was gone. So was Sidney. At the very least he must have driven her to the railway station at Iver because he returned later, alone.'

'That's something to go on. How did his wife react to that?'

Mr Jones lit himself a fresh cigarette. 'Marjorie drowned her sorrows with a few gins at the bar. She likes her drink, I reckon. It turned out she had already told Sidney she had someone else in her life whom she'd been keeping secret for years. Her fit of jealousy was a bit hypocritical, to say the least.'

'Or we shouldn't believe in coincidences?'

'Are you saying that Jolantha had designs on Sidney, detective? You saying her presence that day was no accident? Is she the one we have to look out for now? Is that why you're here?'

'I don't doubt it's connected to the ingratitude Fred showed his brother.'

'What you mean is, she's looking to blame innocent people?'

'I mean she can't forgive or believe Sidney died without just cause.'

'She can't blame Fred for his death, surely?'

'If our theory is correct, Jolantha may well resent anyone who contributed to her fiancé's show of bad faith. She'll hold them to account for his unexplained behaviour in Gloucester Cathedral, if she can.'

'You can't expect me to answer for that.'

'Not you, Frederick.'

'I think I hear him coming now. Please excuse me, I have to tidy up before Wynne gets back with the children.'

DS Biggs stood up to look out the window. Mr Jones was correct: someone was risking life and limb on the creaky old bridge over the river.

His heart missed a beat. He felt a sudden need to recap on what he still couldn't say for sure. Sidney had seen his marriage, health and financial security fail. He'd lost control. This was someone who had, on the surface, appeared to be the epitome of success while underneath there had been utter turmoil. He was filled with righteous indignation at his wife's betrayal and had come to hate her for it? This was not a naturally violent man, but his bottled up feelings were all set to explode.

Or someone helped do it for him?

Lit the fuse?

That someone was still on the loose.

If he were Frederick, he'd keep his father-in-law's shotgun handy.

***

Next moment the whole house shook to much shouting and banging. As for Mr Jones, he appeared confused – he obviously wasn't expecting any more callers. It couldn't be Frederick. DS Biggs didn't like the sound of it. Why would someone hammer on their own front door?

'Are you going to answer that, or shall I?'

He saw Mr Jones pluck a heavy walking stick from the hallway's umbrella stand on his way past – he didn't lean on it so much as wield it like a sword. His reply came back half grunt and half growl. 'What now, I wonder?'

Whoever appeared at the door made no attempt to barge in. He never even noticed what happened next.

All he saw was a shadowy figure.

All he heard was the word '*Die..!*'

Next second Arthur Jones fell flat on the floor…

He dropped like a stone.

…as if somebody had just run him clean through his heart?

THIRTY-FOUR

I'm safely back home in Gloucester and keeping a low profile. Bella stands guard over Jacqueline who coos in her cot in the parlour. Every now and then I lean over and let her grasp my little finger. But don't worry, dear Sidney, the police can't scare me. I'm not about to rest until all those who failed you get what they deserve. Dr Andratschke was kind enough to tell me more about your marriage – you'll be relieved to know I've deleted her name from my list of 'suspects'. As far as I can tell, she did nothing but try to help you, unlike the others yet to be eliminated.

John says I need to forget all this stuff, but he knows nothing of how I really feel. You would never have left me to grieve alone without a reason. I've become very proprietorial – your disloyal wife's letters deserve to be mine since I should have been your only correspondent. I discard one page to seize another. I'm delving deeper into your life right before me. Is that so wrong? If so, I'm sorry. I have to be ready to confront your killer – I need to be able to wave proof of her treachery in her face, so help me God, should she ever be so rash as to open her eyes again...

She, more than anyone, cannot be allowed to escape justice. Someone has got to do it – she's not welcome in my world any more. My fingers are shaking, either from fear or rage. DI Lockett can suspect me all he likes, but I think it's in all our best interests if this case doesn't go his way. Marjorie hated you. You died. It seems crystal clear to me.

It's time to see past the flattery, lies and downright excuses. I intend to show the police, once and for all, that she wanted you dead ever since you and she lived apart too long. The seeds of her evil plan are plain to see in these neat, little blue pages she sent you. It's time to let her damn herself with the flowery loops on all her 'ps' and 'qs'…

I'm ready to study them in detail right now, though I'm not entirely sure I want to. But here goes.

This first missive is dated the 8th of July 1943 when the two of you have already been separated four years: 'My darling Rufus, I was pleased to get your letter, but very sorry to hear you had another "attack". If your own 'quack' is not going to attend I think it would be much better if you tried to get into Kingston hospital, so I could come and see you and it would be easier for you to get here to Claygate to convalesce. Anyway, I'm waiting anxiously to hear the nerve specialist's report, so please let me know directly.'

At first sight, it all sounds pleasant enough as she goes on: 'I enjoyed our week together very much also, but I do wish it had made you feel better in health. I'm afraid, however, a week's holiday was not long enough for you, and anyway your poor tummy needs medical attention.' Except, here's the rub: 'I didn't mind the office once I had settled down to attack the work, as I felt very fit, though lo and behold as the day wore on I developed a pain and by Tuesday morning something happened (not due till Sat.) However, I managed to keep going – no fainting fits this time and am now feeling well again…'

I don't deny your second-rate wife suffers heavy periods each month, which clearly puts her off having sex with you on her sporadic and cleverly timed (?) visits to you, but at what point does neglect amount to malice? Surely even DI Lockett must see how the minx is feigning concern for you while ensuring that nothing occurs to disrupt the alternative life she is leading in Claygate? Your superfluous spouse is really saying she will only visit you in hospital, my love, if it is near enough to where she lives. I, on the contrary, would have thrown up my job at the NAAFI and rushed to help you.

Instead, she's all sugar-coated words: 'My darling Rufus, I think "Anchorage Gardens" is hardly the place to relax and enjoy a month's rest. It seems so cramped and it's miserable not having a garden in which to sit about. Now my suggestions are: I have a week off (I might be able to get more on compassionate grounds – although I shouldn't have a very strong case as you're not bedridden and, of course, for a complete rest you should have somebody to look after you and give you regular meals) and I think it would do you a tremendous amount of good, and myself, if we could afford to take up Kath's suggestion and spend a holiday together at Lyme Regis in the summer. She did say the last week in August would suit them and it would be okay for me. Alternatively, I could come to Cheltenham. Still, it is up to you to decide what to do to get the best results…'

Anyone else might consider my dislike for Marjorie the product of an ill-judged jealousy, but she doesn't fool me when she ends so bright and breezily: 'Aren't you relieved to know you haven't to undergo an operation? Please excuse this short letter, but I'm writing it after lunch at work. I went to the office dance last night (quite enjoyed it – had a dance and a drink with our famous chairman) and tonight we're off to the flicks to see "Above Suspicion". Hope to see you soon, and do hope you haven't had any more "attacks", poor darling. All my love, Marjorie. PS. For your information, your neglectful wife will be 33 on Saturday.'

Surely the police are not so stupid as to fail to recognise that you stood in her way, dear Sidney? Can't have been very pleasant for you. It does not take a genius to see through all your wife's platitudes when she writes to you on the 27th of July 1943: 'My darling Rufus, I'm afraid you'll be taking a poor view of my not writing sooner, but I've been terribly busy at the office and busy at home making a frock for Mother for the Garden Fete at "Milburn House" this evening. Well, darling, another wedding anniversary tomorrow – four years and I'm afraid not much to show for the time thanks to this bloody war. Still things are looking a lot brighter with Mussolini resigning. I hope it means Italy will soon pack up the fighting. Peggy is a lot more cheerful now, though there's no more news yet of husband David from the P.O.W. Camp. He's been away two and a half years…'

To cap it all, she signs off sounding so blithe: 'Hope you enjoyed the Horse Show last Saturday. I'm always pleased to hear you're getting a little from your life. Shall be able to talk to you properly at the weekend. All my love, Marjorie.'

As I say, if I'd been her I wouldn't have suggested some joint holiday with Kath and Bernard, I would have taken you myself in my motorcycle sidecar, only Marjorie doesn't want your company, does she? That's what I aim to get across to DI Lockett – I'll make him see what a charade the whole Lyme Regis thing is. It's the crocodile tears I can't bear. Her note of the 4th of September 1943 makes for a rather bad read:

'My darling Rufus, thank you so much for your letter and I'm glad to hear you got to Oxford to see the doctor by firm's car. Oh darling, I feel so miserable to think of you going into a nursing home and feel so helpless and inadequate. I do wish you were going into one nearer here so I could go and see you often. Isn't everything a mess-up? Can't I do anything for you? I'm full of contrition for being so neglectful and not giving you a better deal in the past, but I'll try to make your life happier in the future...'

She'll throw you a crumb of comfort here and there, but then comes the sting in the tail: 'I did enjoy our brief weekend together, though it was so miserable for you being so ill most of the time, you poor dear. I've got an economy fit on in view of your coming medical expenses and I'm trying to cut down on cigarettes and not fritter money away on odds and ends. I spent 1/6 only in Kingston yesterday. Let me know if you want me to go with you to Stoke-on-Trent (you can't go alone) and I'll drop everything and come. All my love, Marjorie.

'PS. I'm sorry I didn't make it clear about the curse. Hope you haven't been worrying. It happened the day after I returned from Cheltenham but what I meant to convey was that I felt rotten most of the time...'

Is this enough to present to the police? Because your fretful, boastful wife is definitely not a good person. I have in my hand her letter from the 20th of September 1943. I'll read it out loud to Jacqueline and Bella, if no one else: 'My darling Rufus, what a nuisance it is they can't take you at Stoke-on-Trent for at least six weeks, but as you say, if you can get in at Oxford it will be easier for me to come and see you...'

Her letter is all about how important her job is to the war effort, or she's just filling pages to avoid the real matters she should be discussing with you, my love? Of course, I can see that it's very exciting to be able to name-drop such interesting people: 'I started this letter yesterday and now have an opportunity to continue. My two men are very much occupied at the moment with some distinguished visitors – Air Chief Marshal Sir R.

Brooke-Popham (Commander-in-Chief R.A.F. Middle East); A.C.M. Sir Christopher Courtney (Air Member for Supply and Organisation); the permanent Under Secretary (Asst.); and a mere Air Commodore-Director of Air Force Welfare. The Chairman invited them down to lunch and at the moment they have gone to see the NAAFI film. There are also a couple of Canadians about – one is Senior Vice President of Canadian Pacific Railway and the other is the chief purchasing agent for C.P.R. They've been here about a fortnight and have been entertained by NAAFI and they've seen and done everything worth seeing and doing. They've achieved a tremendous lot for NAAFI in Canada and purchased goods there for troops all over the world…'

That's not to say I consider her any less of a liar because her job is so demanding: 'My darling Rufus, I'm afraid you're going to be very disappointed but I don't see how I can get away by tomorrow lunchtime (Friday). The reason – my part-time assistant was away yesterday and again today with a bad cold… The work has simply piled up the last few days and as the Wingco went to the Air Ministry yesterday very little letter writing was done. I hope you will understand and forgive…'

Nor do I believe her to be any less duplicitous just because she, too, is in very real danger: 'My darling Rufus, I arrived home safely at 4.45 after a difficult journey. We had a short, sharp air raid last night but only sat on the stairs for about 10 minutes. There was a similar raid the night before…'

Danger is her cunning excuse to stay in London, if you ask me: 'I found a note on my desk this morning to say I'm down for fire guard duty this evening as I have to take the place of the girl who did my turn the week I was with you. I was livid and stalked round to see the A.R.P. Controller, told him all the circumstances and said I was not on annual leave but compassionate leave for you, but he said he didn't exempt me…

'I wish we could afford a baby (and had somewhere to put it) so I could get away from all this Government red tape…'

Your contemptible spouse can be devilishly convincing, but I won't let the police be fooled by her phoney outrage, my darling. I won't let them believe her over me (30th November 1943): 'My darling Rufus, thank you for your letter and I'm so sorry to hear you're still having bad "attacks" in the mornings. I do hope you'll get to Stoke soon and get on with the treatment…'

The same on the 21st of December: 'I'm awfully sorry to hear you had such an exhausting journey, but I expect you'll be very relieved to be installed at last. I'm glad Ash Hall hasn't a hospital atmosphere, and I hope you'll make one or two friends during your short stay. I felt awfully mean letting Mrs Tuffley take you in her car, but it was a relief as I felt really rotten from Wednesday evening till yesterday morning. I had a stomach pain all that time but nothing happened until the early hours of Saturday. However, after an early night tonight I shall feel normal again tomorrow, thank goodness.

'I had a Christmas Greetings airgraph from Rimmie this morning. I wanted to send him one but I couldn't get a form.

'As you know, we've got four days off at Christmas and I expect I shall spend most of the time with my parents at Milbourne Lane. Wing Commander Bryant is going to the Air Ministry on Friday and he wants me to join in a lunch party up there and then meet some of the people we deal with. I shall probably go for a little mild Christmas merriment.

'I want to catch the 2.15 post, so I won't stop for any more now, but I'll write you again tomorrow. All my love, Marjorie.'

That's the difference between Marjorie and me, I can't bear to think of you spending Christmas without any friends or relatives. It must have felt as if she had stabbed you in the back.

To read her letter from the 22nd December 1943 is to detect a carefully calculated semi-detachment, whereas I would have been worried sick about you. How she loves to torment with details of a life no longer your own! What better way to keep up the charade while pursuing her carefully conceived plans: 'My darling Rufus, I was very pleased to get your second letter written from Ash Hall and I'm so glad to hear you're with a very interesting crowd of people. It should help to pass the time and I'm glad you like your doctor as that will help a lot. It sounds an ideal sort of place and if they put some weight on you as well as cure the nervous exhaustion, I agree it will be money well spent.

'You haven't said whether there is anything you want sent in the way of

197

clothes, though if you can struggle along on two pairs of pyjamas it will be as well from the coupon point of view.

'This will be the second Christmas I've been drinking with the "The No. 7" crowd without you. May it be the last. I think I shall go to the Christmas dance at the club tonight, so that (and Friday) will be the sum total of my 'gay season' festivities but you, poor darling, will have a much duller time, although I believe they do make an effort to brighten up hospitals etc. for Christmas.

'Incidentally, I've sent cards to our old friends, excluding Pam and Mac as I don't know their address. A Happy Christmas to you, darling. All my love, Marjorie. XX.

'PS. I nearly forgot – Megan Lloyd-Jones now has a son.'

When you need her most, dear Sidney, your tawdry wife stays put. I've never read a more damning testimony, but I've gone on too long. Baby Jacqueline grows fretful and whenever she cries Bella soon starts howling.

I know how this must sound. On the other hand, if the police don't agree with me I'll show them this letter from the 27th December 1943. They must be mad if they don't see Marjorie for what she truly is: 'My darling Rufus, I'm afraid I made a rather late start to the sales this year, owing to the fact I first had to go to Bond Street to collect a suit on which I had placed a deposit the previous Saturday. I'm ashamed of myself for having bought new clothes at a time like this and really set out for an odd jacket, but there was such a poor choice and I fell for the suit, which is the shade of blue you like (to wear with my purple jumper) and was quite reasonable as suits go nowadays (£11.0.0.) Hope you won't think I'm terribly extravagant, but having at last spent all my coupons, I really will now sit tight for a while and save some money since you can't work…'

While you were incarcerated in your mental hospital, my love, your wife was keeping up her spirits by simply getting on with her life. I could never have done that – I could never have been so practical. Do these letters not prove that Marjorie only acted the part of your loving bride long after her words meant nothing? I wonder why it was so, but I don't hesitate to call it a symptom of evil. Something led you both on to the bitter end, though. It doesn't look good. Of course the police will blame it on the war and forced separation, except we now know the falling out began long before then. In your youth. Or should I simply take Peggy's word for it and blame it on the 'concoction' that she encouraged her sister to take on your honeymoon?

If Peggy's half right, she's also half wrong.

You once loved Marjorie, dear Sidney and she once loved you, so why am I still not certain who didn't want whom? So far, I have a cause but not a reason.

THIRTY-FIVE

'Police! Don't come any closer! I'm Detective Sergeant Biggs and you're under arrest.'

There could be no doubt about it. Arthur Jones had to be dying? The fallen man lay slumped in the doorway of "Orchard Cottage" – he was gasping for air as he clasped both hands to his chest; shock and pain filled his eyes; he was horribly changed. Pale. Speechless. Paralysed.

Still the killer blocked his exit.

He couldn't see any knife in his hand.

He couldn't see a blade in Mr Jones's body, either.

His first reaction was to protect the victim, his second was that he would be next…

Except the stranger didn't attack – he hopped about in his gabardine raincoat and his face went strangely red; his eyes were ready to pop right out of his head and his chest was heaving where he'd been running as fast as he could. 'We have to hurry…'

That's when he recalled the angler he'd met earlier when asking for directions to "Orchard Cottage". 'Keep your hands where I can see them and tell me your name.'

'My name is James Cameron.'

'What have you done?'

'Me? I didn't do anything.'

'Looks like you did.'

'For heaven's sake, detective, will you help me or not?'

Next minute Mr Jones sat up and groaned. 'What the hell…?'

James rushed to check the old man for wounds. 'Are you all right, Arthur?

Did you hit your head on the door? How do you feel?'

'Never mind me, what about…?'

DS Biggs blinked hard. He'd seen what happened. Now it wasn't true at all. 'What's going on? What are you both so afraid of?'

'There's a dead body in the lake,' said James.

'What makes you think that?'

'I just hooked him out with my fishing line.'

Meanwhile Mr Jones was able to stand with some help, even if he was largely speechless – he was shocked, not stabbed.

DS Biggs still couldn't believe his ears. 'Are you absolutely sure someone's been killed?'

'I've seen enough casualties of this war to know a dead one when I see them, detective…'

Mr Jones began to breathe a little more freely. 'You two go head. I'll catch up.'

'…but I fear we won't be able to do anything about it.'

There was a strange throbbing in his ears. His heart raced. His lungs worked fast. At the same time his legs felt like lead while he hurried along. Bad thoughts filled his head. These flooded quarries were steep with sheer, submerged sides – anyone falling in could struggle to reach safety when there was so little by way of a beach to negotiate the side of the dyke. That water had to be bitterly cold, too. No one would last long if they couldn't summon help very quickly.

They came to the place where James had been fishing and a man's body rested on the ground all right – it lay like a stranded seal half out of the water. Brown hair stuck to its very white face. Its eyes were wide open and a piece of green weed lodged in its teeth.

DS Biggs saw James go to draw the victim further up the bank. 'I wouldn't do that.' Instead he felt inside the man's jacket for his Identity Card.

But there was no need.

Mr Jones arrived gasping. A silent howl was etched on his face as he was instantly transfixed by his son-in-law's empty stare.

Because there was only one possibility…

DS Biggs pressed his finger to Frederick's cold neck. 'He's been drowned a while.'

'Oh God, what will I tell Wynne and the children?'

'I don't see a boat,' he said, scanning the lake. 'You did say he had one, didn't you?'

'…'

'Yes or no, Mr Jones?'

'I heard you the first time, detective.'

'Is Fred good at sailing in all weathers?'

'Er…'

'Well? Just say it.'

'I honestly don't know. I suppose so, yes.'

He continued to study the expanse of misty grey water for signs of an overturned craft, but failed to locate mast or keel. Most likely it lay tangled in weed somewhere among the flooded quarry's many islands and secluded bays. His dislike of this lonely place redoubled as he imagined himself unable to breathe underwater. Next minute, James led them to a small bay.

'This is it, detective. Fred likes to board his boat at this jetty and sail round that island over there.'

'He must have lost his balance and toppled in?' said Mr Jones. 'What else could have happened?'

'I don't know any more than you do.'

'The thing is, Fred couldn't swim.'

'When did he leave the house this morning?'

'About ten o'clock.'

'So you had no reason to miss him until now?'

'None.'

DS Biggs began taking notes. 'What about you, James? It's one o'clock now. How long have you been fishing here today?'

'About two hours.'

'You didn't hear any cries for help?'

'No, I didn't.'

'Because if someone shouted in this quiet wilderness, anyone else would know about it, right?'

James looked offended. 'You think I don't know that?'

'Which means Frederick probably died shortly before you arrived. You sure you didn't hear anything? No engine of any kind?'

'No, why?'

'Because he wasn't alone.'

'What do you mean?' said Mr Jones, fumbling in his pocket for a packet of Woodbines. 'Why are you asking? What does it look like to you?'

DS Biggs crouched by the jetty and ran his finger lightly over muddy ground. 'It looks like we can't rule out foul play.'

THIRTY-SIX

I've decided to go to the police, after all – I'm certain they will believe me now and not Marjorie. I'm lining her letters up on my kitchen table, ready to go over them one last time. Herein lies proof of her duplicity and her criminal plan to get rid of you, dear Sidney, which cannot be denied any longer. Is there anything so dangerous as a vengeful bride with power?

Of course John doesn't see it that way, he doesn't know why I'm focusing all my efforts and anger on ridding myself of your unnecessary wife. I don't expect to have his understanding. I don't need it.

He keeps asking me if I really do believe you're dead due to faithless friends and feckless family?

Due to Marjorie?

Well, *I'm* not about to plead guilty, am I when, out of us all, she fits the bill so perfectly. I shouldn't have to burn in hell for her actions.

John will tell me she's my way out of this.

Easy for him to say. I did want your ungrateful spouse dead, dear Sidney and I do want her to pay.

But I have something very different in mind for her now.

What I need has changed.

If the police won't act, I will; I'll make public the cruelty she wreaked on you throughout your marriage, my love, by showing her up for the two-faced, double-dealing devil she really is. I'll do it for you. I'll do it for me. Until she's shamed.

Jacqueline plays with her rattle in her cot next to the copper which is still warm from the last load of laundry I boiled. Nearby, Bella growls and trots to the front door. She's like me, she won't rest. I'm trying not to lose my temper with her. It does no good to fight anxiety with anxiety and I refuse to reward her bad behaviour with more attention.

Overnight, a mouse has nibbled the corner of the first letter I'm marking for DI Lockett's personal attention. Who'd think your meritless wife could be such a dear and yet so distant? She has the gift of sounding so normal. Does this matter? It matters to me. Can ghosts even listen to the living, dear Sidney? Can you? If so, here goes.

Marjorie starts quite casually on the 11th of January 1944: 'My darling Rufus, thank you for your note and I'm so glad to hear you're getting better – if slowly. Now about coming to see you in Stoke – this weekend is too soon and I shan't feel well enough, next Saturday is Peggy's pantomime (a skit on various departments of the NAAFI and supposed to be very amusing to the staff) and Saturday after that I'm fire guard, though I could swop that. Anyway, darling, let me know what you think and I'll make arrangements…'

So far so brisk, when she adds: 'At the moment I'm acting R.A.F. Member. Bryant and Mrs Coomber are off sick with terrible colds, and our girl at the Air Ministry is also away ill, so I'm the only one left to deal with things. I don't feel very good myself. Nothing much – just a little off colour, and it may not be the beginning of flu… I went to Oxford Street to try and get a roll-on and a brassier but no luck. The things they offered me wouldn't support a fly…'

Are not her letters to you *so deliberately plausible*, my love? Such insincerity has to seem sincere to convince, I suppose.

She almost convinces me.

Won't happen again.

Still Bella barks and growls at the door.

'Bella! Be quiet.' I go along the hall to look out, but no one's in the front garden or on the pavement?

Bella isn't satisfied. She changes from calm to chaotic in seconds. I have, I realised, forgotten to shut the sash window in the parlour. It's not the first time I've found it open, but then its swivel brass catch is half broken….

I'm soon back in the kitchen reassembling the evidence. Do you remember the apparently caring lines that your sly Marjorie wrote you on the 11th of April 1944, dear Sidney, a few days after her visit to Ash Hall: 'My darling Rufus, I'm so sorry you had a relapse last week and do hope you now feel better. It is very disappointing as I thought you were making rapid strides. I'm feeling okay – the cold didn't develop and I just had a sore throat for a few days. Everybody you talk to at the moment says how tired they feel. We've all had enough of this war…'

Dr Andratschke and I are agreed that your fraudulent spouse's few visits to you in hospital did nothing to help you – all they did was to push you over the edge mentally and emotionally as she intended. But then her air of offended, yet teasing neutrality gives the game away (25th of March 1944): 'My darling Rufus, I hope you're not pining too much over your fellow patient Pam, though I've no doubt you felt a great sense of loss when she left – you would feel that for any friend, but I don't know how deeply involved you became…'

DI Lockett must be made to see that Marjorie is projecting her own guilty thoughts on to you, my love? Why else would she then say: 'I thought she was staying at Ash Hall indefinitely, but it is good to know she is now considered well enough to go home. Does it mean they can't do anything more for her? I thought you must be getting rather fond of her. I certainly can't blame you for this as Pam is a fascinating girl and I'm hardly a comfort to you… Did you want to marry her? Or would you have liked to if you were free? I'm not trying to be nasty, but trying to sympathise. Please don't get het up over these questions, as I don't think you were that serious. I think Dora will remain the love of your life, poor darling, and I just snatched you away and made all three of us very miserable…'

Even the police can't deny Marjorie resents even the briefest, most innocent relationship that you enjoyed with another patient? It's due to her appalling jealousy and to justify her own duplicity. I would never be that silly and petty. No one in their right mind should mistake her bland, deceitful utterances for a cry for help: 'My darling Rufus, thank you for your phone call. I was going to write to you after you telephoned on Friday as brief long-distance calls are unsatisfactory and I always think of lots of things I want to say when the three pips have gone.

'I am reasonably happy, except I can't help feeling a little frustrated at times when life rushes along so quickly and I see one after another of my friends having children. If only I were a few years younger, we could see out the war and not worry about such things...'

I trust the police *will not* be captivated by your guileful wife's heartfelt outpouring, dear Sidney, when she adds: 'I'm not blaming you in the slightest. Please don't think that for a moment, as you have always said it is the woman's place to decide whether or not she wants children *though it does help if the man is enthusiastic.* There again it is my fault for not working on you and making you enthusiastic about such things. Everybody agrees they are well worth while although there is no denying they are a great expense and responsibility. Please don't get worked up about all this, but we must talk it over soon.

'I expect you've got your new teeth by now and are struggling hard to use them. I believe it is very painful at first, but I understand one soon becomes accustomed to them. I do hope you get used to yours quickly and they look fairly natural. All my love, Marjorie.'

But even she must tell you the truth eventually when she writes to you on the 15th of May 1944, only TWO days after you were issued with a letter by the doctors stating you were now of sound mind: 'My darling Rufus, how are you today? I'm really terribly worried about you after dropping such a bombshell and feel an awful swine for doing it at a time like this. You were wonderfully kind about it, but this didn't surprise me as you are always sympathetic when people are in trouble. You would have made a very good doctor with a grand bedside manner. In fact, you would have been successful at quite a lot of things and it is a great pity circumstances and lack of money drove you into commerce...'

She really can't help herself, can she, as she continues: 'We may not be suited temperamentally, but I am certainly not blind to your good qualities and brain power. I think a small part of the trouble is due to the fact that I stand rather in awe of you and find it a little difficult to be completely natural. Furthermore, I'm pretty sure you don't feel completely natural with me either, as you like gay and bright women and my woodenness irritates you and gives you a feeling of frustration...'

She's master of all things disingenuous, in my opinion: 'Do you think we could still make "a go of it" if we tried, say in a few months' time when the war situation is clearer and you are better? Of course, under the circumstances, you may not wish to try an experiment and may be very glad to get rid of me.

'It is a funny thing but I feel very much closer to you now, after telling you about things, than I have for the past three years. We must have a good talk soon about our personal problems as obviously we can't go on like this much longer. I've got to the stage where I envy women who have settled down in their own homes and have a couple of children. After all, I'm 34 in July and if I'm ever to have children it can't be put off much longer from the safety angle...'

I worry DI Lockett will not draw the right deductions from how frustrated your wife felt. The nincompoop is bound to take at face value her burning wish to be a mother which you wilfully denied her, my love – he'll fall for it hook, line and sinker? Men are such fools. Next thing you know, he'll think her fair and decent.

So it's just as well someone like me is on hand to dismiss her ridiculous display of pain and dilemma which she wrote you on the 22nd of May 1944: 'My darling Rufus, you stress the fact about the need still existing to tell you about Frank. I think the real reason I did tell you now was not so much that I wanted to do something about it, but rather that I thought the time had come when we simply must settle down to some normal life and perhaps have a family before I'm too old.

'I did not want to tell you last October and November when I came to see you in Cheltenham, as I just hadn't the heart to do it when you seemed to rely on me so. Time and again I was tempted to blurt it all out to you, but quite honestly I just felt I couldn't be that cruel, since you were so ill and depressed. Added to which, I felt that the need to make a decision could be put off for a few months while you were at Ash Hall – the same old cowardly "putting off" Marjorie...'

It's not so easy to smell a rat because all this sounds so reasonable: 'Incidentally, when I did come to Ash Hall to see you, you gave me the impression that I wasn't at all necessary to your happiness and you were quite cold and off-hand with me. Frank thinks it is a very good idea for us to see each other at Whitsun, although obviously he is taking a back seat at the present time and is not attempting to influence me in any way.

'I'm very sorry not to be able to give you something definite as regards what I want to do, but I just don't seem able to make up my mind. I keep weighing up the pros and cons but can't make a decision. I can't even bring myself to talk to Peggy.

'Please try and keep cheerful and put up with me till I come out of my 'coma', darling. Lots of love, Marjorie.

'PS. Zora is the latest to join the ranks of expectant mothers and should give birth on Christmas Eve…'

Your double-dealing spouse has stopped signing her letters to you '*All my love*', I notice. It's a little thing but gives the game away – I shall certainly be calling upon DI Lockett to give it due importance.

I have to say Marjorie's dread of scandal *is* very convincing, my love. But just because she is terrified she will be judged according to her family's and friends' standards of behaviour, even morals, doesn't mean I'm about to cut her any slack. She's a clever schemer – you see it when she writes: 'If you are annoyed about Peggy knowing anything concrete perhaps the following will help to convince you that I have been very careful – when I have known you were coming to Claygate, or alternatively, I have been going to Cheltenham, I have always refused to see Frank for at least a week beforehand and a week afterwards, as I hate the idea of "seeing one man out of the front door and another coming in at the back", if you understand my slang. When I took Saturday morning off work to wave you goodbye at Euston Station upon your return to Stoke, he wanted to meet me afterwards in town, but I said it wasn't decent. We have never been in a Claygate or Esher pub together and just pass the time of day if we happen to meet in the hall, corridors or office restaurant. We wouldn't dream of behaving like Claude and Dorothy etc. and being discussed right and left… PS. Frank is very pleased I've told you. He says the "affair" doesn't seem quite such a hole in the corner one and he doesn't feel so much of a cad.'

She is nothing if not a great actress and she knows how best to wound you, but nothing can detract from the very solid case I now have against her, in particular this note dated the 22nd of June this year: 'My darling Rufus, I've read your letter over and over again and although it points out where my duty lies, I still don't know what to do. As you say, the letter wasn't really very helpful, as of course I had thought of all the points you mention, and further more they referred to the past and it is the future with which we are concerned. You say yourself that if I stay with you we shall have a lot of difficulty in picking up the threads and I must be far more enthusiastic than I have been.

'I must try and pluck up the courage and speak to Mother, although she is not exactly an intelligent person…'

Is it any wonder you began harassing your underhand wife without a thought for her reputation, dear Sidney, by telephoning her so frequently? Her letter of the 28th of June 1944 is one long squirm: 'My darling Rufus, I shall have to write to you every day if you keep ringing – we're not supposed to have telephone calls and at the present moment they're terribly understaffed on the switchboard and extremely irritable. They have been very decent to me but I shall be getting told off soon if you keep ringing. I'm sorry to say this, but anyway it is most unsatisfactory to discuss such a problem on the phone. I don't know what you said to Mother last night (or what she said to you) but she was so worried about the hints you threw out in your Monday call that she asked Peggy point blank what the trouble was between us.

'I had to go off to fire guard with bright red eyes. I couldn't help howling – whether from relief or shock at my people knowing the details, I don't know. It must have been shock, I think, as I shivered violently and had to crouch over the fire. I've got an awful hangover this morning with a splitting headache.

'Have you told Bernard everything? It must have been a relief to talk to someone, but unless you've asked him to keep it confidential I'm afraid it will be all over Ealing as he is rather a gossip and seems to revel in a bit of scandal.

'I'm not looking forward to speaking to Mother and Daddy tonight but it has to be faced now. I still don't think you and I get on at all well together and it wasn't much better before I "departed", as you put it. I know I irritate you and I'm always restless when I'm with you as I know my lack of education is a sore point with you.

'However I must have a certain amount of "gut" to have been able to carry on all this time without cracking up, but I expect you'll say it is not "gut" but lack of intelligence and imagination. And perhaps you're right.

'I'm terribly sorry you have taken this so badly, as quite honestly I thought you would be rather relieved to get out of such an unsatisfactory relationship.'

I can't read any more of her lies. I won't. I have to go shopping for baby food and nappies, though I'm not hopeful there will be much left on the shelves. Frankly, these letters are all tell and no show. I've missed something, I know. It all happened very quickly and yet played out very slowly. You and Marjorie were married for years in name only. Did no one else see it? What did your friends say about you? I will get to the bottom of it, my love, now I'm ready to expose her for the callous killer she is. All I lack is the precise motive… As I said, a cause is not a reason.

When exactly did she decide you were dispensable, I wonder?

I think I might know, only I can't be sure until I pay the last person on my list a visit.

I know I was there and should have helped you, my love, but this time I won't let you down.

'Bella! Come away from the front door.' I go after her and peep past the blackout curtain in the parlour.

Someone dressed in cap and coat scurries off down the garden path. It's my sweet-sucking spy again – he was trying to peer in through the grubby glass.

Bella goes wild. She knows I'm being watched day and night, just when I thought things couldn't get any tenser…

Someone wants to discover, or stop, what I'm doing.

By directing all guilt and blame to those who deserve it more than me, dear Sidney, I'm treading on someone else's toes?

They could be friend or foe.

Well, that's what I'm about to find out.

I'll nail shut the parlour's window first thing in the morning. It's not that

I scare easily, but I urgently need a decent weapon for my own protection. Luckily, I know just where I might find one.

THIRTY-SEVEN

DI Lockett still couldn't quite get his head round what had happened. Any thoughts on why he had seen Oliver kiss another man last night in the urinal at Gloucester Cattle Market still whirled in his brain. He had a good mind to arrest him for indecent exposure. Meanwhile there was a strange knot in his stomach; his legs were restless; his heart was racing. He kept asking himself why it should be so, and whether these feelings were vestiges of love, not hate... He wiped a tear from his cheek even as DS Biggs barged into the office with barely a knock.

'You all right, sir?' The news of Frederick Sheppard's death seemed to have plunged his boss into premature depression this dull wintry morning. He had a bad feeling about it.

'Bit of a cold, that's all.'

'My wife's the same.' He held out a selection of fruit gums in the palm of his hand – he could no longer buy them in tubes or packets, only loose at 7d and 4 points per 4ozs. 'Try a black current, sir. Might soothe your throat.'

'Are you absolutely sure Jolantha wasn't seen at Thorney Weir?'

'Frederick's father-in-law says not.'

'So what *did* he say, exactly?'

'He said Sidney Sheppard had run out of money, not least because he had spent a great deal paying for his feckless brother's two children to go to private school. That's on top of subsidising Marjorie's flat in Claygate and paying his own not inconsiderable medical expenses from his time spent in Ash Hall Nursing Home. He also made regular payments to his mother.'

'Your point is?'

'Sidney was very isolated. The war saw him forced to work up north and cut him off from his wife and all his friends – the '7' they called themselves. More specifically he may have felt out of his depth due to his class, upbringing and foolishness with cash. We all know how financial worries can tip a person over the edge. What if it made him desperate enough…?'

'To do what, sergeant?'

'Not only was Sidney stony broke, sir, he refused to accept that his wife had found herself a new man. He was going to take her to court to fight the divorce because he thought truth was on his side. It's quite possible he lost his temper with her in the cathedral. He had every motive to do her in.'

'Oh really?'

'To be blunt, sir, Sidney was someone of very contentious views. He had strong likes and dislikes and would go out of his way to court controversy. His own brother daren't even tell him his wife Wynne was a Roman Catholic.'

'So what if Sidney was a dogmatist? Was he not also charismatic?'

'He was liked by plenty of people, true enough. As for women, they were all over him for his smart suits and clean looks – I was given the impression Fred was quite jealous.'

'So yes, then.'

'The thing is, Sidney liked to be in control. He felt very strongly that he was always in the right, morally speaking. He called it 'leading a noble life'. From what Fred told me, it's clear that his brother could be very patriarchal, not to say bloody minded… He had plenty of justification to kill himself and his wife, sir, when he found he couldn't get what he wanted?'

DI Lockett shook his head. There were many Sidneys in this world. He was a bit of an argumentative free spirit himself, only for a different reason. It meant you could cut a lonely figure at times. He gave a loud cough. Some people could feel alone in a crowd. 'It's hard to say what anyone will do,' he said darkly, 'when they feel trapped, but I don't believe he jumped because he ran out of money.'

'No?'

'Everyone hates a divorce, sergeant, since they're not considered 'decent', are they? An upright and proper individual like Sidney will feel shamed and humiliated, when we're all supposed to be so correct in our behaviour every fucking day of our fucking existence... But does that make him a suicidal murderer? No, it doesn't. Pah! All this leads us no closer to Jolantha Wheeler.'

DS Biggs cocked an eyebrow. 'Yes and no, sir. I spotted fresh motorcycle combination tracks in the mud by the jetty where Frederick moored his boat. Someone was most likely present around the time he drowned.'

'What did I tell you? Jolantha rides a Brough Superior Combination.'

'With respect, sir, it still solves nothing.'

DI Lockett shifted slightly in his chair. Then he shifted back again. His eyes narrowed; his face looked cagey; both his cheeks blew out like balloons as he emitted a long, low whistle from his lips. With his rapid breaths came anxiety, as if his shirt collar were too tight at his throat. It was the sort of reaction he felt when Oliver had walked into the room generating nervous excitement in him alone.

'Or we can definitely say Jolantha is visiting friends and family of Sidney Sheppard from whom she is stealing mementoes. Now two such people are dead...'

'A coincidence, surely?'

'Oh she's clever, sergeant. She knows how to stage a murder to look like an accident. Now if we could just obtain plaster casts of those tyres...'

'We'd have to come clean to the Middlesex Police to do that, sir. You'd have to make the call...'

'You blaming me for this, sergeant?'

'Technically it's up to them to investigate...'

'Which is why my answer is still no – we'll be the ones to solve Frederick's death by solving his brother's.'

'As I say, no one actually saw her...'

'You mark my words. This widow is the real risk to us all.'

DS Biggs flipped shut his notepad and stood there tapping its grubby cover. 'All this stuff about a spurned, obsessive lover is all very well, sir, but what if she turns out to be quite innocent?'

DI Lockett reached for his pipe and puffed rapidly at hot shag in its bowl – he brought it to an incandescent glow like the fires of hell. 'No, sergeant, Jolantha isn't innocent. You know why? Because she's delusional.'

'In your opinion?'

'She won't stop until she proves herself right and the rest of us wrong. It's the one big thing she and Sidney have in common. They think they occupy the moral high ground. She feels the need to exercise control.'

'Then why don't we bring her in and question her?'

'And let her know we're on to her?'

'What do we know about her really, sir?'

'We know she's a murderous magpie.'

'Not a lot, then.'

'Are you deliberately going out of your way to contradict me this morning, sergeant?'

'No, sir. Of course not, sir.' DS Biggs registered his boss's puzzlement. Each time Jolantha's name was mentioned, he grew more obsessed with it. With that came exasperation. It was as though they were about to join all the dots when she slipped through their fingers… 'There is one more thing, sir.'

'What? You actually take me seriously now?'

'It's about Frederick Sheppard's wedding reception in May. According to Mr Jones no one invited Jolantha – she just showed up and passed herself off as one of the bride's many friends from work. Sidney was able to attend because he'd been discharged from Ash Hall Nursing Home in Stoke-on-Trent only a few days before. Marjorie went to the wedding, too, but she didn't spend much time at her husband's side, which is hardly surprising because she'd just told him that she was planning to leave him. It appears Sidney was feeling weak and nearly fainted at the bar. His wife's bad news had obviously got to him, but on top of everything else he'd recently had a major operation to have all his teeth pulled and fitted with new ones…'

'New teeth?'

'Don't ask. Jolantha was first to help him outside to get some fresh air. They sat in his car where they got talking. Marjorie later tried to pick a fight with her. Gave her a bloody nose, by all accounts. But Jo didn't retaliate, she simply vanished. We think Sidney drove her to the nearest railway station, because they both disappeared at the same time.'

'No one forgets a whack in the face in a hurry. So Jolantha *did* lie to us when she said she met Sidney only a few weeks ago? Why would she do that? Why would she be so deceitful for no reason unless she's guilty of something?'

DS Biggs reached for a cigarette. It was a new pack of John Player and he was hoping for another cigarette card of wild flowers to complete the set. So far he had 41 out of a possible 48. Alas, free cards were still banned to save paper.

'Her treatment in Coney Hill Mental Hospital in 1942 may have left her forgetful, didn't we decide?'

'Or she didn't want us to know she'd been following him for such a long while?'

'Now I know you're joking.'

DI Lockett ripped his pipe from his mouth.

'Don't you see, sergeant? Jolantha Wheeler has been stalking Sidney for at least a year, or more. What was she planning? What will she do next?'

THIRTY-EIGHT

'Mr Wallis, I presume?'

A bald-headed man stands in the doorway of No. 33 Milbourne Lane and peers down his long, pointed nose at me. He's every bit the irritated suburbanite from Surrey. His round silver spectacles make him look like a cross owl. Has he never met a vengeful woman clad in oilskin coat and motorcycle trousers before? Bella and I have disturbed his afternoon snooze.

I'm here to get answers once and for all.

No amount of city chic will save him.

'Who wants to know?'

'My name is Jo Wheeler. I'm Sidney Sheppard's fiancée.'

'Go away! I don't want to talk to you.'

But I'm quicker than he is and shove my toe over the threshold. Suddenly he panics. His head shakes. He stumbles. His puce-coloured face is full of significant meaning. So is mine. He goes to block me, except Bella has other ideas. All dogs like new playthings and she enjoys nothing better than shaking a slipper to pieces. Her best trick is to pounce on it and break its bloody…

'Bella! Leave!'

Huh. Some people have no sense of fun. Time to let go and huff loudly. It was only a bit of sport. The fact that a man's foot is in the slipper is just a coincidence. Better settle for a menacing growl.

I'm first into the lounge which turns out to be a comfy version of my own tiny parlour in Gloucester. Actually, it's no such thing, it's so much plusher. An expensive looking wireless sits on a very large sideboard and comfy cushions line the sofa. Only the blackout curtains at the window remind me we are a country at war. That's not quite true, either. The room smells strongly of melted candlewax – everyone keeps a candle handy these days, in case a bomb hits a power line.

Mr Wallis comes trotting after me. 'The police warned me about you. They say you're deranged.'

I shoot him my sweetest smile. 'Is that so?'

There's something rather phoney about your hoity-toity father-in-law, dear Sidney. He may think of himself as someone rather posh, but no one that grand wears white braces on his trousers like an American gangster. Nobody worth their salt rolls their shirtsleeves above their elbows, either. If he's going to pretend to be something he isn't, he should learn to play by the rules.

'What do you want? We're just a normal family.'

'I want to know what you and that she-devil daughter of yours did to my Sidney.'

'Do? We didn't *do* anything. On the contrary, Sidney did terrible things to Marjorie.'

'Or it suits you to blacken his name to protect your own?'

'My family never hurt anyone. Neither have I. I'm a good man.'

'Oh yes? I know for a fact that Marjorie and her sister Peggy couldn't get on with you. That's why they moved out and took a flat in nearby Claygate. You ignored your daughter Barbara's wedding because she was marrying a mere aircraftsman and you turned Shirley out when she became pregnant. Not my idea of a father figure or a fair-minded person! Okay, there's a quite reasonable, smart, well-to-do suburban image that people like you try to project, except you've added quite a dash of snobbery and social climbing…'

'This is outrageous. I should have listened to the police. I'll go ring them right now.'

My eyes spy a vase on a shelf. Lock on. It's a very nice vase. In fact, it is quite clearly a Royal Doulton Peacock Bird design signed by Fred Moore. I must say I do like its rich red colour under the thick glaze. That doesn't mean I'm about to do anything crazy – I'm not here to be unreasonable, I just want the truth. 'As I was saying before you so rudely interrupted me, Sidney and I were all set to be married until his fall in Gloucester Cathedral left me feeling forsaken…'

'Forsaken? That's an odd word to use.'

'You'd feel the same way if you'd been abandoned.'

'How does this in any way involve me?'

'You and I both know he wouldn't be dead if it wasn't for Marjorie.'

'The police say *you* pushed him!'

'What do you think I am? The wicked widow?'

Mr Wallis is all tippy-toes and can't bear to stand or sit down. 'Please, Mrs Wheeler, put the vase back on the shelf. I bought it for my wife for our wedding anniversary…'

'Not before you tell me everything that passed between Marjorie and Sidney just before he died? What finally drove her to kill him?'

Mr Wallis can see Bella eyeing him closely. 'I was extremely sorry to hear of the estrangement between Marjorie and Sidney, Mrs Wheeler. But I was not surprised in the least since he has consistently – from the very beginning – avoided his responsibilities as a married man and at times left my daughter to fend for herself.'

'That it? That's all you have to say to me?' I still have the precious vase in my grasp – I'm rolling it from hand to hand. The trouble with porcelain is that it can be so fragile. One slip and it's a thousand pieces – this peacock isn't meant to fly.

Your father-in-law is all hands too – he's waving them at me as if his agitation will somehow soothe mine. 'Look here, Mrs Wheeler, does not every married woman have a right to expect a home and children? It is, after all, the purpose of marriage. Sidney did not provide a permanent home when they got wed even though Marjorie was prepared to go to Warrington or wherever else he found himself a job. He ruled otherwise and left her in London for me to take care of, which rendered it necessary for her to get a job of her own…'

'Oh, but there's something much worse than a petty squabble going on here, don't you agree?'

'Your implication is that she has committed an offence which I am forgiving and overlooking. This is definitely not the case – it is Sidney who has done the wrong and made Marjorie's life unhappy *by withholding from her the very things which every married woman has a right to expect i.e. protection, home and children.'*

I place the vase back where I found it, for now. I may do bad things but I'm not a bad person. 'Thanks to your daughter, my Sidney was humiliated, discredited and deprived of his life and I'm here to make you admit it.'

'Marjorie gave Sidney every opportunity over the last five years to do the right thing, but he refused to shoulder his responsibilities. It is therefore not surprising that he lost her love.'

'Is that right?'

'It is an extraordinary thing to me that any woman could be so forbearing and have tolerated such an invidious and humiliating position for so long a time.'

Gimlet-eyed, I'm trying to be patient here. 'What is she now? A fucking saint?'

'Sidney said he still loved my daughter, but on the telephone he poured scorn on the suggestion that anyone could fall in love again at her age of 34. Further, he said that he did not care a damn for her happiness. I think he spoke true on this occasion because, as I understand it, while on honeymoon he accused her of trapping him into marriage. What justification he had for saying such a monstrous thing, when they had only been wed a few hours, I cannot imagine, considering he was hardly off our doorstep from her schooldays to the day of their wedding. He assumed a proprietary interest in her and always made it clear he looked upon her as his future wife.'

'Or she couldn't be trusted from the very beginning.'

'I can't help it if you feel cheated, too.'

'Let's not make this about me.'

Your father-in-law is bold enough to pour himself a whisky. He huffs and puffs, yet it's only right that I let him steady his nerves before I shatter them completely.

'Sidney formally asked my consent to the engagement, Mrs Wheeler. He took the step as a young man with a free will. No one coerced him or brought any pressure to bear on him to marry Marjorie. It's not her fault he made the wrong choice.'

'Oh no?'

'On the contrary, any influence I had would have been used in the opposite direction, because frankly I was not at all satisfied that he had sufficient stability or the necessary qualities to take care of a wife. Events, I think, have proved that I was right.'

'You were never on his side, you only ever aimed to back your vile child.'

'The only villain here is Sidney.'

Something doesn't feel right. This man is clever – he'll have me turn against you, my love, whereas he needs to suffer like all the other so-called friends and relatives who failed you so badly. He may be last on my list but has to be the worst.

'Admit you encouraged Marjorie to bring divorce proceedings? You, as much as her, wanted to wreck Sidney's life, did you not, Mr Wallis? You helped tip the balance of his mind.'

Your father-in-law does his best to swallow his whisky and clear his throat. He's not a big man. One carefully aimed hit on the head might well finish him. But I'm all ears, for now.

'I trusted Sidney would allow his gentlemanly instincts to prevail and not make matters worse, Mrs Wheeler. I was wrong. Marjorie was in a highly strung state of mind and I feared the possibility of a total mental breakdown unless the tension brought about by this unhappy state of affairs was relaxed soon. I therefore asked Sidney to refrain from worrying her or attempting to see her, but instead he arranged to meet her secretly in Gloucester Cathedral.'

'I don't think so.'

To my surprise, Mr Wallis walks right past me and pulls open a drawer in the sideboard.

He's resuming his self-appointed role as master of his own home.

This won't do.

He's being unacceptably cocky.

Won't matter after today.

'If it's proof of his vindictiveness you want, then here it is. Sidney wrote several quite nasty letters to me and to Marjorie which I think you'll agree are proof of his volatile temperament. The man you say you planned to marry was no gentleman, Mrs Wheeler.'

'What's this?'

'It's a letter dated the 30th of June 1944, in which Sidney writes: "Dear Mr Wallis, I am sorry to find you so prejudiced in favour of bad faith, disloyalty and deceit which are the very things that we are all fighting. You are evidently trying to shift a good deal of the blame on to me…" Or there's this note to Marjorie, written on the 6th of July: "Your people make charges of instability against me, yet it is not I who, intentionally or otherwise, did anything to disrupt our marriage". And here again, he writes to her on the 26th: "However unsatisfactory our honeymoon, I came back full of the spirit of endeavour… The difference between us seems to be that whereas I have consistently tried to make any redress and readjustment necessary to our happiness, you have done the reverse. You wrote to me in your letter of 24.2.43: *There doesn't seem anything else to tell you at the moment except that I love you and I'm looking forward to seeing you soon.* Yet when you met me at Easter or Whitsun, you made your extraordinary statement about having no particular desire to be the mother of my children, which has only been explained in terms of your recent confession. Surely it seems fairly obvious that something happened in the interval and equally obvious that it was an extraneous influence and had nothing to do with me."'

'He spoke the facts, did he not?'

'Sidney refused to take any blame for the end of his marriage, Mrs Wheeler, he only took refuge in wild accusations and self-justification.'

'That makes two of you.'

Your father-in-law is apoplectic, dear Sidney. He rolls his head and rattles more letters in my face. He expects me to behave like Bella when I catch her stealing biscuits – he'd have me put my tail between my legs and hang my head in submission. I won't. Much more of this and he's dead meat.

'Sidney consistently blamed Marjorie for his own shortcomings, Mrs Wheeler. Why else would he write to her the following: "It is clear to me that your sense of values is entirely obscured by your obsession for Frank… If this is so, it is just plain weakness to be defeated by war circumstances… When you declined to move to Cheltenham and chose to stay in London, the obligation on you to remain loyal was automatically greatly increased. In the kindest way I can, may I say that surely you realise it is presumption for you or your father to tell me what is best for me…"'

'I'd say he's right.'

'On the contrary, Sidney was incapable of truly loving anyone and that includes you.'

'Rubbish. Women everywhere adored him. He was tall, good-looking and he could choose whom he liked.'

'He always spoke about right and wrong, but he was fundamentally unsound…'

'You'd say anything to shield your daughter from me and the law.'

'…in his heart and in his head.'

'You'd do anything to save her from the hangman.'

'He'd even abandoned his faith in God.'

So now I am furious. This isn't you, dear Sidney. I have so many thoughts fill my brain. 'Save it. I can't stomach your excuses.'

'Listen to me, Mrs Wheeler, the considerate man you *think* loved you is the same vengeful soul Marjorie and I came to know.'

I'm chewing my fingernails to pieces. Your father-in-law's face twists and grows grim. I can only say he looks like a cross polecat. 'Not content with 'vindictive', it's 'vengeful' now, is it?'

'Sidney dug his heels in to make things as difficult as possible for Marjorie and Frank. He wanted to humiliate her in the eyes of her friends by compelling her to start the divorce proceedings. He's been an absolute swine about it.'

I'm biting my nail right down to the quick. '*Oh really?*'

'Judge for yourself. Sidney was not even prepared to pretend to go to bed with another woman to spare Marjorie's reputation, but wrote her the following: "As Frank has all the qualities that appeal to you, surely it is unnecessary to appeal to me to be the 'gentleman'. It is not as simple as just staying in a hotel. I would have to find someone to stay with me, be seen with me, and be cited. Even if it is still possible to arrange this sort of thing through certain agencies (vide 'Holy Deadlock') it costs a lot of money. Apart from this, I fear I am simply not well enough to go through such a performance at this time.'"

I reach for the decanter and pour myself a whisky. My poor Sidney, you should have come to me. I would have let the 'Snapper' snap us naked in bed, I would have given that wimp of a wife of yours all the evidence the court needed, with glee.

'I don't blame him. Faking sex is squalid.'

'You don't understand. Sidney flatly refused to accept that Marjorie was leaving him.'

This I won't believe. You and I had such wonderful plans, my darling. I was going to marry you and go to the south of France with you, I was going to bear your children…

'You say this because?'

'Why else would Sidney write me this only a few months ago: "Dear Mr Wallis, you are of course entitled to your opinion although I cannot for the life of me see how you arrive at it. Fortunately, however, I do not have to accept you as a judge. I am willing to accept the decision of a court of *justice* and if, as you say, Marjorie has made up her mind, the sooner the case gets into court the better. As you will easily understand, there are means of testing the merits of the two sides and I am quite willing to arrange to do this. *Under no circumstances will I admit or assume any responsibility for this sorry business.*"'

'You'll have to do a lot better than that, Mr Wallis, if you want to save your daughter's skin.'

If I had gone to court, my darling, I would have been your star witness.

'Sidney kept writing to me, Mrs Wheeler, over and over. But as I told him, I was not au fait with his correspondence and conversations with Marjorie over the years, so I could not judge the value of what he quoted at me. For instance, he talked of "fighting some adverse influence" for the last three years, except I knew nothing of the state of affairs until recently. As for Frank, whom he appeared to assume I knew well, I was introduced to him several years ago in a crowd at a NAAFI party and have never set eyes on him since, until now. *So much for my influence in that direction.* I kept telling Sidney that he alone was responsible for his wrecked marriage. I took no pleasure in telling him this – nobody likes this sort of thing, least of all a father and mother. I told him straight. I didn't know what would be the end of it, but it seemed pretty clear that Marjorie had made up her mind. It made no difference, Sidney became angrier and angrier. If you ask me, you had a lucky escape.'

'Whatever are you implying?'

'That man was a danger to himself and others.'

Your father-in-law is really rather flushed by now. His face is bright red with fury, or is it the whisky talking? Is mine?

'First you accuse me, then a dead man, of what exactly?'

'Sidney had run out of options, Mrs Wheeler.'

'What?'

'Look me in the eye and tell me that what I say doesn't fit with everything you know about what happened in Gloucester Cathedral?'

'Damn you.' I snatch the letters from his hands and scoop the rest from the drawer. I won't have you shut away in this ogre's house any longer, dear Sidney. 'Here's giving you what you fucking deserve…'

But Mrs Wallis enters the room carrying a shopping bag of vegetables. I can't be bothered with her except to notice that she is wearing the most ridiculous hat and silly white gloves. Who wears kid gloves to do her Saturday chores?

'Is something the matter, dear? Who is this woman? Why is she shouting?'

I take her by the arm and throw her aside. The Peacock vase slips from my hand and smashes into myriad pieces. It's not very seemly but I can't believe Marjorie still had you in her thrall, dear Sidney. Had you really forgotten we were going to run away together? As soon as I get outside I turn and scream at the sky. I'm banging my hands on the brickwork of this smug, stuffy semi. Don't worry, my love, your legacy is safe with me. I'll put this right and prove you're not to blame. Now's the time for your worthless wife to be wiped from the face of the earth.

That reprieve I granted her just got rescinded.

Mr Wallis comes after me – he's thinking of grabbing my arm, but Bella rushes between us. She has her chin on her front paws and her bottom in the air. It's the foot-in-slipper game again. She's growling and straining to have a go – she's curling her lip at him. She's all spit and white teeth while we head back to my motorcycle combination.

Our furious host halts his side of the garden gate even as I pull on my leather helmet and goggles – I'm soon astride my machine, ready to roar off in an instant.

'Sidney did his best to run away from his marriage, Mrs Wheeler. Then, when Marjorie left him, he did the inexplicable – he tried to cling on. When that didn't work he did the only thing he could think of, he lashed out at her because he felt wounded, if only because he'd wounded himself. That's why he did the one thing left to him in the cathedral. He threw himself and her out of the triforium.'

I turn my head his way, eyes blazing. 'No, he didn't. He wouldn't.'

'How can you be so certain?'

'Because you and I both know it was Marjorie who planned it all.'

'Are you mad? Since when?'

'Ever since she married him.'

'Why?'

'She had a grievance.'

'What sort of grievance?'

'The unwanted kind. And I'll prove it. Your daughter had a mind to be rid of him from day one of their honeymoon.'

THIRTY-NINE

CONEY HILL MENTAL HOSPITAL

Dear Violet, I have neglected you so shamefully these last few days, I should not blame you if you had given me up for dead.

I am sorry to confess that I have ignored everyone including my doctors who have written such nice reports about me. Of course time and age have something to do with it, but mainly the reason, however bizarre it may seem, is you. I cannot stand the hypocrisy.

If, as you say many times, you cared about me, you would have come to me at once when I asked you to marry me. But you thought it proper to discuss our love with the new man in your life and decided that you preferred to stay with him. Someone who cares deeply for someone would surely tell him that she wants to be the mother of their child? Contrary to everything you said, you must have known that you were keeping yourself for your new man, yet you kept assuring me that there was no one else and I had no need to worry.

Your past kindnesses to me were solely to keep up appearances, to allay any suspicions I might have and I've no doubt that each time you returned to your new love, you assured him that you remained undefiled.

It is the persistent dishonesty over such a long period of time that I so much resent – telling lies doesn't seem to bother you at all.

Well, that's enough of that and I will retire into the shell of my small world. I will never neglect you for so long again, so I hope you will forgive me. Love, H.

FORTY

'Guess who rang the station last night, sergeant.'

'Who?'

'Mr Wallis, that's who.' DI Lockett looked both vindicated and worried. 'Jolantha Wheeler paid him a visit. He was convinced she was going to kill him. Didn't I say she would? She's going here, there and everywhere scaring the hell out of people. Or worse.'

DS Biggs wound the handle on his 'Crown' pencil sharpener – he did it vigorously until its twin steel cutters hit a stop when the point was produced. It always unnerved him when his boss stood over his deck ready to breathe down his neck, because it invariably meant trouble. 'What did Mr Wallis say exactly, sir?'

'According to the duty officer there was a lot of swearing about us not doing our job properly. It turns out Jolantha has called on his daughter Peggy, too. He's demanding police protection for him and his family. Of course, I've had to tell him firmly that Esher is not within our jurisdiction…'

DS Biggs used his fingertip to test the new point on his pencil. 'What did Jolantha ask him?'

'More stuff about Sidney. What else?'

'Sounds innocent enough.'

'I don't know about that. There's a shadow around her.'

'So how threatening was she? Can we detain her and turn her over to the Surrey Police?'

'She didn't harm anyone this time.'

'So that's a 'no', then?'

'Give her enough rope and she'll hang herself yet, sergeant.'

DS Biggs flinched and looked at his finger. He'd drawn blood. He wasn't always terribly keen on his boss's sayings. Since Josef Jacobs had become the last of eleven men to be executed by firing squad for espionage at The Tower of London three years ago, the rope was the only legal method of killing someone. He didn't like to joke about it.

'If Jolantha doesn't want to be blamed for Sidney's death, why hasn't she left us to call it suicide? Why stir up such a hornets' nest?'

'Because it's not about us any more. Maybe it never was. Jolantha doesn't care about her own fate. She's gone rogue. She wants to punish everyone who failed Sidney. In particular, she won't rest until she has framed his wife for his death? She wants to take her down, no matter what. Only that plan won't work if Marjorie recovers and tells us what really happened.'

'You don't know that.'

'I'm pretty sure I do.'

'So what we do now?'

'Get round to Coney Hill Mental Hospital. I want to discover just how long Jolantha has known Sidney. Did their paths cross when they both fell ill? Go now.'

DS Biggs stood up and reached for his coat. Something about this case saw his boss increasingly on edge himself – all he wanted to do right now was to go after Jolantha as if she were nothing less than the devil's disciple. Or she was the perfect distraction for his own troubled mind.

'Any news about Marjorie, sir?'

'Seems she will survive, but not necessarily with all her faculties intact.'

'Is she likely to wake up from her coma any time soon?'

'Not yet. She's really critical.'

FORTY-ONE

'Brought the brat, have you? You've got a nerve.'

I'm lifting Jacqueline out of the Brough Superior's sidecar where two thick woollen blankets – and Bella – have kept her warm on our way to Sherborne. 'Please don't start, mother.'

But Primrose is all charm. 'I bet you haven't heard from the child's father. No? I thought not. He's had his head blown off or has totally forgotten about you by now, for sure.'

Anyone else might kiss and make up, but I won't lie to you, dear Sidney. Mother and I have hardly spoken since Jacqueline was born. Now that she's heard me arrive, she's determined to demonstrate that she still has the strength to leave her wheelchair and head me off at the door – she's busy reminding me who rules here. It hardly matters, since I won't be long.

'It's cold, mother. You should go back inside because you don't look well.'

'You don't look too good yourself. You're as thin as a rake. It serves you right for turning your back on your own family.'

'I'm here, aren't I?'

'Must you bring that mangy dog with you?'

'Bella goes where I go.'

To think I was born and raised in this grand mansion hardly seems real. Nearby trees cast long winter shadows over Sherborne House as aircraft take off and land at the neighbouring airfield of RAF Windrush. It isn't the place but what it represents that is now so alien, as if I have stepped out of one skin and entered another. War does that to a person, it makes you question everything you ever had. I'm sure it did the same to you, my

231

darling. I could no more live here again than stretch my arms and fly.

Packing cases litter the impressive entrance hall and bare walls up the stairs are already stripped for action.

'Where's father?' I ask brightly and let Bella wander where she wishes, while I cradle Jacqueline in my arms. I don't want to stay too near my mother, even if her TB is deemed to be no longer infectious.

'He's at the deer lodge.'

'That old place? It's a ruin.'

Primrose's long royal blue and green silk dress, embroidered with green sequins and clear beads, hisses like a nest of vipers as she leans on her stick across the stone floor. She has little or no idea what her own husband does half the time, or how he manages the estate. They've always led separate lives, which includes separate bedrooms. She constantly fiddles with her green satin belt as if it somehow constricts her breathing.

'Don't expect anyone to wait on you, Jolantha. Your father and I move out on Monday.'

'That soon? What about Hugo?'

'You don't honestly think I'd leave my only son and heir behind?'

'I presume he has no more say in the matter than I do?'

'Hugo can't manage this estate in his condition, which is why it's up for sale.'

'All the same...'

'You can ask him yourself. He's in the orangery where he always is.'

'Thank you, I will.'

Since her stay in a sanatorium, Primrose has aged terribly. She wipes white hair out of her eyes and proves quite clumsy as she opens a purse with cut steel beads, silvery pearls and half-inch white spangles. Next minute she pulls something shiny from its ivory satin lining.

'I don't really hate you, you do know that, don't you, Jolantha? I just want what's best for you...'

'I didn't come here expecting a cosy chat.'

'Nevertheless, I want you to have this. It's for the baby.'

'Sorry?'

'Please, my dear, take it. I want Jacqueline to keep something of mine, should anything happen to me.'

'God forbid. What is it?'

In her hand is a velvet bracelet decorated with raised glass bead flowers. Its clasp is gilt with green stones. I've seen prettier.

'Jacqueline might like it when she's older, my dear.'

'This is the child you wanted killed.'

'You always make me sound so cruel when I was only trying to protect you from yourself. It's not easy for a woman to bring up a child on her own, especially a…a….'

'Black one?'

'Don't be too hard on me, Jolantha, I can't bear it.'

'Neither can I, I'm going to find my brother.'

As I move past her I deposit the bracelet back in her hand. I know it's not kind, but I'm in no mood for her superior charity. I'm only here to get what I need to make something else right.

***

The orangery is a haven of light and tranquillity after the big house's gloomy corners and echoes. Almost immediately, I see a young man tending to semi-dwarf, citrus fruit trees in pots – he's watering them by guesswork and feel. Heat from a paraffin stove warms the air as I close the door behind me.

I've not taken two steps inside the great glass conservatory when his voice booms. 'I'd recognise the sound of my beloved Brough Combination anywhere.'

'Nice to see you, too, brother.'

'Do I get a hug?'

His lips on my cheek are more miss than hit because he can't see to kiss, but I don't mind.

'If you sit down I'll give you Jacqueline to hold.'

'At last I get to cuddle the latest addition to the family.'

'I'm sorry it's been so long.'

'I take it you've met mother?'

233

'She ambushed me on my way in.'

'Where's that grumpy dog of yours? Where's the adorable Bella?'

There's a loud woof. Bella knows he will be all pats and snuggles. In return she is all licks and kisses.

'She's missed you, Hugo. That makes two of us.'

'Her coat doesn't grow back, does it?'

I replace dog with child on his lap. 'She'll never lose the scars from when she nearly burned alive, I'm afraid.'

Hugo gives Jacqueline his thumb to hold after I make them both comfortable in his big wicker chair. 'What about your scars, Jo? Or has Jacky finally cured your bad dreams?'

'I'm not here to talk about me, I want to know about you? How do you feel? Are you coping better? You were a bit down when we last spoke on the phone.'

'The night trainers from Little Rissington frequently buzz us and the rumble of planes in the sky reminds me of my tank when it got hit. It's been a very busy year. Lots of arrivals and departures both for Flying Training and Coastal Command. A great many Wellington bombers are being stored nearby, mostly Marks III, X, XIII and XIV. This war has definitely taken a turn for the better if the RAF doesn't need them any more.'

'Honestly, though, do you really want to quit this place? Mother told me you're moving out as soon as Monday.'

Hugo stares straight past me. It's slightly unnerving, but he's locating where I am with his ears – his sense of hearing is now his seeing.

'She wants to incarcerate me here to keep me safe, but it's killing me. I can't spend the rest of my days tending to oranges and lemons at a constant temperature of 55 degrees Fahrenheit just to make them fruit. You ran away years ago, so why can't I? I can lead my own life again, I know I can, somewhere new. That's why I'm insisting we sell.'

'*You're* insisting.'

'Mother may make a fuss and pretend to be appalled that the RAF have dug up half the estate for their all-weather runways, but deep down she knows that she and father are too old to manage this place forever.'

I wish I could have shown you my childhood home, dear Sidney, I wish you could have met my fearless Hugo. I never told you much about my family, did I? I was never that forthcoming, not least because I was afraid you'd dismiss me as a spoilt, rich child who might not share your liberal views. If only it were so simple.

Jacqueline wriggles in Hugo's arms, burps and smiles. It's odd to think he'll never be able to see, only know her, yet in some ways it's his greatest strength. If we got to *know* more people instead of dismissing or vilifying them at first sight, we might not be fighting this war now.

'Does our father still have his guns? Is he still shooting pheasants?'

Hugo is too busy cuddling Jacqueline to reply for a moment, or he detects something 'off' in my voice.

'It's the season for it, if that's what you mean.'

'It's been a while since I shot so much as a rabbit.'

He smiles and blank white eyes seem to shine – they could be made of snow or stone. 'My own shooting days are over, I'm afraid.'

'Do you remember that day when we borrowed father's Webley service revolver and took pot shots at flowerpots in the kitchen garden?'

'The head gardener was furious.'

'Don't see why. We hardly hit a thing. That old gun looks fantastic but it's bloody inaccurate over any distance.'

'It made a superb noise, though, didn't it?'

'I don't suppose father still has it?'

'Of course he does. He tells everyone he keeps it in his office in case the 'Jerries' walk through the door at any minute.'

'You received an awful thrashing for letting me use it.'

'Are you in trouble, Jo?'

I throw Bella the fallen lemon she has just brought me. My aim is a bit off, unfortunately. The 'ball' ricochets against an orange tree, to get lost among other potted trees. It's my turn to smile as casually as I can.

'I'm fine. Really I am.'

That German grenade may have blasted Hugo's eyes, but his lips can still curl in disdain. Also, he knows me too well.

'I said, are you in trouble, Jo?'

'Somebody saw me when Sidney Sheppard and his wife fell out of the triforium in Gloucester Cathedral. Now I think that same someone means to come after me.'

'What makes you so sure?'

'I'm being watched. At first I thought it was a private detective or even a regular one, only now I'm not so sure.'

'Have you told the police?'

'They're not exactly on my side.'

'If only I weren't so useless. If only I could look out for you like I always did.'

'Well, you can't. I have to protect myself and my baby all by myself. I've grown up a lot recently.'

'You don't really think someone will hurt Jacqueline, do you, Jo?'

'I can't say.'

'How could it come to this? How can you be so involved?'

'Someone died because of me.'

'Nonsense. Forget the silly coroner's verdict. That fall has to be either accident or suicide.'

'But I'm the one who has to live with the consequences…'

Hugo bounces a laughing Jacqueline on his knee. 'A gun is a bad idea. You're not helping yourself.'

'Are you on my side, or not?'

'Of course I am, but you'll need to get into father's desk in the estate office.'

'Damn, I didn't think of that.'

'Don't worry, I expect he still keeps the key in the usual place. I'll help you on one condition.'

'What's that?'

'Tell me all about my Brough Superior. How's it handling? Did you do that decarb it needed?'

'I did.'

'Then you must take me for a spin round the estate before you leave.'

'First I need to top up its petrol tank with more red fuel from the farm. I've brought a couple of extra cans to fill, too. Will this ban on private motorists never end? Only someone like you can get the necessary 'motor spirit' tokens.' But I'm really wondering how many .455 cartridges I need for my service pistol, for when my stalker and I come face to face any time soon.

FORTY-TWO

'Not again, detective?' Superintendent Beal sucked hard on his cigarette and eyed his visitor with suspicion. 'Seriously, what's wrong now?'

DS Biggs revolved the rim of his hat in his hands in the gloomy office of the administration block of Coney Hill Mental Hospital. 'Something urgent has come up, I'm afraid, sir.'

'But I told you absolutely everything I know about Jolantha Wheeler last time you called.'

'She might not be the one.'

'How so, detective?'

'I have recorded in my notebook that Jolantha was admitted to this hospital on June 8th and discharged on the 20th of September 1942. Did she have many visitors while she was here, as you recall?'

'Her father came regularly, but not her mother.'

'Any others?'

'Not many. Does it matter?'

'I need names. Do you have a visitors' book for the relevant period?'

'Really, detective, you do know how to waste a person's time.'

Superintendent Beal rose reluctantly from his shiny oak chair, then walked over to a row of wooden filing cabinets full of patients' records. There he began examining labelled drawers with a deep sigh at each one.

Meanwhile DS Biggs chewed the end of his pencil. The view from the window was all trees and driveway, a scenic approach to a vast array of wards, kitchens, workshops and farms. There was something unforgettably military about this outpost of humanity, a front line between the sick and the sane. His eye suddenly came to rest on an album of cigarette cards that lay open on the sill. Here, obviously, was a kindred spirit who regretted the paper shortage and the consequent lack of free pictures the same way he did – he counted several blanks where flowers should have been as he thumbed empty pages.

Superintendent Beal slammed a leather-bound ledger on his desk. 'This'll be the year you need, detective.'

'Look for Sidney Sheppard with two 'p's.'

'Sidney Sheppard? The dead man in the cathedral? Why him?'

'Just do as I say.'

'I'm afraid we don't encourage visitors, detective. It unsettles the patients.'

'Can you see his name anywhere?'

'Not right now.'

'Should I look for you?'

'Did I say I needed any help?'

'Just asking.'

Superintendent Beal shut the ledger and looked up. 'Sorry, detective. Nothing.'

'Give it here. I'll look myself.'

'You can't do that.'

'Oh yes I can,' he said and began thumbing the pages for 1942 again, except the superintendent was quite right: very few people bothered to visit sick relatives, they just left them here to soldier on alone. He gave a sigh of his own. There was absolutely no sign of Sidney Sheppard. He hadn't been seeing some other patient when their paths crossed, he hadn't given her some passing smile to ignite her dangerous infatuation... Wherever Jolantha had first started stalking him, it wasn't here.

Superintendent Beal looked at the clock on the wall. 'Now if that'll be all for today detective?'

'Sorry to have bothered you.'

'Goodbye, detective.'

'There is just one other thing that occurs to me. Do patients ever make friends with their fellow patients while in hospital? Did Jolantha? Or was she literally that much of a loner?'

'There is one person.'

'Who?'

'Captain Hector Knevitt.'

'The escapee? What's he got to do with anything?'

'She and Hector knew each other from her early days in Bristol. He visited her shop to buy newspapers and shared her passion for motorcycles. Jolantha took pity on him, I think, because of his injuries sustained in The Great War. She gave him sweets and was generally nice to him. When she fell ill, he returned the favour.'

'And you mention this now?'

Superintendent Beal glanced at the clock on the wall again. Any minute it would be time for lunch which was a tricky period on the wards – a careless nurse could soon find themselves faced with a stampede of hungry people. He was always a little tense until the dinner bell stopped ringing. 'You didn't ask.'

DS Biggs felt his own nerves jangle, but for different reasons.

'Where is this Hector Knevitt now? Let me speak to him.'

'He hasn't returned to us yet.'

'Anything I need to know?'

'I told you, detective, the Captain is a voluntary patient who comes and goes to his private bungalow in the grounds.'

'Anything I need to do?'

'It's out of my hands, but as I keep saying, he's not what I would consider 'crazy'. If you want to see someone driven mad, I could introduce you to a sixty-year-old patient of mine called Martha Jones. The Victorians sliced off both her feet when she was a baby because she was born with club toes. That's madness for you. Theirs, not hers. I like to think we've moved on since then.'

'I know it's asking a lot, but would you say that Hector and Jolantha were close?'

'We have separate male and female wards…'

'What about the gardens? Your patients might fraternise there, surely?'

'There is one incident I recall. Staff were escorting a few patients, male and female, across the grounds as a car was motoring slowly towards them along the drive. Its driver stopped to let everybody cross the road, which they all did except Jolantha and Hector. When a nurse went back and tried to take him by his arm to rejoin the others, he shook her off and threw her to the ground. The nurse cut her lip and strained her wrist. I had to record it in the accident book.'

'Yet you made nothing more of it?'

'Patients have their peculiarities – Hector doesn't like being touched or told what to do.'

'Or he wouldn't leave Jolantha to cross the road alone?'

'As I said, he's quite harmless. He inherited a small fortune when his father died and feels it necessary to spend it on his health. He has also donated cash to build additional chalets in the grounds for other paying patients. He stays with us whenever he feels low. His spell in the trenches… well, you can understand it never goes away.'

'Or Hector admitted himself to get close to Jo?'

Superintendent Beal's eyelids fluttered; his pupils stared; his lips opened and closed. Several deep furrows crossed his brow.

'To do what, detective?'

DS Biggs pencilled frantic notes on his pad. That chill in his spine just rose several vertebrae. 'Hector Knevitt hurled that nurse to the ground to protect his sweetheart.'

'Oh no, detective. You've got it all wrong. He was never in love with Jolantha Wheeler. I already told you – he writes endless passionate letters to someone called Violet. Please don't waste any more of my time on him.'

'You've wasted mine.'

'Whatever do you mean?'

'Did it never occur to you that Jolantha is a variant spelling of the Greek name Iolanthe?'

Superintendent Beal raised his eyebrows. 'You're acquainted with classical myths, detective?'

'Not exactly. Someone mentioned it to me in passing…'

'Then they also told you that Iolanthe was a sea nymph and a daughter of Oceanus?'

'That may not be the point.'

'I still don't see the relevance to Jolantha, detective.'

'Iolanthe is the Greek word for "blue flower".'

'All right, what?'

'Violets are blue, are they not? You can read all about them on page five of your cigarette card album over there by the window.'

FORTY-THREE

I don't know how long I can continue sitting here, dear Sidney, in The Monks' Retreat Bar as I flick my Zippo lighter at a fresh cigarette. It's not as if I'm in disguise in my black lace cocktail dress with its peach-pink slip – it's not as though I'm not feeling sexy in my daywear shoes made from strong black calf with reptile trim. I guess you could say I'm daring the police to come and get me. I wish they would because I have things to tell them. I'm not alone. Half Gloucester is down here in the 'crypt' beneath The Fleece Hotel, it's so noisy and crowded in the vaulted undercroft.

Any other night I might be 'fishing' for dates. American GIs rub shoulders with WAAFs and Land Girls. All talk is about the ongoing invasion of Europe. How soon to Berlin? I'm more than slightly tipsy as I upend a bottle of stout – my third – to my lips, while at my feet Bella sighs and places her nose on her paws.

'Shouldn't you be getting home?' John strokes his thin black moustache and rolls his big eyes at me. It's a rhetorical question since we already know the answer – he asked me the same thing half an hour ago.

'Mrs O'Brien never goes to bed before midnight.'

'All the same, Jacqueline must be missing her mum…'

'I don't like to be on my own, ever since I've started carrying my gun.'

'You know what I think about that. It turns out meeting Sidney was the worst mistake of your life.'

I stare at the line of green-painted beer barrels that prop up the bar and wonder if I should brave the throng to fetch another round of Guinness. 'I still can't believe he isn't coming back. It doesn't seem possible.'

'Then call it a day?'

'Somebody has to be held to account for what happened and we both know who.' I pinch finger and thumb in the air. 'I'm this close to plucking up the courage.'

'It's not as if Marjorie can defend herself…'

'So?'

'So why are you doing it, Jo? It can't be for justice?'

'I've had enough of losing people I love. Don't forget I was a real bride once. Who'll want me now?'

'You can't stay wed to the dead.'

'The dead don't choose to abandon us, John, it's we who abandon them. No one can die unless we let them. Can they?'

'You talk as if the living and the deceased want the same thing? Isn't that a bit scary?'

I wriggle hard on my chair. Suddenly the stone arches of the undercroft seem far too low. I'm sweating profusely.

'The dead don't frighten me.'

'What if they should?'

My brain is reeling and I know my speech is slurred. All this talk of ghosts sees my thoughts fly back instantly to Bristol and its Blitz in 1940….

I close my eyes and straightaway I'm fighting my way through bombed streets – I'm doing it to feel closer to the slaughtered, which is where you are, dear Sidney, you're in a world where those who still live and breathe are unrequired…

I'm straight back in Castle Street four years ago, in my previous existence. What does it take not to feel totally banished from all I've lost? Alcohol does that to me, it lets me revisit a wasteland of thoughts, sights and feelings that don't belong this side of the grave. My husband Jack and I are standing in the Regent Cinema's Crush Hall inside the main entrance – we love to walk up the wide staircase to the auditorium and stand beneath the impressive dome that now lies shattered in a million pieces. We order food and drink from the Tea Lounge and arrange to have it brought to us on a neat, little tray. He and I can't wait to snuggle up together to watch a film.

I'm picking my way past red, purple and gold paint on the walls and ivory pillars whose fierce griffins taunt each other with their gilded beaks at the end of the balcony. In my mind I can see the organist seated at his organ, playing something suitably dramatic, but it's all over now. No music plays in the smoky debris. The cinema's mighty steel and concrete walls might have preserved its skeletal shape, but the audience is long gone.

Because there's something I have yet to tell you, dear Sidney. As it happened, Jack and I left Emmy with his mother while we watched 'Rebecca' on Saturday, the 23rd of November. The fire bombs pierced the cinema's dome twenty-four hours later. It seems so perverse for the three of us to cheat death one day only for Jack and Emmy to die the next, in the comfort of their own home while I sat in church on Sunday. Why did God spare me, only to have me suffer ever afterwards? Since then I've learnt that, for the first time, films had been scheduled to be shown throughout the following weekend which would have been carnage – we're talking about 2,014 seats with more standing room for another two hundred or so at the back of the stalls…

John is trying to say something to me, but I'm too busy searching for something familiar. It's a smell. Lower Castle Street always exuded exotic scents such as pomades, brilliantines, liquid shampoos, paraffins, lime creams and all kinds of toilet goods. I'm outside the Eclipsol Laboratories, except they're all gone as if the whole place has covered itself in one of its own vanishing creams.

I'm looking for Mrs Sarah Hayball's sweets and tobacconist store at No. 38. Like my own shop, though, hers has been flattened too. At No. 40, on the corner of Ellbroad Street, I can once more envisage myself entering the "Rising Sun". I dream of standing at its long narrow bar that runs along its Lower Castle Street side. At five storeys high it stands tall and defiant – I don't know how it has managed to survive so well…

The curve of the castle wall is where I go when I enter Broad Weir, I'm doubling back on myself because if I were a ghost this is the route I'd take now – I'd be forever bound by the limits of where my husband and daughter died in this, the oldest part of the city. Four people stand one above the other on the rungs of a very long ladder as someone else passes them an undamaged mirror from an upper window of a gutted building. Union Street isn't much better. Facades have collapsed and interiors have gone until shops resemble empty brick boxes. On the air comes the taint of burnt cloth and singed leather. A delivery van lies abandoned with its driver's door wide open and its bonnet buried nose down in the road....

I'm treading six inches of ash deposited by red-hot storms that have whipped though windowless buildings – these are not fires as anyone knows them but some hellish tornado that has flung tiles and timbers to the wind and scattered bricks about like the devil's playthings. It's not all gloom and doom. One sign reads: WE ARE CLOSED FOR DURATION OF WAR. HAVE GONE TO SERVE TROOPS IN OUR TRADE CAPACITY. WE SHALL RE-OPEN WHEN HITLER'S FINISHED.

You'll think me hopelessly sentimental and stubborn, dear Sidney, but I'm looking for BELFIELD'S in Union Street where I'm trying to buy Emmy's first Christmas present. A few flimsily made paper and card toys still line its window while the roof is missing. When I look through the door I see myself just before disaster struck... John says reliving my memories like this only fuels my burning, even murderous anger. But how do I stop, now you're not with me, my love, to put out the fire? I'm burning in my own private hell.

I keep going. That's the point about dreams, they continue to roll from a never-ending reel – I'm obliged to watch night after night an all too familiar film of my own making, only to relive the same horrors with the same bitter ending...

But to revisit the lost is to forge a connection. By learning to walk and talk with my own family I'll soon learn how to walk and talk with you, my love? We'll finally share the same language?

Because they're all like you, dear Sidney, they're waiting. This is what they are. This is what they want – to see me on the other side.

'Your love for Sidney didn't kill him, Jo, if that's what you're thinking? In the same way, your love for Jack and Emmy didn't get them bombed.'

It's John again, shaking me out of my drunken reverie.

'What? Oh, well, no, but...'

'You have to stop thinking you can freeze time. None of this will go away until you let it all go.'

My cigarette, I realise, has burned to ash in my fingers.

'Except the police won't let me drop it now. They absolutely think I'm a killer.'

'What did you think would happen, since you've started acting so oddly?'

FORTY-FOUR

CONEY HILL MENTAL HOSPITAL

Dear Violet, you know better than I do what happened, how you abandoned me as soon as you left hospital, how you fell for or became infatuated by your GI. When that didn't work out, you did it again with Sidney: you ignored our love and then vilified me.

Yet long before that, as I've said before, you told me in Bristol, 'You're the kindest man I know.' I knew then that I was the right one for you. It was such a lovely and reassuring thing for you to say to me that I felt all was well between us – well, wouldn't you? In fact, I'm sure it was and so far as I know (and certainly you have not told me otherwise) it still is.

You may well blame me for our parting, yet to do so belies not only the facts but my dozens of letters to you over the years. For all that I have said or done we can still be married by the time this war ends. It was you who found other lovers, not me. It was all so unexpected by me and I was not even given a hearing. It is equally reasonable to say you were hoping to rekindle our passion when, on one of my visits to you in hospital, you told me that I would always be your dearest love.

Never mind that you could wound, betray and abandon me with never a twinge of conscience. Well, my darling, this war marches inexorably on, but bittersweet memories remain and always will till the end of time. Any damage done, it is my most earnest intention to repair.

We'll be wed soon. Only then will we be happy ever after. Love, H.

FORTY-FIVE

I'm sitting on the floor in my bath before the fire in the parlour – after my shift at the Shirt Factory, the infernal racket of sewing machines no longer clatters in my ears. I can feel the few inches of water growing colder under my knees as I listen to loose tiles drip rain in the attic. None of these modest, Victorian houses in this part of Gloucester are in brilliant shape, to say the least, but is it only mine that has to leak like a sieve?

There's a cruel draught blowing smoke back down the parlour's chimney and I'm running short of coal again. I've taken Bella for a walk and collected Jacqueline from Mrs O'Brien next door. There's no fire watch duty for me at the cathedral tonight and I've put the bin on the pavement ready for the ashman to empty in the morning.

What I should really do is light the spring-loaded candle in my Arctic lamp and go up to my bedroom where Jacqueline is asleep in her makeshift cot. But I don't. Instead, I rest my head on the metal rim of the bath and look into the fire's dim coals where I dream of you, dear Sidney. I must have fallen asleep because when I wake I feel terribly, unbelievably chilled. But it's not just cold skin that strikes dread into my bones – I can hear Bella barking frantically elsewhere in the house.

My first instinct is burglars. Many a home gets robbed these days on these dimmed streets and I fear the worst. I'm out of my bath in a jiffy with only a towel round my chest.

'Bella? What's wrong?'

There's a great deal of noise coming from the scullery and then a yelp.

I call again.

But that's not enough.

I'm advancing through the darkness when I should fetch my gun before proceeding so rashly…

As it is, I'm weaponless.

Still want to go?

I walk more slowly into the scullery.

Don't make me regret this.

Everything has gone quiet except Bella – she's lying panting on the worn linoleum… I'm fumbling about trying to light the gas mantle on the wall. I can see what looks like blood oozing from her mouth where she has been struck on the head with something heavy…

So far I'm rushing about with no thought for my safety.

I retrieve the fallen flat iron from the floor, ready to use it on whoever lurks in the shadows.

The scullery door stands wide open to the freezing night. My No. 8 torch is on the table – I use my teeth to tear off its blackout tape and shine its white beam at the cobbles, privy and Anderson Shelter in the yard beyond, but to no avail.

Whoever broke in just escaped over the brick wall?

What have they stolen?

Do I even want to know?

My priority is Bella. I pick her up very gently and cradle her in my arms. She's breathing far too quickly and rolling her eyes. As far as I can tell, she could be dying.

Fact is, I have only myself to blame. I should never have dozed off in my bath. Suddenly I'm at sixes and sevens. I should have thought of it before…

I'm up the bare wooden steps to my bedroom in a few leaps and bounds.

I'm holding Bella in my arms, but she's not my baby. I'm kneeling aghast before the drawer-cum-cot on the floor and frantically raking both ends with my hand.

It's worse than I thought.

Jacqueline is gone.

FORTY-SIX

DI Lockett had it all worked out, even if his sour-faced driver did openly disapprove. 'Drive straight in, sergeant. What are you waiting for?'

DS Biggs steered the police car through a pair of somewhat forbidding, black and gold Gothic gates and started up the red-gravelled drive. Monkey puzzles grew into ugly, twisted shapes on each side of them – their spiny, leaf-like scales resembled claws in the rain. They had at last arrived at Cassel Hospital and Nursing Home in Stoke-on-Trent. 'Does this place give you the creeps, sir? It does me.'

'Don't worry, sergeant. With any luck it'll be worth it.'

'You really think it will tell us more about Jo Wheeler?'

'Sidney Sheppard spent six months in Ash Hall, recovering his sanity. Wherever he goes, she follows.'

'Concerning Captain Hector Knevitt, sir...?'

'We're about to prove one thing and one thing only, that Jolantha is a very dangerous and calculating person. What better way to do so than to talk to doctors who have witnessed her in action? If she has come here making wild accusations about how her dead lover was treated, she must have made a strong impression on somebody – she will have let slip her mask, I'm sure. We'll be able to confirm she's more criminal than crazy.'

'I just think...'

'All in good time, sergeant. If Hector Knevitt has known Jolantha for five or six years, ever since he visited her sweetshop in Bristol, why would he present a threat to her now? What's changed?'

He took an increasingly behavioural attitude towards Jolantha. If she wasn't crazy, she had to know exactly what she was doing. Nothing

251

therapeutic could save her. He was here to challenge her sense of omnipotence. Call it intuition. It's who he was.

DS Biggs was no longer listening. His buttocks ached from hours of driving, but that wasn't why he slammed his foot on the brake. The Austin 10 skidded to a halt in a slither of stones as his eyes nearly popped out his head. A large red Dennis Pump Escape fire engine blocked the way.

'What the hell!'

DI Lockett was equally lost for words. 'Just when I thought things could only get better.'

'Do we stay or go, sir?'

'I want answers.'

They abandoned the police car in a hurry and advanced side by side towards the three turntable ladders and labyrinthine hoses that surrounded the burning building ahead. Tongues of flame licked at oriel windows and pointed gables where the conflagration had taken hold in the building's roof despite the showery rain. Firemen from the newly formed National Fire Service walked the Hall's Flemish parapets and sprayed jets of water over scorched balustrades – smoke spiralled from gable-lit attics in whose slates they were punching holes to reach blazing rafters. DI Lockett's first thought was that it had been hit by a bomb. Into his nostrils came the acrid smell of soot and cinders. He made as if to hasten towards the three Gothic arches, turrets and battlements of the front portico, when he felt a hand on his arm.

'It's no good, sir, the whole place is a gonner...'

'Uh-huh.' He changed tack and made a beeline instead for a red bus-like vehicle that was parked on the lawn. A door stood open in one of its windowless sides on whose bodywork he read Emergency Tender/Control Unit. 'Who's in charge here?' he demanded, thrusting his head and shoulders inside the doorway.

A smoke-blackened fireman, dressed in waterproof tunic and trousers, looked up from a table on which lay plans of the hospital and gardens. 'Who wants to know?'

He flashed his warrant card in the air. 'My name is Detective Inspector Lockett from the Gloucestershire Police.'

'Can't you see I'm busy?'

'I'm here to investigate a possible connection between a recent patient and someone called Mrs Jolantha Wheeler.'

Goggles had given the Fire Control Officer's sooty face white saucers for eyes. 'It's too soon for that. We have the blaze contained, but I can't yet declare the building safe to enter. Doctors only just evacuated all patients in time.'

'We talking German rocket?'

'Absolutely not.'

'So it could be arson?'

'All these heavy blackout curtains at the windows are a real hazard...'

'I didn't ask that. Is it or isn't it?'

The officer scowled. 'That's what I'm investigating right now, Inspector. I'm trying to pinpoint exactly how and where the fire started.'

'So you're not ruling out an accident?'

'As I said, all these black curtains burn so damned easily...'

'When will you know?'

'By tomorrow we should be able to sift through the ashes.'

'But I...?'

The Fire Control Officer waved him back out of the truck. 'Ask me again in the morning.'

DI Lockett stopped to unscrew the lid of his baccyflap and began to refill his black Bakelite pipe with Fine Shag tobacco. Meanwhile DS Biggs watched firemen use their axes to expose more blackened timbers.

'You look as if you could do with a cup of tea, sir.'

He kept walking. 'I need to take a look for myself.'

'You don't have to do this now, sir. Better come back when things are a bit calmer.'

'Don't you start.'

DI Lockett led the way to the terrace at the back of the house and stood there gazing out over the surrounding countryside towards Bucknall and Hanley.

'Nice view,' said DS Biggs, ignoring the scene of mayhem behind them. 'If I were ill I wouldn't mind being treated here myself. It seems so tranquil.'

'Don't be a fool, sergeant. This place is full of people who've lost control over their lives. On the surface I bet they can seem nice and stable, but next minute they're wracked with insecurity which makes them highly unpredictable.'

DS Biggs frowned. His boss's mood of semi-confidentiality today was something he didn't dare fathom.

'We should try over there, sir. By the look of it the fire hasn't spread to those outbuildings.'

Several nurses sheltered under umbrellas outside a service wing which was attached to the right of the Hall.

'Excuse me, I'm Detective Inspector Lockett. I'm here to see Dr Andratschke.'

A smoke-stained nurse peered at him from under her umbrella. 'All doctors have gone to the police station to give statements.'

'In that case I'd like to know what you witnessed…'

'Can't you see? Someone tried to burn everything down last night.'

'Who would want to do that?'

A fellow nurse with singed hair and eyebrows chipped in. 'It seems the caretaker heard a noise in the night and went to investigate. He saw someone dart across the terrace…'

'Man or woman?'

'Whoever it was wore leathers, helmet and goggles, but they got clean away on a motorcycle.'

DI Lockett shot a look at DS Biggs who said nothing. Then he focused on the nurse again. 'Was it a motorcycle and sidecar, by any chance?'

'Yes, it was.'

'Did anyone get the registration?'

'No, it was too dark.'

'Where is this caretaker now? What's he called?'

'His name is Jim Whittaker. He's with the other witnesses at the police station.'

'Thank you. You've been most helpful.'

He returned at once to their Austin 10. 'What did I tell you, sergeant?

Jolantha was here. She set fire to Ash Hall, mark my words. She came here last night looking for trouble and this is what she does.'

'So we corroborate what the caretaker says he saw, do we, sir?' asked DS Biggs, as he sat in the driver's seat and clasped the steering wheel.

'No need. We have what we want.'

'Aren't we at least going to tell the Staffordshire Police everything we know?'

'Don't see why a lot of Midlanders should get all the credit. Now let's drive, shall we?'

'Is the sighting of someone on a motorcycle combination enough to say it was Jolantha, sir? I don't think so.'

'It's enough for me.'

'You do recall that Hector Knevitt has a passion for motorbikes, too?'

But he was a man inspired. He exhaled hard on his pipe to fill the car with thick clouds of blue smoke.

'I haven't forgotten, sergeant. Hector is as unhinged as Jolantha, but I don't think they're in this together, do you?'

'In what, exactly, sir?'

'When love between two people is somehow prevented or forbidden, it can lead to a frustration that borders on madness. It's not the love that's crazy, it's the not-loving. Jolantha behaves like a cheated sweetheart. Fate has been doubly unkind to her. People have been unkind to her. That takes some forgiving. This isn't love any more, it's a mania.'

So saying, he popped the stem of his pipe back in his mouth and worked his hot cheeks again like a pair of bellows.

DS Biggs didn't reply – he only wound down his car window as fast as he could before he started choking.

FORTY-SEVEN

'I'll ask you again. Where were you between the hours of six and seven a.m. on the day in question?'

The directness of DI Lockett's inquiry completely throws me. I need time to think. I'm in his office in Bearland Police Station to report my missing baby, not answer questions on where I spent my weekend. Glossy brilliantine lends a sheen to his hair that gives off a strong aroma of scented violet, or is it white lilac – he smells too nice to be a policeman? As he jabs his finger at my face, the bare bulb above us catches an impressive, mother-of-pearl stud on his shirt cuff with its sapphire centre. He's looking and sounding very sure of himself, I must say.

Everything I've done so far has been about you, dear Sidney, about getting you justice. Suddenly it's all about Jacqueline. I don't know what else I should be doing since I found her cot empty. It's all an awful mess-up. At least Bella was only bruised and bloodied and not bludgeoned to death. If she's rather quiet at my feet right now, it's only to be expected.

'What does Sunday morning have to do with anything, Inspector? Jacqueline hasn't been seen for the last two hours. I need you to go after whoever has taken her... Now.'

A peculiar look fills his brown eyes; his hands tremble; his chest expands inside his buff-coloured cardigan, so much so that he frees the top two of its buttons to relieve the pressure. It's sheer anger, evidently.

'You know what I think, Mrs Wheeler? I think you've hurt your baby the same way you set fire to Ash Hall Nursing Home.'

'You're not making any sense. What do I care about any fire? I need to find Jacqueline.'

'Did you, or did you not, drown Frederick Sheppard at Thorney Weir?'

'Who, me?'

'Did you push Mrs Tuffley off a cliff the same way you pushed Marjorie Sheppard out of the triforium in Gloucester Cathedral?'

I reach for my packet of cigarettes in my red, fox fur coat. I cross and uncross my black calf shoes with reptile trim and fire up my Zippo lighter – I'm steadying my nerves with a ciggy so as not to scream. 'You really need to ask me that?'

'Do you deny being in the vicinity?'

'Could prove nothing.'

'We've been on your trail wherever you go, Mrs Wheeler. We've seen you systematically hunt down Sidney's family, friends and doctors one by one.'

'Listen to me, Inspector, I've just walked through the door of my own free will, haven't I? I'm here voluntarily. I'm simply begging you to help me find Jacqueline before something bad happens to her…'

'We know you threatened Mr Wallis in his own home.'

'So what? He's a snob and social climber.'

'No, he's a perfectly respectable citizen of Esher in Surrey.'

'Same thing.'

The only way I can make this right is to find Jacqueline. Instead of which, I'm trapped in this dreadful interview room with this incompetent imbecile who thinks he's got me beat with his tactless questions.

'Several people have died or suffered horribly since the day of Sidney's fall, Mrs Wheeler, yet you don't seem very concerned. On the contrary, you threatened and stole from them. Isn't that a bit odd?'

'I haven't said I'm innocent.'

'So you're admitting it's you? You set out to kill four people?'

'No, I'm definitely not saying that.'

'So it isn't you?'

'You know I'll never tell you, even if it is.'

DI Lockett goes to fill his pipe from his baccyflap. He shows a great deal more tender consideration for his shitty piece of black Bakelite than he does me. The longer we sit here wasting time, the further my baby's kidnapper is getting away.

'You think the world revolves round you, Mrs Wheeler, but you're wrong. I'm going to keep you here until you confess to your crimes. No confession, no daughter.'

'I'm not sure that'll do it.'

Actually I'm not as confident as I sound. My baby is missing! Why does it feel as if I'm the only one taking this seriously?

'You bear a grudge against Sidney, his friends and his family. That goes for his wife and her family, too. You hate them all. Why is that? Did he break some promise or other to you? You should tell me everything immediately.'

This chair I'm sitting on feels much too rigid and hard suddenly – it's no way to treat a distressed mother. 'Why should I tell you? What good will that do?'

'I'll be the judge of that.'

'Sidney and I were madly in love. We were going to run away and get married any day now. That's all you need to know.'

'Except he wasn't about to divorce his wife for you without one hell of a fight, was he?'

'Don't say that! Don't ever say that!'

For such a well-groomed detective DI Lockett appears strangely louche as he fixes me firmly in the eye. 'This great passion of yours didn't turn into paradise, Mrs Wheeler, it turned into torture. Sidney didn't *want* you as his bride if he could keep Marjorie. You misread the situation completely. Is that why you pushed man and wife out of the triforium? It is, isn't it, because you felt so jealous and betrayed?'

'If you could see into my heart, you'd know.'

'Your black heart.'

'You know what I think, Inspector? I think I'm done here. Charge me or let me go. I need to look for Jacqueline.'

'Let's start again at the beginning. Why did you steal a box of photographs and postcards from Dorothy Sheppard at 149, Waverley Avenue?'

'I should have asked, I admit.'

'Please answer the question.'

'I knew it was a bad idea, but I couldn't bear to feel I was losing Sidney.

I don't know what else I thought I was doing.'

'Don't tell me you weren't gathering information on his friends and family to do them some harm.'

'Are you deaf? I don't know why I did it, I tell you.'

DI Lockett bangs his desk and scatters his pens. I'm horrified. An untidy desk equals an untidy mind in my opinion. 'I want to help you, Jolantha, I really do.'

'Then send every policeman you have to scour the city for my daughter.'

'Truth is, you lied to us about when and where you met Sidney. You failed to tell us that you already knew who Marjorie was when you came face to face with her in the cathedral. Nor did you tell us that you voluntarily admitted yourself to Coney Hill Mental Hospital. Instead, you blamed your mother.'

'Are you calling me a liar?'

'You've lied to us about things you had no reason to lie about, right from the start. Any idea why that might be?'

'I can't even pretend to know what you're getting at.'

'Here's what I think, Mrs Wheeler. Your own spell in a mental hospital has left you with a grudge against those who gave you Ediswan Electric Convulsion treatment to induce seizures in your brain? That's why you identify so closely with Sidney who experienced similar advanced treatments – in his case doctors tore out all his teeth in a vain attempt to curtail his bouts of vomiting. That *is* why you went all the way to Stoke-on-Trent in order to burn down Ash Hall Nursing Home, isn't it – you wanted to get back at Sidney's doctors on his behalf? To settle a grudge of your own?'

'*Interesting.*'

DI Lockett squints at me through the haze of smoke that pervades the air. Anyone would think I suddenly don't like him.

'Okay, but I do have one other suggestion for you. This all really begins with the Bristol Blitz in 1940, doesn't it? It destroyed your family, your mental health and your livelihood. You act like a grieving widow of one man – Sidney Sheppard – when you're really grieving for another one, Jack Wheeler. After you lost your husband you took a GI for a lover, but since

D-Day he's gone missing in action. Sidney was meant to heal all that, only he ratted on you at the last minute, didn't he? When you heard him refuse to sign those divorce papers something in you flipped. It wasn't planned. You gave in to a momentary rage.'

'Bullshit.'

'Jolantha Wheeler, I'm arresting you on the suspicion of …'

But I'm out of my chair and through the door in seconds.

I can't believe anyone can be so cruel and unsympathetic as to deny me some credit in all this. I can't believe he can dismiss all my hopes and happiness. Not in that way.

DI Lockett is slower than I am – he's not as slick as his hair-do suggests. 'Stop her!'

Except I have everyone at a disadvantage. Many a younger policeman has been called up to serve in the army, to be replaced by compulsory conscription into the force. These Police War Reserve men aren't too quick off the mark, either, what with the recent dreadful increase in crime – they're all too busy trying to catch up on their paperwork to stop me in time.

I hit the street running. Whoever's been shadowing my every move really has convinced the inspector of my guilt? I have to admit I didn't see that coming. I thought I was smarter than that.

I'm going home to see if anyone has discovered anything yet about Jacqueline. Only I have a better idea. DI Lockett is determined to prove he's been right about me from the very beginning. I can't allow that. I must think what to do.

Who'd believe it? He actually intends to see me hang in Gloucester Prison instead of Marjorie?

We'll see about that.

Hopefully I still have one friend I can rely on in this world.

Run rabbit, run, rabbit, run, run, run…

FORTY-EIGHT

John Curtis didn't see who rushed by him from the presbytery, but he heard them. Their feet tapped the tiled pavement in front of the shrine with its saint's relics in the sanctuary – they skittered beside the raised stone platform on which the high altar stood and dodged between him and the ritual choir. Somebody had just fled into the cathedral's north transept in a great hurry. He smelt the rain on their Rayon raincoat...

There was no reason to suppose it was the Very Reverend Dean Drew or the librarian, Canon Bill Jones. It certainly wasn't the Chapter Steward Peter Marshall because he always crept about the place like a snail. If it was all a bit of a blur it was because he was balancing a tower of hymn books in front of his face as he went about the job of sprucing up the choir's sixty seats in time for Christmas.

He had already inspected the ten return stalls at the western end. Now he was about to work his way along the north side as far as the tomb of Abbot Parker. He was on a search and destroy mission. It was a deplorable fact that ever since American GIs had 'invaded' his country, many a young chorister saw fit to deposit blobs of masticated chewing gum on the carved misericords under their hinged seats. He was having to go to no end of trouble to raise each wooden perch to remove pellets of Double-Bubble pressed to foxes, knights, dragons and lions, not to mention Adam and Eve.

He deposited his books carefully in a nearby chapel and turned to investigate. Whoever had just evaded him had been skulking behind the altar like a wild animal. The most cursory examination of coats-of-arms, lion rampant and an eagle beneath his feet revealed something else unexpected on the tiled pavement.

To his astonishment he found himself staring at a gold ring.

The intention was clear. Somebody thought they could hide from him. He couldn't allow that. Was it not his job as verger to maintain the minster's security at all times?

John hurried down the steps into the north transept, crossed sepulchral stones which had once been adorned with brasses to honour the dead and got ready to flush out anyone who might be lurking in a place known as the reliquary. Nobody quite knew what function this ancient piece of stonework really served – it may have been an old entry porch moved here centuries ago from the original Lady Chapel. He could see why his mysterious visitor might mistake it for an exit rather than a dead end.

Too late. His quarry had moved on. From here he should go straight to the nave's north aisle or veer right into the cloisters?

Honestly, he didn't know.

He had a bad feeling, either way.

For someone of his size to rush about like this was scarcely sensible. Next minute his ears detected another short burst of hurrying footsteps. He knew that sound – it was a distinctive echo to be heard only in the former cloisters.

It might be nothing, but…

This was where monks once sat in silence at their carrels to read by light from the garden. He continued at a brisk pace along the stone flags of the south cloister alley, each loud footstep echoing off the fan-tracery vaulting in the ceiling above him.

Perhaps he was wrong to assume his anonymous intruder was up to no good?

At the very least he must return the ring he had just found to its rightful owner.

He slowed his trot to a march. 'Is anyone there? Who are you? How can I help?'

But there was nothing to be gained by shouting too officiously. He unclenched his fists and lost his scowl. Comic book Flash Gordon he was not – too many heroics would only make things worse.

The alley led him up a flight of stone steps into a dark, vaulted chamber where he normally never ventured. Above him lay the deanery. It was here that monks could break their vow of silence in what served as an extra parlour. Since this was the main entrance to the cloisters from the outer court, there was every chance that his quarry had given him the slip. Here, too, merchants once came to sell trinkets and pets to the abbey, only now the door to the outside world was well and truly locked.

He was on the verge of giving up when he registered something in the shadows close beside him.

'What the hell...?'

A single blow sent him reeling. It could have been a fist or a piece of metal. There was an instant ringing in his ears; one eye almost popped from its socket; his lungs felt fit to burst; his legs crumpled under their own weight. Then, with an avalanche of pain he clawed at the cold stone wall to slow his fall...

A riot of thoughts shot through his brain. Did his assailant intend to finish him off there and then?

'What do you... want?'

Instead, walls wobbled and paving sank underfoot – drunken steps saw him make it as far as the west cloister just in time to see his would-be killer dash across the garth. In their arms was a bundle. If his eyes had been better, he might have seen what it was.

After he ran along the south cloister past its carrels, he could turn left and cut the intruder off as they re-emerged from the garden...

Beads of blood bled into his eyes. His head felt on fire. He fell from one side of the passageway to the other, yet somehow he didn't stop moving forwards.

He reached the 90-degree angle where east and south cloisters met in time to see somebody disappear, it seemed, into solid wall...

'I've got you now. That doorway leads to the library.'

His blood was up. He thought nothing of his own safety. How dare someone attack him in his own cathedral!

Stairs led to an ancient room whose animal smell of ancient, leather-bound books immediately hit his nostrils. He was in a museum enriched by the gifts of countless Canons which contained both treasures and oddities. No one sat here perusing a fourth folio of Shakespeare, though, or the very large collection of Puritan newspapers. A Coverdale Bible lay open at its 1538 frontispiece, but its reader had simply failed to place it back on the shelves while they went to lunch?

Then he remembered. This long room or gallery had been the Abbey's chief dormitory. The cubicles where the monks once slept were long gone, but not so this other, ancient door. Whoever just fled here had done what the brothers did when they came up to bed by way of the newel staircase from the cloister – they'd descended again by this second, stone staircase into the church for night prayers.

John felt his way down the spiral of sharply descending steps to emerge from total darkness into the north transept.

No one. No tell-tale footsteps rang out on the stone pavement. Whoever had passed this way a moment ago had already left the cathedral?

He wiped blood from his lip like a bitter pill as he felt a sudden need to sit down.

He still had the solid gold ring in his pocket.

With silence came relief. If somebody had attempted to steal anything, they were long gone. He'd scared them away and that was fine.

So how was it he could hear what sounded like a baby crying?

FORTY-NINE

DI Lockett stepped from his car and donned his hat in the drizzle. He was not unhopeful. 18A Edwy Parade stood in a cluster of narrow streets that contained no more than thirty terraced houses. Such an area was small enough for his men to surround. The Parade had once been called Snake Lane, which was not inappropriate, given his quarry: their fugitive 'bride' could not have gone far.

'Search every backyard and outhouse.'

DS Biggs was less gung-ho. Instead, he smelt fresh air this far from the city's smoky chimneys where north Gloucester merged with marshy countryside. He might have his handcuffs ready, but all anyone on the run had to do was to head for St Catherine's Meadow at the end of the road and disappear among the riverside reeds and grasses. They might hitch a ride on a barge at one of the sawmill wharves or boatbuilding yards along the east channel of the River Severn – they could sail right by the high stone walls of His Majesty's Prison and cock a snoot at justice.

No one answered his urgent knocking. 'Jolantha will have seen us coming, sir.'

'Then we keep looking.'

'Should we really beat down her door?'

'Sorry, but this can't wait.'

'What if she really does have good reason to fear for her baby?'

'It's not that simple.'

'You think she's a murderess?'

'I'm glad to hear you say so.'

DS Biggs pointed to the bottle on the doorstep. 'If she is at home, sir, she hasn't taken in her milk yet.'

DI Lockett fitted one end of his crowbar between door and doorframe and began to lever at its lock. He pushed and pulled until he went red in the face, but to avail.

Suddenly a voice piped up from the house next door. 'You here about the baby?'

'What do you think?'

'I think, young man, that you should wipe your feet before you go in. Jo likes to keep a clean house.'

He stood there swinging his crowbar from his hand, somewhat menacingly. 'And you are?'

'Mrs O'Brien.'

'Then please mind your own business.'

'That's a pity.'

'Why's that?'

'I have a key.'

'Jolantha Wheeler left you a key?' he replied, wiping one hand over his scented hair.

The broad-faced neighbour's own greying locks were tied in a stuffed stocking to make a roll. 'Jo pays me 6d per day to look after baby Jacqueline for her when she's at work or doing fire guard duties at the cathedral.'

'When did you last see your neighbour?'

'Early this morning. Is there any news yet? She was in a frightful state. She came hammering on my front window and said that her baby had been stolen. Said she was going straight to the police. She would have left her dog behind, too, but Bella raced after her.'

'Then you won't mind if one of my constables searches your house?'

Mrs O'Brien raised her stern chin and her chest swelled. 'And why would you want to do that?'

DI Lockett stepped up to the garden fence and held out his hand.

'Let me make one thing clear. If you're hiding anything from us it will go badly with you – it'll be considered an obstruction of justice.'

With a flounce, she yielded the key at once. 'You don't really think the baby is in there, do you?'

'I'm not looking for any baby.'

'You mean that?'

'I'm looking for its mother.'

'Then you should question that shady-looking bloke who's been watching her house lately.'

'Bloke? What bloke?'

'The one who stands over there on the pavement after dim-out time every evening. Mark my words, he means her no good.'

'How do you know about that?'

'I see everything round here.'

'Did you get a good look at his face?'

'He always wears his collar up and his hat down over his eyes.'

'So nothing?'

'He stands very upright and marches about like a military man. He's forever sucking sweets, is all I know.'

DS Biggs felt his heart quicken. There was a dryness in his throat; his brain began to buzz; he was seized by a sudden conviction.

'Sir…'

'Not now, sergeant. We have a house to search.'

'But sir…'

DI Lockett pushed open the door to 18A and went inside. The first thing that hit his nostrils was a dank, almost metallic odour. Clearly the single brick walls weren't proof against rising damp.

'Police! Give yourself up!'

A pale blue linen scarf printed with Army and RAF badges hung off a hook in the hall, next to a trilby trimmed with ribbon. But there was no coat. Jolantha had last been seen wearing her red fox fur coat in Bearland Police Station.

Before the fireplace in the parlour sat an empty tin bath. Its owner had dutifully painted a white plimsoll line round its sides so that she never used more than five inches of hot water to save fuel.

'Take a good look upstairs, sergeant.'

DI Lockett advanced as far as the scullery-cum-kitchen. Here, two tins of Spam, some flour, suet, tea, cocoa and plain biscuits sat on the shelves.

There was fresh bread in a bread bin and some homemade jam, as well as cakes made from leftover porridge and breadcrumbs ready to fry with some bacon. Was this to have been her breakfast this morning, he wondered?

DS Biggs soon returned. 'I found these, sir.'

'What are they?'

'A lot of photographs of Sidney and Marjorie Sheppard taken, I'd say, in the South of France.'

DI Lockett dealt several black and white pictures from hand to hand, then threw them on the scullery's wooden draining board. 'As we thought, she's obsessed with him.'

DS Biggs shared his frustration. It had to be a bad omen.

'There's an empty cot on the floor in one of the bedrooms, sir. It's lined with newspapers and an old nightdress, but there's no sign of any baby.'

'Check the Anderson Shelter in the backyard.'

'Jolantha has made her escape on her motorcycle, sir. She could be anywhere by now. I think she's telling us the truth about the baby. I don't think it's an elaborate charade to cover her tracks.'

'What makes you say that?'

'No mother leaves her child's milk bottle and nappies behind. Not with this war on. She wouldn't risk not being able to replace them any time soon.'

'You'll understand if I don't take your word for it?'

'Maybe we've been looking at this all wrong, sir.'

DI Lockett led the way back through the house. As he did so he took out his pipe with every intention of lighting it to soothe his frayed nerves. 'Is that what you think, sergeant?'

'Jolantha may be a bit of an odd fish, sir, but why would she lie about her own baby going missing? Then Mrs O'Brien reports seeing this shady character watching the house. It has to mean something.'

'Mad or sane, she's an inveterate liar.'

'No liar, sir, only a bit lost.'

'What are you trying to say?'

'She may need our help.'

'So where is she now?'

'She wouldn't have left town without first finding her child. Not even to save herself.'

'You sure about that?'

'I just don't know where to start looking.'

DI Lockett tucked his pipe back into his pocket. That smoke would have to wait. 'I can think of one place, sergeant.'

'Which place is that?'

'Come on, let's get cracking.'

FIFTY

I spy the dark blue police vans the moment I reach the east end of the Parade – I have to open the throttle wide on my Brough Superior to effect a sharp U-turn as I head back into the city. It's as I suspected! Instead of taking me seriously, DI Lockett doesn't believe a word I've said. He considers me dangerous now because I've been dangerous before, he doesn't think me a credible witness.

Which is why I can't go home.

Anyone else might simply hand themselves in, only I know you wouldn't want me to be so stupid, dear Sidney.

The police's stance is that my side of the story doesn't matter.

It matters to me.

In the same way I was all set to have and to hold you, my love, for better or worse, for richer or poorer, in sickness and health, I can be sure you'll never betray me, not even from the grave.

You, at least, know what happened in the cathedral triforium.

If only I could look into your eyes one more time I might see…

Why you fell?

… your secret.

As it is, Bella and I are riding about looking everywhere for my baby girl. I'm hoping against hope to see her dumped in a doorway or on a pavement. I think I spot her in a pram outside the Princes Hall on the Cattle Market side of George Street, but it's not Jacqueline, it's some other mother's GI baby…

Next minute I'm following the remains of the Roman walls on King Street, because there can be no yesterday and no tomorrow until I have my baby girl back in my arms.

I'm trapped in this perpetual now.

A shabbily dressed woman pushes a pram just like mine in front of the Guildhall. Another stands gossiping to a friend outside the "Lemon and Parker" Pub where you and I used to go for a drink after an evening's dancing, dear Sidney....

But one box-like Utility pram is very much like another.

It's a similar story in Southgate Street where two teenage girls are showing off their babies to each other outside the "Berkeley Arms".

Don't tell me one of your friends isn't paying me back for what I've been doing? Don't tell me my baby's kidnapper doesn't know it's wrong.

My greatest fear is that I'll never be allowed to be Jacqueline's mother again because of you, my love.

No one will trust me?

They'll say I've put you before my other responsibilities.

As if that counts for anything.

They'll never understand.

And why wouldn't they be sceptical?

I've let myself down.

If I can't continue and can't go home I have to come up with another plan and a place to lie low...

If I had you by my side, dear Sidney, I could do so much more, I know. But the dead can't look out for the living, can they? You're useless to me now.

FIFTY-ONE

There it was again – that petulant protest. It plucked at his nerves and got under his skin. He, John Curtis, might not be an expert on babies but this one sounded angry and hungry – no cry like that should be ignored. Why bring it here, though, as he hurriedly crossed the middle of the cathedral in the direction of the south transept?

Whoever had the child might be about to abandon it at any moment? What did they want? How could he help? He really didn't know yet. If it was the last thing he did, he had to find out where. His heart raced and he was gripped by a reckless urgency; his head throbbed; more blood trickled down his cheek and he couldn't think straight. But he'd be a fool not to wonder....

He was about to leave the south aisle of the nave when he slowed to listen. He usually liked to distinguish between rash and reasonable, but this was different.

It was hard to know if he felt relieved or disappointed. The chapel tomb of Abbot Seabroke, builder of the cathedral's great tower, stood a few feet to his left side... But no baby wriggled and waved its arms beside the alabaster effigy of the vaguely smiling abbot. No distressed parent accompanied the gypsum figure in long white vestment, silk stole, tunic and linen cap as he rested his head on a cushion supported by two decapitated angels.

He was at the point where the aisle opened in all its glory into the south transept. Next minute, footsteps sounded not far behind him.

Again the baby cried, more softly this time, then dwindled into part whimper.

'Wait, whoever you are! Show yourself. Now!'

Each yell, growing fainter, sounded from inside the cathedral's very stones, without a doubt…

Such plaintive complaints appeared to be trapped between the early, plain Norman masonry and the later, fancy Perpendicular tracery that overlaid it.

He ran to the transept's southern corner where a door opened on to unlit stairs. That bruising encounter with his attacker had to be a dire warning. His heart missed a beat as he dived into pitch darkness.

Whoever had the baby trod the steps within the walls just above his head…

FIFTY-TWO

'Bella, come.' Not even two extra hours of wartime "double summertime" have proved long enough to find Jacqueline so far. I'm abandoning my motorcycle combination on College Green and heading straight for the cathedral. Bella may not know it's my father's Mark VI .455 service revolver that hangs by its lanyard round my neck, but I'm in no mood to explain right now. As it is, she's alert to my every wish and signal, which is unlike her.

Anyone else will think I want to settle more scores.

But this is not about that.

I'm done doing what I did for you, dear Sidney – no one can be allowed to distract me now.

This is about my daughter only.

John should be here somewhere, doing his rounds of nave, crypt and garth. Only he can give me sanctuary for the night until I begin scouring Gloucester's streets again in the morning.

That's not to say I know where to start.

Whoever has my baby may be long gone.

Doesn't bear thinking about.

I'm in a cold, dead cavern of stone where the dying sun pierces the windows behind me: its star-like pattern bursts faintly on one of the nave's piers as I approach the east end of the north aisle. Its reddish rays seem to show me the way – I'm in a place once painted with fleurs-de-lis, emblems of the Trinity and golden crowns...

Still no verger with his rattly bunch of keys. A quick look at the stalls in the choir produces nothing. I can't give up now... I won't have anyone put me in jail before I'm done.

Next minute Bella utters a bark. It's a sharp, shrill shout that means business. I know that sound: she's off before I can utter a word.

Because she's found something.

I follow her up the steps to the north ambulatory where pilgrims once queued to view the sacred tomb of King Edward II. Bella has turned her egg-shaped head to the row of mighty Romanesque pillars and arches – she's wrinkling her nose skywards at something or someone in the high stone triforium that runs round the top of the walls at this end of the cathedral. It's the same sort of open-sided corridor from which you fell to your death in the nave, dear Sidney, only it's much longer and broader.

'John? Is that you? It's me, Jo.'

The wide stone apertures directly above me remain a mass of shadow. Whoever Bella can sense up there chooses to lurk within the massively thick walls beyond the reach of anyone at ground level.

To go up is to go back.

I'm soon treading the almost vertical stairs that climb from the south transept.

Something isn't right.

Bella and I reach a secret part of the minster where only stonemasons usually venture. Half-barrelled stone thrusts act as flying buttresses inside the building at my shoulder. I can feel them counteracting the great weight of the choir walls and the groined roof above us, without which the cathedral will surely pull itself apart. If the tension is in the stone, it's also in me. My brow throbs. There is a constant pounding in my ears; my lungs can't keep pace with my rapid breathing. I wonder at what I think might be fear.

I'm soon at the end of a gallery that crosses from one side of the choir to the other by way of its flying bridges, ever since this end of the church was demolished to make way for the great east window hundreds of years ago – I can hear the gallery magnify the urgent whispers of two people.

The first voice is unmistakeably John's: 'So tell me what this is all about.'

'No.'

'It's not too late to...'

'I don't want your help.'

'Just tell me what you want and we can work this out.'

'Or that's what you'd like me to believe.'

'Don't be silly. Hand me the child.'

But I don't wait any more, I'm using my thumb to cock the hammer on my Webley revolver. I'm advancing with six bullets in the chamber and the tip of my finger on the trigger...

FIFTY-THREE

The first thing DI Lockett saw parked in the cathedral's close was a 499cc Royal Enfield sidecar combination. Suddenly his face was all frown. His heart sank. His feet turned to lead and he nearly stumbled.

Next minute he regained his grim smile.

He wasn't mistaken, after all. Beyond the older motorcycle stood the much rarer and more impressive machine he was looking for. Here was the Rolls-Royce of motorcycles all right – very few people could afford to ride something as expensive a Brough Superior Combination.

He set his grey felt hat squarely on his head and began to cross College Green. He was advancing towards the south porch with rapid steps. Jolantha had given him the runaround for long enough, it was time to get tough with this phoney bride until she confessed her crimes.

DS Biggs hurried to catch up. 'The deanery is the other way, sir.'

'I don't need any dean to tell me what to do.'

'We should at least alert the Chapter Office.'

'Damn it, sergeant, I'm here to arrest a dangerous fugitive.'

'All the same, the dean is the head of the cathedral. He should be informed of…'

'No time, sergeant.'

'You honestly think Jo Wheeler is in her right mind?'

'I can't be sure what she is or what she believes, but I know she's gone too far this time.'

'Maybe if we'd listened to her a bit more, sir?'

'Don't be naïve, sergeant. "Hell hath no fury like a woman scorned". Jolantha is a malicious and unusually manipulative person. She thinks only she has the right to avenge any wrong done to her.'

DS Biggs watched his boss tap his pipe against the stone font just inside the cathedral's door, ready to refill it when on the move. 'She might say the same about us, sir.'

'Why does that not surprise me?'

One of them took the north aisle, the other the south. Working as a team they advanced along the nave as far as the choir and transepts. DI Lockett's first puffs on his pipe grew more rapid. A cathedral could no longer be considered a sanctuary, which was ironical since in the eyes of both Church and courts he could be considered a criminal, too. His feelings for Oliver had to remain a total secret in a place like this where he would be doubly damned. Was he venting his frustration on someone else? DS Biggs seemed to think so. It didn't matter what he thought. Not so much. What mattered was the 'madness' that came with not being allowed to love the one you wanted.

His train of thought was interrupted by a shout.

'Over here, sir.'

'What is it, sergeant?'

'Fresh blood.'

They met at a doorway situated in the corner of the north transept. 'Go up, sergeant. Find out where it goes. Meanwhile I'll follow the trail down here. We'll meet back at the font.'

'Very good, sir.'

He didn't like the look of this one little bit. As the detective in charge he should keep DS Biggs with him. There was no saying what a desperate Jolantha would do next. This could be kill or be killed. It really could.

But he already knew that.

FIFTY-FOUR

The gun in my grip weighs a couple of pounds but right now it could be lead or stone. My eyelids twitch, as does my mouth. I'm grinding my teeth before I go giddy with vertigo...

I'm high above the Lady Chapel on one side and the choir on the other. This far along the whispering gallery Bella and I are edging towards hushed voices where the east window should be. We're following voices that hover all round us on account of the very strange acoustics – they're like winged demons in the air and in my head...

The first thing I see is John slumped against the base of the wall with his feet wide apart. Bloody froth leaks into his mouth from a bad cut on his scalp. He's mumbling something as he dips in and out of consciousness. One arm hangs limply at his side and looks broken. His entire appearance is that of useless but defiant opposition. I wonder why anyone should hole up here. Then I recall how the exit from this part of the choir's triforium to the north transept is blocked by the organ's thirty-two feet long pedal pipes laid on the floor.

Before I can reach my friend's side someone else emerges clearly, distinctly, ever more recognisably! A rasping breath sounds each time he expels air from his lungs. Even his handsome blue eyes look haunted as though they have never fully recovered from some former blindness. I'm looking at the ghost of a soldier whose youth got left behind on the battlefield. He could be some lost creature from a medieval depiction of hell – he resembles a tormented soul being tossed into flames at the Last Judgement, without hope, love or even pity.

He's not so old as to be entirely grey but has to be about fifty in his shabby army uniform. It's his skin that really has my attention. Pockmarks dot his cheeks where his face has been all but obliterated and replaced with a mask of pitted scars and holes. Wounds left by pustules and spots point to a hideous disease. In another century people might say he had the plague.

'Captain Knevitt?'

'You found me.'

'Hector?'

'I knew you'd come.'

Which is when I regain my senses. His ravaged visage is really the result of leading men into battle in The Great War. Back then, poison gas caused his cheeks, throat and neck to erupt in hideous black blisters like pestilential boils – oozing yellow fluid melted his flesh where the vapour touched bare skin or soaked through his woollen uniform. His breathing is bad because the gas turned to acid in his lungs.

He wields a rifle bayonet in one hand, while with the other he clutches something wrapped in a blanket close to his chest. My heart is in my mouth. I don't need to be told who's in his grasp…

I'm torn between talking and doing something really stupid. He's scared and confused. As am I. Possibly he'll detect something friendly in my forced smile? 'Listen Hector, you don't have to do this.'

Meanwhile John gives a groan. He struggles and falls in a lame attempt to rise. I would go to him, only I daren't take my eyes off the bundle Hector embraces so hard. Is my baby asleep? Why isn't she crying?

'What do you want with Jacqueline? Tell me you haven't hurt her.'

'You ignored my pleas.'

'What pleas?'

'I've written to you constantly these past few weeks. You've always been my very own Violet.'

'You know we agreed you wouldn't send me any more letters.'

'I knew if I took your baby you'd have to listen.'

'What? Why? None of this makes any sense.'

'Not to you, maybe.'

Our paths may have crossed several times but I never realised his bouts of delusion revolved solely round me, I never reckoned he would make me the centre of his universe.

'First give me my baby, Hector. I need to know she's unharmed.'

'Let me think.'

'You still have a choice.'

I try edging forwards until he waves me back with his bayonet: 'Sidney Sheppard was never going to run away with you.'

'Are you serious?'

'Why else do you think I put an end to it?'

'End to what, Hector?'

'You should never have listened to all his promises. He was never going to leave his wife to marry you, he was going to fight his divorce every inch of the way because he couldn't face the public humiliation.'

'No, that's not right. Sidney loved me more than Marjorie. You have to stop this right now.'

But he isn't finished. 'I told him he couldn't have you because you're promised to me.'

'I am?'

'No other woman wants me because I look like a monster. I had to tell him how kind you were to me years ago. Until I met you I had nothing to live for after I was discharged from the army. Why else do you think I've made it my mission to watch over you day and night, ever since?'

It's true I briefly befriended him years ago, dear Sidney. Why not? I wanted to spare him mindless rejection. He fought and nearly died for his country, but what thanks does he get for it? He has been left to wander the earth like one of its unwanted, when every night he relives the attack that hideously disfigured him. He seems genuinely relieved to see me, yet the way he stares and the erratic urgency of his movements suggest this is not the same gentle person who once sucked sweets in my shop in Bristol.

'If you want to protect me, Hector, you have to pass me my baby.'

'Not before you say you're mine.'

'...?'

'I had to stop Sidney from making your life a misery – I wanted him to answer for the way he was stringing you along with all his lies.'

'You had to stop him? When? Where?'

'Here, in the cathedral.'

My head reels and there's a deafening throbbing in my ears. At the same time my blood curdles.

I'm all too aware of how the choir yawns beside us and its horrible void. 'That was you on All Saints' Day when he fell?'

'Because I love you, Jo.'

I should put a bullet through his head this instant, but Jacqueline is still asleep on his arm.

'You had a hand in what happened?'

Tears roll down his face even as he stares long and hard right through me. There's something pitiable about his eyes, not least because they look so needy.

'You should never have listened to him, Jo. He was no good. He deceived you. That's why I had to act as I did.'

'What did you... do, Hector?'

'I saved you from yourself, what else?'

FIFTY-FIVE

The line of bloody splashes did not come to an end at the top of the spiral staircase, but led him into a long room which housed all the cathedral's reference books. He adored libraries. If he had not become Detective Sergeant Biggs, he might have been a bookseller. He paused at a copy of Frocester's Cartulary, which he liked to think was so old that it belonged to the church before its abbey was dissolved and reborn as a cathedral…

The crimson trail didn't stop at the shelves, either, it descended a second, newel staircase to exit again into the east cloister.

A red starfish stained a stone carrel where the walking wounded had passed along the south aisle and left behind a crimson handprint. He was in one of the most beautiful places in the world with its fan-tracery ceiling, if only he cared to pause and look up….

Another day, perhaps.

The long line of bloody spots on the ground took him to a vaulted chamber of considerable size at the far end of the alley. It was very old, dark and unrestored. Other buildings stood above this tunnel which ended at a locked door to the world beyond.

He struck a match. Another red starfish turned black on the wall – the victim had slid down cold, grey stones to leave a long angry smear behind them.

'This is where it happened, all right. This is the place where someone tried to kill you, whoever you are.'

He was at the beginning of the trail, not its finish! Which meant he must get back to the nave in a hurry. His boss was in danger.

FIFTY-SIX

'Save me from myself? I'm sorry, Hector, but I don't understand you.'

He shifts his weight uneasily from one foot to the other. His eyes seem to stand out of his head, so intently do they stare at me. 'I arranged to meet Sidney here, in the cathedral, on All Saints' Day, because I had something important to tell him.'

'*You* arranged to meet him?' My aim is to keep him talking. For as long as he's speaking to me he's less likely to harm Jacqueline.

'Instead of which his wife appears. I had no idea she would show up waving divorce papers on that very day, at that very hour. I don't think Sidney did, either.'

'You're right…'

'That's when he saw me signalling to him from the nave's triforium and hurried to join me.'

'…Marjorie travelled all the way from London to confront him.'

'Except neither of us expected her to run up the steps after him.'

I've taken one pace nearer Jacqueline – I can see her little brown face poking out of her blanket. She's blinking at me.

Next minute Hector and I have gone full circle. His grip on my baby redoubles but he's hampered by the heavy blade in his hand. That's what concerns me – he might have to decide at any moment which one to drop. I see to my horror that he has his back to the balcony, beyond which gapes the chasm of the choir. I've done a bad thing, I've spooked him.

'Please, Hector, it's not too late. Tell me everything. I'm sorry, I really am. We've both been through a lot, you and I. If it's one thing we don't need right now, it's another casualty.'

'Sidney assumed I was a private detective hired to spy on him by his wife and wanted to confront me. But before I could explain I was only thinking of you, Marjorie appeared at the top of the stairs and began arguing with him. Of course, you being present was a bonus because it was my chance to demonstrate how far I would go to help you.'

'So much for my hiding behind pillars.'

'She wanted his signature on the papers in her hand, there and then. He vowed never to give her what she wanted without a humiliating public appearance in court. Marjorie couldn't understand why he wouldn't be photographed with some other woman – any woman – to give her legitimate grounds to annul their marriage. He said she was the adulteress, so she should do it. Neither would back down despite my presence. She just flew at him as if I didn't exist. He snatched the papers from her fingers. She resisted. Very soon they were wrestling in one of the triforium's open windows before I could do a thing to stop them...'

'It's as I thought. The bitch pushed him...'

'Sidney was holding the divorce papers high over his head while she was reaching up, trying to grab them before he tore them to pieces. The further he leaned back the more she leaned after him until their arms became entangled. Suddenly Sidney seemed to go giddy. Lost his balance. Fainted? Before I could do a thing he took her with him.'

My brain is spinning. I could be in freefall myself. Blood races to my temples and my eyes burn. There is disbelief in my bones. Hector is clearly confused and struggling to recall what really happened? The nave's triforium has less room to manoeuvre than where we're standing. I can see why he might be mistaken as to who pushed whom when you fell, my dearest.

'Think very hard, Hector. Did Marjorie not say she wanted Sidney dead? Did she not say she'd see him in hell if he didn't sign the papers? You admit she was furious. She considered herself in the right but she took revenge by pushing him over the edge, only to have him take her with him. That's what really happened, isn't it? *That's what you're going to tell the police.*'

'...?'

'*You'll do it for me, won't you?*'

285

Now I have his attention I'm already within reach of Jacqueline – I just have to lean forward to pluck her from his crooked arm and she'll be free.

'Everything's going to be just fine now Sidney's gone, Jo.'

I freeze. A frisson of fear chills me. How can I deal with a madman when I'm feeling crazed myself?

'What do you mean, Hector? Why don't you say?'

But he isn't saying anything, he's trying to feel in his pockets when both his hands are full.

'I have it here, ready.'

'Why don't you put the bayonet down for a moment?'

Carefully, almost tenderly, he takes my advice and lays his lethal blade on the low wall beside him. The bayonet is beyond my reach, but now it's out of his grip he can't harm Jacqueline.

Yet he's becoming increasingly flustered. He's feeling in every pocket he can reach with his free hand without finding anything, apparently. 'Where is it?'

'What?'

'Your ring.'

'For me?'

'I purchased it specially.'

This is my chance. The dismay on his face is crucial to my success – this is meant to be his big moment.

'Calm down, Hector, it has to be here somewhere. Let me help you find it.'

'You will say yes to me, won't you, Jo?'

'Let's find the ring first, then we can do this properly. Why don't you hand me Jacqueline for a moment?'

Except he's suspicious. He needs to find the ring before he can go down on one knee to propose.

I'm almost there when a voice booms behind me.

'Jolantha Wheeler. You're under arrest on suspicion of murdering Frederick Sheppard. You don't have to say anything, but anything you do say...'

DI Lockett is standing there determined to spout some ridiculous spiel.

As if that matters right now.

'Stay where you are, Inspector. Can't you see? This man has my daughter…'

'Of course he has, he's trying to save her from you.'

'No, he kidnapped her this morning. I have to get her back.'

'On the contrary, Mrs Wheeler, it's over. You must accompany me to the police station this minute.'

'Are you mad, detective? I'm trying to save my child.'

But all he can see is the gun in my hand – it confirms everything he believes about my mental wellbeing.

'Did it ever cross your mind that I'm only trying to help you, Jo?'

'Did it ever cross yours that I'm the victim, not the suspect?'

'If you'll hand me your weapon we can resolve this peaceably.'

'Don't be ridiculous.'

'It's time to tell me what you did to Sidney, Jo.'

'Ha!'

Bella growls at my feet. In another second she'll have him by his ankle, no matter what.

'You realised Sidney didn't love you, despite your ridiculous demand that he should walk you down the aisle? You attacked him because he refused to give up his wife even though their marriage was over. It meant you flew at him in a temper. But killing him wasn't enough. Marjorie had to suffer, too, as did his friends and family. Except it wasn't a just cause at all, it was desperation because he didn't want you.'

'Doesn't mean I'd ever hurt a fly, Inspector.'

'You tried it before. You fired a shotgun at your own mother.'

'So you *do* wish to use my past against me.'

'Isn't that why we're here?'

'I'm only here for my child.'

Except Hector is gone. While DI Lockett has been distracting me, the captain has seen fit to start running.

So has Bella – she's after him like a shot.

DI Lockett leaps towards me, but a dazed John comes to just in time to stick out a foot – sends him flying.

I'm chasing after Hector because I don't know what else he'll do. I'm going as fast as I can from one triforium to the other, where I can see Bella already has him pinned up against one of the nave's stone apertures. A terrible sense of deja vu grips me. Everything I've done to right your wrongs, dear Sidney, has brought me back to the place where all this began – I'm at the lofty window in the wall where you plunged to your death as if I've condemned myself to relive that day all over again.

'Hector! Wait! Let's talk. Did you hurt people on my behalf? You did, didn't you? Okay, I shouldn't have spurned you in favour of someone else. Forgive me. I wasn't thinking straight – *I do still want you.*'

Gone is any look of love and longing in his face, to be replaced by horror and anguish. He's glancing at the stone pavement far below us, while everything else about him suggests he has forgotten that he lured me here to ask me for my hand in marriage.

Or he's changed his mind.

Now he wishes to teach me a lesson?

He could be me, a moment ago. He wants to fight fear with fear.

'Hand me Jacqueline, Hector. The police are everywhere. You can't escape. I admit I did harbour thoughts about revenge, but you had no right to act on my behalf. Now you can't simply walk away from what I've started, so let me help you...'

'Shut up. What kind of woman are you?'

'I'm your best friend.'

'How much of what you say is ever true?'

'I suggest you and I sit down and talk it over.'

'You suggest?'

Bella won't let him leave. She's growling and snarling. Without the bayonet he can't fend her off. I'm poised to raise my revolver. I can get a clear shot at his head, I'm certain.

'Don't you want to marry me, then, Hector? Isn't that what you set out to ask me, ever since a bomb killed Jack and Emmy in Bristol?'

'It was. Now it's not.'

'But you came here today to do just that. So what changed your mind?'

'You set a trap for me.'

'No, I didn't. You heard DI Lockett – he's here for me, not you…'

'You just said it yourself. I'll be the one who hangs, when I only did it for you.'

'What are you talking about?'

Hector glances first into the void then along the passageway. DI Lockett is converging on us in the narrow stone corridor and causing him to panic. 'The only reason I drowned Sidney's brother and set fire to Ash Hall was to do what you wanted…'

'How was *that* what I wanted?'

'I couldn't stand idly by, not when I could see how much you longed to pay people back for what they did to your precious Sidney. I understand. I feel your pain. But how can you fight your enemies when you are at war with yourself? That's why it takes a real soldier.'

'You literally killed Frederick for me?'

'Didn't he leech off Sidney? Didn't he make him pay for all sorts of things that helped to drain him financially and bring him down? His own brother did nothing to help him in his hour of need. Just like all the others on your list.'

The list. He's copied my list of your so-called friends and family, dear Sidney, along with their addresses. He must have burgled my house or searched my motorcycle sidecar…

'Is that why you pushed poor Mrs Tuffley off the cliff? To help me get even?'

'That wasn't me. That must have been an accident. Unless you know better?'

'If you really want to help me, Hector, you'll give me Jacqueline. See, she's awake. She'll be very hungry. Has she even been fed today?'

'I never intended for things to happen like this, Jo. I did want to give her to you. Now, I'm not so sure I should.'

'Why not?'

'Because you want to ruin everything.'

'No –.'

There's no time to cock my gun, I have to use the double action trigger. Jacqueline utters a scream. It's loud, disconcerting and fills the whole cathedral. She's exhausted, frightened and aware I'm here…

Already Hector has one leg over the balcony – he's swaying into open space high at the top of the nave's mighty pillars – he refuses to let go of my baby before the great empty gulf.

DI Lockett has him by the shoulder, except it's not him he's after. He's heard what Hector said.

I squeeze my finger. I'll blow both their fucking heads off. I pull through on the trigger to both cock and fire in one swift move, only nothing happens.

Instead, the lanyard catches in the hammer – it's preventing the firing pin from reaching the primer in the base of the cartridge. I should never have worn it round my neck like Hugo showed me.

It's misfired.

I have the gun free in a moment and look back at the opening in the wall to the sheer drop beyond. DI Lockett has both arms over the stone parapet – he's leaning so low he's half into open space. I can't see his head, only how his heels are two inches off the ground.

One push and he's gone.

It's so easy….

There's no sign of Hector or Jacqueline.

'For God's sake, Jo, pull me back.'

I have him by the collar in a jiffy, I'm clawing at him so he can't topple over. He doesn't look too good. When he collapses in a heap at my feet I think he might have a heart attack, he's struggling so hard to get his breath and turns very pale. He'd have me restrain Bella who's licking his face as I hear him mutter a few words: 'I'm so sorry, I tried to grab her…'

But I don't have time for him. I'm yelling and crying. I'm staring beyond the parapet at the vast, grey floor of the nave directly below me. Hector lies spread-eagled in a growing lake of red that quickly spills across cold stones. Next to him stands DS Biggs whose face is frozen in horror as if he's been paralysed or something.

His gaze meets mine.

'Are you all right, Jo?'

I would reply, if I still had a voice. I should cry, but I don't, I go on screaming. Right now I'm only concerned with what he has in his arms…

FIFTY-SEVEN

Your useless wife has unaccountably emerged from her coma, dear Sidney, though her sight is hazy and her speech may yet turn out to be a permanent slur…

Marjorie has both her arms and legs in plaster, which means I can do what I like to her – I can tweak a limb or two to my heart's content? I always knew you didn't *choose* to jump to your death and so leave me alone, my love, only I still find it incredible that she didn't push you.

So incredible, in fact, that I'm with her right now in Hammersmith Hospital to suss out her barefaced lies once and for all.

This isn't over.

'Remember me? I'm Jo Wheeler. We last met in Gloucester Cathedral.'

There is an urgent flutter of her eyelids; her pupils look fit to leap from their sockets; her head shakes and her lips begin to utter strangulated cries. They remind me of something and I wonder if it isn't a drowning kitten. Then, with a failed attempt to work her strapped limbs, all inner resistance collapses and she breathes more steadily. She has realised she can't move a muscle in my presence, poor dear.

'I'll call the nurse…'

Too late. I'm closing the curtains round her bed before some busybody makes us their business. We don't need any sudden dramas.

'I've come to give you my condolences, dear Marjorie, since Sidney was my sweetheart, too. Did you know he and I were going to move to France? Yes, it's true: the moment this dreadful war ends he was all set to try and get his job back with JAZ, the clock manufacturing company at 46, Rue Eduard Vaillant. All he had to do was to telephone Longchamp 08-77 or

292

send a telegram to REVAJAZER-Paris for another interview, I'm sure. Monsieur Pen told him so... If he was successful we were going to begin our lives afresh in a new country with no awkward questions.'

Your redundant wife is all genuine apprehension, but my boldness doesn't quite pique her the way it should. Instead, she looks slightly baffled. Nor do I care for the twinkle in her eyes. That curl on her lips could be a smirk, not a smile?

'I remember when he first got that job. The letter arrived on the 7th of August 1939 while he and I were still on honeymoon on the French Riviera. I watched him open it in Hotel du Prince in Cannes – it invited him to start work in Paris on the 16th. That was to have been the beginning of our new life together, only war broke out three weeks later. You didn't really think it was going to be your life too, did you, Jo?'

I don't care for the tone of voice. Someone that helpless should watch her Ps and Qs.

'You always had it in for him, Marjorie. Now I'll never know that joy...'
'Of being his bigamous spouse?'
'If you hadn't shown up in the cathedral like that he'd still be alive.'

Red hair falls over one eye. The ironical glint in her hazel irises changes to disbelief, or it could be something else. For some dreadful moment I think it might be pity.

'Is that what you think, Jo? You literally believe you could have made it work with my Sidney?'
'He was maverick, mercurial, obsessive, but always passionate about things.'
'Things aren't people.'
'He had a great mind. He wasn't boring like most men. I believed him when he said he wanted to be prime minister...'

Your irrelevant wife starts to laugh, but has to stop when it hurts her ribs. 'You didn't know him at all, did you?'

Her newfound spirit of resistance irritates me because she's so damned cocky. 'I never met a cleverer, smarter or more courteous person than Sidney. He could make anyone happy.'
'If it's happiness you want, Jo, he's the last man you should look to.'

That's not cockiness, that's bitterness. She's deeply troubled by something.

Guilt does that to some people.

She can't forgive herself.

'Listen to me, Marjorie, I'm far from convinced that you didn't arrange for Sidney to die on All Saints' Day. I'm also inclined to believe you preyed on poor Hector… Well, I have bad news for you. He's dead.'

'Who?'

'Don't play games with me. You exploited Captain Hector Knevitt's infatuation with me to manipulate and use him to your own advantage, didn't you? You wanted him to force Sidney to sign those divorce papers. He was your back-up plan. Did you ply him with sweets, too?'

'Nothing you can say can change the facts, Jo. This Sidney you're pretending exists isn't him.'

'Tell me why I shouldn't finish you off while I have the chance?'

Marjorie doesn't laugh this time, she only stares straight back at me. She's behaving as though I'm more afraid of her than she is of me. 'I've never told anyone this before, but I don't consider that Sidney and I were ever truly husband and wife. Oh, we got married all right in 1939, with lots of people at our posh reception. We said our vows and were photographed looking happy as we took the train to Paris where we stayed overnight. But that's when he flew into a rage for no apparent reason. He told me that I'd ruined his life. He was ranting and raving and was very cruel to me….'

'Honestly? On your wedding night?'

'I thought that was the end of it, only I was wrong.'

'Yeah, yeah, I know all about it. Peggy told me. You took some awful concoction to stop the curse while on the French Riviera. So what?'

'When we reached our hotel I knew it would be a problem. And you're right, my sister Peggy did give me some quack's potion to suppress everything for up to a week to save my blushes.'

'Except it made you terribly sick and gave you diarrhoea. Blah. Blah. Blah. You fell ill and as a result Sidney didn't make love to you on your honeymoon, which made you think he didn't want you ever afterwards…'

'Oh no, that's not it at all.'

'But your sister distinctly told me…'

'Sidney had no right to go through with the wedding and then turn on me immediately afterwards – the very next day. He had no excuse to accuse me so bitterly of having *forced* him into it, leaving him nothing to live for. I was completely wholehearted about our marriage until he gave me such a dreadful shock… He convinced me there and then that he didn't want me. No matter what he said later about being utterly exhausted by the wedding and train travel, I'm convinced he *deliberately* intended to convey the impression that I'd somehow cornered and trapped him. When I remember – and I'll never forget – how he loathed me, I go hot with shame, but it might have blown over and come to nothing, except for one thing…'

'You're only angry because that's how you choose to remember it.'

'I was a disappointed 29-year-old virgin when we returned to England. I was confused and humiliated. Wouldn't you be? I couldn't think why he should suddenly take against me for no apparent reason. But he made his feelings so clear that I felt the only thing I could do to keep my pride and get reasonable happiness out of the future was to stay out of his way as much as possible. But you're wrong to think the honeymoon was the cause of it. So was I, as it turned out.'

I'm still suspicious. She'd have me think she can outwit me. Anyone else would dismiss your wife as a skilful liar, but something about the disbelief and hurt etched into her face, even after all this time, rings horribly true. She's in more than physical pain, she's embarrassed.

That doesn't mean she doesn't want to tarnish your good name when you're not here to defend yourself, dear Sidney.

'If he really behaved so coldly towards you, you would have left him straightaway.'

'I didn't have to. Sidney abandoned me, in all but name, when his newly acquired job in London saw him evacuated to faraway Warrington. But I still hoped we could make a go of it – I hadn't given up on him entirely, until one day…'

I can hear nurses moving towards us on the ward which could spell trouble, so I have to speed things up. 'All right, say I believe you. What *does* explain Sidney's sudden dislike of you, physically? After all, you'd been courting for years and years. You were like brother and sister.'

'One day, when I had the idea of converting some of his old clothes for myself, I dug out his old blue suit. Quite casually I looked through the pockets to see if there was anything there he might want and to my horror I found two letters he'd started to write to a mutual friend called Dora.'

'To Dora?'

'You know her?'

'We recently bumped into each other for the first time in Gloucester Cathedral.'

'You can imagine the awful shock it gave me, but after a while a wave of pity swept over me – I thought of all he must have gone through marrying me and loving her so terribly. I worked it out and I came to the conclusion that it would be less damaging to our future if I kept it to myself and let sleeping dogs lie. It was very difficult not writing straight off and telling him that I knew. What made it worse was these letters were written just after his new job again saw him evacuated out of London, this time to Wilnecote, near Tamworth – I remember the time vividly because that's when we were still managing to spend a few weekends in our Ealing flat. I thought, poor fool me, because I hoped he might yet become fond of me again. Truth is, I was too weak to do anything about it until I found somebody else who really appreciates me and loves me as I am. My husband didn't keep changing jobs to get back to London for my sake. He did it to get close to *her*.'

Your wife looks pathetic in her bandages but there is a steeliness in her voice that is hard to dismiss. It's not sour grapes. Still I think she hated you enough to want you dead.

'Are you really saying Sidney didn't wish to live with you right from the start?'

Marjorie looks flustered. When someone can't get her story straight, she must expect to be cross-examined. 'He was flirting with one girl – me – while deeply in love with another, so it was no wonder the storm burst on me after we were married. I was the only one he could turn on. It doesn't make me the villain.'

'I'm pretty sure it does.'

'You don't know Sidney as well as you think you do…'

'All right, what?'

Marjorie winces and tries to persuade me to take my hand off her broken arm. 'As I say, I did think he might calm down when we returned from honeymoon and settled in our flat for a while, but the war spoilt all that. He went on disliking me for at least a year. In fact, for quite a time he made no bones about it that he really hated me for marrying him. He riled me in very bitter tones for going through with it, while all the time *he* was the one with such very strong feelings against it.'

'You can fool everyone else but not me. In the end you cheated on Sidney quite shamelessly and broke his heart.'

'I agree I should have told him earlier about Frank. But as I've said before, I didn't tell him as I thought we might come to have some deeper and more real affection for each other. I was wrong. With separation I just drew farther away from him and realised he wasn't cut out for a family man, and would be far happier without heavy responsibility. In the cathedral he told me he now wanted responsibility, but that was quite a change of front as he had always bemoaned the fact that he had no one to fall back on if anything went wrong with his job etc. Neither have millions of others.'

'Or you couldn't see another way out of your marriage? Don't tell me you and Frank didn't hope a bomb would drop on him and make things easier for you?'

'Sidney, on his side, always gave me the impression I irritated him. He was always restless when we were alone together. We were totally unsuited and should have parted years ago. A handful of friends was the only thing we seemed to have in common. I was very sorry to do this to him, in spite of my genuine grievances over the first part of our marriage, and particularly after he had been so ill, but I thought it was much better to cut my losses than drag out our lives together without harmony. You've had a lucky escape, Jo, thanks to me. *You could have been an unwanted bride like me.*'

I'm dumbfounded. Your wife is a dab hand at turning the tables on a person. 'Don't flatter yourself. Sidney and I had it all planned…'

'He might have married you, lawfully or unlawfully, but he didn't desire you, Jo. All he wished to do was to prove to the world what a charlatan and whore I was. I was really shocked at the way he changed his views – for years he had always said the divorce laws were scandalous and that if people can't live happily together there ought to be a quick and decent way of breaking a marriage. He would say that, of course, when his adorable Dora was married to her violent husband. Then he swung round completely and was very vindictive. All this was bewildering, as in spite of what people said about all his pontificating – and I'm not referring to my family exclusively by any means – I always believed in his theories and had even been accused of believing in them blindly. Now to find the model had feet of clay was rather shattering, and consequently I'm afraid it was impossible for us to go on together when I'd lost my respect for him.'

'You mean you wanted revenge.'

'I honestly can't understand Sidney's sudden change of attitude. When I first told him about my new love he said it was 'rather a relief' to him to know that he hadn't the responsibility of providing for me etc., and it was a great load off his mind to know that there was somebody else willing to do it. He also wrote a calm letter to me last June and said: "It is not my intention to discuss THE problem because I am satisfied that you have a very definite preference for Frank, and in any case you have completely departed from me. It is therefore a question of getting you free as quickly and quietly as possible. It isn't practical for me to run off with somebody else, and I don't know whether these things can still be faked or not, but I can try and find out if necessary..." In the end I was the one who had to go to the Hotel Russell for the weekend. *I* had to give *him* the hotel bill so he could instruct his solicitors to take the necessary steps to put an end to our marriage and leave me free to start over. That's how self-deceiving, destructive and cruel he was. As I said to him in the cathedral, my decision to leave him was absolutely final and he must know that by now.'

'You're making no sense. Are you saying that Sidney *did* want you, after all?'

'*No. He didn't.* Not in any real sense. He and I never had sex once in five years of marriage. Only, he didn't like the idea of another man doing what he wouldn't. How long was I supposed to wait? I'm thirty-four already. I want a family.'

'But you admit you went to the cathedral in a final bid to beg him not to contest the divorce and it all went wrong?'

'He left me no choice. He forced the issue by bumping my friends into it with his awful letters and telephone calls to mother and father. He passed on the news to all the Ealing busybodies before it was really necessary. He was trying to scare me with the threat of scandal, to the point where I lost the deep sympathy I once had for him.'

'What were your final words to him before he fell and took you with him?'

'I again asked him to set me free. As I'd told him previously, my opinion was that our marriage had turned out to be a complete failure and since I'd left him I'd seen no reason to return. In fact, my love for Frank strengthens each day and I'm quite convinced he's the man for me...'

'And?'

'He tried to rip up the divorce papers. I went to stop him. I can't remember anything after that, I simply woke up here.'

For a murderess your wife can still shed a genuine tear or two when she tries. I'm almost at a loss for words. 'Sidney didn't deserve to die – he was no monster.'

'We cling to the idea of love because it promises us the world, Jo, but promises alone don't mean a thing. It's not what a man says, it's what he does that matters.'

'No, you're wrong. Sidney was a passionate person who lived life to the full.'

'I bet he barely even kissed you.'

'But we had the rest of our lives ahead of us.'

'Is that what you really feel?'

'We were going to try.'

'Wake up, Jo. Here's what I know. Why do you think Sidney spent years hankering after Dora? It was because he knew he could never have her. She was married to George and she wouldn't leave him. The only woman Sidney ever truly loved was his adoring and fussy mother – it can't be a coincidence that when she fell seriously ill he had a mental breakdown. Sex between us was never on the agenda, but unconditional love is what he always clung to…'

'Go to hell.'

My most fervent wish right now is to suffocate Marjorie with her own pillow, but people are coming our way. Your wife is just getting into her stride, it seems. She's not about to spare us both total exposure as I raise my hand to the bedside curtains – I can hear a trolley rattling across the ward. All this ridiculous chit-chat means I've missed my moment? 'Admit it, Jo, he wouldn't fuck you either, would he?'

'I said go to hell.'

'Or he couldn't.'

She's still mouthing off at me as I go to leave. 'He didn't want you any more than he wanted me. Are your eyes open now, Jo?'

'….!'

I have to quit this awful place before she makes any more of a scene.

'You and I are like two pees in a pod, Jo. There never was a more unwanted bride than you, or me.'

FIFTY-EIGHT

It's a lovely sunny Sunday morning and I should be at 10.30 matins in the cathedral. Instead I'm standing by the bonfire I've built in the backyard of 18A Edwy Parade, where John is helping me dispose of the last of your belongings, dear Sidney.

'You don't have to do this, Jo.'

'Yes, I do.'

'It's a fire, not an expurgation.'

'I'm right about this, I know I am.'

'This isn't who he is.'

'It's all he is.'

'And I thought I was the emotional, sentimental one.'

'Don't make this any worse than it has to be.'

John strokes his arm in a sling, looks doubtful. 'The only person you can hurt now is you.'

'What else would you have me do?'

I'm about to toss your 6-franc "Handy Guide for Seeing Everything in Paris and its Environs" at the burning dustbin, my love. Do you recall how, one day in the Cadena Café, you unfolded its red and gold covers on the table and we planned all the places we were going to visit – we were definitely going to see the Chateau de Versailles and Chartres Cathedral...

The map misses the fire by an inch and lands at John's feet. Now he's holding it up between finger and thumb like another piece of damning evidence.

This won't take long now, then you'll be gone. I have a few more oddments to add to your inferno. Here's your school certificate from 1925 detailing all the subjects that you, Sidney Arthur Thomas Sheppard, passed with credit at Ealing County School. You were so good at French and Latin. I have, too, confirmation of a job you gained at Cement and Steel Co. Ltd in 1928, while a letter from Jantzen Knitting Mills in 1937 gives you the authority to sell swimsuits in Denmark. I love the elegant diving girl in red bathing suit at the top of the page. Here's a pair of rusty ice-skates as well as your shaving kit, your PRONTOR II camera, and all the letters Marjorie ever sent you.

But right now I'm staring open-mouthed at these cream-coloured pieces of paper that have your scratchy handwriting on them.

'What is it?' asks John, seeing my face pale.

'Proof.'

'Proof of what?'

'Marjorie was right. She was right about a lot of things. Sidney was strong in words but weak in action. That mysterious look in his clear blue eyes that I thought so interesting turned out to be fear.'

I'm holding letters dated June 24th 1940.

John hurries round to my side of the fire. 'I think you'd better sit down, Jo.'

'I'm okay.'

'You're clearly not. You've come over all giddy.'

'I really haven't.' I don't know why I'm standing here half paralysed when this is old news.

John has his hand on mine. 'Allow me.'

I confess I'm scared to dwell on your passionate declarations that should have been solely for me, dear Sidney. Your address is Wilnecote Hall, near Tamworth in Staffordshire just as Marjorie said. You wrote it less than a year after you got married. I do as John bids and give him what you wrote years ago.

'Please.'

'Sure?'

'Sorry, but I have to know.'

'Then I'll begin: "My dearest Dora, I love you. You probably thought I was never going to write, but you have never been out of my thoughts. The delay has been almost entirely due to lack of opportunity and a sort of perverted frustration due to the fact that I really didn't want to write at all. I want to be with you.

"I could write, and probably will write at length shortly about life here, but I'm afraid that where you are concerned, I think only of you and everything seems unimportant unless I am sharing with you.

"Sometimes I think you have outgrown me…"

'Why have you stopped? What else does he say?'

'Nothing. But there's another letter stapled to it. It's also dated 24th June 1940. He clearly had two attempts at writing the same thing.'

'Read that one to me, as well.'

John makes a face. 'What is this? Why do this to yourself? Is it because you think you were the love of his life, not her?'

'Not after today.'

'Okay. Here goes: "My Dearest Dora, I love you more than ever. I will probably write shortly and tell you of life here, but for now I only want to know that you still love me. I expect as usual you'll tell me not to be so silly, but I do like to know.

"I'm away from you so much and I do envy the people who are able to spend their time in your company. The fact that I don't like most of them overmuch only makes it worse. Do you still feel the same, is it really one of those never dying flames of the novels?

"I am feeling particularly expressionless today…"

'And?'

'It just peters out like the first. He doesn't sign either. Perhaps there's a finished version somewhere else…'

'I know for a fact he never sent any of them.'

John holds both pages over the fire. I nod and he lets them drop into the flames.

'It's not your fault. You didn't know what you were about to get yourself into, Jo. You could never have guessed where his love really lay.'

'Don't you see – it makes me my own worst enemy. I thought I'd found my dream man who could solve all my problems for me. I was mistaken.'

'Everyone deserves to have a dream, but not every dream comes true.'

'I was wrong. I was wrong about everything. I won't be charmed again.'

'Don't be too hard on yourself. Thanks to you, a deranged stalker-cum-murderer is no longer roaming the land. Even DI Lockett has had to admit you were right about Captain Hector Knevitt. Now he's gone he can't do any more harm.'

'That's not how I wanted this to end.'

'How did you want it to end?'

'I was so focused on what I wanted that I couldn't see I'd already lost it.'

'You were grieving. You still are.'

'Because of me people are dead. Does no one have to answer for that?'

'Not you.'

I take a step back from the fire to rearrange a blanket in Jacqueline's pram. She's smiling and happy to hear the sound of my voice. Meanwhile Bella hunts rats in the Anderson Shelter nearby.

I'm staring at the DEBARQUEMENT stamp in your passport, dear Sidney, dated the 30th of July 1939 at Calais in France. I can't find the corresponding return EMBARQUEMENT stamp anywhere, which is strangely fitting – I don't think you ever came home, not in spirit, you never really understood the enormity of what you failed to do on your wedding night. Had I been there, I would have been your vilified bride, too?

Your passport is not so quick to burn. Its hard blue covers will be the last to go. Instead the flames eat into the photographs of you on page three, above the blank square ready for the face of your wife never now to be filled. Even on your honeymoon you and Marjorie must have travelled as separate people. You look so smart and young – your brow is unwrinkled and your cheeks smooth as marble. Your hair is very short and your ears stick out a little, until there's something about you I don't recognise: you look confident, happy and very handsome, not like the ghost of a man I was courting.

John watches your passport curl and crumple, too. 'Don't think of today as the end, Jo, think of it as the beginning.'

'Don't insult us both. Without an end there is no beginning.'

'You think?'

'Sidney lived in an emotional never-never land of his own making – he had me trapped in a moment of perpetual promise.'

'So what did he promise you?'

But my eyes are transfixed by a photograph of Marjorie that you took while on honeymoon, dear Sidney – she's standing on a set of steps beside some sort of stone balustrade as fronds from a palm tree frame the top of the picture. She squints heavily in the French sunshine, yet gives you a broad smile. I never realised how slim she could look in her long black skirt down to her ankles and her short-sleeved, white blouse – that white belt round her middle almost cuts her in two. She holds one arm across her stomach and raises the other above her head in a carefully contrived wave. You'd think she didn't have a care in the world.

I can see why you said you'd take me to Cannes straight after we got married. Its tennis courts, restaurants and cinemas are open all summer and winter. If we were there right now I imagine we would be strolling hand in hand on its long sandy beach or visiting the de luxe Palm Beach Casino – we'd go to its theatre, restaurant and gaming-room or enjoy its large open-air "Piscine". We'd be clinking glasses, laughing and listening to the latest music. Or we'd go along the coastline where red porphyry rocks dip down in a rugged mass to the sea below and swim at Agay or Le Dramont.

Instead, here's your real bride again, dressed in floral top, shorts and white sandals. She stands half way up some shady garden steps and rests one elbow casually on a wall, where her smile is seemingly radiant. In the next photograph I rip from its album she sits astride a pretty balustrade, against a backdrop of more palms and spiky succulents. She poses for you while wearing a one-piece swimsuit and high-heeled sandals. She has on her thick red lipstick which exaggerates her smile – she's smiling for you and your camera. I'm guessing this terrace must belong to the Hotel Du Prince where you said we, too, would stay after the war.

You said I could be her one day soon. As your new wife I would enjoy the sun-baked Riviera from Marseilles to Mentone – we could have taken the boat along the coast streaked with coral-coloured rock or gone walking in hills sprinkled with groves of pine and olive trees.

They say the camera doesn't lie, but each one of these pictures is a fake. Marjorie smiles outside the hotel or down on the beach – she wears a dozen different outfits including a very fetching white jacket and knee-length skirt with white shoes, but by now you'd quarrelled with her, hadn't you, my love? Strictly speaking, you were at war with her. Yet she looks nice enough in her top and shorts, even if her thighs are fatter than mine. She looks as though she's enjoying herself as she climbs a rope or poses beside Le Pedalo No. 35. It's all to show friends and family back home.

Does it even matter any more? You'll never take me there now. The doing can't measure up to the dream.

I should simply consign your life to the fire with one final throw of the album, but here you are in other, earlier years – I'm looking at a prelude to your marriage when the fantasy must have still seemed real before the onset of war. And yes, it does look as if it could go on for ever. I have in my fingers photographs you took of Cannes's Midi Plage with its forest of pyramidal beach tents, parasols and canoes as well as swimmers at the Monte Carlo pool. I know from your passport that you and your friends went there in the summer of 1935, '36, '37 and '38.

Even in black and white you and your friends look as brown as berries on the hot sand. I'm fascinated, even now, because this is your life as I'll never have it. Here you are, holidaying with Dora and George. Marjorie wears a big sun hat down her back, held on by a string round her neck. In this next picture of you in your swimming shorts you look very thin beneath your shady sun umbrella – you're smiling with your eyes half-closed and I can see your ribs. Scarcely anywhere else do you exist in your own album, as if you've become a ghost of yourself already. I'd say you had a very good time before you met me, except you were already being duplicitous. You're lying on the sand looking happy, but you're harbouring some great passion for another man's wife who is stretched right alongside you.

Yes, the camera does lie, most definitely. It can also be evidence and a warning. I duped myself when I thought I could be your next great passion. No lover should have to be someone's idea or ideal, I refuse to play your nervous virgin any longer....

'What about these?' asked John, holding up the final album. 'This one is full of wedding photographs.'

'Not helpful.'

'So what do we do?'

'Pass them to me.'

I've seen these pictures of your big day before, dear Sidney, so I hardly need to view them again. Only this should have been our album, too. I think you look very dapper with your white gloves and shiny top hat. Marjorie looks positively divine in her white trailing bridal gown, flowers in her hair and a bouquet in her hands. It all looks so perfect, which is why I don't hesitate to consign you both to destruction. Until this judgement day it's as if I've been asleep, but now I'm awake and not about to go to hell.

John pulls me back from the heat of the flames before I singe my brows. 'You've dropped something, Jo.'

At my feet lies a small picture of you, dear Sidney – it has fallen from the album and lodged beside my heel. It shows you smoking a cigarette at your reception? The camera has caught you in half-relaxed pose. Your cheeks are in shadow which exposes your bones. You look tired, uneasy even, as if the day really has been too much for you. Were you already thinking of Dora? Were you angry and screaming on the inside? It's hard to tell. At that moment you woke up, too? Your marriage was a terrible lie and ours would have been no different.

You may not have been the man I remember, but I'm not the person you thought I was, either. I can make it without you, I'm going to be just fine. You made me part of your grandiose, romantic plans, except you didn't fully understand them – you ran away from your marriage and tried to hit back when you hurt yourself.

'Let the fire do its work, John. It's time you and I went for some fresh air.'

'Finally! I'm sure Jacqueline would like a stroll, too.'

'This time you get to push the pram.'

John lights a cigarette off the blaze. 'You seem different today, Jo.'

'Different, how?'

'You've spent the last few weeks chasing a ghost as though you were gripped by some special spirit, but now you're prepared to see him go up in smoke.'

'I was so sure a crime had been committed against him. In the end he did the committing.'

'Sorry, I don't follow.'

'Is there such a thing as a crime against love? I rather think there is, but you can't go to prison for it.'

'I feel safer already.'

I'm holding Jacqueline in my arms and give her a kiss on the cheek. I nearly lost her because of you, dear Sidney. That's what happens when you try to cling to the dead, you forget to look after the living. That's not who I am. That's not what I want to be.

John brings the pram and Bella follows. Maybe we'll go to the cathedral and light a candle for you, my darling.

You'll always have a special place in my heart, but there has to be more to it.

'What made you think Sidney ever loved you, Jo?'

'And you mention this, *because*?'

'I wouldn't ask if it didn't matter.'

'After everything that has happened to me, I guess I needed to believe that someone could still want me. That I had a future. I placed my trust in him and forgot to trust myself. He was very convincing. I made him the one hope of my life, but it turns out he was only a mirage of myself.'

Bella trots ahead, sniffing lampposts. John pushes the pram along the pavement as Jacqueline smiles at us both. If this is a better future, then I already have it.

He slows to light a second cigarette from his. Hands it to me.

'Did Sidney really vow to marry you before he fell, Jo, or was it all in your head?'

'Better. He said he would never let me down.'

Printed in Great Britain
by Amazon

38539054R00187